BAGATELLE·
GUINEVERE

BY

FELICE ROTHMAN

EDITED WITH AN INTRODUCTION, ETC.

BY

NANCY 'BOGEN

THE TWICKENHAM PRESS

First published in 1995 by
THE TWICKENHAM PRESS
31 JANE STREET, SUITE 17B
NEW YORK, NY 10014

The graphics for John Milton's "l'Allegro" and *Gilgamesh* first appeared in the second edition of Ms. Bogen's *How to Write Poetry* (Simon & Schuster, 1994).

Library of Congress Cataloging-in-Publication Data
Bogen, Nancy, 1932 —
    Bagatelle•Guinevere / by Felice Rothman, edited with an introduction etc. by Nancy Bogen
      p.   cm.
    Felice Rothman is a fictitious character created by Nancy Bogen.
    ISBN 0-936726-05-9 (cloth) — ISBN 0-936726-06-7 (pbk.)
      1. Young women — United States — Fiction. 2. Women poets, American — Fiction. I. Title
    PS352.0434B3 1995
    813'.54—DC20   94-4038

The paper in this book meets the guidelines for permanence and durability of the Committee on Production Guidelines for Book Longevity of the Council on Library Resources.

[Ed. This page has been deliberately left blank pending the return of our author, Ms. Rothman, when she will provide an appropriate dedication, hopefully to me, her sole support during her years of hopeless travail.]

Contents

Introduction
by Nancy Bogen, M.A., Ph.D.

Normally a piece of fiction of this nature would speak for itself and require no preliminary statement from me or anyone else. However, the circumstances surrounding its composition are such that I feel duty-bound to offer one.

The author makes claim to having undertaken an exploratory mission to a world beyond our solar system on behalf of the United States government — obviously an impossibility, at least as of the time when this is being written, the last decade of the twentieth century. Even the combined technical resources of every nation here on earth would not suffice to send a fellow human such a vast distance.

On the other hand, the work is not *simply* fiction either. There is a kind of truth to it all, though not in the ordinary sense. As Hamlet said, there are more things in heaven and earth, Horatio, than are dreamt of in your philosophy . . . according to geometrist Lobachevski, I take it, a straight line may not always be the shortest distance between two points.

The question is how did someone like myself — a professor of History residing on Manhattan's Upper West Side with patent attorney husband and a fine son in medical school — become involved in such an enterprise.

It began quite unexpectedly one day late in the Spring of 1984. I was up in my office at the University adding a few afterthoughts to a term paper after turning in my grades. Suddenly the telephone rang, and there on the other end was this person with a voice that was youthful but belonging to someone past her twenties seeking to make an appointment with me. Probably it's one of my students of bygone years, I thought, though off-hand neither "Rothman" nor "Felice" rang any bell.

What did she want? That she couldn't say except that it was "personal and rather urgent." Since I had no plans to return to the campus in the immediate future, I asked if she minded coming to the apartment, not an unusual thing for me to do with students past and present when classes were no longer in session. No, she wouldn't mind at all, she said, and we made a date for the following afternoon.

The individual who stood before me at the door — short and slight with hazel eyes and long, dark hair — was totally unfamiliar. Her outfit, peculiarly mod — including a jeans miniskirt and Grecian sandals with the thongs crossed over aquamarine pantyhose — likewise offered no clue as to when and under what circumstances she had studied with me.

Well, people whose ages are closer to thirty than fifty have a way of changing rather dramatically these days, I reflected. For instance, a few years ago she may have been given to wearing suits and sensible footwear like me, and had she continued in that vein, might now have been easily recognizable.

Only no, that was not the explanation I learned, after we were seated opposite one another in my study. While she was indeed an alumna of our graduate school, her field had been English literature, and to her knowledge we had never crossed paths.

So what brought her to me, was she looking for a job or what, I next inquired, understandably a little irritated at her not having enlightened me sooner.

No, a job she had, came her response — as an instructor in English at Greenburgh State across the river in New Jersey. What she wanted was someone to lend a hand, in an advisory capacity of course, on a book that she had begun working up from a diary of hers.

One can well imagine my feelings when I heard that the book was about a mission — her mission — to outer space, which, it should be understood, she delivered with not so much as a blink of the eye. My heart even sank a little in fear as I recall, on my realizing that I was alone in the house, my husband and son not yet home from office and classes.

All the same, my curiosity got the best of me — what had led her to feel that she needed the services of a historian for her project? Wouldn't a plain garden-variety editor or even a professor of English have been more suitable?

She had the answer all ready. Ordinarily, yes, someone along those lines would have been just the thing. But in this case, no, neither the one nor the other would do. Why? Because her work was a "real-life story" and as such required the services of a person who regularly dealt with the like.

So where did I fit in, after all an ancient historian?

She smiled ingenuously — very simple. She had recently come across a paper of mine on early Aegean shipping capabilities, in which I had offered the speculation that ancient Cretan vessels had penetrated eastward as far as China — which happened to be one of her pet theories. And the next I knew this odd-looking visitor was explaining, with positively glowing eyes, how Minoan ships could have reached the Persian Gulf via the Euphrates, after first being portaged to it in sections, then sailed on to India, hugging the coast as was their wont, and around it to Indo-China. As for the lack of concrete evidence that the two cultures had met and mingled, could not ancient Cretan merchants have used long-since-lost *objets d'art* from their part of the world to barter for precious but perishable Chinese goods like silk, she reasoned. Most assuredly speaking in favor of this as a possibility was the existence of many a piece of early Chinese statuary and ornamentation with a Mesopotamian or old Egyptian look to it, in particular the celebrated *t'ao t'ieh* mask, which in certain instances bore a striking resemblance to the millennia-old Eastern Mediterranean motif of the two upright animals facing one another in profile. There was also the matter of the rather sudden appearance of writing in China circa 1700 B.C., the Middle Minoan heyday.

Tenuous as her argument was — for example, Ancient Near Eastern artifacts could have reached China overland through a slow process of dissemination — I couldn't help but marvel at the range of this curious individual's knowledge, especially considering that she was a non-specialist. Even so, what has this to do with the matter at hand, I reminded myself.

Seeming to read my mind, she cut short her development of that last point. Now the light in her eyes faded and the lids fell; at the same time her voice dropped, almost to a mumble. There was another reason for desiring to enlist my assistance. According to a capsule biography of me, found in some directory, I was twenty years older than she and thus the same age as her late mother. That my parents had fled with me from our dear Vienna in 1938 when I, a half-Jew according to Nazi notions of race, was eleven reinforced the connection in her mind. In the early days of the century, her mother's people, who were Rumanian Jews, had come here to America under trying circumstances as well — the father a victim of a vicious anti-Semitic slap in the face by an officer while serving as a recruit in the Austro-Hungarian army.

I felt a little sorry, but again failed to see what one thing had to do with another — and this time told her so, then got up, expecting that she would too.

That she did, only not at once. First her face took on an earnest expression, and withdrawing a bankbook from a leather sling bag of a purse, she said that she was ready to part with the amount given there as the balance — a tidy sum in four figures — if I would see her through this "present crisis," as she now put it.

The whole thing was foolish and preposterous. I put my foot down as delicately as I knew how.

At the door she looked so discouraged that I found myself questioning whether she wasn't exaggerating about the necessity for professional assistance. Surely she was no novice, had something of hers in print by this stage of her career, I suggested.

Well, no, to be perfectly frank, she didn't, and as if that weren't bad enough, she'd left school without finishing her dissertation. Indeed, if the truth be known, she could boast of having brought only a single work to successful completion since then — on the subject of King Arthur, his queen Guinevere, and her lover Lancelot, "in verse or prose depending on how one looks at it," and "well regarded in some circles," but, alas, still in manuscript.

And that was that. I took in those greenish-brown eyes subject to their quick changes of mood for the last time I thought, and counted my blessings that I had not yielded.

Later, over dinner with my husband, was another story. It seems that between our son's educational expenses and a weekend hideaway we had purchased Upstate, which was constantly in need of repairs, we had overextended ourselves somewhat financially, according to the master of the house. And the upshot? The unconventional one's offer coming at this time was like a godsend. How about it, why didn't I try it out with her at least? After all, aside from seeing a recently-completed opus through galleys, I had nothing of any consequence on the boards, so it wouldn't be as if I were taking time away from something else.

Most reluctantly and with many misgivings, I telephoned her the next morning — she having thrust a card with her number on it into my hand before departing — and we arranged to meet that day after lunch. She was to bring with her an outline or summary of the proposed work, and I, provided that I approved of it, would then establish a *modus operandi* for us — which, to make a long story short, is what happened. Her plan appearing reasonable, all things considered — including her continued eccentricity of dress — we agreed that she would mail me a chapter at the beginning of every month and then appear a few days later for a critique, after calling first to set up a date. Payment was to be made on each of those occasions, with it clearly understood that the arrangement could be terminated by either party at any time on becoming dissatisfied.

At first everything went well, my part of the work at least proving not at all onerous and her company, thanks to a naturally cheerful disposition, rather pleasant. . . .

I can still see the two of us laboring away together, I at my desk, where I am now, penning this, she before me in the old grande dame of an armchair I keep in here, with a clipboard in her lap. The afternoon light filters in through the glass curtains — it grows duskier outside. Soon it is dark and time to switch on the overhead light and Tensor at my elbow; and then another session is at an end and we are that much closer to the goal. . . .

Yes, that is how it was with us — but as I said, only at the outset. Suddenly, after four such meetings, came trouble, those good spirits of hers giving way to anxiety and this in turn deepening to despair. And to such depths of it did she descend that as the deadline for Chapter Six approached, I was beginning to fear dire things for her (about which more will be said in its place). Suffice it to say here that in due time she somehow managed to pull herself together — only to suffer another decline around the time when I expected to see Chapter Ten (concerning which I shall have something further to say in time too).

At long last, though, I received her final submission (an autobiographical sketch that figures in the next section). However, all was not over between us — quite the contrary. Later that day there came by parcel post a large jiffy bag containing the entire manuscript plus a small collection of school children's composition books — the kind with marbled black-and-white covers and sewn-in pages — which turned out to be the original notes or diary on which the whole of it was based. To these materials was appended a handwritten note from the author advising that she would be out of town for a while and proposing that in the interim I "do something more with the thing," she didn't know what except that she felt that something more was needed. After I had attended to this, she asked only one additional favor — that I send the work on to some people whose names and addresses were listed on the back. A certified check for twice the amount due me was attached to take care of any extra trouble or inconvenience I might be put to. The note concluded with her apologies for such a precipitate departure and assurances that she'd write before long.

Indignant at being treated in such an abrupt fashion, I

hurried to the telephone and dialed her number — to find that it had been disconnected. The dean of faculty at her college, whom I tried next, gave cause for further alarm — Miss Rothman had come to his office a few days ago and just like that without warning handed in her resignation. Did she give any indication of where she was going? No, and the place for explanation on the form had been left blank. There was nothing for it then but to try and reach her through the mail. Accordingly I posted a letter to the address that I had for her, down on West 19th Street, marked Please Forward — but as I now expected had no luck with this stratagem either. The letter was promptly returned, indicating that the party had moved without leaving a forwarding address.

As a last resort, my husband and I decided to pay a visit in person to the place — a seedy tenement as it turned out, but not without a certain charm it struck us, the doorway flanked by a pair of sweet grey stone Dianas gazing fondly down on two glossy black lionesses guarding the stoop. But here too we met with no success. The superintendent, an old black man encountered creating order among the garbage cans out front, informed us that on the day she left Ms. Rothman had handed him her key and told him to dispose of her stuff as he saw fit; other than that, she had kept her own counsel — he had no idea where she'd gone off to. And the building agent had rented her apartment again almost at once to someone who had absolutely no connection with her.

What was there to do after that but wait, and in the meantime for lack of something better carry out her wishes.

Around a month later a letter arrived from some remote corner of Texas — without a return address. Everything was going well, it said; that was about all. A month after that, a second letter arrived, from another part of that state to judge from the map, with more or less the same message.

Naturally, I tried to get in touch with her care of General Delivery each time — and naturally, these efforts proved to be of no avail like the others; the letters were sent back unclaimed. Then no further word coming from her, there was one final ploy — my husband appealed to the local sheriff there. But this too was in vain; the man wrote back that while yes, he had run across a party by the name of Felice Rothman, as he saw it a person had a right to remain incommunicado if they so chose, even if one did have a vitally important new prescription for them that had to be put into their hands personally.

That last communication was longer ago than I care to remember. And now — now one can only hope that news of the author's good fortune regarding the acceptance of this work for publication will somehow find its way to her, and that she will then come forward at least to claim such emoluments as may accrue from it — after all hers, the work of *her* hands.

I should like to take this opportunity to express gratitude to my colleagues in other disciplines, too numerous to mention here individually, for their help with technical matters.

A special note of thanks is due to my typist, Mr. B., for devotion above and beyond the call of duty.

And last but by no means least, there is my dear companion in life, Franz, who took his medicine like a good soldier and has promised to do yeoman service with the proofs.

About the Author

After reading through the last chapter, I began to feel that readers would be well served if the entire work were prefaced by an account of the author's life prior to her mission. Accordingly, I mentioned this to her at our meeting, and several days later my wish was satisfied. However, on perusing the piece, I soon perceived that much of what I had thought of as essential had either been omitted or utterly overstated, and rang her up to apprise her of this; a revision was promised but never materialized — the author was gone a few days after that.

What follows then is the best that I was able to do under the circumstances — her text in substance paraphrased by me for the sake of brevity and where appropriate fleshed out by additional information remembered from our conversations, together with passages from those children's composition books, the Diary.

Her opening statement stands —
"I'm not sure how to style myself. Prose poet would seem to be the closest thing, but it sounds funny, like a dunce cap.
"Poet with a small 'p' then — ₚoet?
"Anyway, my life in so many words—for what it's worth."

Her beginnings were ordinary, almost to the point of being laughable. Born in Brooklyn, she was the only child of Flora nee Engel and Barney Rothman. He owned and operated a modest retail toy store on Flatbush Avenue, which he still did until shortly before the author's mission. They lived a short distance away on Ocean Avenue, in a snug two-bedroom apartment.

Her mother's parents, the Rumanians from Austro-Hungary, continued to make their home in a tenement on the Lower East Side, where they had first settled, and sold hosiery in a little shop downstairs from them. Flora was their sole surviving offspring.

Barney, her father, had lost his people when very young and grown up in an orphan asylum. Nothing was known of them except that they came from the neighborhood of Kiev in the Ukraine.

"That's the lot," as the author said at this juncture.

A prodigy she wasn't, unless one is willing to acknowledge as a sign of something unusual to come a penchant in her pre-school years for covering sheets of paper with loops and squiggles that she insisted to one and all was writing.

A special fondness for serious music she seems also to have had then, particularly for opera and German lieder, the credit for which goes to Flora, who was forever singing snatches from one or the other while attending to her daily household tasks and at night generally tuned the radio beside the little girl's bed (a cheap plastic model but fine for the purpose) to WQXR or WNYC, often staying on a while to hum along.

Flora was "most striking-looking" as a young woman, with "Carmen eyes, fresh cheeks, and lips like a delicate bow," set in "pearly white skin" framed by "dark brown waves that became all fiery in the sunlight." Her voice, "an exceptionally rich soprano," she probably could have done something with, "if not at the Met then surely on Broadway," had matters turned out differently.

She and Barney met at a settlement house dance in the final days of World War II. Just turned 21, she was in her third year of vocal training at the Greenwich House Music School and working as a salesgirl at Macy's. He was a returning G.I. who had spent the war in England "repairing LST engines or something like that."

What Flora saw in him, outwardly at least, was anybody's

guess —"already at 26 with a receding hairline and bulging paunch" (as evidenced in their wedding picture). At any event, after several months of Saturday night movies and Sunday outings to museums, they became engaged, and then with the blessing of her parents, "who didn't see any harm in it, that being their way," were married.

The music lessons soon ceased, replaced by homemaking and motherhood. And then with him working as a clerk in some store and the two of them stinting and saving, before long they had enough to set up the store, which he figured would provide them with a decent living.

As far back as the author could remember, Barney "had to have, hands down, the world's sourest disposition." He was "forever bellyaching," if not about one thing, then another — the "shoddy" games and dolls lining the store's shelves, the "fancy" prices the jobbers "soaked" him for them. Flora came in for her share of it — "always picked on for the least little thing," the breakfast toast not done enough or too dark, teacups insufficiently scalded, and so on. Seldom did he have a pleasant word to say even when something turned out exactly to his liking — like the meat for their evening meal seared through and through.

As for her warbling as he called it, that too came in for criticism — he couldn't stand it and absolutely forbade her to sing when he was at home. "In fact, when you come down to it, I don't think he even liked her, let alone felt something more profound for her. 'Least he never once that I recall kissed or so much as touched her in my presence."

Our author Felice used to wonder from time to time through the years why her mother continued to put up with such treatment, "why she didn't just clear out, and take me with her of course." But generally so blinded was the daughter with fury against the father at those moments that not until later, much later — after Flora had finally gone and done it — did Felice, in her 20's, obtain a glimmering of the reason.

They were standing together on the sidewalk in front of

her mother's apartment house in the glaring morning light of southern Florida — Felice with suitcase in hand after a short stay, Flora in housecoat and slippers to see her off ("as people'll do down there").

Just having hugged and received her hug in turn, Flora stepped back, and all of a sudden "that pretty bow of a mouth sort of puckered into a smile" and out it came, very softly —

"Does he ever ask about me?"

Felice's early education, in a local public school, was "one big holiday," thanks largely to a knack for dealing with manipulable symbols — "that is, those then in fashion."

She did not seem to have many friends in those days, though.

Poetry was discovered at age 7 in the Twenty-third Psalm, probably heard in Assembly at school, as the family was not at all religious. Anyway, turning to it in their Bible one day (which was located between *The Complete Works of Shakespeare* and H.G. Wells's *Outline of History* in the living room bookcase), she soon had it by heart and was reciting it to Flora, who was "tickled pink," especially when she came to the part about walking through the Valley of the Shadow of Death, which was pronounced with "special fervor."

In junior high school there were *Macbeth* and *Julius Caesar* to savor, that is, as the teacher and Barney, from his own school days, apprehended them — "the ambitious one's treachery and blood-thirstiness counting for nothing because of his Tomorrow, and Tomorrow speech, and Brutus, despite his readiness with the knife, truly a noble sort."

Her own first efforts, in verse, date from that period too. However, so convinced was she of the "all-around silliness" of those little poems that for a long time she told no one about them — not a soul.

In high school there were *King Lear* and, more important, Milton, his "organ tones" as she later learned to call them, and Thomas Wolfe, discovered on her own. And then later in college she encountered Keats, whose "Eve of St. Agnes" more than any other work she felt "fed into" her own first major one, yet to come. . . .

When nine or so, the author also showed herself adept at learning foreign languages, or so the rabbi at the neighborhood synagogue where she went several times a week after regular school led her to believe, able after a single year to sound out all the words in the Bar Mitzvah preparation book.

One Saturday morning during that period she went off to the local public library intent on doing the same with Chinese. But once within its familiar portals, her "luck ran out" — they refused to give her the much-needed book because it was in the Adult Section.

She consoled herself on the way home with the Morse Code — found inside a bubble gum wrapper.

NYU's Washington Square College was selected "for the most ridiculous reason that anyone could think of" — the spirit of him who had engendered *Look Homeward, Angel* haunted its halls, Thomas Wolfe having taught there.

Even so, it proved a fortunate choice, for Felice was soon to be beset by difficulties and it is always best then, as she herself pointed out, "to be in a place you're at least a little familiar with instead of off somewhere in the middle of nowhere."

To be brief, shortly after the beginning of the first semester, her mother suddenly announced the "parting of the ways" with her father and proposed that Felice accompany her down south, where she intended to settle to be near her parents who had recently entered a retirement home there, arguing that while the University of Miami did not have the same allure, they would be together. But our author was already happily settled in a studio on Thompson Street, with other students in the building, and so chose to remain — which meant that except for small sums that her mother might be able to send from time to time, once having obtained a little employment, she would be on her own. For certainly nothing was to be expected from her father, who was "not exactly thrilled" at the notion of more education for her to begin with and at any event could not afford to contribute to the upkeep of both wife and daughter.

A sudden yen arising to "feel free, utterly free, even to fail," if that were her pleasure, Felice decided to treat the matter of survival as a challenge and instead of applying for a scholarship, found a job waiting on tables at a luncheonette near her place. This step neither parent was pleased with. Barney in particular wished to go on record as being firmly opposed; his daughter should forget about the "college bit," he maintained and go to work in an office, where there was a "sure-fire chance of meeting someone."

Still getting the hang of it when the new term began — at a second luncheonette after having been fired from the first for being too slow — Felice found herself with not enough cash put by for tuition and thus "was forced" to go to her father for a loan.

He gave it all right, but first let her have it in no uncertain terms, "as never before —

"WHY DO YOU ALWAYS HAVE TO BE LIKE YOUR MOTHER!"

After that, our author did not have any contact with him for a good long time — not until he was on the point of remarrying, when his wife-to-be, a widow and his general factotum in the business, "in all fairness, a decent sort," insisted on their patching things up.

The second Mrs. Rothman subsequently had our heroine over for dinner at the apartment. But so strange did it seem there, "lonely somehow," without Flora her mother, that when asked again, Felice politely declined, giving some excuse, and took to dropping by the store to see them from time to time — that is, until Barney found fault with some new "crotchet," and then she didn't bother anymore. . . .

Flora in the meanwhile was doing just fine to judge from her letters and occasional telephone calls. The best piece of news, she had begun studying voice once more, at the Y in Miami. Also of interest, she too had met someone — but, alas, he "shot his mouth off too much about having show biz connections," Felice warned her.

Flora on her part continued showing a motherly concern — her child should not fall behind in school, difficult though things might be, and by all means should "go on with the poetry writing," which Felice had finally admitted to.

●

As our author's junior year drew to a close, she began giving serious thought as to how she and "the work," still in conventional verse, might be supported later, and coming to feel that the job should be related in some way, fixed on teaching, which hopefully could be in a college.

Graduate Faculties uptown seemed the best choice that was closest to hand for preparing herself to enter this profession. In time, "after getting the lay of the land there," she chose the Eighteenth Century as her area of concentration, particularly in its "mellower moods," and a rather unusual Master's thesis topic — Ossian as a Verbal Analogue to the Paintings of Fragonard — which, when worked up, earned her a recommendation for a doctoral fellowship from her advisor.

And who knows, Felice might have gone on to distinguish herself. But now came the Vietnamese War and all the trouble that went with it here in the United States. Like many another young person then, she could not keep from questioning the established norms. But at the same time a dissatisfaction uniquely her own arose with the "ethologically absurd" way in which languages and literatures were being taught at Graduate Faculties and everywhere else as well, and it wasn't long before her voice was raised in favor of instituting a Pan-Germanic department "to include English and all dialects, like Black English, as well as regional literatures, all complexions," and a program entitled Indo-European or Occidental Studies to parallel our East Indian Studies, which contained "all sorts of ethnically unrelated things," or else — her own brand of absurdity — one language and literature department "with everything subsumed there!" As she put it in the Diary, *Mind you, I'm not ipso facto advocating an equation of Rudaki with Homer. Let's just see for ourselves, damit!*

Even more deplorable, all thoughts of broadening and deepening her background in the Eighteenth Century went by the wayside, as a list of alternative dissertation topics in the Diary, consisting of such gems as *Chekhov's plays: Bourgeoigrified Shakespeare; Lesbian wish-fulfillment as ursprung of The Tale of the Genji & something else — maybe the sexploits of Odysseus, haha,* bears witness.

And that is how, what with taking part in demonstrations and sit-ins in addition, she ended up with ABD after her name (for all but dissertation) — "like a scarlet albatross."

Her rescue came about from an utterly unforeseen quarter, her former Master's thesis advisor, Luke, a Southern gentleman of a certain age. Now Chairman of the Division of Humanities at the Institute for a Liberal Education in Weehawken, a new, unusual upper-level college that was more interested in talent than in credentials, Luke somehow heard of her situation and getting in touch by phone, offered a full-time job "with no strings attached," meaning no commitment from her to resume studies. She, "weary of the whole mess," accepted at once.

Different about the place, among other things, was the fact that all members of the instructional staff could do more or less as they pleased with respect to selecting courses to offer. And this opportunity our author lost no time in taking advantage of, with courses like Blake and Shelley: Apocalyptic Humanists (after scholar Harold Bloom's book of that name), which seasoned veterans at traditional institutions would be hard-put to obtain approval for nowadays even in a more relaxed atmosphere.

Also unusual, there was a good deal of consorting of faculty from different fields — all except the teacher education people, who were universally regarded as "dummies." To this mixing and mingling the administration gave active encouragement, looking forward to interdisciplinary programs as the fruit, which were mandated in the Institute's charter.

Smooth sailing did not always prevail there, however. On one notable occasion, for instance, the social scientists split into five unequal parts as the result of an ideological falling out, which necessitated some rather laborious counting every time a vote had to be taken by Division at Faculty Council. But no one seemed to mind much, at least where that matter was concerned — "just a few soreheads from Pure Sciences who complained about having experiments cooking in the lab that couldn't be left untended for so long."

At the end of our author's third year with the Institute, Luke, now a friend, announced that she was being awarded a Certificate of Permanent Eligibility (CPE), the equivalent of tenure for junior teaching staff. By way of celebrating she set to work on a new poem, something "on a grander scale" than anything that she had yet attempted.

This preliminary sketch appears in the Diary:

Theme — the utter waste and uselessness of war

Setting — the Middle Ages, specifically the campaigns of King Arthur

A note several pages later illuminates further:

Have this unquenchable yearning for sight-sounds (good ole onomatopoeia) — like Keats's "silver snarling trumpets" in "St Agnes." Am going to try and push it — as far as it'll go.

The following fall, while in the middle of that precious labor, Felice had another stroke of luck — she met a man, not the first in her life by any means, but indeed "the only one who counted."

She was living in a regular apartment by then — on Bank Street in an old elevator building with brass fittings on the front door — and had acquired a slightly battered light blue Volkswagen beetle, which she kept garaged several blocks away, near the Hudson.

We were in the midst of our first fuel crisis here at the time, with very little gasoline to be had anywhere at any price. Arriving to pick up her car one morning, she found this "newish" forest-green Cadillac pulled up on the sidewalk beside the entrance and José the attendant telling the driver, who didn't rent there, Sorry, the "juice" inside was only for their own people. She would need some, she said in passing.

There was a thumping of feet from behind. The stranger yelled after her.

She turned to face him. His wallet was out.

Slapping his registration on her Volks's hood, he offered her an even swap.

She gave him a lift down to his office, on Wall Street. . . .

His name was Dave, and he was a widower, her father's age give or take a few years, short, heavy-set, with "an extreme penchant for green," which matched his eyes and complemented his hair, "colored bright carrot."

He began stopping by the apartment once in a while after the Market closed. Soon it got to be just about every day (when she was home).

He was especially fond of strutting and crooning, and had an extensive repertoire of routines to regale them with.

After she let him have a key, he tended to favor one in particular, usually performed on his arrival:

"The front door would open, then his mouth. Generally I was at my desk writing in the bedroom beyond —

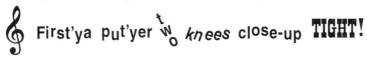

"A squeak would sound from the rack in the closet there, him disposing of jacket and tie.

"Now in the living room, he would go, 'Oof!' and make a clump — his shoes coming off

"Rustling would follow — his shirt and pants.

♪ Now that's what I call BALLIN' THE JACK!

"A pirouette, and there he was in the doorway with a clink — bottle and glasses."

Ordinarily, at the first sign of life out there, she would have begun hurrying to bring that part of the poem to some kind of completion, and would now be swiveled toward him — in which case he would treat them to an encore. But sometimes it did not work out that way — she was "maybe stuck on something" and had to see it through — and then he would tiptoe over to wait quietly behind her chair until the pen had stopped moving.

Once when that happened, he murmured in her hair, "You know, I'll probably never fully understand what you're doing, but I don't care. It seems to give you pleasure and that's enough for me.". . .

It wasn't long before the two of them were speaking of marrying, and with the blessing of Flora, thankful that her child had found someone who would tolerate her "creative endeavors," they had gone so far as to decide on the quietest of ceremonies at City Hall. However, realizing that a move to a new place was going to require her full attention for a time — what with his W & J Sloan one-of-a-kinds from his house, in Hartsdale, and her "beat-up" white Parson's table of a desk among other things — she asked for more time to finish the poem first.

The matter of the difference in their ages also appears to have been of some concern — to each of them in their own way, as this entry from the Diary indicates:

Last night I was at the stove stirring some red clam sauce from a can (to which I'd added a few fresh ones), when all of a sudden out it popped just like that — Dave, one day we might find ourselves at a kind of crossroads.

He was standing beside me — had just finished testing a strand of spaghetti with a loud zup, from a rumbling pot of same. Eyed me

blandly — So, we'll get us a houseboy.
  I wasn't sure what to think. Did he really mean it or what?
  Whatsa problem, he said with the same calm look on his face. His eyebrows went up, lips parted —

DEW!

  Just to keep her from the foggy, foggy
  He trucked on out to the foyer.

●

"We all have a load to bear, I know. So I won't try to make any special claims for myself where that's concerned —

"Well, maybe in this one respect, once it all got going, one thing seemed to come on top of another without let-up."

So the author began the concluding section of her account.

One day in the dead of that winter there was a telephone call from a social worker in Miami Beach's Mt. Sinai Hospital. Mrs. Rothman had been admitted the day before and wasn't doing too well — would her daughter come down immediately.

Flora sick! Very sick! It took Felice's breath away and filled her full of guilt and remorse. Ever since beginning work at the Institute, she had made it her business to fly down and be with her mother twice a year, during intersession in January and after June commencement. But that year, with the poem to be finished and Dave somewhat impatiently marking time, the summer visit had been put off to Rosh Hashona, and then to Thanksgiving, when the last line was finally penned. Only even then she had delayed — Dave having insisted on their finding an apartment first.

Now en route to the airport, Felice was truly angry with herself for not having stayed abreast of developments, especially since she had come away from the two previous visits with a certain uneasiness — her grandparents having passed away one after the other not long before and her mother's

boyfriend having disappeared. When Felice last went down,
Flora was considerably heavier and the voice lessons had
ceased; most of her time seemed to be spent indoors in front
of the television, singing along when some piece of music
suited her fancy — dancing too, as space allowed in her tiny
efficiency.

As if that weren't bad enough, so wrapped up in her
own affairs had Felice been that she only now realized that
few letters had come from Flora in recent months, and no
phone calls whatsoever. To make matters worse, the letters
were merely collections of set phrases — I'm feeling fine, the
weather's great and so on — and so too had become the
daughter's responses.

As soon as Felice walked into the hospital room, the
whole situation revealed itself. Her mother's face was very
pale and thin, her hair white.

How did she feel, Felice asked — an "asinine" question
under the circumstances.

Everything hurts, Flora answered, faintly.

When it was over, Felice had the body shipped North, to
be buried here, "foolish as some people thought it," meaning
Barney, her father.

.

One afternoon some months later, Felice was at her desk
at home trying to make selections from two lists that Dave
had drawn up for her, "one headed by an upright Hoover,
the other a Sunbeam canister.

"The key sounded in the front door. I heard —

 Oh, the **SHARK**, Deah–

and a heavy sigh. That was all."

After the funeral, arranged by his son, an iron-haired

Army officer, she began going to the office every day — "to hang around there till it grew dark because it was so quiet at home."

•

Such solace as our author derived from this was short-lived, however. For suddenly — or so it seemed to her grief-stricken mind — the Institute was no more. Deeming it "a losing proposition," with expenditures far exceeding what it thought they should be for a rather small student body, the New Jersey Board of Regents had gone and combined it with the junior college nearby, a "going operation," to form the relatively conventional four-year Greenburgh State.

As a result, Felice found herself, along with others from the Institute's Division of Humanities, including Luke, as "commoner," assigned to an already overcrowded English department that was seething with resentment at having to "take in" the refugees. You guys will sweat for it, looks everywhere promised — over freshman compositions, "oodles" of them.

•

Somehow managing to rise to the occasion, our author vowed that she would not let the situation demoralize her any more than she already was, and as soon as everything had settled down to a "kind of normalcy," took up her pen one morning as of old at the scarred white table in the bedroom. However, while her hand fairly shivered to begin on something, not a word came — only a desire that this next work be more sweeping yet in scope than the last, that long piece set in the Middle Ages about the horrors of war.

After remaining poised thus for some time, she stepped over to the nightstand, where that seventy or so pages was kept, and removing them from the drawer, lay down to read, hoping that the piece would provide some sort of inspiration — if not, it now occurred to her, then she ought to try and decide what to do with it.

No sooner did her eye glance over the opening lines than she began to read in earnest, marveling — "at how all those sight-sounds piled on top of one another worked, the thing echoing and re-echoing with the clangs of broadswords, thwacks of pikes, whizzes of arrows, and humanity crying out in agony over it in rising crescendos."

Or rather they worked and did not work—an element was missing, she soon felt — "something intrinsic, some necessary dimension."

And then all at once she was lunging for her copies of Chrétien de Troyes and Malory in the bookcase! She would overlay all that carnage with the "curiously intricate" tale of the passionate queen, her aging husband, and young lover — indeed fashioning it anew as Tennyson and others had done in the past!

Here is the gist of it from the Diary:

Guinevere — deeply attached to each of them, in EVERY way.

They — aware of it & heartily disliking it but unable to do anything about it: Arthur needing a sure arm for the continued success of his kingly enterprises (bald-faced territorial expansion), Lancelot (a bit of a show-off) unwilling to do without that arena for displaying his prowess.

The denouement (on a fine note of irony) — she's very unhappy at the thought of the terrible suffering they've caused, but at the same time sadly sensible that one of them would eliminate the other or possibly she might lose both, if there were no such "distractions.". . .

In six months she had a first draft; by the end of eight, a second was well under way. But then suddenly one day it "didn't sound right anymore." And for a few after that she just sat trying to figure out what the problem was . . . at a loss.

Finally, at 3 a.m. one morning it struck her — *It's the lines. I've loosened some of them into prose — normal sentences — a big improvement.* Now, returning to the beginning, she made rapid progress over the next few months, "stretching out" the rest of the lines to the end.

A week went by, in which "the dust was allowed to settle"; then taking the whole thing up, she went through it with a coldly critical eye — to find that "it was good, quite good — it sang!" And then, not entirely trusting her own feelings, she "tried it out on Luke," who with her permission passed it on to two others from the Institute's Humanities, whose judgment they respected — the three of them were highly enthusiastic, confirming her in her opinion.

The next step was to try and get "Guinevere" published, for which a literary agent was needed, according to one of its new-found admirers. Our author sent it to a woman he suggested who was "likely to be sympathetic." But curiously, while that agent seemed to be quite positive about the work — going so far as to call it "dazzling" — the thing was neither a novel, nor strictly speaking, poetry, she went on to say in her letter, and more to the point, there was "no market for it."

"Disappointed but not cowed," Felice sent it to another such individual recommended by the same friend, but the reaction was much the same — "I adore it," that second agent wrote, "sorry."

Who would not have felt bad.

Even so, Felice persevered further with a number of literary journals, hoping to interest one of them in printing at least a part of the work. But no success was to be met with in that quarter either; as the comments on the rejection slips made it woefully clear, the passages that she had chosen simply "did not hold up by themselves" even with new, explanatory material added.

What then was there to do?

Let our author have the last word:

"What, but as with its UR," the original anti-war piece.

"And there in that drawer by my bed the whole shebang has been stuck away to this day, except for a period of time now to be considered, when it was put in a vault box for safekeeping along with some other important papers belonging to me, like my birth certificate."

A Note About the Text

The author's wording was faithfully retained throughout, but placing the broadest possible interpretation on her mandate to do "something further," I filled in with explanations according to my understanding of things as well as excerpts from the Diary where they seemed called for. Here and there the pages resultantly took on somewhat of a patchwork appearance, for which I apologize.

I am responsible as well for the title, strangely among her omissions. The section dividers with their quotations are hers, however — designed from her original sketches.

BAGATELLE·GUINEVERE

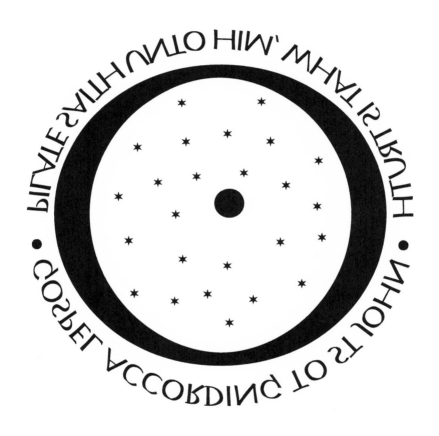

GOSPEL ACCORDING TO JOHN • PILATE SAITH UNTO HIM, 'WHAT IS TRUTH' •

[over]

[Ed. The idea here is to turn the book this way and that in the mirror while at the same time observing oneself doing so — great fun and very revealing, if not absolutely devastating.]

Chapter One

It was the beginning of July, 1976, the month and year of all that red-white-and-blue hullabaloo over the American Bicentennial, and there I was sitting around my place turning the pages of *The New York Times,* a habit I'd gotten into to pass the time when there were no compositions to read.

"Hey, look at that!" I cried out one morning. An article about the upcoming Space Shuttle had caught my eye. Expecting to need new astronauts for it, the powers-that-be at NASA were inviting anyone who thought they had a chance of qualifying to apply, including women and ethnics.

You know, I said to myself, might be just the thing for you, even if the trip's nothing world-shaking — amounts to just going round and round the Earth.

Why make a long story longer — I sent away for an application and a brochure, and when it turned out on my reading the fine print that NASA wanted candidates to have a degree in math or a science, I sent back their form filled in along with a carefully worked out letter asking them to make an exception in my case.

[Ed. This outline from the Diary gives some indication of the tacks that she took.]

1. Raw talent & a willingness to learn should count for something!

2. Am in A-1 physical shape — thanks largely to running up & down in the apt., which I've been doing for years.

3. A born collector of artifacts & stuff — one period in childhood was dedicated exclusively to rocks — 'case they ever change their minds & decide to send some of us minority types to the Moon or something after all.

4. Unlikely as it may seem, I've done a bit of flying in my time —

cross my heart, 12 lessons won in a raffle while I was in college. They can check it out if they want — the instructor was a WWII hotshot by the name of Murdockson or Murchison. He spoke with a funny twang, maybe came from Canada.

5. There's one big advantage to taking on someone like me. Have the ability as a writer to delineate the unmeasurable aspects of things. (Attençion: take it easy with this one or sure as shootin' you'll end up in an office doing you-know-what.)

Maybe it'll come to something, maybe it'll be like everything else, I thought after dotting the last line at my good old Parson's.

    A few days later, came a call from a Ms. Ruth Koviak, secretary to Mr. Willard Watson of NASA. He wanted to see me right away, she said in a gentle voice, would I fly down to Washington the next day?

"Well, yes, I guess so," I answered, almost dumb-struck.

Good, she would meet me at the airport — and oh yes, would I bring along an overnight bag. . . .

When I got off the plane, she was right at the door — willowy, green-eyed with blondish hair in her mid-30's, neatly decked out in a beige blouse and chocolate skirt with two-toned bag and shoes. "Welcome to our nation's capital, I trust your trip was uneventful," she said in her same mild way, with a terribly earnest look. Her car, a cream-colored Ford, was waiting in front of the terminal with the blinkers going.

In no time flat we were at NASA headquarters and she was ushering me into one of the offices in the executive suite, all grey with chrome against stark white walls — here and there a splash of blood and egg yolk from colored blow-ups of blast-offs.

Mr. Watson was waiting behind his desk — trim, fair of face, with pale blue eyes and a full head of ivory hair, in his 50's for sure. Had on a suit of that medium shade of blue all the men seem to go for down in Washington, his tie, lemon stripes outlined in salmon on a navy background, tastefully complementing.

Ms. Koviak did the honors in barely a whisper, then after

getting me settled in a cushy chair opposite him, left us alone.

Watson was not one to waste words — began at once, in an accent redolent of corn and soybeans. NASA had been considerably impressed by what I'd sent them and he was glad to see that, initially at least, I was everything I'd said I was. Seemed particularly taken with my small size and the fact that I had no relatives to speak of.

"Well now," he said at long last — those very light blue eyes fastened on me, mouth became set. Something was in the wind likely to have much more of an impact in the long run than the Shuttle, was I interested?

My breath came up short. Yessirree, do believe I'm feeling better already, I confided to myself. "I most certainly am," answered.

He was happy to hear that. His lids fell — would I then be willing to undergo NASA's battery of tests, justly famed for their rigor?

Some minutes later Koviak and I were back at the airport boarding an Air Force jet transport, bound for the School of Aerospace Medicine at Brooks Air Force Base outside of San Antonio.

The testing lasted almost a whole week.

How did I make out? Quite well, I learned on the return trip, including the psychological part, 'case anyone's wondering. When it came to things like giving twenty answers to the question, "Who am I?" — simply leaned into the psyches of John Glenn and the other boys, as remembered from TV interviews, put down as they would have in my place, "A poet of sorts, likeable, good company, etc."

There was only one problem, and that a slight one Koviak emphasized — my performance on the centrifuge or Wheel as they call it, which measures one's tolerance to gravitational fields, something like that. The best I was able to do before blacking out was $5\frac{1}{2}$ g's, whereas it should have been 7 or 8. "It just needs some working on, that's all," she reassured. . . .

"Yes, we're certainly pleased," Watson echoed when I was before him again. His chin jutted out — it was time to fill me in on things. Wanted to know if I'd ever heard of Explorer 49, and when I said, not really, guessing that it was probably something we'd sent up into space, he went on to tell me, yes, it was put into orbit around the moon in 1973, loaded with sensory apparatus — to act as a kind of celestial watchdog.

I could hardly contain myself — that must mean, his reason for bringing it up, it spotted something!

"That's correct," Watson acknowledged — picked up actually, pulses . . . two weeks ago . . . coming from beyond a cloud of cosmic gas a little to one side of our solar system . . . a sun and a planet at least, the one a class G^2 like ours, the other somewhat larger than our Earth and further away from its luminary. To put it in a nutshell, there were two sets of those pulses or glitches as he alternately termed them, one regular, the other not.

My nails dug into the chair's armrests — was someone signalling from there then, is that what the irregular beats represented?

"No, not that our people have been able to make out anyway," Watson said. Nor did those odd glitches seem to be interchanges back and forth either, no answer-and-response pattern being evident — was "more like a passel o' folks fiddlin' with the dials on their TV sets and radios, and flittin' around in taxicabs and squad cars with their squawkboxes on."

I assumed we'd tried to establish contact.

That we had and were continuing to do so, saturating the area with meaningful beeps day and night, but so far without any result whatsoever — not the slightest alteration in all that "chattering."

I leaned forward — "So where does this leave us?"

His jaw tightened — "With you in the driver's seat if you care to be" — meaning that they were fixing to send someone out there to see what was what and wanted that someone to be me.

"Well, I'm — I'm certainly honored."

Watson continued — he didn't mind telling me that it was no easy thing getting a green light for this project. Seems that the Joint Chiefs of Staff had been firmly opposed to even an unmanned probe at first, believing with some scientists that the ruckus out there was due to an unknown natural cause. Wasn't until NASA had pointed out what a splendid opportunity the situation gave them all to try out a brand-new super-duper mode of rocket propulsion that the Chiefs had agreed to go along with it.

All fine and good, but why had I been singled out rather than one of their regulars, I wondered out loud.

Watson's lips parted . . . came together again, his face a little paler than usual.

So, I surmised, too much dough and time's been invested in them, the risk of losing them's too high.

"'Course," Watson made haste to smooth over, "we'd do everything in our power to — " His eyes found mine . . . split away. . . . "Listen," he said finally after a longish silence, "why don't you think it over for a few days."

"Unnecessary," I announced straight out. My mind was made up, had been all along, and once it was, that was that.

He slumped a little in his seat, relieved, then shot me a look — "You sure?"

"'Course." I grinned with parched lips — kept the saliva building.

•

Lift-off was scheduled for January 2, the next best time for entering the trajectory or Window, so there wasn't a moment to lose. I hurried back to New York, and three days later, after getting rid of the Volks and my furniture, and obtaining a leave from the college as Watson wanted it, for reasons of health — mum was the word — reported for training at Houston's Manned Space Center.

Soon as my gear was stowed — in this sweet, little apart-

ment they'd had done up for me — Watson was at the door
in one of those white jumpsuits everyone wears down there,
with Koviak peeping twinkly-eyed behind him, in a fetching
shirt dress of dark green.

I'd changed into jeans, a T-shirt, and sneakers, by the by
— to be my outfit from then on, for the record.

The first order of business was to introduce me to the
staff, for which purpose a meeting was being convened.
However, as it wasn't to take place for a while yet, Watson
suggested that we wander around for a bit while he filled
me in some more about the flight; Koviak, who only wanted
to know if I needed anything, promptly skedaddled.

There was no end of passageways there at Houston as I
was now to find out, all of them long with the same immaculate white walls as in the HQ building in Washington. . . .

The spaceship would consist of four parts, Watson began to instruct — a mission module (MM) in which I would
live during the trip, an excursion vehicle (EM) for maneuvering around in Planet X's atmosphere, and two of the new
kinds of rockets, which had gaseous nuclear cores. Saturn V's
with boosters would lift the MM and EM, each connected to
one of the GNCR's, into earth orbit. There the two greater
units would be joined, after which one of the GNCR's would
be activated for insertion into the trajectory. Watson paused
— did I follow him?

Well, I had and I hadn't, my mind'd sort of gagged at
"gaseous" and "nuclear." But why be a killjoy. Must be a
library somewhere around here where one can bone up on
this stuff, I schemed.

Watson quickly picked up the thread — once the vehicle
had made it through the cloud, the instruments would provide more definitive data respecting Planet X, whereupon if
an orbit was feasible, I would briefly have to take over the
controls, otherwise auto-guided. Should it come to a landfall
as well, I'd be happy to know that the EM was heavily armored and capable of delivering an ultra-speedy getaway. But
no need to worry, the gang both at Houston and Cape
Kennedy would see to everything — every possible contin-

gency — in due time.

Fair enough, it seemed to me.

"I suppose you'd like to know about your accommodations in the MM," Watson threw out.

"Well yes, naturally" — as who wouldn't have liked to in my shoes, about to spend a goodly time in it as I understood.

The ecology was to be completely closed, meaning that everything — food and water as well as air — would be recycled. Watson stared hard — "Do I have to draw you a diagram of what your diet and beverages'll consist of?"

I shook my head — nothing new there.

In addition, whenever a hankering arose, I could enjoy a little respite from complete weightlessness by pumping on an exercycle, whose pedals were connected to a gravity simulator. "How's that for comfort?" Watson crowed.

"Fine, just fine. Very good to know." Thank goodness for a draft from a ventilator shaft we were then passing. . . .

The meeting was about to start, we were approaching the door to the main auditorium.

"One other matter," Watson put in — his voice became husky. Mum was really the word about all of this, if for no other reason than the panic it might cause if people found out at this point. So if it was alright with me, they'd send me up at night, fast, with communication, by coded blips, kept to an absolute minimum. Should someone from the media or another busybody make inquiries, they were to be told that this was a military affair, ask no further questions, please, get lost.

Whatever they at NASA said, was my feeling.

"Ah yes, one more thing" — the right corner of Watson's mouth curled up into a half-smile. "Ruth felt it only fair that you be the one to give the operation a name, the MM and EM too if you've a mind to."

"How very nice of her," I cooed — meant it. "And I'll certainly give it some thought."

Later that night, when I was alone in my place, just the thing came for each: Project Guinevere . . . Arthur . . . Lancelot.

From the next day on, beginning bright and early in the morning, every waking hour of mine was spent in some form of prepping, including stuffing myself to capacity with highly nutritious food, usually prepared by my own hand since the patient knows best.

[Ed. But, alas, the author became sidetracked — in conjecturing a romance between Ms. Koviak and Mr. Watson, who wore a wedding ring — and never did elaborate on what her new regimen amounted to. Let the following entries from the Diary serve to give a general idea.]

July 20. Day 2.

6 a.m. 3 miles around the track — 1 walking, 1 jogging, ¼ sprinting, rest walking.

7 a.m. Brkfst — Freshly squeezed oj, stone ground whole wheat, corn oil marg., skim milk.

8 a.m.-12 On the Wheel, trying to beat that damn 5.5. Maybe soon. Tomorrow at this time the tech says I'm scheduled for loops in a specially-rigged jet, supposed to accustom body to shifts of gravity. Day after to be spent "brushing up" on my flying with an instructor from the AF Academy, hoo hah.

Noon. Lunch — Roast white meat chicken without skin, salad with olive oil and vineg. More bread, milk, etc.

1-5 p.m. Acclimatization to the deep-dark in the Apollo 8 flight trainer. I'm to go thru all the missions!

6 p.m. Dinner — More of same.

8-10 p.m. In the water tank in diving gear with lead weights. Somehow makes you weightless, don't ask me.

Certainly takes one's mind off things. . . .

Aug. 15. Just back from 3 days of pitching tents in the wilderness of Wyoming, under the tutelage of Sgt. Michael Henriquez of the US Marines, scion of Cochise (through his mother).

Fun, fun! . . .

Sept. 20. More fun, 4 steamy days in the swamps of Panama, shepherded by Lionel & Sanford Johnson, both black, no relation, from the AF survival school there.

I bagged a wild fowl (?) all by myself, we cooked it in a cookie tin.

A far cry from chicken soup, but. . . .

Oct. 12. Out bobbing around in the Drink today with a mock-up of Lancelot, my trusty Explorer, & frogmen.

Veree saltee.

Once everything settled down to a routine and everyone was convinced that I could handle long periods of darkness alone, I spent the afternoons in the Apollo trainer trying, with the help of simulation tech Charles Wong and a contact of his at the Library of Congress, to get ready to meet face-to-face with X's intelligent beings, should there be any and that prove possible. The deal with Watson was that I should push for this only if they and I hit it off well first over the air waves, naturally. After meditating on it, I added the following conditions: their normal way of communicating had to be by means of sound, and the sounds in some way had to resemble our utterances, or else they somehow had to be capable of seeing.

[Ed. The account of her course of study occupying many pages in the narrative, I have substituted this concise version from the Diary.]

1. Language — I want to condition myself to deal with strange intelligible sounds. The way I'll do it is to study a number of foreign languages conversationally on tape, beginning with the not-too-difficult German because it's close to English (both in the Indo-European family) & I'm already familiar with it on a reading basis from school — and progressing by uneasy stages (haha) to the "impossible" — Hebrew, which while belonging to the Hamito-Semitic family, is Western, and which I know somewhat too; Chinese with its killer-diller tones (but "normal" word order); and finally Japanese, where the verb comes after the object on top of everything else. The goal is NOT fluency, remember.

2. Drawing — I want to become "literate" in it (as opposed to accomplished or even competent at drafting). Copying is the answer. I'll do it only from the best, nat'rally — Rembrandt & Goya. Try parts of a given work first, finally render each one faithfully in entirety, do it over and over until I can make a pretty exact copy with my eyes closed practically.

But my studies didn't end there. Seemed to me I had to have something to say to X's intelligentsia — something besides how fantastic our technology is, which would speak for itself in the fancy-schmancy stuff I brought along, first and foremost in my means of transport.

3. Humanities — I want to fill in the gaps left by my schooling so as to make my background more representatively human — to become conversant with the best that was thought and said in the whole human past, not just Western European. I'll read or re-read —

a. History

1) Earth history — especially vertebrate, mammal & primate evolution, both psychological and physiological, in other words as a background to human hist. To be on the lookout for boo-boos, both scientific & theological.

2) Human history — post-neolithic developments! With a keener eye for lopsided views (Western, male, etc.) than when I was in school.

b. The literary masterpieces of Russia, the rest of Eastern Europe, Islam, India, China & Japan; also the Bible and the Kalevala.

c. Illustrated studies of non-European art, particularly Near & Far Eastern and to some extent African, Mayan, Incan, American Indian, Polynesian etc. (That'll have to do the trick for "art"; music I can't do anything about obviously.)

But Rome wasn't built in a day, as Flora used to say. To be continued on shipboard, Watson and I agreed.

•

On December 1st we all moved bag and baggage to Cape Kennedy.

From then on until practically the moment I left, there were constant dress rehearsals of the different phases of the space mission in look-alikes of Arthur and Lancelot, including simulations of X and its sun under a variety of conditions with — boop boop dee boop — the actual glitches piped in as an added touch. And in the water tank every night, among other things I practiced snipping off the tip of a toothpaste-like tube and squeezing a puree from it into my mouth — to be my only form of sustenance on the trip.

At last the big day rolled around. At 5 p.m., Koviak came to drag me off for my physical, the last one. At 7:30, after a quiet meal with Watson and her, during which we toasted my success and well-being with a little wine, it was on with the suit and off to the real thing in the van.

"Sure is something," I sighed, the two rocket shafts standing tall, but I mean tall, against the dark starry sky . . . the tails of the Saturn V's on the bottom venting snowy billows . . . Arthur and Lancelot perched way up like two pimples.

"Mm," Watson agreed, something on his mind.

Koviak sneaked me a smile, a thin one. . . .

"Last stop!" the driver called, as we pulled up to Arthur's gantry.

"Boy," I said quietly — struggled to my feet, burdened with all that gear on plus my ditty bag.

Watson got out first, hopping slimly down, so as to give me a hand. We walked in silence, with me in the middle, to the elevator, got on it, and Watson pressed for the top.

"This's as far as I go," Koviak announced in a quavery voice when the door slid open. "Take care" — she put her arms around me, squeezed, her eyes two leaky pieces of jade.

I took off along the walkway — Watson followed right behind. Gads, it was scary, such a long way down to terra firma.

The hatch there at the other end was waiting, a black hole. I crawled in onto my couch. Watson bent over me from the outside and began fastening the straps and so on. Finally, done — I was ready.

"Well," he said all sorry-like, took my brown-padded hand in his bare one, very white — "'Luck." Smiled a full smile, both corners of his mouth turning up. . . .

[Ed. The Diary provides a more graphic account of the final moments.]

I'm all alone now — hatch is sealed. The thing below me — the super-duper nuclear firecracker on top of the Saturn V — is weaving, waving — in the wind, I guess. Feel like a monkey in a palm tree, real lofty one.

The guys in Mission Control keep blinking for my "Fe" (signature). There they are again, nervous maybe. . . .

I can see the lights of several towns and hamlets hereabouts, including the one across the bay. Wonder what they're making of this, did they buy the story about this as being military? I suppose — as long as it didn't get out about the glitches —

Lift-off! We had lift-off! I'm up (¿), the world is sailing by below (?). Boy, what a lot of rattling sound & fury.

Now for the hook-up with my Lancelot and the other firecracker. Gonna be one lon-ong dogtail, is all I can say. . . .

So this is it. They're after me for my "Fe" again — "All set?". . .

My whole life just passed before me. But not really, just a sense of it . . . Flora . . . Dave . . . the things I'm capable of doing . . . writing . . . still.

What do you say, give this crazy business up and tell Watson and his tootsie to go shove it or what? . . .

Nix.

●

[Ed. As the voyage out was rather uneventful and the account once again overly long, I have selected highlights from the Diary to stand in lieu. Quite a few of the items represent intellectual epiphanies and have a bearing on subsequent developments, so perhaps the best thing to do is glance over them now, saving them for closer perusal at a later, more appropriate juncture.]

Day 2. Arthur's been going juh-juh-juh-juh terribly since I don't know when — vibrating. Watson warned that something like it might happen, but I never dreamed it would be like this. Can anything be wrong? . . .

Day 8. No let-up yet, and I got a period this "a.m." — as luck would have it, an extra lousy one. Can hardly hold a thing down(?). Only consolation: Koviak told me on the q.t. in the van that women who are in the air over considerable periods of time — like airline stewardesses — quite often get a long holiday from it. Good riddance to it. . . .

Day 10. Peace at last, my innards too — hooray!

Now back to school — Hebrew I, Rembrandt III, the T'ang Dynasty. . . .

Day 60. Can't understand people who say they're losing touch with their emotions. A character in a novel I read once — "The Golden Notebook," I think — goes to a shrinkeroo because of it, and now & then I've run into real-live folks who've done the same.

Me, mine are too much with me.

The only thing is, my memory's not what it used to be (except, of course, when it comes to the computer commands, down pat forever). . . .

Day 83. It was they who failed:

— the editors & their bosses, asses all of them

— "The Times" with no choice because of the gelt — the gelt from the Advertising — but to knuckle under

— the public too, even with the disastrous results before their eyes — cheap junk that passes for literature. . . .

Day 253. There's no denying it, I miss Light.

One frigid afternoon last January, when that piece from "Guinevere" came back from that last journal, What's-its-name, I watched the sun go down from the roof — go down in Jersey.

Afterward, an orange glow remained on the horizon, which little by little turned to red and deeper red, finally purple.

I leaned with my head against a metal pole there.

Day 254. Contemplating the Stars

In bed at night when I was a kid, a streetlight used to send a pale-golden gleam in at the window, and another — softer, warmer — would peep in from under the door, where Flora was turning dishes over in soapy water. . . .

Day 269. By the by, 'bout time you went & paid your respects at the graves — if & when you return.

And don't go bolloxing everything up the way you usually do — Mama's in Beth David, he's in Woodlawn. . . .

Day 380. Now that I've read a bit —

On Structure

The beginning, middle, and end that we here in the West take for granted as the basis of structure is surely Indo-European in origin

*(besides the Germanic — Greek, Latin, Sanskrit, Gaelic, Slavic etc.)
stemming from their preoccupation with Time, as reflected in their
verbs, which in turn may have been influenced by a temperate zone
setting, where the seasons are constantly changing and in extreme contrast to one another.*

*The Hamito-Semitic community (Ancient Hebrews, Arabs, Egyp-
tians, Mesopotamians etc.) has always been aware of this beginning-
middle-end mode of organizing things and has even at times paid it lip
service by using it in a minor way, but never made a great to-do about
it (like the Ancient Egyptian pyramid builders with respect to geome-
try, which they employed of course but saw no reason to write about
meaningfully, leaving that to the Greeks, who took credit for it). The
Hamito-Semitic idea of structure, by contrast, is a seemingly endless
repetition of things and larger units incorporating those things — the
Old Testament & Koran being excellent examples of it both in content
and style. Correspondingly, this idea of organizing by "bead stringing"
might have taken root in a more equatorial clime, where one day is
much like the other.*

Day 381.

On the Origin of Sex Distinctions in Language

*While there's no question that sex distinctions in language are
initially owing to a recognition of the perceivable biological dif-
ferences between males and females, maybe their subsequent elabo-
ration — in the original Indo-European and Hamito-Semitic at least
— started with those two groups going in for animal domestication on
a grand scale, the one primarily horses, the other sheep and goats.*

*One thing's for sure, the distinction is stressed somewhat more in
Hamito-Semitic than in Indo-European — it crept into the Hamito-Semitic verb; certainly is there in the Hebrew ones. Perhaps the difference
is due to the kinds of livestock that each group favored. That is, while
for the Indo-Europeans there was always the option of hunting with
their steeds, the Hamito-Semites had to concentrate more on breeding
(& hence pay more attention to the sexes of animals) in order to keep
up with tribal consumption of their flocks. . . .*

*Day 411. Earthly life seems early on to have separated into heads
& tails, the one for getting somewhere (& eventually ratiocinating
about it), the other ka-ka. It's tempting to wax witty where we humans
are concerned, not excluding yours truly — but let it be. . . .*

Day 618. Some beliefs in an after-life must simply have arisen thru a conviction concerning the efficacy of a good night's sleep after a day of crisis & pain — all the better if under the sharp-eyed vigilance of a mama or an old geezer of a Chief. . . .

Day 856. And if this more or less twelve-billion-year-old universe of ours is after all but a megastar, indeed one of many, and each of those megas is at a certain stage of development (like the stars proper) and all of them together form a greater, supermega, of which there are others young & old . . . and so on. What then?

Day 857. On the other hand, let's say that this is It, only instead of the Big Release with the galaxies flying off in n-teen million different directions, supposing — well, it looks as if a massive explosion took place but actually there's something all around, pulling.

That last day in New York, while sitting and waiting in my place for the Salvation Army to come and haul away all my "finery," I saw in the window, where the morning sun was pouring in, a thousand, thousand golden specks floating down. Or so it seemed — was really Gravity getting 'em.

·

"Now we're talking!" I sang out, right after breakfast on Day 981.

The computer had winked on, screen was reading —

ENTERING GAS

Also gave its chemical composition: hydrogen, helium, and something else — I don't remember anymore.

I tapped out another "Fe," that being a part of the arrangement, and hiked myself up for a look-see.

Sure enough, was pitch black outside — well, charcoal grey.

So what's new on X, I wondered. A new message had recently been added to those being beamed there, in a variety of formats including Lincos, an artificial language some scientist cooked up based on semantics — "Something different but harmless is coming your way, over please." A special yellow light on the panel was supposed to indicate when an answer was being made — it was still dark. I tip-tapped on the keyboard again.

The glitches were going the same as ever.

Well, tomorrow's another day, as Flora was fond of saying. . . .

"Aha!" I cried about a week later, while half-basking on the exercycle.

The stars were out again — yessirree, all that murkiness was in the past, blown away like candle smoke in a breeze. And one of those white pinpoints seemed a little larger and brighter than the others, in which case —

I "swam" over to the keys. "What do you say?" my fingers queried.

Absolutely, came the answer, and there was more: the planet was number two of three, and it had two moons . . . something . . . something . . . the combined mass of the two aforementioned celestial bodies was slightly larger than that of Earth's Moon.

"Now how about it?" I lectured the yellow answer light, still "silent." And the pulses?

Were the same, except more intense now that we were closer. . . .

"Oh joy!" I whooped, first thing on waking a month or so after that.

A lime-colored crescent was out there flanked by a pair of tiny bluish drops — X and its moonlets — gum drops.

"Okeedoke, what's the story now?" I asked with the keys.

I got plenty of interesting dope, the machine answered: the atmosphere is bearable, there's negligible radiation and minimal volcanic activity, the surface consists of proportionate amounts of dry land and water, day and night are a cool 20 hours.

Now came the clincher:

NOON TEMPERATURE = 70° (AT POLES)

100° (EQUATOR)

"Hot dog!" I just about screamed out — my whole being

was positively yearning to stand firmly on something, you understand.

But hold on — the screen'd scrolled to a second page:

G-LEVEL = 1.65

Darn, old Gravity again, I brooded, higher a smidge (by +.65) than back home. Oh well, first things first. Unless I hear otherwise from mine hosts, we'll go for an orbit at least, definitely.

Mine hosts were still keeping their own counsel according to the yellow one, and as for the glitches, they were unchanged too. . . .

"Now how 'bout that," I trilled in a few more weeks.

Overnight that sliver of lime kid-candy had turned into a circular disk, showing a single continent of bright emerald green — vegetation for sure, the instruments said — and a greyish-brown ocean.

And the pulsing?

Was something fierce now — coming from the land only.

"Okay, Glitchers, here we go, now show your kissers!" I hollered out on 1046, having successfully achieved orbit, by golly.

I'd fixed it so we'd start swinging round on the dark side of X, as Watson and some of my instructors had suggested in this event. Our course lay across the continent, beginning with its extreme western edge, like where California'd be.

"Just don't shoot," I added under my breath, "if that's what you've been fixin' to do all along."

Everything below lay in darkness, not so much as a flicker anywhere. The only light was coming from above — two violety rays from the moonlets.

We were cruising along just fine now, though actually speeding. "No, no, no," I sang in time with the scanners. The sky began losing its gloom . . . more . . . more . . . and giving portents like back home before dawn.

Now all at once my eyes were filled with mother-of-pearl — daylight! Theirs but no matter. My mouth opened:

Hail holy Light, offspring of Heav'n first-born!

It's by Milton, 'case you were wondering. Wrote it when he was blind. . . .

What's going on below now? Not a blessed thing. It was extremely overcast all over, and in between the fluff, as far as I and the sensors could make out, the ground was pretty uniformly green, that was all.

As for the glitching — out of this world, as it should have been since we were right on top of it now. . . .

Maybe they make their homes underground, I speculated as the eastern shore came into sight. If any human had a shot at such a prime piece of real estate with such ideal conditions, she or he certainly wouldn't behave like that, you better believe it. But as the old saying goes, what's sauce for the goose may by no means be etc. Even so, wherever mine hosts are, how is it they haven't said boo yet? With all that equipment they have, capable of making such a fracas, they surely gotta be aware of my existence by now, no? . . .

You know — we'd just crossed the wispiest white line, a little beach at the waterline no doubt, and were heading out over the sea, like a piece of muddy brown slate — you know, it's just possible the Joint Chiefs of Staff were right after all, there is no one.

I looked . . . and looked. My battery of electronic eyes did the same.

Wasn't anything on the water or in the air either. . . .

So what's the good word, I canvassed myself, as "California" appeared on the horizon in the waning light.

Well, to tell the truth, that extra bit of gravity or no, I sure would like to stretch my legs, enough is enough already.

Still, didn't do anything hasty-like, it's important to realize that — waited for us to complete two, three more passes, 'case they were playing possum, never having laid eyes on a mechanical contrivance aloft before.

After that, was only a matter of suiting up, sending them back home a last "Fe" peck, crawling through to Lancelot, sealing off — and blast off!

Destination: "Long Island — Jones Beach."

•

'Course in my eagerness to romp in the dunes I totally forgot about the extra big build-up of g's that I was bound to meet up with on the way down, and the next thing I knew, or didn't know, I was out but good.

Came to just in time to see through the monitors — five of them, all black-and-white — that we were skimming low over the water, cutting through many a curlicue of white cloud, and heading straight for a sandy beach indeed, whose tree-line we would surely plow into if I didn't take some kind of action at once.

"Lancelot, looks like you're gonna have to attend to this all by your lonesome," I groaned, still out of it, zonked — just managed to reach up over my head to flick a special auto-landing switch.

Lickety-split the plane made a sharp turn to go southward over the strip of sand, and moments later touched down with a thump-squeak — then raced along with a roar as wide-leafy foliage streamed by on the right.

Soon as we rolled to a standstill, I struggled up, clutching my heart, and fell on the controls, threw them into reverse — backed up with my old Volks touch — *Yeeeek!* —into a little indentation in the trees, so that Lancelot would be visible only from the front if anyone should happen by.

I'd expended my last mite of energy I felt — activated the warning system and auto-evac, shut down power. Out.

"So, whada we have here?" I sighed from the couch after a while.

Focused on the first monitor, studied the contents of the

screen carefully, went on to the next . . . and the next.

Ahead was sand with rocks perhaps sixty feet wide between me and the water — beyond, the sea, with nothing on
it and hardly a ripple in it. The beach on either side, alas, was
visible only for a hundred yards or so, as we'd ended up on a
curve in the shoreline.

To my rear — no surprises there — was a choked tangle
of bush as quiet.

Overhead only white-seeming sky with no sign of sun and
absolutely nothing flying, not even a "sparrow."

And the air, what's that like? I pressed to open the vent
near me a crack and took a sniff. Had a slightly swampy
smell, but seemed otherwise alright. Still feeling poorly with
the same load on my chest, I opened that one and all the
other vents wide, still on my back, and cut off the air condi-
tioning.

[Ed. The next two weeks were spent inside the ship pulling herself together while hoping that the intelligent indigenees would not try and make contact until then; her wish
was granted. Once again, the Diary provided a most necessary shorter distance between two points it seemed to me.]

Day 1. . . .

p.m. Good'n gloomy out, like Coney Island off season with the
lights from all the rides & stuff turned off. The moonlets are up there,
frizzy-like, but no stars — hasn't cleared yet. . . .

Achtung! Some "animal" sounds here & there from the woods —
bleepings, hootings . . . soft.

Day 2.

a.m. Everything shrouded in thick fog. No sight of the sea, only the
immediate greenery behind. . . .

"noon." It's lifted, but the sky's overcast again.

The trees are much like they were in Panama: eg, palm-like with
a pineapple-husk trunk & blades for leaves; sort of hairy bark with
oodles of needles resembling our conifers; having elephant skin plus
feathery fronds & long whips hanging down. BUT — they're all pretty
short — the tallest 30 feet at the most — and very thick at the base,
with a broader spread of "arms.". . .

Some branches have bounced, leaves twitched several times, but I *couldn't see anything, whatever it was well hidden. Gotta be on the small side.*

Boy, I sure am itching to get out, have a look around in natural light instead of this misleading black-and-white. But that's got to wait till I get myself in shape again. Tomorrow I'll start on Pete Saito's exercises. With a little luck, my g-tolerance should be up to snuff in a week, maybe 10 days given this added burden of weightfulness.

p.m. Like last night. Two more "animal" sounds (I think): a hollow clacking like a pair of 2x4's being knocked together; a shrill tsip, anguished kiss.

Day 3.

a.m. The fog again.

"noon." Pretty much gone, like yesterday, but cloudy still. Beginning to wonder if it isn't this way all the time.

Some things're moving around in the trees again, but I've yet to see anything spread "wings" and soar. . . .

p.m. The same, the same. . . .

Day 8. . . .

"noon." Exercises're coming along fine, bless that tech Saito. Tomorrow, running in place . . . in a few days, with the knapsack and stuff in it.

"Okeedoke, alleyoop!" I sounded out at midday on Day 14, feeling infinitely improved. [Ed. However, this sanguine appraisal of her physical condition should be tempered by the following, made retrospectively during the flight back: *Never felt entirely comfortable there on X, even after making self really fit later on. Always had the urge to slump when standing, sink into a bottomless pit sitting or even lying down.*]

As you can imagine, even after all my vigilance, I wasn't exactly dry under the armpits at the thought of taking this next step — sticking my head out — and when I stood tiptoe after disengaging the armored plate, my knees began to jitter plenty. All the same, I did it, to find — well — everything not much different from the way it had been on the video: the sky off-white with the sun showing through a luminescent smudge; sand and rocks various shades of light grey; water like lead in color; greenery dark and dull.

No one was around . . . no one turned up.

I poked my upper self out like that a few more times that day and on and off the next, on the off-chance that a welcoming party might be lurking thereabouts in the brush in a state of shock. No luck.

p.m. Moonlets, an anemic sort of blue.

Day 15. . . .

"noon." It's something at least, some "ants" marching along the ground single file — I trained the binoculars on'em. Bodies are long & thin, legs (6 or 8) very heavy. Couldn't help a tee-hee, reminded of racing cars, the kinds with the big, fat tires! Grand Prix ants.

C'mon, this is foolish to hang around like this, I nagged at myself when Day 16 dawned. Go on out there already. You've got work to do, then we'll go home.

Like before I waited till the "sun" was well up for the sake of maximum visibility on everyone's part — mine hosts' as well as mine, should they exist and some of them be in the vicinity after all. And I'll tell you it was something climbing down with my back exposed like that — thought I'd split a gut.

"Now then," I murmured with heart knocking, and feet planted at the bottom of the ladder.

Not so much as a pebble anywhere was out of place.

I advanced the few feet to the plane's nose . . . pushed on to Lancelot's other side . . . came round the tail to the ladder again.

You know, I'm really beginning to believe there's no one, I confided to myself. Now — slapped my hands together — time for serious business.

I went back in for the sample bags, and came right back down with them slung, nifty black leatherette. "First some a-a-air" — I drew out a test tube, uncorked, waved, re-corked and tucked away. "Next ur-urth" — I bent over and scooped — "'n rocks" — grasped, chucked."Now lea-eaves" — hopped over to the nearest tree, which happened to be a "fern" — pulled, stuffed. Stooped, plucked from a "rhododendron" bush — crammed.

Just some water, then we're done, I told myself breathing

hard, all bags but one piled at my feet. But boy oh boy, I sure don't relish this part, being separated from the ship.

Hurried forward ten paces, whirled round with shoulders braced — everything was the same. Hurried another ten — ditto.

I can't go on like this, I thought, I can't, the tension is too great. Decided to cover the remaining distance in reverse. Took out another of those test tubes with a pair of tongs and rubber gloves, waterproof of course, in preparation. Kept a close eye peeled . . . ahead . . . right . . . left . . . as I scuffed each foot back.

"So, " I exhaled, when finally there was a lupping of wavelets from behind me. Spun round, dropped to my haunches, and plunging the thing in, pulled it out overflowing — hopped up, re-spun, stoppering.

Enough excitement for one day. . . .

Back on the top of the ladder, before sliding into the ship and battening down, I held the tube up to the light.

The water had many black specks in it — like flakes of grimy dust. But for all I knew those pieces could have been churned out of some slimy creature's bowels. Yuck.

•

So what's next on the agendy, I inquired of myself the following morning, all cozy on a parachute plumped up with marsh grass close by the ladder.

Breakfast was in progress on a square of green vinyl — saltines topped with almond butter and guava jelly, and Earl Grey, brewed on a can of Sterno with water from the ship's tank, naturally.

Well, go tomorrow I guess, what else.

My eyes focused on the sea, as grimly grey and desolate as ever. Imagine, I thought, a perfectly decent world and utterly without intelligence it seems — which all at once struck me as being very funny, so much so that finally I had to dry cheeks from laughing so hard.

Eh, what's the rush, why not hang on a bit, it came to me.

There's plenty of stuff left in the ship's stores yet, have your-self a little vacation at governmental expense. You deserve it, no? . . .

Boy, it sure beats correcting compositions, I congratu-lated myself along about dinner time, with operations shifted to underneath a "palm tree."

Purling away nearby was a wee pot of macaroni, to which I'd add, after it was done and drained, a pack of dried beef and a bouillon cube — on deck a handful of marshmallows to be toasted for dessert.

Do I dare go for a swim tomorrow? No, too much of a risk of swallowing those noxious-looking specks, whatever they are. The same applies to paddling around in the ship's life raft — though how it could possibly turn over with so little breeze and such a minuscule tide I can't conceive. . . .

Well, maybe the thing to do's to stretch our legs a bit, I concluded at nightfall, see what's what beyond the curves in either direction. Probably more curves, but what the hay.

I took a sip of brandy-for-emergencies, the eyecup from the first aid kit doing nicely for a snifter, thank you . . . glis-tening with the final licks of the Sterno. And then there's the laundry.

An idea came, like a seizure! I could stretch the water supply out if I washed everything in the sea, wearing the rubber gloves and galoshes of course!

I considered, sipping some more . . . the two moonlets all fuzzy blue on high.

Okay, I'll do it, it's a deal. Hauled myself up — "Hoo-haha! Hooray!" Threw the empty eye-thing in the air, leapt up after it, sort of.

It'll be a real beaut, you'll see, I promised, on my fourth trip out the next day, in my underpants, everything including the jeans spread to dry.

Draped around my neck was another parachute, and in hand two hooks like for cups I'd found lying on the floor inside. Was only a matter of screwing them into the bark and winding the parachute cords around them good and tight —

voilà, a hammock fit for a queen, just like in Survival.

"Darn!" — just as I was stepping off the bottom rung of the ladder, one of those hooks got away from me. "Oh no, I don't believe it!" — it had disappeared in the sand soon as it hit, pulled down by that extra .65.

"I gotta find it, just gotta, ain't no more," I mumbled. Dropped to my knees, began to sift, with the other hook parked between my teeth.

Just then the oddest thing — suddenly from the left on the beach came this *pom-pom-pom*, as of many feet pounding, bare feet on sand!

I looked up!

About a dozen darkish two-legged beings ran by, say halfway between me and the sea . . . roughly my size . . . wearing cape-like garments of different colors, hanging from the shoulders to the waist, nothing more.

"Oh wow!" I let out, my hair nearly standing on end — it was the suddenness of it, you understand.

But strangely not one of them took the least notice of me — or so it seemed — they all kept right on going toward the other bend.

"Oh wow!" — I couldn't climb back into the plane fast enough.

Chapter Two

Then felt I like some watcher of the skies
When a new planet swims into his ken;
Or like stout Cortez when with eagle eyes
He stared at the Pacific — and all his men
Look'd at each other with a wild surmise —
Silent, upon a peak in Darien.

Keats wrote that, 'case someone doesn't know, about a translation of Homer's *Iliad* done by a Renaissance poet named Chapman.

I wish I could say I was musing in a similar vein that day after diving into the ship and jamming the armored plate into place after me. But no, all I did was sit and shudder.

Didn't even remember about the monitors for a good long while. Boy, you sure are a ninny, I took myself to task then. For all you know, those alien types turned right around and are now busy gathering brushwood to build a fire or something. I reached up, pressed. Flick-flick-flick-flick-flick — all the screens flashed on.

No one was there.

So what's the good word, stay or go, I queried after an hour of watching some more.

Go, I think. Only there was the matter of the wash. Jeans I had another pair of up in Arthur, but all of my T-shirts, underpants, and socks except those I had on were on the sand outside, and as you know, it was going to be a long trip back. Go on out and get them, I urged, then blast off.

I'll tell you, it took the better part of that day just to get up the nerve — every time I was on the point of sallying forth, my knees began to give way just like when I was fixing to pop my head out at first. And at long last when I did steal out, toward "sundown," practically tumbled down the ladder going, and again coming back with all those things clutched tight. . . .

There, it's over, you did it, I soothed myself quite some time later, sucking on a good ole tube of puree by the light of a single little lamp.

Had the jeans on, rest of the stuff stowed. Everything'd still been damp, so I'd had to string a line across the length of the plane inside, drape it all, turn up the blower, then just before each item was completely dry, give it a good shaking out the top to get rid of those pieces.

So what's the good word now?

Go tomorrow — too tuckered out tonight.

•

You know, this's foolish, I told myself, with another tube in hand the morning after — eyes re-glued on the TV sets. If those aliens were returning or others had decided to come, they would've been here by now surely. So why don't you just relax.

Good reasoning, but I couldn't — simply couldn't.

Aw c'mon, my better self nagged, what is there to be frightened of actually? They didn't offer you any harm, did they? Matter of fact, if the truth be known, you really took fright because of their weirdo appearance. I was reclining on the couch by then, hands behind my head, legs folded. 'Fact, may even have been a little prejudice there on your part, their skins dark, admit it.

So take it easy, will you. And while you're awaiting developments, try and think back and remember whatever you can about them.

[Ed. The author provided a fuller description in the Diary.]

Alleyoop, thinking cap on.

Generally speaking — they were all definitely my size, at most an inch or two taller. Narrow at the shoulders, widening downward to the hips — like an hour glass with all the sand settled to the bottom, as men say of big-assed women. Definitely had one head, 2 arms, and 2 legs.

Heads — smaller than mine by a good third I'd say. Hairless I'm sure of it (possibly no hair anywhere else on them either). Had 2 eyes and a mouth apiece, where ours are. As to a nose??? Ears???

Arms — skinny. Hands — elongated, with a number (?) of tapering digits.

Thighs & calves — thick, like wrestlers' or handballplayers'. Feet — long like hands, & flattish. With each step, they all raised a knee almost to their bellies, maybe to keep from tripping over'em, feet (!?).

The skins — tawny, yes, but not all the same color: some brown, but others green or else purple.

Garments — let's call'em capes, also of three colors: red, yellow, and white.

So how is it no one's here to investigate further or something, I wondered at nightfall, still holed up.

Held a tube, half-finished, poised in the air. You know, there's one thing that troubles me — not one of those individuals who ran by so much as looked our way.

I considered — could they not have spotted us? Possible. If one's not on the look-out for something, especially something really way out, it could simply escape one. Supposing, for instance, they were all out for some exercise and particularly intent on it. Conceivable to pass right by and see but not see. That is, if anyone caught a glimpse in the process, they could have mistaken me, hunched over like that in the T-shirt and undies with the parachute round my neck, for a part of the terrain, the laundry lying there spread out too.

It's a possibility I guess. But Lancelot's nose high above ground-level? Did they all miss that as well?

[Ed. Another idea occurred to the author in the wee hours.]

Couldn't have been dummies or robots — too lively-looking.

How about this? They're for real but not smart at all — instead, some other brainy creature's pets or herd, the capes like our dog & cat collars, or nose rings for cows!

•

Well, you can't stay cooped up like this forever, now what's it gonna be, I asked myself bright and early the next morning, with still no one in sight.

I say, on with the show, the holiday that is, a voice like Flora's piped up within me.

I don't know, I debated uncertainly, I think I really want to go home.

Clearly it needed mulling over.

[Ed. The Diary presented the argument in a nutshell.]

What if some of those runner types do come back eventually & kill me?/ Well, once it's over with, it's over with.

How about mutilation? For instance, what if they get hold of you and tear off an ear or something, what then?/ You'd have to learn to live with it, like loads of other people back home with their physical handicaps.

And rape?/ There is no guarantee they're divided into sexes as we know 'em. But even if they are, remember how that bunch shaped up at least, the floppy feet! It'd still be like —

DUCKS'N APES!

I'm still not happy about it, I sort of whined, out there at last in the full light of day, such as it was (still cloudy). Had my behind perched on the edge of the hammock (up with a makeshift hook). Was all for putting my head in my hands.

The Flora-voice inside me spoke up again — So do us all a favor, take off already.

No, no, I protested, I said I'd stay and I will . . . for a spell. Swung my legs around, lay back.

But things certainly didn't improve over the next several hours — every time a leaf stirred, my eyes shot open. . . .

Eh, let's get the circulation going a bit, I suggested by and by. That's what we had in mind to do originally, before we were so rudely interrupted.

I went inside for the binoculars. Started off trudging to the right curve, around which they'd disappeared. After that, I'd go and look beyond the left one, where they'd come from.

Begging to report, as suspected —

Right — visibility 10 miles to another peninsula. I stood there for maybe 1/2 an hour — not a soul, nothing abroad./ Left — the same story, 5 miles vis. . . .

Should I change the location of the ship perhaps, I put it to myself, plodding back. For security purposes?

No, let it be. The thing moves only once far as I'm concerned, & that's when I give this place — X, that is — the heave ho.

•

Now what would it take to make you feel really at ease once more — was swinging slightly in the hammock the following day after breakfast.

I dunno, maybe sketch for a while, that's pacifying. Went and got a pad and pen. What'll it be? I know, a gazebo! I'll design it, and then later maybe try my hand at erecting one.

Now lemme see — I shifted into an anchoring position. I'll drive some saplings into the ground like so — made six x's in a circle. Then get hold of some twigs and lay them out like spokes, punch a hole in the ends, tie them all together, and then —

It was no use, I couldn't go on with it. WHERE ARE THEY? my being cried out. WHAT'S HAPPENING? . . .

Now what, I asked, once the being had calmed down.

You know, there's such a thing as bringing the mountain to Mohammed, my better self reminded.

Yes, that's a good idea. They won't come to me so I'll go to them — I'll go and find them.

Gonna be the trick of the year getting it all in, I crooned to myself not long after.

Had everything to take with me piled on the other chute around the knapsack and canteen.

[Ed. The Diary yielded a more or less complete inventory.]

food tubes — enough for one month. Don't think I'll be away anywhere near that long, but one can never tell — might be held up somewhere. Also, I'll need something to tide me over till something else to eat, if anything, presents itself should Lancelot (God forbid) be swiped or destroyed(!) in my absence.

pads & pens — lots, a must
flashlight
matches
green vinyl tarp — useful for everything from rain shield to pup tent
toiletries
sunglasses — on the slim off-chance
week's supply of underpants & sox
extra T-shirt
first aid kit — modified
compass
mini-tool kit
Swiss Army knife — for non-violent purposes
small hank of nylon rope. . . .

Just a matter of persevering and I think I can do it. If not, if it doesn't all fit, there's always a plastic shopping bag to accommodate the overflow.

Tantarah! In!

●

"So, here's another parting," I murmured, standing on the edge of the left-hand curve at day's dawning.

With one more step Lancelot's familiar aluminum-foil glint would be lost from view. I'd gotten it in apple-pie order just as the maintenance people at Cape Kennedy'd shown me, with the sheathing in place all over, so someone could get in only by pressing five pseudo-rivets that belonged to different series of genuine ones in a certain sequence.

I shifted away. My foot went up — came down in the same place. I faced toward it once more, homesick already.

'Course, if you'd rather not, Flora offered in my mind.

No, I'd rather, I assured.

"'Kay, here goes" — I turned again, stepped forward for real. Northward ho!

[Ed. A plan of sorts turned up in the Diary.]

Why go that way rather than the other? Just feel I should, that's all. I'll keep at it for 3 hours tops. If I come upon a settlement or some such in that time, I'll try & establish relations with'em, whoever the indigenees are. If there's no luck or can't make any headway with'em, I'll return to base . . . then decide whether to pursue it further & if so, how. . . .

When I got to that next peninsula five miles leftward and rounded the curve, lo, the coast was straight for a good long stretch — the sand, sky, and sea all silent grey in the still early light, the line of trees with a veil of mist over them.

An hour later by my watch (which, you understand, was not a true hour what with X's twenty-hour day) I spotted a trail — no question about it, a vrai one — into the woods.

"That's the ticket," I said as I approached it nice and easy like. Stepped in, began slogging up it.

Nothing, just trees all around at first. But soon there was a rare, beautiful fragrance in the air, exuded from I couldn't tell what . . . which somehow brought Flora to mind.

[Ed. This charming vignette from earlier in the Diary seemed to fit here.]

She used to keep a small, round powder box, like a tiny hatbox, on her vanity table when I was a kid . . . pale peach dotted with lilacs.

My mitts were forever itching to sink into that soft, cool, heady stuff inside. And she knew it too, kept a sharp lookout, always singing out whenever during the course of her dusting and so on she spied me near it — Don't tou-ouch, Felice.

Can't I just pick it up & smell, I begged once.

Alright, she said. But remember, she wagged a finger — DON'T open it.

Before long I heard skittering overhead on the branches and on either side in the bushes, and now and then got an actual gander at something — a wisp of tail and once for sure hindquarters, little ones.

Now look at that, I crowed to myself at a certain point.

Was a whole creature right smack in the way directly ahead — lizard-like, upright on its hind legs and all of a foot high, and get this, brown all over with reptilian-like skin except for the "armpits," where some tufts of hair were sticking out, flaming red.

Just for a moment it stayed there, sizing me up, then scampered off like everything else.

•

In another fifteen minutes, paydirt — what looked like some white domes the size of large wigwams were showing through the trees.

I put on steam and moments later came to a clearing, where maybe as many as fifty of those round, marblish structures were clustered together. Each had a single entrance covered with dangling strings of greenery, reachable by a short cement-like ramp down — meaning that the rooms or room inside were somewhat below ground.

No one seemed about in the unpaved footpaths between them.

Is everybody still asleep or what, I wondered, after waiting a while at the clearing's edge for someone to come out. Went down to the nearest doorway. "Hello!" I yelled through the vines (for lack of something better).

Was no movement inside or anywhere else.

Maybe those who live hereabouts are not at home, I theorized. Let's try another location.

I went back to the top of the ramp, started up the path there. "Hello, hello!" called out.

Silence, all over.

Possibly they're all away somewhere — I was in the center of "town" now. Cupped my hands — "HALLOO!"

No change. Was spooky.

"A fine howdya do," I grumbled after some more skulking around in the byways.

Well, let's have a look-see inside one of these places —
only not here, go on back to the one nearest the trail 'case
you have to get going in a hurry or something.

I returned to the doorway of that house and parted the
vines this time, stuck my nose in — I was alone. Added rest of
self.

Was rather chilly in there, like a wine cellar, but considering there were no windows, not as dark as expected, light
coming in through the wall(s) it seemed, which were an inch
or so thick.

I was standing on a landing, of cement like the ramp,
with a five-step stairway directly ahead. Below was a single
room, circular naturally, with a number of pieces of furniture
disposed around it — a large oval bed at one o'clock, a low
round table resembling a bass drum surrounded by three
bongoish stools at five, and a bulgy hamper like for laundry
built out from the wall at seven. All of it was white and looked
to be made of the same alabaster stuff as the place itself.

I stepped down and tested the bed, which had a bare
mattress of cottony texture — it gave like foam rubber. Noted
there was a ceiling-to-floor white drape behind the table,
concealing a cupboard I conjectured, but refrained from
snooping (which somehow struck me as going too far then).
Instead opted for lifting the lid of the hamper a smidge,
which turned out to be empty except for a small pile of soggy
leaves on the bottom, which was of dirt. . . .

Well, why don't we mosey on out and into some more of
these dwellings, see what's what in them too, I proposed,
after postulating from the size of the bed and number of
stools that three individuals resided there, parents and a
child perhaps.

I tried 3 in all — are absatootly identical inside! Only the ar-
rangement of the furnishings varies:

#1 — bed at 10 o'clock, table & stools 2, hamper 4

#2 — bed at 7, table etc. 12, hamper 3

#3 — bed 5, table 11, hamper 9

What can be? Every couple with one kid apiece, or do they all live
in menages a troises?!

There we are, now what? Was back out in the footways once more.

Why now, let's go and sit somewhere and have us a wee bit of well-earned refreshment, like in that first dome. We'll give'em one hour to show. If during that time I hear a sound as of the occupants or someone else in the village arriving back, I'll hop right out and begin my spiel. . . .

Inside I decided on the hamper as the best place to settle down, which, remember, was at seven o'clock in that particular house or foot of the stairs left as you entered.

"Boy, I sure am bushed," I sighed, with the pack off, canteen beside it. *Yuff,* yawned. The heat was partially to blame, it'd grown sultry by then.

I rested back against the hamper's curve. But the floor was so hard. If only — I considered the bed over there to my left, its big ovalness. Do I dare?

Who's been slee-eeping in my-y-y-y etc., Flora's voice sirened, crazily, in my head.

"Okay, okay," I pacified. I'll just stretch out here for a few secs, no harm in that, is there? . . .

Leave it to me, I fell fast asleep, for considerably longer than that hour. Woke with a start to find it much darker in there and not much brighter out to judge from the color of the sky through the vine-strands — was dusk.

Now you've done it, better get a move on right away — I jumped up, bent over for my stuff. Flashlight or no, didn't relish tramping through the woods at night, pulling up late like that at the ship either.

Uh oh — there were footfalls outside, no doubt about it . . . very close by, like on the ramp.

"Yessirree, really done it," I muttered, stock-still there, trembling a teeny bit.

An individual clumped in . . . then another . . . and another. They seemed to be of the same species as those runners from what I could make out in the gloom, with the same smallish head, narrow shoulders, and wide hips.

"Hel-lo-o," I said with a catch in my throat.

Nothing, no one uttered so much as a grunt back.

Clunk, something went, like a wrench on a zinc pipe, up there on the landing . . . something I didn't catch sight of when I entered. The three of them changed places. *Clunk*, the same thing went. They shifted round again — *clunk*.

Maybe they hear in another register, I tried to guess. "Halloo-oo!" I repeated squeaky-like.

Still nothing.

Deaf altogether then?

They began coming down the stairs, more or less side-by-side with those same heavily muscled legs and long, flat feet making those same high steps.

I sucked in my breath. My heart went pitter pat.

Having reached the room's floor, they veered right, and passing within a few feet of me, made for the table — leaving behind a foul stench, like from rancid butter, pyoo.

No sooner did their bottoms touch the seats than, of all things, the walls began to glow, reaching to nothing sensational — maybe sixty watts total — within a few minutes.

There was a brown, a green, and a purple. They had on those capes — the brown's red, the green's yellow, the purple's white.

"Hi," I said — gave a wee wave.

Again there was no acknowledgement — truly, it was as if they hadn't heard. But hearing they most assuredly had, and speech. Began making sounds to one another with their mouths — but such sounds, like a bunch of gurgles and gargles — and using their hands a lot in conjunction, which had five fingers apiece by the by.

They know I'm here and must've heard me, I argued with myself. But then again who knows, anything's possible, let's see what this brings. I slid a foot forward — oh, I'll tell you, I was having a thousand fits — slid the other foot up to join it.

The conversation broke off, the hands fell.

So there, I tweaked myself. Now for the routine. I took another step toward them. "Hul-loh," I gruffed as low as I could go.

They seemed to be waiting.

I went forward some more . . . slowly. "Hul-loh."

Despite the difference in color, they resembled one another to a T, at least to my inexperienced eye, the faces hairless like the tops of the heads, with two coal-dark eyes and a wide, narrow-lipped mouth that curled up at the corners like a serpent's, underlined by a minuscule chin and framed by no ears far as I could see. As for a nose, there was none whatsoever — instead, a hole like a navel where our nose is, which one assumed served the same purpose.

Here we go, I primed myself, at the table finally, come to a halt in the space between the brown and green. Drooped my shoulders (like one of the submissive types in Desmond Morris's *The Naked Ape*). "May — I — have — your — attention — please," hoarsed out like before, my idea being to convey the sense, then rush back to the hamper for a pad and pen in the pack.

Their cheeks puffed out like footballs inflating, and there was that rotten butter stink again but much stronger than before — from their skin, behinds, goodness only knows.

"Oh boy, message received," I murmured — turned away with itchy nose, teary eyes. . . .

So what's the story here, and what should I do now — was back at the hamper. The good-natured banter among them — for so it seemed — had resumed in the meanwhile, their cheeks the normal size again.

Well, happy 'bout my being here they're not, but not overly so, or they'd have hopped right up and chased me the hell out by now. But my standing close to them is another matter, obviously not to their taste for some reason — like my smell! So let's keep our distance and see if we can spend the night at least — which it was by then. And who knows, maybe they'll soften up in the process. Maybe I just need getting used to, like a new baby in the house. Some baby. . . .

What happened next! Believe you me, it's lucky I didn't have my back to them, or so help me, I would've been shot clean through the heart without a gun's ever going off if you know what I mean. Suddenly there was a CLICK!

Had to come from the table, I reasoned, still standing

and all woozy-like with the fright. What can they have in there?

Didn't take long to find out. One of them began turning the table's surface, which was round, you'll recall. Unscrewed it like a jar lid and stood it on end on the floor, held it there. The other two reached inside and lifted out three trays with bowls and cups on them, everything white. Then that first one putting the tabletop back on and receiving one of the trays, they all three set them down and began eating what was in the bowls.

But such eating! With a sort of thumb and forefinger, of their left hands as it happens, they picked out small chunks, which were off-white and fleshy, and flicked them in the air, then scrolling out their tongues (to a good three inches), caught the bits plummeting on the tips and — *shlup* — recoiled the tongues with the pieces of food on them in the manner of frogs on Earth.

Hahaha, I had to laugh inwardly, still by the hamper, leaning against the wall, all eyes. The tongues were the same color as the capes — the brown's red, green's yellow, purple's white.

Shlup, shlup, shlup — what manner of food're they eating, I wondered yearningly . . . lonely-like. Looks like some kind of seafood, maybe this world's version of lobster or crab, yum. Guess I don't dare eat anything here on X, do I? Too much of a risk from germs . . . possibly the stuff has a different chemical content, poisonous in some way to humans.

But what's this? Now almost at the bottoms of the bowls, they'd begun letting fly at each other's mouths with the remaining morsels, at the same time making a whole lot of cackly "Khee-khee's" way down in their throats as if they were really enjoying themselves.

Fini . . . now each had a cup in hand, drained it to the dregs, drinking as we do. . . .

Well, looks like I'm in, I sighed inwardly some moments later.

They'd stowed the trays with their dishes, were on their feet — the walls were beginning to dim. Pulling the capes off over their heads, they put them on the seats, and then neatly folding them, set off with those knee-steps in the direction of the bed, one o'clock.

Try and do likewise, I directed myself, seeing them recline back there. But just a sec — had to pee. Took the flash and stepped outdoors in the vicinity of the trail for a moment; then back inside, sucked up lunch and dinner — and then eased down so I lay flat, dragged the pack under my head.

One of them uttered something lowly; it sounded like "gluglug." Another seemed to answer louder: "Glugluglug." The third perhaps had something to say too: "Glugluglugluglug."

Now what can that be about — I listened with my eyes.

"Gluglug! . . . Glugluglug! . . . Glugluglugluglug!"

Hm, things seem to be heating up a mite, I alerted.

Smack! went something, a hand probably, as if on bare flesh. *Smack!* went another hand perhaps, the struck one striking back. *Smack-smack!* possibly the third party chimed in, taking sides with the one or the other.

I strained to see over there, the room being completely dark by then.

Smack! Crack! "GLUGLUGLUGLUGLUG!" one seemed to accuse. "GLUGLUGLUGLUG!" another flung back in that one's teeth — scratched, bit. "GLUGLUG!" went the third, perhaps pursuing a middle course. *Thud!* — someone spilled onto the floor. *Thud!* — a second came down. *Thud!* — the last.

Boy oh boy, I sure am glad to be out of that melee, I told myself.

Too soon — the next thing I knew, they'd all three rolled on top of me in a frenzy!

"Hey, what's going on here, what's the big idea!" I yelled. Pushed, tugged — wrestled. "Whew!" — finally got myself extricated. Crept away on my hands and knees to the wall behind the table, and the drape there.

The sillycrazy battle raged on — "GLUGLUGLUGLUGLUG!" *WHACK! SOCK!* Then all at once came to an end —

the three scrambled up and kneed back to bed. Became utterly still there.

Let's play it safe, stay here by the table for the night, I cued myself. Just, quickly, go back for the gear. . . .

Well, that was a wise decision. A while later just as I'd fallen soundly asleep there on the floor, one of them got up and stomped over to the hamper, lifted the lid and — *bang!* — slammed it down.

"Leave it to you to land in a home with an unstable family," I muttered.

●

I sure would like to give those three a piece of my mind, I grumped the next morning, they've got some nerve involving me in their troubles. Had a sizeable lump on my forehead and a beaut of a black-and-blue mark on my left shin, it felt like under the jeans.

But they'd awakened before me and silently come to retrieve their capes from the seats, the purple stepping over me, now were on the landing about to issue out through the vines.

Well, let's see what's what, where they're going at least — I sprang up. Except that by the time I got to the top of the ramp, they were nowhere and everywhere. Those narrow paths of packed earth were filled with trios of browns, greens, and purples wearing red, yellow, and white capes from all the other houses thereabouts, who seemed identical down to the oversized legs and flipper-like feet.

No one paid the least attention to me, no more than mine hosts had.

Are they all off to some kind of work or something, I speculated. From what I could make out, craning my neck, the whole crowd of them was heading for the other end of the village, probably the woods beyond, as I'd encountered no structure there large enough to accommodate that many in my explorations of the day before . . . only the white domes all of the same size.

So should I follow or what, I considered after a while. No, let's pull ourselves together, take stock here.

You know, it's not a bad set-up they have here, I acknowledged, back inside, on the purple's stool with the draped wall behind me, from which I had a view of the bed and hamper as well as door.

The table before me beckoned especially — how does it work, do you suppose? I scrutinized the side, looking for a seam, but couldn't find one — put my hand there to feel. "Ouch!" — got a shock I did. Tried another place lightly with a fingernail. Got another — drew nail right away.

Must be a security system, I figured, probably meant for animals that might wander in during the residents' absence.

As for other matters, betcha dollars to donuts the lights are controlled by the seats. That is, they're activated with the application of pressure when it gets dark out — because that's what happened yesterday if I rightly remember.

Be interesting to know how they get the food and liquid in there, whatever it is. Wouldn't be surprised, now that I think of it, if the catch holding the top on is likewise released when they sit down.

Now we'll see what the rest of the situation is like here, I announced, breakfast in my left hand, the rubber-handled screwdriver from the tool kit in right. Twice burnt, three times if one counted the head lump. 'Course this is trespassing, what I'm about to be about. But what choice is there if nobody communicates with one.

"First things first," I said, as I'm fond of doing.

I faced round to the drape — thrust the screwdriver shaft under it, hiked it up.

A cupboard was there; that is, there were shelves with things on them. ('Case you're having trouble visualizing this — ledges attached to a curved surface — think of the balconies in the dome of the Capitol Building or St. Paul's Cathedral.)

The things were as follows:

— three metallic nets the size of my fist, each attached to an end of a silvery rod, two to three feet long.

— a partitioned white wooden box resembling the ones we use to keep silverware in, except that it was missing one of the short sides.

— a disk a foot in diameter, also of wood painted white, with an inch-long peg protruding from the center by a half inch.

— a softballish ball of the same hard white stuff as the building and furniture.

Either toys or *objets d'art*, I hypothesized. Certainly the disk and ball, but maybe not the nets and box. . . .

"Next case," I chirped.

I turned toward the landing, where they'd all made clunk yesterday with something that escaped my eagle eye. "Aha!" I just about roared. Was something to the side of the left doorpost, on a level with my hip I gauged. Reminded of those pneumatic tubes you used to see in department stores once upon a time.

One-two-three I was up there, had the cover pried. I looked — was nothing there, just a hole. I skipped down and returned with the flash, shined it — still nothing. Tried the driver in it — *jiggle-jiggle-jiggle*. Still.

Eh — I let the cover drop, *clunk*. It's just a clunker, that's all.

"What else?" I addressed the air, the rubber handle itchy in my palm, empty tube stored in jeans pocket for burial later.

Ah yes, the hamper. Now was that individual who slam-banged the lid last night having the last word in the argument or what?

Step-stepped down, wedged the driver tip in, jacked the lid up.

"Ho ho!" I sounded out. "Whadya know."

Something was in it, resting on the bed of decomposing vegetable matter on the bottom . . . whitish, flatly rounded, say two and a half inches long, one and a half wide, a half inch thick. Like a sea-washed stone.

I put my hand down there, rubbed the surface with a fingertip. Was delicate, fragile . . . yes, no question about it, like our own eggshells. So that wasn't an altercation they were having last night — those were love taps they were giving each other!

Some dust had fallen on it, or so it appeared — I blew down there, gently. "As I live and breathe!"

Wasn't dust at all, but speckles, purple ones.

Gonna take a peek in some of the other hampers hereabouts, see if they have the same thing. . . .

Done . . . they do, but with different colored specks. #1. green. #2. purple. #3. purple. #4. brown. #5 green. #6. brown.

Think I'll 'vestigate a few more. . . .

Couldn't help m'self, did the whole village. And boy, talk about hard work, I'm all done in.

The score: found them in all but 4 houses, with the speckles continuing to be fairly evenly distributed. . . .

Next on the agenda, a little shut-eye, after which I'm gonna go and wait outside for them all to return, which let's assume'll be around the same time as yesterday. Want to study 'em a little more carefully, see if there's any reaction to me anywhere, among those who live in this part of town anyway.

As for the future, I'll spend a few more days here, see if I can effect a break-thru, 1st of all (unless there's reason to act otherwise) with mine hosts since they know me already. If it's no sale nohow, I'll go back to the beach and push on northward a bit more . . . possible these here're not the only fish in the ocean.

•

It was just before the twilight hour — the mists were coming on, the two moonlets purply peeping through. Everyone was hi-stepping it home.

"HUL-LOH!" I boomed out top of the ramp to mine hosts and their neighbors coming along the path. "Lovely evening we're having this evening." Smiled smearily, sans teeth.

The neighbors went down to their respective doors, mine hosts continued on to ours.

"Ahem," I made for real as they brushed by, letting out a spurt or two of that skunky butter gas.

"Here I am again!" I gaily greeted, bouncing down the stairs inside a few minutes later (after going to that place beside the trail to powder my nose).

The walls were alight, trays'd been doled out . . . meal was in progress with fingers lofting and tongues reeling in.

"Got one more trick up my sleeve," I said, back in my place by the hamper, seated there now on the floor. I dug out a tube from my pack, smartly nipped off the tip with the special scissors — held it up high above my head, stuck out my own tongue, dripped the puree onto it. "Pretty neat, huh?"

No opinion about that either.

The dinner game began, the three of them once again catapulting tasty tidbits at one another. Soon as it was over and they were on their way to bed, I ducked back to the drape in the fading light, rather expecting they'd be at the love-game afresh before very long.

Sure enough . . . within a minute or so . . . *bim!* . . . *bam!* . . . *bam!*

What do they do when they do it, I asked myself, while they pounded on, warming up for it I supposed. And what do they do it with?

Who knows, it could be anything anywhere. I'd given them the once-over several times earlier, outside and when they got up just before, but didn't notice a thing. Certainly their "groins" had nothing tell-tale on them, they were perfectly smooth in that area of their bodies in fact . . . like little girls' dolls.

I'll try & get a bead on their upper torsos tomorrow in the a.m. when they're putting on the capes.

●

Day 3.

Wish I could report some success of some kind, but nothing doing. Woke at the same time as they & said, Good Morning. No response. They came & got their capes, the purple again stepping over me. More old butter-stink, that's all.

Was too dark to make out anything clearly on their chests or backs. Seemed smooth there too. . . .

They went straight outside & I followed like yesterday. No change in the footways either — I might as well not exist for them. Correction: I have a sneaking suspicion they all look upon me as one of those animals that come wandering in for food from time to time, to beg for it, and if that doesn't work, possibly to snatch it. Something like that, betcha. . . .

Inside here, found a second egg in the hamper, exactly like #1 only with brown spots.

Went & looked in 'bout a dozen other hampers around . . . same story except for the empties, which are still. . . .

So what are we going to do today? What else — chase after'em, see where they've gone, what they're up to. . . .

Here's news. I picked up a trail on the other side of the woods. Guess what — work, my foot. Found'em all at a pond, just having a good time lounging around or swimming — with kids!

P.S. The water's clear — it doesn't have any of those disgusting black pieces in it!

[Ed. I found this next by the author on a page by itself later in the Diary.]

The Pond

A blaze of milk-green . . . surrounded by slatey ledges.

Dazed eyes looking, just staring . . . out of skins all pastel pink, chartreuse and lavender in that broad light, iridescent every so often as the clouds shifted.

I intoned, with Byron —

   The isles of Greece, the isles of Greece!

Where burning Sappho loved and sung. . . .

In the water here and there, some skimming along with easy scissor strokes.

Underneath, not far below, small dark-greyish forms flitting, in and around swaying bands of filament.

Now and then one such hopped on a great back and rode for a while, wagging a tiny rosy tongue.

p.m. Late, by flash, under the tarp.
Nothing further to tell really. Came home & waited for'em again like yesterday. Everything the same. . . .
Decided to re-bunk with mine hosts, hoping against hope. . . .
Scene identical to last night's down to the hamper-lid-bang . . . that'll be lil green dots I reckon, & there'll be the same or brown or purple just about everywhere else. . . .
What will tomorrow bring?

●

No two ways about it, something different's going to happen today, I know it, can feel it crackling in the air, I primed myself soon as I opened eyes, which was extra early in the a.m. Best get well out of the way of major traffic, was my advice. Scooted over to the wall, 11 o'clock, bag and baggage.

After going for the capes and donning them as usual, mine hosts pushed aside the drape and took up those nets on their silvery rods. Then proceeding to the hamper, each in turn scooped up one of the eggs and began moving toward the vines with it.

With those precious burdens hanging before them and that walk of theirs, to say nothing of the flounderish feet, they made one think of three giant chickens just home from fishing with the catch of the day.

Needless to say, I was right behind them, at a respectful distance 'course, and on reaching the outside, noted without a blink that the neighbors all around had emerged with their eggs. Everyone seemed to be heading leftward.

What were they going to do? Well, was only one logical possibility. Up a few rows to the left was a dome with only a landing inside the door and water like an underground stream below, where the room was situated in the others. (Meant to mention that one odd house before, sorry.) Anyhow, as I now saw it, the stream had to lead to the pond and each trio approaching the edge would empty their nets there.

I created the rest of the vision in my mind —

And there on the bottom of the stream the white ones with their brown, green, or purple speckles'll lie nice and peaceful-like, until one fine day they'll all burst open. And away in the current the funny new creatures — the infants — will sail, maybe spluttering at first but soon paddling along just fine.

Then on another day even more gala, after they've grown and grown and become socialized by consorting with the parents swimming, including learning the lingo, and perhaps made some "friends," they'll all crawl out and push themselves up on their feet — knee-step away. . . .

And then what? I don't know. But one thing's for certain, unless these individuals here've got a stockpile of equipment stashed in the woods, they won't go rushing to help the newly formed trios, their common offspring, put up houses and so on.

Even then, if they did have cement-mixing machines and the like somewhere, I have a feeling. For when you come down to it, the only know-how this lot seems to possess is for eating, drinking, and making merry plus being a little testy from time to time. And then, let's face it, that paltry glow the walls make, together with the wattage the tables and security systems use, could not possibly account for all that glitching in the air waves, even if there are a hundred such similar villages. So yes, it must be, it seems plain now, you have really known it in your heart of hearts all along — others're in charge here.

No use in hanging around any longer, enough of watching there from the top of the ramp. I went inside to get my stuff.

Only — only something was different when I came out

again. The whole tribe was still inching forward in the paths, with mine hosts somewhere among them. But now everyone's throat was going, and from them were issuing sounds other than those they normally spoke with . . . it was like a burbling. They were singing! Gradually it swelled to a squawkish yowl.

Boy, what a racket! Let's get going out of here in a hurry. Stepped onto the trail.

As for them, the rulers, leaders, wherever they are — I sent up a hand, fluttered it.

•

Well, my own daily routine had been disrupted that day — I hadn't even tasted a morsel yet. And now in the heart of the woods nursing a tube, suddenly I had to go — like real bad, couldn't wait until I got to the beach.

Bushes, forget, I'm not one for doing it in them. Wasn't even as a kid when there was Flora to stand guard (in Silver Lake Park on Staten Island, to which she and I and Barney would make a pilgrimage every June of a Sunday by subway, bus, and ferry). Was always worried that something vile and slithering might come sneaking up on me in the midst — with TEETH.

There was only one solution, to try and find another place out there just off the trail, where the undergrowth was relatively sparse. Why not simply do it right there in the way? Well, call it habitual delicacy for one; for two, I guess I felt it would put me in the same class as horses and dogs, so on.

Fine and good, only in my haste to pull down the jeans, do it, and return, I must've gotten mixed up as to the right direction.

"Now look what you've gone and done," I scolded myself a few minutes after getting under way again. The round white heads of the domes were showing through the trees. Right back where you started, how dumb.

Chapter Three

But was I actually back at the place I'd just left — was it the same village? I don't know, I said to myself, bumbling along, the lay of the land didn't seem quite right. Possibly in my jitteriness I'd stumbled onto a new trail.

Sure enough, when I had my first clear view of things, it turned out to be another village, with the domes close together as in the first one but tinged with grey as if older and with clumps of grass growing in the footways.

All was still, not a soul about, but the silence seemed of a different quality. Could be this one's really deserted, I theorized.

Oh well, just a matter of retracing your steps and picking up the other trail. But first, before you do, better have a sip of water, I cautioned.It was getting on toward "noon". . . beginning to heat up.

I hefted the canteen. "Hm" — there was just a sip left. I'd meant to fill up at the pond before my departure, chance it with a water purification tablet (water after all being water as long as it's clear, unlike eatables, which can be poisonous). But in all the morning bustle that particular chore had slipped my mind.

Well, you certainly can't go traipsing around the woods without something to drink — may not find your way right off, and then what. There was only one solution, to try and locate the odd house with the stream running through it, likely to turn up among the others as in the first village, everything else being more or less equal.

Nice going, I praised myself, stepping onto the landing a while later.

I knelt down near the edge, unslung the gear, got out the hank of nylon rope from the pack, tied one end to the ring on the canteen strap — with a double knot, of course — wound the other end round and round my wrist, good and tight. As an afterthought, polished off those last few remaining drops inside. "'Kay, here goes" — began paying out the line.

Plush-ull, the canteen splashed down. *Bongo!* something shot up out of there — and narrowly missed flying smack into my face! "Oh wow!" A purple praying mantis-like thing the size of a kitten with white antennae!

Out it scrammed through the vines as fast as its spidery legs could carry it. Good riddance. Boy oh boy, for company I'll take that little brown "lizard" with the red underarm hair any day, confided to myself. . . .

Now to the matter at hand. I pulled the canteen back up, poured a little water into my palm.

"Oh nuts!" — it was full of black specks, those ugly specks again. . . .

Don't see that we have any choice, I reasoned after a moment or two. Dropped in one of the purifying tablets, oscillated, brought the canteen's mouth to mine, took a tiny bit in. Tasted a trifle bitter, like soap. I swallowed, it went down alright. Well, might as well be hanged for a sheep etc. — I took a deep breath, tilted head back. "To the gods!" — chuggalugged.

The most important thing is to banish all thoughts of what those nauseating curlicues might be. . . .

More easily said. . . .

Gonna stick around here for a while, don't ask me why. Guess it is because if anything bad should happen — like I should croak — prefer that it be in a settled place, even if it is one of theirs . . . .

+10 mins. Have a slight feeling of queasiness in the gut, but don't think it's of any consequence — probably due to the IDEA of them being inside me, something like that. . . .

Eh, why not take a little walk in the byways, leave everything here, I suggested at long last, still uncomfortable. Got up and sort of lurched out.

Singing has sometimes proved beneficial to people in similar tight spots, I reminded. Unsealed my lips a crack, and broke into song, more in Flora's vein than Dave's, dear Dave —

𝄞 Sah ein Kna-ab ein Rös lein stehn

Rös lein au-auf der Hei den. . . .

It's a *lied* by Schubert, based on a poem of Goethe's called "Heidenröslein." About a boy who sees a rose and plucks it in spite of the flower's sharp warning. Ends up with him sobbing with pain from a thorn in his finger —

Rös- e -lein, rot

Rös lein, Rös lein,

𝄞 Rös lein,

Rös lein auf der Hei-ei-ei den.

•

So it looks like I'm okay, I acknowledged in another ten minutes or so on the ramp of the stream house. If something were going to happen, it would have already, no?

Let's pop into one of the regular houses and grab a bite — have it at a table like a civilized type — then be on our way. . . .

"But what's this?" I mumbled, on pushing the vines aside at the next dome over.

Someone of the same species as the first villagers was there, all alone, sitting on the edge of a narrow oval bed straight ahead facing me — a green a bit shorter and slighter than the other villagers, just about my size. Had on one of those capes, of yellow. Seemed to be gazing back at me as if in expectation of something.

[Ed. Hereafter the author used the masculine pronoun with respect to these individuals, but it should be clearly understood that males they were not in our sense — "just reminded me of them generally at times," as she explained during our conference on this chapter.]

The rest of the furnishings in this puny green's house ran true to form, except that the table (at three o'clock) was on the same small scale as the bed and there was only a single stool by it.

Are they all bachelors here then? I had stepped right out again, feeling somehow as if I'd intruded.Let's look, discreetly, into a few more.

#1 — a lone brown in it, tall and very thin. Also sat on the bed as if waiting, but with eyes on the floor.

#2 — a double, vacant.

#3 — another single, ditto.

#4 — two chubby, pint-sized purples, like identical twins. They were standing together in the center of the room — at the sight of me, quickly sidestepped toward one another. Scared?

#5 — full complement but off-sized too, the green big & fat, purple another starveling, brown very tiny. They were standing against the wall in three different parts of the room all talking very loudly at the same time — till I showed, when they stopped & stiffened like to attention.

Now that was a real argument, betcha, I wryly reflected, withdrawing again.

Eh, let's have another look in on that first green, I proposed. The way his eyes met mine when I came in had stuck in my mind. Possibly he'll be amenable to a little conversation, who knows.

I found him just as I'd left him — sitting on the bed there, at twelve o'clock, with the same expression, if one can call it that.

What the hay, I thought, let's have some fun. "Hello," said in a normal voice. Thumped my chest — "I'm Felice."

His left arm stirred skinnily under the yellow cape, fist rose to his brow, bumped. "Gluglug," he said back.

So, I cheered myself, all things come to those who etc. . . .

"May I come in?" I asked, after marking time on the landing for ever so long, hoping for an invitation of some kind. Motioned from my behind to the floor in front of him, back again.

His eyes seemed to check out the spot, that was all.

Go on 'n do it anyway, I urged myself. If it turns out to be not to his liking, he'll make it known soon enough with that stinky gas, like mine hosts when I got too close for comfort. I skipped down the stairs, plopped there where I'd indicated, unloaded the pack and canteen on either side of me, and faced him with legs crossed yoga-fashion. Thumped my chest again — "Felice."

He, who'd paid strict attention, re-saluted — "Gluglug."

I cocked an ear, thought I'd caught something that time — sounded like Laleekh (the "kh" like the "ch" in "ich" in German but coming from much deeper in the throat).

[Ed.Highlights of the language are presented later in this chapter. Suffice it to say here that henceforth all foreign words are given twice — casually spelled for easy reading, followed by a more exact rendering in the International Phonetic Alphabet. As there turned out to be a superabundance of gutturals, some of the IPA symbols had to be qualified numerically. Let the rendering of this individual's name serve as an example—$\text{la} \cdot \text{l} \, \text{i}' \chi^{12}$.]

"Laleekh," I tried — almost gagged on that final consonant.

He put up his index and middle fingers (still using his left), repeated more emphatically, "La-leekh!"

So, not quite up to snuff it seems. I tried again, "La-leekh!"

The same fingers went up, but they were crossed now, and his mouth stayed shut.

It's better, I interpreted, but far from perfect, sensed. "Now me," I said. Banged the left side of my forehead as he had his — "Felice."

He hopped right to it — "Pelice!"

I showed two fingers for a repeat — "Fuh-leese!"

"PUH-LEESE!" he produced with great effort.

"Haha," I laughed, no f's in his repertoire evidently.

"Khee-khee," he echoed lightly.

That's something anyway, he's got a sense of humor. . . .

Now what, I considered after some more moments of silence. Well, one of the high and mighty in these parts he's clearly not, but for all one knows might turn out to be useful one of these days as a go-between with those who are, should they ever lose their aversion to me or whatever and be willing to have a confab.

I dug in the pack for an ever-lovin' pen and pad, got to work in my best Rembrandt-Goya manner. "Look, Laleekh," I said in a matter of moments, with a drawing of Arthur going from our solar system to X's and Lancelot hovering over land with both villages below. Showed it to him and pointed to myself in either cabin — "That's me, Felice."

The small, dark eyes in the green face with its nosehole where our nose is and serpent mouth fixed on it, then on me, then it again.

Does he understand, I wondered. Inclined to think not. Okay, let's try another approach — I turned to a fresh page, rushed with the pen once more, this time sketching out a small body of water with humans and fish in it, and a city skyline in the background. Displayed it like the first — "See, that's where I come from. Traveled a long distance to get here." I looped through the air with my arm, using the pen as a nose.

He simply stared . . . no capeesh, definitely.

And now? I prodded myself. "Here" — I held out the pen and pad with the sheet turned over again — "you try now."

"Alright, if that's what you wish," he seemed to say in his gluglug way — reinforced it with a raised finger. Then clutching the pen close to the tip, as some human children do, examined the point, from a greater distance than we would normally — and then scratched in a corner of the sheet with it to test it(!). Finally got busy, eyeing me from time to time as if he were doing my portrait, but not so.

"Not bad, not bad at all," I appreciated, adding my finger, when he showed — was a copy of my first opus of the space ship and lander. And it certainly was impressive, just about every detail there.

My reaction seemed to please him, but the at same time he appeared to have grown tired or bored, or maybe glum or troubled.

Enough, I alerted myself — took the things back and put them away. . . .

The afternoon was petering out, I noticed, glancing toward the door. Hope he'll let me spend the night, but if not there are those empty houses I came upon before, reminded myself.

"Hey, Laleekh, how about some chow?" I sang out before very long. Pointed to my mouth, then to his table, at three o'clock, remember.

He seemed to snap out of whatever was bothering him, stuck up a finger — fine with him then.

[Ed. Henceforth all signed dialogue will be indicated by ✋, the author having so ordained it.]

✋Only hold on a sec, he made — like a stop sign(!). Sprang to his feet, scooted forward, high-stepping hurriedly by me, going all the way to the landing, and about-faced at the left doorpost — the pneumatic-tube-like clunking device there that was on a level with my hips.

Oho, I joyed inwardly. Hauled myself up, followed after him.

Clunk, went the cover.

"What is it?" I asked, pointing to the thing and shrugging.

He gave me a funny look.

I asked again, same way.

He faced around, somehow with this attitude of I'm not liking it but if we must, we must.

"Oh my!" I exclaimed.

He had a small tail or flap just above the base of the "spine" — say three inches long by a half in diameter. Was so flush with the contours of his body in a groove there —

unless he raised it, which he was doing then — that I probably never would've spotted it on my own.

"And so?" I pursued it.

He turned so his back was once more to the clunker,
wedged up the cover with that "tail"'s tip, slipped it in the
hole, and drew it out again — *clunk.* "Bagaba" [b h a · G^{13}a'·
bha], he said, clapped his hand over his nosehole.

I stepped around him and lifted the cover—bent over
with my nostrils. "Phooey" — it smelled like mouldy onions
in there. The thing was a toilet then and the "tail" was what
he made with, Number One and Number Two together it
would seem.

"Bagaba," he repeated, meaning "excrement" obviously
(to put it politely).

"Ba-ga-ba," I imitated, having as little luck with the "g" as
with the "kh" before in his name.

[Ed. The following by the author, which appears to fit in
here, turned up on a scrap of foolscap stuck away between
some blank pages of one of those children's composition
books belonging to the Diary.]

*My first word, and what a boon. Yes indeedee — considering this
life of ours, and how things untoward have a way of suddenly descending on us in its progress — a gem for the permanent collection. Sitting
here now at home, I dub it the very Prince of Words. Why if there were
any spirits around — I've run out & it's in the wee hours of the morn
— I'd toss off a merry glass to it, so help me —*
            BAGABA!

On with the show — the meal, that is. Laleekh took his
place on the stool, I came and sat opposite him on the floor,
dragging the pack. The lights eased on, and he struck up a
conversation, chatting agreeably with much use of his hands.
I grunted throatily out of politeness. . . .

Click, went whatever it was inside the table. His spindly
arms got the top loose with a few smart twirls and deftly stood
it on end beside him. Out came another of those white trays
with a white bowl and cup on it, lifted carefully by him with

long green tapering fingers.

I sat up on my knees and leaned over —"Whadya got there? Can I see?"

No objection.

The bowl was full of whitish lumps like from crayfish claws plus minuscule dark green legs and gelatinous dots, possibly something's eyes. A little steam rose from it, so it was warm, but, disappointingly, I couldn't smell anything, somehow expecting garlic, ginger, something on that order.

The cup contained plain water — of the specky variety.

Laleekh fell to in the manner of mine hosts, choosing out morsels, flicking them in the air, picking them off plummeting, and enveloping them with a yellow feather of a tongue. I fished out a tube, which he noted, that was all. . . .

Some minutes later, when we were about done, he uttered what seemed like a question.

✋ Not receiving you, I told him with two fingers.

He said something more — (?)"Let me show you what I mean" — and selected a tidbit from what remained to him, launched it at me.

I reached up and grabbed it with my hand. "Sorry, no can do," I said, showed him why, my (surely to him) pathetic little pink tongue — fired the tidbit back.

His own snatched it handily. . . .

"So where does all this bounty come from?" I asked, indicating the table in which the tray had just been replaced, and the rest of the house.

He understood or seemed to, but gave me a strange look, as with the clunker before.

I was not to be put off— "Where?"

He began speaking, harshly I felt. I heard my name mentioned several times — Pelice — as if he were chewing me out.

"But where? Who?" I insisted.

Clearly exasperated, he jumped up. His arm swept round — "Gagloo" [$G^{12}a'\cdot G^{11}$lu]! The walls were fading. He whirled in the gathering dimness — "GAGLOO! GAGLOO!" Pulled off his cape, slapped it down on the stool disgustedly — was completely dark by then — began moving toward the bed, still at it, like muttering — "Gagloo-oo-oo."...

So there we are, and I guess I'm in, again, I said to myself in a congratulatory way. I'll just step outside for a moment — one of those clusters of vegetation in the path'll do — then turn in too.

Before lights out (the flash).

I really like this green one — he's asleep now — because of his pluck I guess. Have bedded down on the floor close by him, where I sat at first — my head's parallel with his feet. . . .

Gonna hang around here for a coupla more days, see if I can get some additional data on his Gagloos. Till then, maybe it's best not to say anything more 'bout myself. . . .

Be interesting to know one day who or what he takes me for at this point.

●

The most curious thing, Laleekh and I both opened our eyes at the same time in the morning. And thankfully, there was no trace of last night's rancor in his.

"Whadya say to a swim?" I threw out, made a sidestroke.

🖐I'm with you, he answered, supplementing the finger sign with a lowering of his chin, such as it was, to his left shoulder, their way of nodding it appeared.

I popped out to do my business. On my return, he was all ready, with cape on.

On the way, along a trail close by the one I arrived on, I sucked up breakfast, not a good idea before vigorous exercise, but then the puree was ever so light.

Within minutes we were at his village's pond, which was much like the other one in layout, with grayish-brown slate ledges all around for basking, but murky-looking — because of those bits I imagined, which turned out to be so.

Some of the other residents were already there, lying ar-ound . . . a few gliding sleekly along in the water, but with-

out any "fishes," kids. At the sight of them, Laleekh muttered something under his breath and ushered me to the
opposite side.

Off came his cape. I stripped too — what the hell, took
off everything. Gave his chest a quick once-over, then his
back as he turned to go in — where indeed there was nothing, at least to my naked eye. He did likewise to me, I had the
feeling . . . my boobs, hairy triangle.

In the water we swam up and down by our ledge side-by-
side till I grew tired, which was pretty soon, that extra .65
pull of gravity still getting to me. Spent the time waiting for
him a short distance away, rinsing and spreading to dry some
underwear and so on, which I'd brought along for the purpose in a plastic bag.

"What's with them?" I asked when he came out, concerning the neighbors, still on their side.

Immediately he grew all hot and bothered again, and
yacked and yacked, now and then tapping the side of his
head as we would of someone who's nuts.

Back home Laleekh had some chores to do, he informed
me in his fashion, and after I'd re-spread the wash — what
better place than on his roof — he bade me stay out of the
way by the drape.

*Bed — he peeled a paper-thin layer of something, some plastic, off
the mattress . . . changed the sheet, in other words. Gathered the dis-
carded layer into a heap and began pushing it together with his hands,
compressing it — until it was down to the size of a golf ball. It worked
fine up to the final phase, when the stuff became gummy & started to
stick to his fingers, which brought on another fit of muttering, good
natured this time. When he was done, he got on his knees by the bed
with it, raised up the dust ruffle & held it there — something sucked it
away with a hiss.*

*Floor — scuffed sand, wisps of vegetation etc. toward the same
place, doing it with a shuffle almost in Dave-style & "Sih-sih-sih,"
extent of his singing, thank heaven. After he had it all there, pried the
edge up with his foot — s-s-s, it was gone. . . .*

Now what can he have in the hamper, I wondered —

which by the by was at nine o'clock as in mine hosts'.

He'd gone there, pulled up the lid, now was bent double in it, stirring with his arm . . . sounded like water. "Something, something, something," he said. My ear isolated the word "khreekho" — [$\chi^{18}{}_{\text{в}}{}^5{}_{\text{i}}$'· χ^{17}o] — repeated several times. His hand emerged with something whitish and flatly rounded in it.

But it can't be, I assured myself, it simply can't without his having mates. I went over to join him. "So, Laleekh, you have a khreekho, may I hold it too?" — extended my palm.

He sized me up — was it alright? Saw that it was, dropped it there.

It looked genuine in every respect, down to the green flecks — except that it had seemed heavier, tipping my wrist slightly when he handed it over. So it's not for real, as I said, a phony . . . was probably made of that same plaster as the walls, with particles of leaf embedded in it before it hardened. Yes, another *gift* from his Gagloos it appears — and chances are as in the German word gift, namely "poison."

The false egg back in his possession, Laleekh put it to the side of his head — a tiny button of flesh there, I now noticed, with a corresponding "pimple" like that on the other side — and shook it, "listened" again. ✋Maybe yes, maybe no.

Boy, some kettle of fish.

•

"Well, Laleekh," I said, having come to sit beside him on the bed, to which he'd transferred himself after gently immersing his khreekho again. *I didn't mean any harm —HONESTLY.*

I picked up his hand. The skin was salamander soft . . . beneath it cartilage-like bone, hard but pliable. I detected a faint coursing like a pulse under the pinky . . . there was an extra joint at the tip of each finger, for food-flicking purposes probably, or maybe it was vestigial, needed by his kind for grubbing in tree trunks and the ground once upon a time.

I grinned like a jack o'lantern to show teeth. "Now let's see yours" — I touched his lips, dark and narrow.

They spread into Cheese in a way — he had a row of uppers and lowers, all of them very white and small and even, like so many immaculate toothpick heads.

I tapped my nails there on the front ones — "Ya got any more?"

His jaws clamped, he looked perturbed.

"Aw c'mon, Laleekh, be a good sport!" — I poke-poked.

The tiny points widened a smidge. There were grinders on either side, on the bottom row anyway, likewise without the least sign of wear-and-tear. . . .

"Whadya say, can I look under your little cape now?" I inquired, after allowing us both a breather. It was his "armpits" I was after. I applied my hand to the yellow fabric . . . was very silky, another peeler like the mattress it wouldn't have surprised me.

(?)"I'm not exactly thrilled by this new idea," he said, something like that.

I smoothed it down — "It won't take long."

He was still not happy — (?)"Don't like this game, no, not at all" — moved away from me by an inch or two.

I quickly closed the gap, caught hold of some of his fingers, lifted the arm in the air — was just flesh there. I hopped to his other side — "No more after this, I promise!"

He squirmed — (?)"I'm gittin' outta here!"

Too late, I had that arm raised. And there it was, or rather they were — a small cavity, and an inch below it a protuberance of equal size, like a young human female breast without a nipple.

Well, I couldn't let it go at that with only a third of the picture, could I? "Listen, Laleekh," I said on my feet — gestured to myself, the door, "Be right back, okay?"

First stop that lean, lone brown a few houses down.

As on the day before, he was facing me from the bed, at one o'clock, studying the floor before him.

"Hello!" I called from the landing.

He didn't move a "muscle."

I stepped down the stairs, got hold of both his hands, swung them up together, his red cape along with them.

He also had a cavity and protuberance, only under his right arm and in reverse order, bump on top. . . .

Next, the two porky little purples.

They were standing side-by-side at ten when I came in.

"Hiya!" I yelled out — cantered toward them.

"Khee-khee," they tittered, grasped hands.

I pounced on their free outside hands — "Whoops!" — and pulled them up with the white capelets. "Whoops!" — yanked up the other hands, with stubby fingers twined.

They were the same on the left as my pal, identical on the right with the brown. . . .

To sum it up, understanding that r and l stand for "left" and "right," P for "protuberance," and C for "cavity" —

green		purple		brown	
r	*l*	*l*	*r*	*l*	*r*
	C	P	C	P	
	P		C	P	C

As for the act itself, try to imagine three Russians doing the Kazatsky with their arms fast around one another . . . the bumps and holes fitting together like dress snaps. Beyond that, don't ask me. Some seminal-type fluid must have passed from one to the other of them through the protuberances I guess, and the eggs would've come out of the cavities, where else? . . .

So the mystery unraveled to a certain extent, I told myself out in the footway. But I don't know, suddenly something got into me, I just had to see more — MORE! And next door lived that freaky-looking trio, you'll recall — the midget brown, emaciated purple, and giant green — who'd been in the middle of a domestic quarrel when I last set eyes on them.

As I galloped down the ramp, the same kind of enraged talking was coming from inside there, plus a new sound —

a *bam-bam-bam.* Didn't matter, I charged in. "Khreekhos!" I trumpeted — steered for the brown on the right, who was the closest and making that extra racket with the hamper. "I wanna see where your khreekhos come from!"

"Khyee-ee!" the shrimp howled, flung himself across the lid and held on to it for all he was worth.

"Khyee-ee!" the toothpick joined in from the table, left, rattling in all his "bones."

(?)"What in hell ya think ya doing!" bellowed the mighty one, the green, from the bed, two o'clock — standing on it. He stepped off, glaring(?) — began lumbering toward me, making a harsh grating sound in his throat!

"Uh oh" — I braked hard. But before I could spin fully round, a stream of spit from his mouth flew onto my left cheek right below the eye with a sharp sting!

"Oh no!" I tore out of there.

Serves you right, you got your just deserts, I scolded myself, pounding down Laleekh's ramp seconds later.

Never mind that now, my other self interposed, do something, quickly! Had wiped that beast's venom away with my shirt sleeve, but the place where it had landed still burned, terribly.

Practically leaping from the landing, I grabbed up the pack, stacked earlier by the hamper — dumped everything out of it. Where? Where? Sifted for the first aid kit and relief in the form of A&D ointment, little hand mirror etc.

Laleekh had just sat down at the table, it being the dinner hour by then. Watched as I shmeared and examined, just watched. Sad? Concerned? Certainly wasn't peeved anymore over my prying and probing before, that was for sure.

Well, it's the best I can do, I sighed at long last, resting with my back against the hamper, the stuff from the pack scattered all over the floor around me.

Laleekh began speaking, a bit more softly than usual it seemed. I thought I heard "Gagloo" more than once — as if he were saying over and over in different ways, "Much as I dislike those types, I'm positive they could be of assistance in this crisis. If only some of'em would drop by."

He kept it up all through the meal, between shlups, till bedtime.

●

Well, certainly looks alright, I had to admit, outside with the mirror in the superior light the next morning. Wasn't even a hint of pink on the cheek.

The only thing was, felt a twinge in the eye now and then — meaning possibly an itty-bit of that nasty spittle had gotten into it without my being aware.

I pulled the flesh down, pushed the lid up — was nothing there that I could make out. Put some drops in to soothe, in the other eye too for good measure.

Think I'll stay in and take it a little easy today, was my decision. . . .

Inside, propped against the hamper again, I broke the news to Laleekh. "You can do whatever you like" — pointing to himself, the door.

He gave me one of those "chin"-to-left shoulder nods, stayed put on the edge of the bed — and began talking in the same commiserating manner as last night, with more "Gagloos" thrown in. . . .

Must have been a nervous tic of some kind, I concluded around midday, the irritation in the left eye entirely gone.

Except, except — Oh, that devil, Imagination. What if a little of that awful stuff had seeped into my bloodstream via some itty-bitty microscopic lesion in my skin, I worried. A picture reared itself up in my mind . . . ghastly pimples appearing all over my body and erupting into putrefying sores, a dry, wracking cough beginning, which would soon turn bloody with lightning streaks in the head . . . my succumbing finally in dumb delirium.

I'll tell you something, if you know what's good for you, you'll quit this line of thought, my better self advised.

What more appropriate way of getting one's mind off

something stupid like that than with — "Say, Laleekh?"

He looked alive.

I pointed to him — "La-leekh," pronounced. Shifted my finger to the table — "How you say?"

He did not seem to understand, I repeated it, he gave me another of his funny looks.

"C'mon, Laleekh" — I gestured at the table once more, the bed.

HOkay, he agreed at last. (?)"But I really think this is foolish," qualified, I sensed.

p.m. We've made good progress. I now know the words for "cup," "bowl," etc. plus those for some simple actions involving 'em, like "lift."

Patient's condition is stable, no change for the worse yet, and I don't think there will be, I'm basically alright. But am going to continue with the lessons — would have to learn the lingo sooner or later, might as well be now.

Lal's realized that it's agreeing with me, has become more willing. . . .

A really nice guy, he means well. Someday we'll get to the bottom of that look of his . . . & a good deal else.

Day 4 (chez his place).

Except for utter "necessities," I've decided to remain indoors for a soupçon longer on the off-chance that some droplet of the poison did find its way into my veins & is lurking there . . . waiting for some triggering effect from prolonged exposure to broad daylight. . . .

Day 5.

The language is really a snap — I'm picking it up fast. Get this: subj-verb-obj word order, almost no case endings, basic tenses with simple markers. . . .

Day 6.

Well, a few little hitches, but in the end really nothing that I can't handle:

A. Gender — four of them, one for each type of individual plus a neutral for animals.

B. Number

1. personal singulars for "I," "you," "he" and "it" according to gender.

2. the same situation for duals.

3. the same situation for trios.

4. plurals galore — besides a general one, for one + one, one + two, two + one, two + two, one + a group, etc., also according to gender. . . .

P.S. Laleekh uses the same gender to refer to me as to himself — the khlag [χ^{13}l̥aG^{10}] it's called. Do I look green to him, or what? . . .

Day 9.

Let's face it, the major stumbling block is & I fear will always be the pronunciation. . . .

Here's the pitch —

A. Vowels and diphthongs — on a par with ours in English but presenting enormous problems when coupled with #2 type consonants below.

B. Consonants

1. "b," "ch" (as in "church"), "j," "l," "m," "n,", "p," "s," the hard & soft "sh"'s, and "z" are okay — except for the "b," "l," & "p," which are always breathed and therefore I give in International Phonetics as b' *or* bh, l̥, *and* p' *or* ph.

2. A whole bunch of others pronounced in different places in the throat, which I have gone ahead and subdivided to the best of my ability as follows:

letter	*IPA*	*as in . . . .*
g	$G^{1\text{-}13}$	*"goon" to "geek"+*
h	$h^{1\text{-}7}$	*"hoop" to "heap"+*
k	$q^{1\text{-}15}$	*"coop" to "keep"+*
kh	$\chi^{1\text{-}19}$	*Spanish "junta"+*
r	$\textsc{r}^{1\text{-}5}$	*French "rue"+*

•

"'Kay, Laleekh, believe I'm ready to go out today," I said the following morning after coming in from the usual, still with much waving of the hands.

Boy, you never saw a being so happy — he bounded out of bed, had his cape on one-two-three.

"But just for a while," I qualified. "We'll gradually increase it.". . . .

Hope everything's alright back at the ship . . . should be trotting along there one of these days, if only for a look-see. . . .

Day 12.

At the pond this day. I sure needed it, bath plus a real work-out. . . .

Afterward, Lal insisted we detour onto another trail, came to a place in the woods full of jabba [ʒáˑ b a] trees, whose fruit was good to eat, he said. Color, ocher; the size of one of our medium plums, except that it's shaped like a fat pancake, the pit inside like a half dollar.

We piled the "silverware box" (dragged along this a.m., I wondered why) high with those jabbas. On our way again, Lal gorged himself, biting into each juicily & chewing it up, but once in a while for fun taking a piece out of his mouth & spinning it above his head to catch with his tongue.

The air around us grew all nectary, which made me think of the phrase "petal wine" — and his skin got sweaty-like. Let me tell you, my own tongue was hanging out a-plenty, & for a brief moment there, I was on the point of weakening & digging in myself. But there was Flora's voice ringing in my ears, as it had once when I was a kid, with respect to some luscious-looking berries behind our summer bungalow in the Catskills — "Don't do it, Felice! It'll make you sick, give you a bellyache!"

I tried to justify then — "But I drank the waw-ta!" I tried now again, appealing to that mental image of her — ". . . the waw-ta."

No use, no more than it was then — "Never you mind," she lectured. . . .

Day 13.

Lal & I took another long way home today, stopping by a quagmire full of dark-grayish stuff like clay, in a small clearing surrounded by bushes.

The stuff's called khalala [χ¹⁷aˑ l̥áˑ l̥a]. He picked up half a handful & began kneading it . . . turned the lump into one of those "lizards" with hairy underarms. After a few minutes of showing it to me, it became chalky white and rock-hard. So probably it's a material similar to the one the houses & furniture are made of, maybe the very same.

His handiwork expertly done, truly. Reminded me of those slender, long-necked things of Modigliani; also, of those Modigliani-like sculptures of the ancient Cyclades.

I complimented him — "Nice."

What do ya think — he tossed the thing over his shoulder so it landed in among the trees somewhere!

I opened my mouth to protest, but he immediately scooped up some more of that khalala & in no time flat was holding another vunderpiece for me to see — a sort of turtle with a goatee!

"Nice too," I said.

He threw that one away as well, then made several others — a spiny "crab," that praying mantis — and each time, though he delighted in fashioning them & obviously went to considerable pains, they met the same fate. . . .

[Ed. This next was written in pencil in the margin of the page on which the above appeared.]

Am I capable of doing the same where my own work is concerned . . . my "Guinevere"? And then of walking completely away from it? Good question.

●

Day 16.

Before reveille. I really should think seriously about getting back to the plane. . . .

"Say, Laleekh, isn't there anything else to munch on in these here woods?" I nagged in pidgin fashion, as we were leaving the jabba grove, for the third day in a row if memory correctly served me, bearing the box.

Glad to let me in on it, he gulped down a big juicy hunk in his mouth and allowed the rest of that sure-to-be honey-sweet "plum" to drip on the ground, the stinker — "Let's see." But then, suddenly, he froze and pinched his throat under the "chin," meaning for me to be quiet.

"What is it?" I asked in a hushed voice.

"Regee" [ʁ⁸ɛ̱·ɢ¹⁰i], he whispered, which I doped out to stand for "something serpentine." He pointed to a hole at the base of a tree to our right, where one of what he meant, a rather fat one, had just slipped in apparently.

I thought I had gotten a glimpse of a dark snake-body, maybe two inches in diameter. Jeezy-beezy, do they have horrible slitherers like that in this world too? "Are there many big regees hereabouts?" I inquired.

"Oh sure," he answered, but there was no reason to be concerned, because they were all burrowers.

Now there was something interesting, some new matter to cudgel my head over. The word he'd used for the latter seemed very similar to "Gagloo," about whom, mind you, I'd tried to pump him for information before on several occasions, but was each time treated to one of his looks, which I'd recently learned signified, "You must be kidding." Here, as we were on our way once more with him happily slurping again, was a fresh opportunity — "Hey, Laleekh, is that what Gagloos are by any chance, are they regees of some kind?"

His face took on that same scornful expression, as if to say, "C'mon already, how many times are we gonna go through this?"

But I wasn't going to be put off this time. I'm gonna find out no matter what, told myself. "Well, are they or aren't they?"

Muff, he went through his nosehole, a sign of utter impatience. "Honestly, Pelice!"

"But I mean it!"

I'd stopped in my tracks; he had too.

"'Course not, 'course they're not regees," he said dryly.

"So what are they then?"

He became particularly adamant. "Why, if that isn't the silliest thing I've ever heard! Pelice, you know it as well as I do! Why — they're just like us!"

What! Us? But how could he — ? Us? My flesh turned to goose bumps. Of all things, he thinks that I'm — But let's set this matter aside for the moment and get to the bottom of the one at hand, I prompted myself. "Except that they live under the ground, isn't that right?"

"Pe-li-ice," he whined, "surely I don't have to spell that

out for you."

✋Okay, okay, I agreed. "Only supposing for some reason I don't know that, where are they" — I motioned downward — "precisely?"

His left fist went up to his "sinus" — betokening concentration when held there. He'd originated among them like
everybody else . . . but that was long ago. No, he didn't know
either, finally had to confess, not even how one traveled
back and forth from there — only that when visiting here,
which was generally in groups, they always emerged out of
the woods to the left of the pond, where indeed I'd come
upon another trail in my wanderings one morning . . . leading to a small clearing like the one the khalala pit was in, that
was all.

"When's the next bunch due to show up?" I asked.

Well, there was no way of telling for sure. But now that I'd
brought the matter to his attention, there hadn't been any
around of late — "So pretty soon I guess."

He and I had pushed on again in the meanwhile, the
village was now in sight. I decided to wait a while with the
other matter — that of my supposed identity according to
him — until we were facing one another, pinko-white nose to
green nosehole, across the table. . . .

"Laleekh, I'm a trifle confused," I began. What was his
drift before when he said etc. etc. I made it clear I was
absolutely in earnest, so he wouldn't launch into another of
his tirades.

Well, seems as if I'd had him really puzzled at first —
he'd actually taken me for one of them, yes, even in spite of
the fact that they seldom appeared alone as he said and that
I looked — I should pardon him — somewhat peculiar, by
anybody's standards. How so? My bearing for one (whatever
he meant by that, I let it slide). For another, my getting him
to copy one of those pictures with that drawing instrument,
which was not unlike what some of them made him do at
times. And then there were my "fluffy leg coverings" (jeans,
in other words), which generally resembled the lower garments of those who administered the tests. However, when I

stayed on overnight, which was absolutely unheard of for them to do, what else could he conclude but that —

I beat him to the punch — but that I was one more they'd sent to live up here. . . .

So, now, it's time, let me make a full breast of everything, I nudged myself, with dinner dispatched, his pretty well finished too.

Only that wasn't to be yet — he still had some words for me on another, related topic, which he'd been meaning to broach for ever so long but had been reluctant to because of my condition. Now that I was fit again, though, it was hoped that he could avail himself of the liberty without my taking offense — "Are you aware that you're having problems with your memory?"

"Well — I — "

He stopped me with a palm — knew what I was going to say, his own memory wasn't always all that one would wish. "But, Pelice, you seem to have difficulty remembering the least little thing."

"But — "

There was also something else, now that we were on the subject of me — I seemed to have a serious speech impediment, it was almost impossible to understand me most of the time.

"Look, I can explain — "

🖑 I'm not done yet, he signaled irritatingly. Now whether I wanted to do something about those troublous areas or not was entirely up to me. Still, one would think that I would, in which case as I knew or had an inkling from what the Gagloos had taught me down there —

I was beside myself — "Laleekh, please!"

'Course, one had to exercise extreme care as to who among those awesome ones a body petitioned, he went on to say, many of them being worse than useless. But obviously he'd be more than happy to help out with advice and so on whenever I felt up to it. Not only that. . . .

It needs the ship, definitely, I saw, soon as his mouth closed for good. But Lancelot's not just around the corner, so let's see if I can make out without it — "Laleekh, would you step outside with me for a moment?"

Well, that proposal certainly took a little wind out of his sails. This unusual one wants to do something different, his expression seemed to say, this individual would like for us to go outside at night, which one never does.

"Just to the other side of the vines," I assured. Took along the flash so we wouldn't break our necks after, coming back in. . . .

"Do you see those two things?" I asked of the moonlets overhead. "What are they?"

He was quick to respond — "Why everyone knows that, they're lights, blue ones."

"And the thing up there during the day?"

"Day?" — both of his fists sought his brow, signifying intense concentration. The answer came after a minute or two — "Oh yes, that. It's a light too, white one."

So much for his knowledge of astronomy, I sighed inwardly.

Back inside. It's worse even than one imagines — the word he used for the moons is a compound made up of "khalala," the term for purple-skinned individual, and a khalala particle, and that for their sun is along similar lines. In other words, both heavenly bodies're defined exclusively in terms of things here on the surface.

Must have a long think about this. . . .

Before shut-eye. The words are a hold-over from a primitive past & the G's with their technical expertise will know better, betcha — and THAT, if ever they & I meet, is all that counts. So no, the ship's out far as my friend here's concerned, I'm not gonna take him there. Either it won't have any meaning for him & he'll look upon it as something given to me by them regardless of what I say, or worse yet, if he does manage to understand, it could upset him, badly.

•

The next morning I'd awakened feeling somewhat stale, in need of something more vigorous than my slow swim. "Hey, Laleekh, how about a little run today for a change?" I

asked from the landing, improvising with the word for "walk"
plus "very quickly" — trotted in place.

He looked his look from the bed.

Well, what is it now? I came and took my old place on
the floor, facing him. ☙Sorry, I twiddled. "One more thing
you'll have to familiarize me with again I guess."

He blew through his nosehole, lightly — *Muffle.* "One en-
gages in that activity only once in a lifetime, Pelice." He lay
back, went limp — let his tongue dribble out of the corner of
his mouth.

"But — I don't understand!" I complained — told him
about the runners I'd seen that day on the beach.

"Exactly," he said — sat up again.

"You mean that was a run to the death?"

His "chin" descended to his left shoulder, sure thing. Was
the Gagloos' doing, they ordered it.

My scalp tingled — Can you beat that, a death run! And
then I remembered something curious that I'd noted in passing in the other village — pairs of white plastiform legs the
size of middle fingers hanging in the doorways of the four
houses without any eggs. I'd thought at the time that they
were trophies or lucky charms put up there by the missing
occupants, who were one and the same with those runners,
still off loping somewhere. I mentioned them now —"What
are they, notices to vacate?"

You bet. Folks here get them too!

*Important: The other village is off-limits to him & his neighbors,
seems. There are only these two. . . .*

p.m. Another day at the pond — ho hum. . . .

*Have been mulling things over & I believe the wisest course is to
return to the ship asap, like tomorrow, & stay there, await further
developments . . . like the arrival of everyone's landlords or doctors or
whatever from below, see what's what with'em respecting me. And, of
course, I'll certainly do my darndest to make amends for the intrusions
etc. — after all, perpetrated before I had any idea of the true state of
affairs here.*

The question is, what shall I say to him, Lal. . . .

Nothing, that's the answer. I'm not keen about it, but clearly it's

*the thing to do. Will simply take off before he gets up, explain as much
or little as the G's tell me is advisable, if & when they let me come back
for a spell.*

"Hey, what is it, whatever is going on here?" I squawked,
roused out of a sound sleep early the next morning.

Laleekh was on his "knees" on the floor, leaning over me,
which he'd never done before — was plucking at my sleeve.

I heaved myself half up — were they already there, the
Gagloos? Revolved my head one way, the other, squinting in
the gloom — no, were only the two of us, inside there anyway. I listened — no, wasn't a peep outside either.

Laleekh pulled on my sleeve again. "Please," he murmured. Wanted me to get to my feet, it looked like.

"Awright, awright" — I did it. "What's up?"

He didn't answer — instead, took hold of my hand, began tugging me in the direction of the stairs.

You know, I do believe he's throwing me out, confided to
myself. "Hey, hold on, Laleekh!"

But no, he was in no mood to listen to anything, and
dragged me harder yet.

"Okay, okay, only let me get — " I wrenched myself down,
looped my free arm through everything, including the sneakers, tied together.

He redoubled his efforts toward the door.

You must've hurt his feelings in some way, I guessed, as I
was being towed along like that. Try and find out what it was,
at least apologize. . . .

Out on the ramp, I swiveled round to face him, on the
other side of the vines — "Laleekh?" — searched the now
familiar nosehole, smear of a mouth, chinlet. "Oh boy!" I
gasped. Something was wrong, very wrong, with his eyes!
They were like full of milk! "Laleekh, are you sick?"

He said nothing — his left foot jittered up, massaged the
right leg.

"Laleekh, what is it?"

Nib-nib-nib, the foot went, rubbing in earnest. Celluloi-
dal shreds were falling from the place, a patch of fresh skin

the color of our baby leaves in Spring showed there.

So, nothing to be alarmed about, I saw. Only Mother Nature calling — in a manner of speaking, there being no mothers here. He'd grown a new epidermis apparently and was shedding the old — was molting in other words, like a multitude of our creatures on Earth. Still I was sorry because of his discomfort. "Laleekh, is there anything I can do?"

≰No, thanks, he responded limply.

"You want to be alone, is that it?"

"Just — for a few days," he choked out. "Take — one of the empty houses — in the meanwhile. Hope yours — isn't as — severe!" His hand leapt to his back, he rushed inside.

•

A pity he has to suffer so, I reflected, making progress up the trail to the beach not long after. All the same, look at what it saved you from, walking away without so much as a word of leave-taking — what a stroke of luck.

But what have we here? Now all at once I didn't feel so well — a little light in the head.

Eh, you probably need some food, you're hungry. The mists were still heavy — a few feet to the left I spied this overturned log, and trudging over to it somewhat unsteadily, eased myself down and dug out a tube from the pack beside me.

Hm, now that's odd — my mouth was full of saliva, too much of it. Is it a period coming on maybe? I patted my chest, pelvis — no, at least it doesn't seem like it, though one should be coming along any day now. Boy, I ruminated, sure hope it's not a delayed reaction from that spit in the eye or ingesting the water, those pukey pieces. Couldn't be after all this time, could it? . . .

Well, let's see what the story is now, I proposed, a couple of minutes later.

I pushed down hard on either side of the log with the heels of my hands. Up, up, I got. Ah, Whitman. Unclamped my jaws —

When lilacs last in the dooryard bloomed.

That's all I remember.

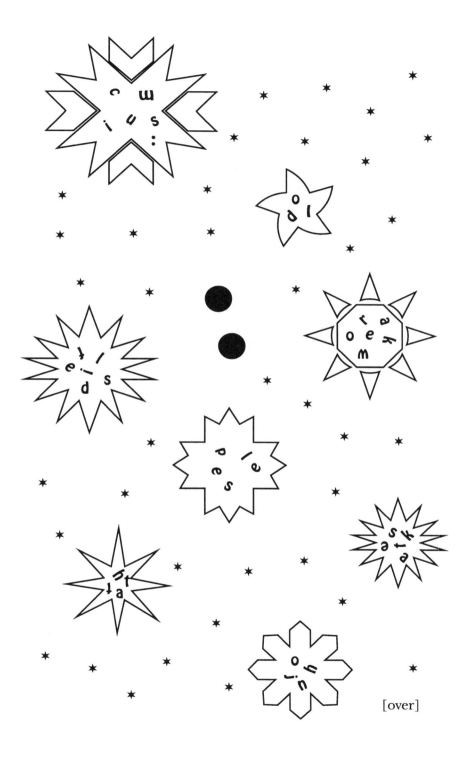

[over]

[Ed. For those unable to spare the time to work it out –
"Fled is that music:– Do I wake or sleep?"
John Keats
(from his "Ode to a Nightingale")]

Chapter Four

I was having this dream.

I'd just dance-walked through the portals of this huge building like the World Trade Center, only it was very long rather than tall, as if one of the WTC towers had been laid on a side.

The name of this structure was similar but different too — the Trade Center of the World (TCW).

It as well had lobbies galore, with banks and banks of bronze-doored elevators. The only thing is there was no need of lifts there, at least so many of them, and drifting along beside someone, an attendant in an official cap and overcoat with lots of gold braid and white gloves, I kept on trying to point this out —

"What's the use, it's just as easy to walk up!". . .

Could be this is a clue as to where you are, I prodded myself, lying outstretched on something, half awake. Below the surface somewhere for sure. Also, suggests how you got there — an up-and-down conveyance of some sort.

I was fully up, on a narrow bed in a corner, walls on my right and behind my head.

Now let's see — I parted lids, looked. It seemed just as bleak-black as with them unparted. Is it that pitchy in here or am I blind, Samson-blind with my eyes put out? Well, let's say for peace of mind's sake it's very dark, okay?

I touched the wall beside me. It was cool and smooth like nickel, that is, the nickel of our coin of the same name if that's what it's made of. The wall in back of me felt the same, but they did not meet at right angles it seemed — was a curve there. . . .

Mm, have to go — I sat up. Turned out I had on only a T-shirt, without the bra, and underpants, the jeans were off. I slid to my feet — they were bare too and the floor under them was also like silky metal. I took a step forward, another. You've done this before recently, I remembered. . . .

"There," I announced. I'd reached a wall parallel to the one against which my bed stood after ten paces or so. I squatted down, put a palm up against its surface for better balance. It was truly chilly — or else I'm burning with fever. I fell to laughing.

Finished with my business, I half-blindly reached out for a hand shovel from a pail nearby, both of them icy — scattered sand over the wet place. . . .

On my back again, I dimly made out a fourth wall ahead beyond the foot of the bed, and gauged from this that I was in a room roughly ten by twenty feet. Only it was vaguely rectangular, the corners were all rounded probably.

"But my things!" I suddenly cried out. Where was it, what had happened to it? I sat back up, peered hard.

"Ah!" — everything was on the other end of the bed . . . the jeans, bra. Sneakers will be there on the floor, betcha. When did I eat last? I reached out for the pack and canteen, sank back drawing the straps with me. Well, there in the woods near Laleekh's village, whenever that was. My hand snaked in among the first aid kit and stuff, found a tube. But did I actually consume the contents of that other one? I don't think so.

I bit the tip off this one, squeezed into my mouth. "Yum,

sick food," I mumbled. . . .

Now for some fluid—I brought the canteen to my lips. It was still full, as I'd taken it to the stream house the night before I left. I've been here only a while then, it would seem — unless someone, like whoever undressed me, also —

"Sleepy time now," I cooed, after a few small sips. But somehow I wasn't comfortable anymore, felt clammy from old sweat.

"I know." Slipped off the bed, got on my knees in prayer-fashion. Dug out a wet wipe, cleansed hands and face. Took off the T-shirt and pants, swabbed arms, chest, etc. Changed to fresh things. The old ones'll have to be rinsed out soon.

Now it's the sheet's turn. I scraped up a bit of the edge near the bed's head with a fingernail, peeled the whole thing back like a banana skin — wadded it with difficulty into a gummy-sticky ball, remembering the trouble Laleekh'd had at this stage, his good-natured curses. I raised the dust ruffle, held the ball there. It went off to wherever, *poof!*

I pulled away another layer of sheet — slipped back into bed under it, daintily soft like fine gauze. Bandage, told myself.

•

Someone's here, I warned toward the end of another dream — in which I sensed Dave had figured. Opened eyes slightly.

It wasn't quite as black as before, the walls were a deep gray. Two individuals were there, like two dark shadows. One was by my peepee place opposite me, brushing or sweeping on his "knees"; the other was standing at the wall extending leftward from behind my head, maybe five or six feet away, fiddling with machinery I imagined. That is, every few seconds from his direction came a bip followed by a faint whir-ring.

The motor or whatever was too loose in its chassis or something; the whirring trailed off each time to a squeaky squeal.

It's the Gagloos, I alerted myself. My stomach churned. Let's stay put for the moment till we have a better idea what they're up to. . . .

Now what? A short time had passed.

The sweeping had petered out; he who had brushed was upright on his feet now, with my sand pail in hand. Went, high-stepping, to the corner of the room beyond the foot of my bed, manipulated there with his left hand. A door, consisting of upper and lower portions, widened — *clang!*

Light from outside fell on him — he was a green, a trifle shorter and thinner than Laleekh and me, wearing a green cape and a knee-length skirt.

He stepped out, in green pumps with floppy toes!

The door parts came together again — *clang!* . . .

Next case, I pronounced to myself sometime later.

A metallic clap, as of a plate being pushed into place, had sounded from the direction of the fiddler with the machinery. Now that one was moving closer to me.

He came to rest about a foot away. Just stood there like that, facing me, my head.

Time to unveil. "Hello," I said, quavery-like, employing the obligatory lone-one-of-one neuter form, since there was no telling in that near-dark to which type he belonged.

His body gave a sort of jerk, the way ours do when we're startled.

"'Lo-oh," I sort of warbled.

He didn't answer a word, just took off, high-stepping, toward the door. And the next instant — *clang!* — he was out of it like the sweeper — *clang!*

Was also a green, likewise short, but bigger-boned with more flesh than that other . . . had on the same cape, knee-length skirt, and funny-toed shoes.

Why didn't he respond? Did I say something wrong or what? And why did he stare at me so? What was going through his mind then?

It's getting to look more and more as if this is some kind of jail. Can it be? . . .

So, time to see what's what here, I sighed inwardly after a spell more of lying there. But am I up to it, that's the question — the fever had abated, but I still felt very weak, like on my last legs.

Well, let's give it a college try — suitably equipped, of course. . . .

First things first. I bumbled over to where the fiddler had fiddled, shined the flash there. The wall was indeed grey, with a sheen, but I couldn't make out the least little mark on it. Scraped the driver across the place to pick up grooves to indicate seams — there was nothing, it was or seemed perfectly smooth. I felt here and there with my fingers, pressed — still couldn't detect anything. Eh, the hell with it, I dismissed, for the time being anyway. . . .

The doorway was next, what else. I went over to it practically reeling, let me tell you.

On the left in the corner were three things:

— a ball of crystal or glass the size of a doorknob, parallel with my shoulder

— a horizontal switch to the left of it, which invited pushing leftward

— one of those pneumatic-tube-like toilets, below them on a level with my hip

Possibly the Gagloos' minds run along lines similar to ours in these matters, I posited — applied my thumb to the switch in quest of more light.

"Oh shit!" — the "door" began to divide. I punched the switch right back. The upper and lower door-parts rushed together again — *clang!* I held my breath with hot cheeks. There was not so much as a pin drop anywhere.

Since that was the case — nobody running to 'vestigate — why didn't I go ahead & have a peek out?

Very simple, wasn't ready for that yet. Wanted to take in the rest of the room first, thoroughly — and digest it. . . .

The see-through knob must be for controlling the lights then, betcha. I gripped it and with the leftwardness of the switch in mind, turned counterclockwise a smidge.

Yes, the walls appeared to be a mite brighter.

I turned the knob some more, to the end.

Was still dim in there, 40 watts I'd say, but why look a gift horse etc.

The room was about twelve feet high. Everything from the ceiling down was that same shiny grey. . . .

Can the walls be all of metal, I wondered. Ticked the one catty-cornered to the "door" with a fingernail — *tonk-tonk.* Ticked in another spot, same wall — *tonk-tonk.* Tried a third spot — *dick-dick.* One more — *dick-dick.*

So there's metal in some places, but in others something else — that khalala or another cement compound, wouldn't surprise me, tinted and polished to the same glossy grey.

It's reasonable to suppose there are alternating panels of each. I went through the routine of scraping the driver and pressing with my fingers again in search of grooves. Also in vain.

[Ed. Obviously a point was being made here about the stage of civilization at which these individuals were — that it had reached its prime and was beginning to decline. During our discussion of this chapter, the author launched into two digressions that seemed to offer analogies. One was respecting the then recent find at Xian in the People's Republic of China of seven thousand life-sized terra cotta statues of warriors and horses dating from 221-206 B.C. (well past the Shang heyday); Ms. Rothman gave it as her opinion that they were redolent in their modeling of earlier stone figures from New Dynasty Egypt, Assyria, and Archaic Greece. Her second digression had to do with a photograph, taken by a historian colleague on vacation, showing a modern shopping-plaza style ice cream hut in the Peloponessus, home of the Mycenaeans, with a triangular hole gaping uselessly over the front door; this was in imitation of the space of the same shape that the builders of the citadel at Mycenae had left above the lintel of the main gate out of engineering necessity, and ingeniously filled in with the well-known triangular bas-relief of the lions.]. . .

I lowered the lights to where it seemed they'd been originally, and made my way back to the bed, really rocky now.

One more mystery to try and unravel, and that's it for now. Namely, each time before when the door had clanged, the room'd trembled slightly.

I jump-rope jumped. It did it that time too.

Well, why not, I considered, off my feet once more. But don't elevators usually have a hole in the top for getting out in the event that something goes wrong?

I clicked on the flash, aimed it upward. Was just more of that glittery gray metal and khalala or whatever.

The roof is solid then . . . the room's sealed off.

●

Someone's come in again. I was emerging from another dream — about my mom, Flora, fat and with streaks of gray in her hair as she was in her middle years . . . chasing after Barney, my father, with bald head, and paunch as big as ever.

Someone had entered indeed, turning the lights up in the process, though by no means all the way. It was a willowy brown reminiscent of the kookey lean-lone brown in Laleekh's village; he was dressed in a cape, skirt, and floppy-toed shoes of his color like the greens before in theirs, only his skirt was considerably longer, covering to mid-calf. In his hand was this object that looked like a small folded beach umbrella.

Must be some kind of official, I cued myself, already sitting and about to swing round so my back was resting against the wall — and feet were sticking out. Now we'll see what's what around here, just what my status is. I felt a little funny about my legs being bare, but thought it would be more awkward yet if I started scrambling to put on the jeans.

The brown had proceeded to the center of the room — oh say, four feet before me. Now he touched the tip of his "umbrella" to the floor, and — *wip!* — it unfolded into a brown "director's chair," replete with armrests and legs of brown metal tubing. He eased his bottom onto it.

My facial muscles tightened — okay, look alive, here we go.

Not quite — he got to his feet again, shifted the chair a little to the right. But then no sooner down than he was back up yet again, shifting it leftward to where it had been before. . . .

After the fact: he was trying to put my peepee place and its odor well behind him more than likely. His nosehole kept twitching.

Anyway, the fuss 'n bother with the chair gave me a chance to size him up. My impression was: he's not very high in the pecking order. 'Fact, I have a sneaking suspicion that he's rather young & not too experienced at what he was about to do.

[Ed. It might as well be further noted that the author was never to become privy as to how the individuals of that world reckoned their ages and other extended periods of time, save that their calendar was *based on something of a natural nature regularly occurring below there.*]

Finally, he was settled. His mouth opened, a whole lot of words poured out.

I listened — very closely — and I must say that I recognized most of them. But crazily, for the life of me, I couldn't put them together . . . couldn't make head or tail of it all!

Maybe some extra light would help, I felt after a time. ✸I'm not following you too well, I signaled. Can you hold on a sec.

He stopped, looked.

I scooted over to the door, spun the knob all the way, scooted back. ✸'Kay, carry on, I twiddled.

He started talking again, more slowly.

To no avail. I spoke up now — "Sorry, still experiencing difficulty."

Again he stopped; then his expression changed, as with a realization. He gave a sharp little blow to his left brow, the way we do sometimes when we've suddenly remembered something — "Oh dear, of course!" he said quite distinctly. I'd been expecting to hear Geegloo, the language of the surface, whereas he'd been addressing me in Khakhloo, their related but different tongue down there, he went on to explain.

"Oh well, no harm done," I chimed in. As long as I haven't completely lost my wits, soothed myself.

He regarded me as if with new interest — "It's good of you to feel that way." Why didn't we continue in Geegloo for the moment, he suggested — though it should be clearly understood that I would have to get some of their Khakhloo on board as soon as was practicable.

🖐No problem, I assured him. But how come, since we appeared to be doing just fine in Geegloo, at least from where I sat.

Well, it seems there were a variety of reasons, not the least of which was that most folks down there were hardly familiar with Geegloo — indeed, his own grasp of it was rather tenuous. And certainly this held true for the Supreme Council (literally "a group of purple friends of the First Stage meeting together for the sake of talking things over"), to whom I was to be presented. Of more importance yet, in preparation for that event, I had to answer a question that could only be phrased in Khakhloo, as Their Honors were bound to demand an accounting with respect to it then.

The brown allowed time for this to sink in, then added confidentially — "I must tell you that everybody has been most eagerly awaiting your recovery because of the question" — among others his ultimate superior, the Head Archivist. [Ed. To anticipate, the archivists, exclusively brown, were for the most part responsible for the storage and retrieval of public information.] Just a pity that the big boss didn't foresee the problem of the language, but it was an understandable oversight — "So much on his shoulders, you know." To complicate matters, the Council's next session was coming up very soon — as luck would have it, just before a major holiday when everybody was too busy with their own concerns to be bothered. So we'd have to make haste with the Khakhloo — "we" meaning he, the Head Archivist's Third Assistant, and I. He'd endeavor to instruct me, having no idea of what else to do under the circumstances.

🖐Quite all right, I assured again. What can I say, goes

with the job, consoled myself. Still, I felt a little je ne sais quoi uneasy. "Look" — I narrowed my eyes—"you do know who I am, don't you?"

"Oh yes." They knew about EV-rything.

I winced — boy oh boy, the indiscretions too I suppose. Oh well, guess they've been forgiven, after all he's so very pleasant.

"Shall we begin?" he posed.

✋I'm all "ears," I waved. Also had some questions for him — among other things, first and foremost, where could I find a sink or something for when the canteen began to run low and to do the wash.

✋All in good time, he palmed, very decently. I'd have answers to each and every one just as soon as we were done with our lessons.

Apres Lesson One. He's giving us both a "breather," said he'd be back in a while — whatever that means. Their time words are full of all sorts of odd qualifiers.

As a teacher he's better'n Lal any day — though I'm as fond as ever of that little green bum & miss him muchly. Very strict, doesn't let me get an unnecessary word in edgewise, but thorough & utterly engaging into the bargain.

The language: turns out to be not as grim as feared, everything much of a muchness with Geegloo except for the consonants, which seem to have shifted (just like with the vowels in English once upon a time, the Great Vowel Shift, Bowel Shit, haha). Ex: jabba (Lal's favorite fruit) = chappa in Khakhloo. Jabba in Khakhloo means "itch." Here's the whole shmear in a nutshell:

Geegloo		Khakhloo	
Letter	*IPA*	*Letter*	*IPA*
b	b *or* bh	*p*	p *or* ph
ch	tʃ	*j*	dʒ
g	ɢ$^{1-13}$	*kh*	χ$^{1-13}$
h	h$^{1-7}$	*k*	q$^{1-7}$
j	dʒ	*ch*	tʃ

k	q$^{1\text{-}15}$	*h*	h$^{1\text{-}15}$
kh	χ$^{1\text{-}19}$	*g*	G$^{1\text{-}19}$
l	l̥	*r*	ʁ$^{1\text{-}5}$
m	m	*n*	n
n	n	*m*	m
p	p *or* ph	*b*	b *or* bh
r	ʁ$^{1\text{-}5}$	*l*	l̥
s	s	*z*	z
sh	ʃ (*"shut"*)	*sh*	ʒ (*"measure"*)
sh	Z (*"measure"*)	*sh*	S (*"shut"*)
z	z	*s*	s

My primary task, as I see it then, will be to acquire a new basic vocab. . . .

Gotta get some rest, sleep fast . . . then memorize word lists till he shows. I don't much like doing it this way — better to use the words, learn'em that way — but there's no choice. Will have to make-do with little chit-chats with him in that regard. . . .

Lesson Two down (with me suitably attired for the occasion). Two more to go, mentor says, still with his nosehole problems. That's all there's time for.

Very important, don't forget:

— green individ. = glakh [G^{9}laχ^9] (think of the initial "g"'s)

— purple individ. = shkhurza [ʃχ^{7}ɷ'ʁ^5·za] (here remember the "ur"'s)

— brown individ. = eekhal [i'· χ^{8}al̥] (no hint there at all here, THAT's the HINT)

Food for thought: he uses the green (glakh) forms re me just like Lal (his khlag forms). What can it mean? Do I appear green to them here on this world or what? Never mind, sleep, sleep. . . .

Lesson Three fini. Ouch, the verbs. But I think I can finesse it, & Teach (twitching worse'n ever) is inclined to agree.

Get this: there are two modes, one for an action occurring or state of being existing under the ground, the other for above on the surface. However, the latter can also serve as an intensifier of the action or state of being. Ex: "to think" = zagochee [za·G^{2}ó·tʃi] in Geegloo, but in Khakhloo it's either sakhokhakhlojee [sa·χ^{2}o'·χ^{13}a·χ^{11}l̥o'·dʒi] or *sakhokheekhlojee [sa·χ^2o·χ^{13} i·χ^{11}lo '·dʒ i] depending on where the thinking is being done or how deeply. . . .*

Lesson Four & that's all, folks. Seems there are two other modes (vestiges from sometime long long ago, offering hints as to the origin and development of the species), involving:

— khokhl — lit. "in the water," for very grave occasions

— khookhl — lit. "up a tree," for frolicsome ones

Attençion! Also veree important: "The distinction between these two modes, alas for the novice, has become somewhat blurred of late," quote unquote.

He's just left. Returning "tomorrow" with The Question, by gum.

I'm worried about the water situation. There're only a few drops left & I've gotten no hint from him as yet as to where to find more. Need a bath bad. When was the last swim with Lal, who knows. Have to nail the guy down about it as soon as this travail is over — without fail!

Clang-clang! "So how are we today?" the tall, thin brown, my teacher, called out, breezing in the "next morning." He didn't wait for an answer — high-stepped it right to his spot, unfolded his chair, took a seat, and unlike the other days, stayed put, somehow managing to keep his nosehole under control.

I was up. What with the worry over The Question — did I really have everything down pat — I hadn't actually slept . . . just dozed some. ✋Fine, just fine, I motioned.

There was something different about him, this Third Assistant to the Head Archivist . . . his manner. But I couldn't quite put my finger on it. "All set?" he asked.

I pushed forward from my place on the bed, so my feet were planted firmly on the floor —✋Check.

"Just answer yes or no."

"I'll — I'll do my best," I gulped.

He seemed to take a deep breath, a brown noseless scarecrow inhaling — "Do you believe in gleego" [G^{16}li'·G^8o]?

"Gleego? Gleego?" — fear gripped me. We had never covered that word, I was sure of it.

"Answer," he said curtly.

"But — but how can you — ?"

He sprang to his feet — "You answer at once!" He looked as if he were about to storm out and report me to someone, or something.

✋ Okay, okay, I tried to pacify.

He sat back down.

"Just give me a few moments," I pleaded — put the knuck of my left forefinger in my mouth. It isn't fair, I brooded, but what other alternatives are there? Now let's see. . . .

For lack of a better idea, I tried transposing gleego into Geegloo, and lo, there was our old pal kreekho, "egg." But obviously it couldn't mean just that. "Do you believe in egg?" didn't make any sense. Further, since the question could only be asked in Khakhloo, the term had to have some special significance to these individuals here below, I reasoned. Here are two possibilities that occurred:

— an abstract concept like the name of a god, the Mundane Egg etc.

— a principle, like democracy

Then came this chilling thought — it was conceivable that I could be right & still answer incorrectly. For instance, supposing it stands for "life" & I said yes & it turned out they were in the middle of a population explosion here. . . .

"I'm still-ill wai-ting," the Third Assistant singsonged — scuffed his shoes, with the silly toes.

Well, here goes, I primed myself. At least it isn't multiple choice. I removed the knuck from my mouth — "By all means."

He was, or seemed, ecstatic — "Good, that's all I wanted to know!" Shot up, with a flick of the "wrist" transformed the chair into an umbrella again . . . made a bee-line for the "door."

"Hey!" I yelled after him. "Hey, what about my turn?"

No sale — *Clang! Clang!* — he was gone.

•

Now what the hell, was my first reaction. The guy tricked

you, hustled you, the nerve of him! I was beside myself.

And YOU, I scolded, why did you have to answer so positively? You may be in a real jam now on account of it. Really, what's the matter with you, howje let yourself get sucked into such a deal? I stood up, paced over to the peepee wall, paced back.

And what about the water situation? I bounced down onto the bed. May be a long time before somebody else appears again, do you realize that? . . .

"A mess," I muttered before long, with arms behind my head, eyes staring at the ceiling. What're you going to do?

I conjured up Donne. Licked my top lip . . . bottom . . . aridly —

Shee, shee is dead; she's dead: when thou knowest this,
Thou knowest how poore a trifling thing man is.

You know, this is downright foolish. All you have to do is go to the door, open it, if it's still possible to, which one assumes it is, and voilà, the solutions to all your problems, or at least the most pressing, could be right outside there in the form of someone to ask — or, for all you know, a waterfall!

I took up the canteen and hopped to it. After all, that eekhal (brown one) never expressly forbid you to go out there. The subject simply never came up, that's all — thanks to your close adherence to his conditions — and you simply assumed that you were confined here, just as you and you alone got it into your head before that this is some sort of prison.

He shouldn't have walked off like that, I grouched, at the "door." So if his boss or the Council are unhappy when they hear about what I'm doing now, that's tough. I thumped with my thumb — *Clang-lang!* — poked my nose.

What can I tell you — it was a big disappointment. There

was just a narrow grey-walled corridor there, extending rightward for maybe thirty feet, with a black rubber-like mat on the floor, and at the end of it, before a door that looked to be another clanger, five glakhs or greens reminding of the small sweeper, in the same green capes and knee-length skirts, and shoes with flexible toes.

They'd been passing the time o' day among themselves; now they stopped and turned toward me, expectantly.

"Hi, to you three plus two of your own kind," I said — put a foot over the threshold, lifted the other and placed it beside the first.

They remained as they were, still waiting.

Well, they certainly are on the tame side for goons, if that's what they're supposed to be, I mused. [Ed. Which, to anticipate once more, they most certainly were not — rather they were maintenance workers, or conservers as they are later called, all green individuals down below there having been so employed, in every field, from the janitorial to medical.] "Mind if I have a look around?" I asked.

They didn't say boo.

Well, it's easier that way, I comforted myself.

Ranged along the wall opposite my "door" were four more doors that looked to be as ours normally do, except for having leatherish loops like curtain ties for handles.

Where can they lead to, I wondered — stepped up to the first.

On it was a tiny green circle, say a quarter of an inch in diameter, with a yellow dot in the center.

I took hold of the loop, pulled the door open.

Of all things, inside was a narrow room with a row of hip-high "pneumatic tubes" on either side. It was a toilet room for glakhs, in other words.

The small greens were still holding their breath, so to speak.

"Bagaba," I said, pointing in there.

They all burst into hysterical laughter — "Gee! Gee! Gee! Gee! Gee!" — their throats, bellies going.

What's so funny? Oh yes, of course, how gauche of me —

"Pakhapa," I corrected. (Do so hate to make careless mistakes like that, don't you?) And what might bagaba signify here then, I wondered anew — closed that door, pushed on to the next.

That one had a larger brown circle on it, let's say a half inch in diameter, and in the center was a red dot.

Very likely a toilet room for eekhals, I figured, and tried it.

Yes, indeed.

Looking ahead, I saw that the fourth and last door — that closest to the gigglers — bore a purple-and-white insignia, three-quarters of an inch, and so had to be a facility like that for shkhurzas. But the door before it, the third, coming up, was bare.

This should be interesting — I visualized a broom closet with maybe a slop sink. I tugged with the loop.

Now howdya like that! There were a dozen or so stairs going down — baby-bluish grey in color, more of that dyed khalala or garara as they'd say here — and at their foot a landing with a promise of more stairs, the railing, a black pipe-like affair, curling there.

Those glakhs were watching again, fascinated it seemed.

"Say" — I held up the canteen — "do you know where I can get some water?"

The green ones looked, simply looked.

They must understand me, that's for sure . . . they're just being stubborn or something. "Water," I repeated — I shook it, canteen.

There was no change, they just kept their eyes fixed on it.

Well — I shrugged — all roads lead to etc. "Be back in a while, 'kay?" I sauntered out, drew the door behind me with another of those leatherish loops on that side.

Now — I stood stock still there — will they or won't they follow me, or go and snitch to someone? . . .

All clear, I made it out to be after three, four minutes. "Yippee-yai-yo-kai-yeah!" I whooped, not too loud.

Lickety-split (the +.65 assisting), I was down on the landing, and sure enough, there was another flight of stairs, which led — wouldn't you know it — down to another ordinary door in the same place as the stair-door on my floor . . . with more stairs below it to another landing.

On the other side of that stair-door there? Another corridor, identical with mine in every respect, down to the black mat — except that only two of those sweeper-types were there. I found 'em busy at a small rectangular hole opposite the Shkhurza (Purple) Room — one using a "monkey-wrench" on a fat pipe inside it, the other holding a plate of nickel or garara to fit over. So busy were they in fact that when I called over to ask if they had any water there, they both jumped as if to hit the ceiling, not having heard me come in apparently!

Water, I emphasized.

They just looked, like the glakhs upstairs — mesmerized at the sight of the canteen, & also of my watch. Boy, I sure hope I'm not going to have any trouble with pilfering down here. That'd be a fine howdyado. . . .

Down, down I went to another door and corridor like that with small green ones in it, again a twosome, engaged in swabbing down the mat with something resembling a mop. Same story.

What can I tell you — there was another floor of the same below that one, and when I met with the same treatment from yet another pair, I decided that it was an office building or something like that and just kept going down without stopping anymore, figuring it would come to an end sooner or later.

Sure enough, finally, after four more stories, I came to a door on the between-floors landing that gave onto a small, rail-less platform on the "outside." Boy, I'll tell you, it was gloo-oomy out there — with a kind of pinkish-brown sky overhead and the facade of my building all cliff-like grey rock.

Four or so more stories down were a whole lot of roads sort of radiating out in concentric circles, one beneath another, to a horizon. They were all single-laned & unpaved, I think, with figures in groups kneeing along here & there . . . no vehicles, at least while I was standing there. . . .

I went back inside & started descending again, hoping to find a way out to the uppermost of the roads, which I did in time. My building curved, the roadbed with it, in both directions almost at once. Nobody was around.

I opted for a leftward course, to follow in the wake of the pedestrians I'd noted above. But first, before I set off, I grabbed up a handful of pebbles from the ground, took them to a little extra-dark area near the door (like where I'd go pee if I had to), & arranged'em in a circle with an arrow the way that nice Sgt Henriquez taught me when we were doing Survival in the wilds of Wyoming.

As I went along, the exterior of my building was on my left, you understand, with a sheer drop of several hundred feet on the right to the inner side of the road on the next level down.

Eliot's "Prufrock" came to mind —

LET US GO THEN, YOU AND I,
WHEN THE EVENING IS SPREAD OUT AGAINST THE SKY
LIKE A PATIENT ETHERISED UPON A TABLE.

That's what it felt like, it was that bleak. . . .

On the other side of the bend was an entranceway of sorts — like a barrier in a bullring, except that it was of stone, or if you will, like the opening to a giant snailshell. It's possible that this was the main entrance to my building & the one I came out of was a back one.

Around the bend was yet another jutting stone barrier like that, and around the next another, & around the ones after that, more. They all had writing on the protruding part, but this I didn't spot right away 'cause the letters, which resembled random scratches, were only an inch high and almost the same gray as the facades. The words go from left to right, I have a feeling. . . .

Finally, when it began to look as if the road would never come to an end, I got up the gumption to take a peak inside one of the doorways. And what do you think I found? A large hall, dark throughout except for down front, and packed to capacity, with the whole place gabbing away like crazy. Down front were highlighted, would you believe it, three huge doohickies of violet, magenta, and taupe, about ten feet by ten feet, hanging from the ceiling. They looked to be like loosely wound-up scrolls. [Ed. Alas, the author never did share the secret of what was transpiring in there, and unhappily, I did not think to inquire. An anthropologist colleague of mine has suggested that the objects were stylized representations of white, red, and yellow tongues tinged with purple, and theorized that in progress was a game of chance requiring strictest secrecy, or else a cooking class or family planning session.]. . .

Well, well, just what the doctor ordered maybe, I rejoiced, after a few more bends.

A trio had just come out of a doorway and begun heading up the road leftward ahead of me.

Let's catch up with them and try and sound them out, I proposed. Maybe they won't have the same antipathy toward me as those small glakhs and show themselves more kindly disposed than that back-stabbing Third Assistant.

They were all three stepping along side by side, the eek-hal, another lanky one, in the center, in a brown get-up identical with the Third's down to the calf-length skirt. The shkhurza, on the left, was as tall as he but much heavier, and dressed in the same outfit in purple, only with his "toes" peeping out from beneath an "ankle"-length skirt, while the green one, on the right, who was larger than the sweepers but not quite so large as the fiddler with the machinery, wore the same short green skirt, only topped by a long-flowing cape of yellow.

What should I do, should I call out or what, I wondered, hurrying after them.

When I got to about a car-length away, the green sensed me I guess . . . turned his head.

✋ Hey, wait up, I diddled, huffing and puffing.

His tongue flicked out — *shlup*.

Now what kind of an answer is that, I meditated. ✋ I mean it, I'm serious, I made it clear.

His right hand point-pointed to his left side beneath that copious yellow cape, where his "organs" were, the cavity and protuberance (same as on friend Laleekh). His tongue flashed again . . . waved like a yellow flame!

Ugh — I grimaced — a pervie. So they have them in this world too, how disgusting. I slowed down, as I would have, faced with a similar situation on a New York City street.

The cheeky devil kept at it, but then suddenly tripped on

his own feet, and knocked against his brown-mate, the eek-hal, who in turn bumped into the big, fat purple one, the shkhurza.

The three of them came to a halt — I too, at a considerable distance to the rear now.

(?)"Who do ya think ya pushin' around?" the shkhurza gave it to the brown, nosehole to nosehole with him.

(?)"Whadya mean, pushin'!" the eekhal protested. He was not about to take the rap for somebody else! Etc., etc!

The dandyish green renewed his pledges of "affection" for me, digitally and lingually.

(?)"I'll be DAMNED if I will!" the brown one roared — whirled on the jackass, the green, and — *smacko!* — lashed out at him with the flat of his hand.

"Ookh!" the culprit screeched, clutching his right ear button.

Boy, you sure can pick'um, I chided myself. Hope and trust all marrieds aren't like this here.

🖐Onward, the hefty purple motioned crankily.

Eh, let's follow and see where they're going, I suggested. Maybe you'll encounter some more wholesome types there.

Boy oh boy, no sooner said than that glakh was at it again. Still nursing his button, he fell to mimicking one or the other of them, alternately waddling and mincing along, and turning round now and then to see if I was appreciating. . . .

At last, after another bend or two, they ducked inside another of those entranceways. I marked time out front for a few minutes to let'em get to wherever they were going, then went in myself . . . to what could only be a lobby, a fairly well-lighted one as things went in those parts.

What a layout — the walls were all silvery with the softest of patinas. If they didn't consist of real silver, betcha it was titanium, pricier yet by our standards — and 'case anyone's interested, I know titanium when I see it. The nitrogen storage tanks of one of our orbiters in the Smithsonian's Space Museum are made of it. . . .

There was only that room & another smaller one in the back to the right, like an alcove. So the question was, where did that unholy threesome disappear to? I made a very costly mistake snooping around — walked into that second room, thinking maybe there was a door in there not visible from the lobby proper. A second later, a wall slid across behind me — with a clink! I turned right around, tried to do something . . . push it back, pry it with my fingernails. Not on yer life, & worse yet, suddenly I felt myself beginning to rise. That smaller room was an elevator, it seems.

Controls, controls, it has to have controls, I told myself, in a sweat. Go find them — I looked on the left, gave it a real once-over. Couldn't see a thing. Has to be here, somewhere, I know it. Sure thing, I found after feeling around. The "room" jerked to a halt — took off again with a zoom — sideways!

Oh brother! But did I let it go at that? No way. I began slapping all over the left side there with both hands. And the result? The thing switched to going left-right-down-up!

Realizing that something was there and I just couldn't make it out, I tried pressing lower down, & that did it, sort of. The "room" switched again to going straight up — with jolts every 20 feet or so, & either that "door" or another to my rear opening & closing — clinkety-clink! — on what to all intents & purposes looked like living rooms.

I was plenty worried — maybe there was a law against it, intruding on folks' privacy, that sort of thing. But was curious too, and tried my darndest to memorize details to write down later for posterity. Had no luck there either — now as I sit here with pen in hand chez moi again, it's a jumble, & all I can remember with any clarity is the following from the first of those rooms:

— 4-large, medium, and small plastic-seeming chairs, shaped like sliding ponds, in a semi-circle — glossy black, hot pink, and orange

— a cocoa-colored carpet with foot-high stalks of brilliant green "shrubbery" rising up from it here & there, cloth on wire probably.

— on the wall, which was dazzling white, the pièce de résistance . . . a five-by-two-foot turquoise blob with navy polka dots, reminding of a fish belly. . . .

The other rooms were either more subdued — though not much more — or louder yet, with bloody reds & what looked to be chests 'n cabinets dangling from the ceiling. No matter, gaudy or not, the whole kitnkeboodle of them had a certain something in common . . . hard to put a finger on. . . .

They were all empty 'cept one, where an eekhal was just sinking wearily into a canary-yellow sofa-like affair with a cup of something in

*his hand, and not a stitch on — as if he'd just come home from an
extra-long excruciating day at the office. He stared at me for that moment before the "door" clinked to, flabbergasted! You better believe it, I
had visions of his calling the police or something. . . .*

*I finally made it back down to ground level, don't ask me how.
Maybe someone came along & "pushed" the "button," then got fed up
with hanging around & decided to hoof it instead. . . .*

*Outside on the "street," it was the old story — what was I going to
do about the water situation, the canteen was bone dry. Oh, I was in a
state, let me tell you, mouth all pasty, on the point of wringing hands
and sniveling.*

Glory be, are my ears hearing right? A hollow plashing
sound, such as a pool might make, was coming from within
the entranceway I was just then passing.

I rushed inside without giving it a second thought — to
find just that, an indoor pool.

But what a pool — it was obviously intended to resemble
the pond belonging to the first village above on the surface,
with the same ingenuity used as in the living rooms I'd just
seen. That is, the water was a glaring cloudy green, thanks to
a whole lot of ill-concealed lights on the bottom; it was surrounded by greyish-brown ledges, fashioned from that garara
no doubt; and the ledges in turn were ringed by a clutter of
lifeless bushes, more cloth on wire for sure, with a concave
gray baldspot overhead topped by a white curl.

No matter. Not a soul seemed to be in sight, so one-two-
three I was on my knees at the edge, shoveling water into my
mouth with one hand and keeping the open canteen mouth
glugging with the other.

My chin rose at last . . . itchy with specks. Those specks
again — I imagined the lower half of my face dotted with
them, like black chickenpock marks. Olé!

Eh, might as well take a dip already, I thought. Reeled in
the canteen and capped it, set it aside — stood up, unzipped
the jeans.

Uh oh — there were voices . . . from the opposite end, in
among the "vegetation."

There was a door in the back somewhere in all likelihood. A number of individuals had come in, that was certain. I narrowed my eyes, listening.

The voices became louder . . . were there, issuing from a bunch of what could only be kids, who had emerged onto the ledge — tubby purples, beanpole browns, peewee greens, all of them in the raw.

They started horsing around, evidently unaware of my presence.

Go or stay, I debated. Eh, I'd like to have that swim. "Hel-loh!" I hallooed, to you four three's etc.

They broke off, peered.

"Hi there!" I followed it up. "Is it okay — do you mind if I — ?"

"Gyee — ee!" they all cried out — began pedaling my way as fast as their legs could carry them — every one with a spitting face on him!

"Curses," I muttered — scooped up the flask, made tracks myself with a good headstart. ✺Sorry, to you etc., I sent them, behind me, with one foot in the "street."

Boy oh boy, I sure will be glad to lay me down and rest my head once more, I conceded to myself, on the top stair of my floor quite some time later, with the canteen weighing down my shoulder like a rock.

I pulled open the door, looked left.

There were only three of those green sweeper-types in the corridor now. Part of the same lot from before? Who knows.

"Here I am," I said cheerily, "back safe 'n sound."

They kept their own counsel. I went on my way, rightward toward my room.

"Council's meeting tomorrow," one of them said to my back.

Oh? Now there's something of moment. I stopped and turned around.

They'd been clustered together before; now they were standing abreast of one another facing me. "Would you like to see the room?" the one on the left asked.

Eh, why not, was my feeling. Every little bit helps, grist for the mill etc. ✋ 'Kay.

As I came up, they stepped aside, the spokesman to his left, his pals right.

I stepped to the door there, definitely another clanger.

"Look," the leader said, close behind my left ear. He reached for the switch.

The door-parts slid away from one another noiselessly. It was inky-black inside.

I'll just go in and spin the light-knob quickly, I schemed. Raised a foot, lowered it — onto nothing! There was no floor inside there . . . just a sheer drop of hundreds or thousands of feet to judge from the echoes.

I just managed to get hold of the doorframe and drag myself back in.

"Gee! Gee! Gee!" they hee-hawed.

I got myself on the other side of them in no time flat. "That wasn't very nice."

"Gee! Gee! Gee!"

I started heading for my place again. "Some fun," I muttered in English — blinked back the tears. . . .

Well, no sense fretting over it, I tried to buck myself up with, once inside. Dropped the canteen on the bed, plopped myself. . . .

C'mon, you did it, you got the water, I made an effort to reason, still weepy. You're all set . . . at least for the moment.

Chapter Five

[Ed. This chapter like the previous one was late in forthcoming, but this time by a good month instead of several weeks, and again with an excuse from the author of being overburdened by student papers. However, when the manuscript arrived, I saw at once that something was very much amiss; in a word, the strategy of the narrative was entirely different. I rang her up to register my serious reservations — which I did as delicately as I knew how. Even so, Ms. Rothman grew indignant. "What's the big deal?" she said, rather morosely. "Everyone else and his brother changes the rules to suit themselves, whenever they feel like it — look at publishing and the other arts industries, to say nothing of academia." Uppermost in her mind, of course, was the failure of her long prose-poem "Guinevere" to find a publisher in spite of its being universally admired, and her having been transferred elsewhere, practically overnight, without having any say in the matter, from an unusual institution with a special educational mission to another, ordinary one that had no need of her unique qualities. "Why should I be excluded from the privilege?" she went on. As for the prospective audience for this work, to whom at least a modicum of consideration was due — "Believe you me, they'll survive."

Caveat lector.]

Clang!

Felice sat bolt upright. "Who?" she hoarsed out. "What?" It was the "door" obviously, the two parts had widened. But no one had come in.

She slid off the bed, was before the empty space the next moment. Put forth her big toe.

"Yooow!" She was hurtling toward the other end of the corridor on her back, the black mat under foot having taken off in that direction and swept her along with it as soon as her toe touched.

"What's the big idea!" she barked, nose to nosehole with the Third Assistant the next moment. He was standing in front of that other clanging door like hers, which she'd nearly stepped out of into nowhere last night, thanks to those nasty little green ones. It was open, maybe still open, from then.

The Third Assistant regarded her with utter impassivity — "Quiet, please. Council's in session."

And so it seemed — there was a well-lighted room behind him now where that black hole had been, to 60 watts at least, and a discussion was in progress, somewhere to the left beyond her line of vision.

Felice swallowed her fury. I better do as he says, she thought, and made efforts to compose herself.

Straight ahead stood an eekhal and a glakh, in the usual skirts and capes in their own color, paying very careful heed. Both had a mature look to them somehow; the brown was extra gaunt, the green built along lines similar to the fiddler with machinery — who he may well be to judge from a certain tilt of his head, she felt.

She tried to listen too, but, tantalizingly, the voices — five or six of them at the very least — were just out of earshot. . . .

The eekhal spoke up several minutes later, the mumbling having petered out — "I take it that we may move on to the next item on the agenda, Your Honors." He turned Felice's way and beckoned.

What, like this, she screeched inside, suddenly conscious that she was wearing only a T-shirt, without a bra, and underpants below — that her legs were bare!

"Go ahead," the Third urged her, under his breath — jerked his "thumb" leftward.

"But — " she began to protest.

"IN!" he ordered.

Her mouth wrenched itself into a smile — the ludicrousness of it all, to have to appear before the Council in this fashion. Her hair was all bushed out too. A new fit of rage made her eyes smart.

Leftward, once she'd entered, was a long, glistening, mahogany-like table, rectangular in shape with curved corners, standing lengthwise close by the right wall. Along its sides and far end were twenty purple figures, all of them big and fat like the member of the trio she'd encountered on the "street" — all with behinds perched on quarter-backed stools like typists' chairs. Before each was a small piece of black apparatus the size of a shoe-box, with a three-by-five-inch display, also rounded at the corners, and a minuscule keyboard; ready for each to use, in their left hands of course, was a black xylophone-type hammer.

Above each of the purples seated with their backs to the wall were portholes offering a view to the outside — the facade of a building a short distance away. That is, as far as Felice could tell, the lower edges of those round windows being on a level with her eyebrows.

"That's enough, turn around this way," someone behind her said, the older brown probably — after she'd proceeded past three of the enstooled ones.

Do it, she told herself, with everything pretty much under control again . . . done.

She was facing him and the older, more filled-out green, the pair of them side-by-side with a few feet between them. Behind each, on top of head-high dark-metal platforms full of struts, were two much larger box-like contraptions with screens, say thirteen by fifteen inches, their corners likewise curved.

The brown began to sound off: "As some of you are already aware, this individual was transported here from above by our last inspection team, after they discovered her lying unconscious in the woods. [Ed. One must imagine the glakh-forms being used for her here and below.] She had apparently fallen a prey to some affliction — "

Hey, hold on, let's get everything straight, Felice cued herself. "'Scuse me," she interposed, and looked left. "Your Honors, permit me to intro — "

"Ga-ga-ga-ga-ga!" went the Third Assistant from the doorway, his station — plucked at his throat.

Felice looked searchingly at the older brown, clearly the Third's boss — maybe even the Big Boss, the Head Archivist. "Listen, all I wanna do is — "

"Would you get her to be still, please," the purple beside her at the table said. "It's very annoying."

Felice stared at the floor — what does it all mean, what's going on here? Best do as they say for the moment and listen, try to figure it out.

The head brown resumed — "On the same mission, as you may also have heard, a few of our little conservers, happening to become detached from the main party, stumbled on this." He glanced toward the green, who stepped back to the platform behind him and put a hand up to the side of the box there. The screen brightened, in tones of sepia and tan. The plane materialized on it.

Hah, Lancelot, Felice joyed. Seemed all in one piece, as good as new.

"I'm sure you'll be happy to learn," the brown in charge added, "that our conservers delivered it into their purple superior's hands exactly as they found it."

"I should hope so," Felice muttered, though naturally her mind was considerably eased.

"Most commendable of them," one of the shkhurzas under the portholes toward the table's near end rapped out. "But where is it? Why isn't it here?"

"It was too unwieldy, sir," the eekhal answered. "See for yourself."

The green fingers of his glakh associate rose to the tv's side once more. A ribbon of dark brown scratch-like characters began fluttering along under the image of the plane, from right to left — in the opposite direction from the writing that Felice had seen on the various building marquees during her walk down below. Must be data respecting Lancelot's dimensions, she surmised, the leftward writing being reserved for ordinary text.

"Some bagaba," someone else at the table remarked.

Felice bristled — what, Lancelot's a piece of shit? Then she remembered — oh yes. But whatever can "bagaba" stand for here?

"Where is it then?" the original purple-asker persisted, his patience beginning to wear thin.

"Right outside, sir," the eekhal answered — meaning outside the portholes.

Felice swiveled that way, gave a tiny hop.

Sure enough, the craft was there, on a surface just wide enough for it; the building wall was directly behind.

"Can't you keep her from fidgeting?" the shkhurza next to her complained again. "Really, I can hardly hear myself think."

"Sorry," Felice said, in a low voice — re-directed her eyes frontward. . . .

"You must have something on her too, no?" someone on the end prompted, when the ribbon of hard facts trailed off.

The eekhal gave a nod to the glakh — doing so in their style, with chin to left shoulder, remember.

Someone else under the portholes interrupted — "Just — one — moment!" His voice rang out harshly — "Conserver, before you begin, I want it clearly understood. You are to speak plainly, use no technical terms unless you absolutely have to, define'em when you do, and above all — "

"There are to be no jokes or other funny business!" his neighbor to the left finished it for him.

Jokes? Felice could hardly contain herself. Fancy that, they crack jokes here, jokes crack.

Without a glimmer of a reaction, the glakh went and turned on the other tv set. A brownish "x-ray" [Ed. possibly a sonargram or thermogram] flashed on the screen, with a line of more of those leftward-slanting scratches at the bottom.

So that was what the fiddler with machinery, if this is he,

was up to, Felice realized.

The technical one explained matter-of-factly from what angle the shot had been taken, then pressed to bring up another, which he did the same with, then pressed again, and so on.

Looks like he got every bone in my body, some organs too, was Felice's conclusion when he was through.

A fresh series began, of photographs now, also brownish, of the canteen followed by the pack and its contents, with guesses, some of them pretty shrewd, as to the functions of the unfamiliar articles — like the comb, for instance, which had somehow wandered into the tool kit.

"I should now like to call your attention to a number of curiosities relating to the subject's person," the glakh very soberly announced after the last slide. "First" — he paused for effect — "she appears to have dual excretory systems."

Felice got all hot under the collar again — now that's going too far. "Your Honors," she said, appealing as much to the eekhal — "if I might just — "

"Hakh!" warned the Third Assistant, clearing his throat from the doorway.

What in the world, she wondered.

A film began to roll, featuring a bearish silhouette in a darkened room, herself obviously from the rear. The Bear lurched up from a bed, tottered forward, hunched down by a wall, padded back. The glakh offered commentary of a general nature.

"So what's she got there, Conserver, two appendages or what?" the one on the end asked, after the same thing was repeated several more times and the green one threatened to drone on ad nauseam(?).

"Well, not quite," he answered. "That is, I'm not entirely certain."

A second on the end picked it up — "Not quite? Don't know? Well, let's have a look for ourselves then."

⚘Take that off, the Third motioned to Felice, meaning her undies.

"Huh?" she said. What in the hell, what is this? "Look

here — "

✋OFF! the Third gesticulated.

Well, I won't, I just won't, Felice decided, and folded her arms.

The Third started toward her — "Ha-a-akh!"

✋Okay, okay, she defended. Her fingers crept down to the elastic band — face struggled to control itself.

"Show!" the Third gruffed, when the pants were down on the floor.

She shifted toward the table.

Everyone around it convulsed — "Gee! Gee! Gee! Gee! Gee!". . .

"What's the hair for, do you suppose?" the second on the end asked, himself not quite recovered.

The glakh's eyes practically danced in his head, he was so happy — he had a hunch, he said, but of course it required a more thorough investigation before he could be certain. The hair, he proposed, was an instance of duplication for the sake of self-defense — he indicated the mop of hair on her head. Analogous phenomena obtained among many lesser species, he offered, their termini outwardly similar to confound their enemies. [Ed. Self-mimicry of a like nature here on Earth is made much of in Desmond Morris's *The Naked Ape*, especially as a means of sexual signaling, and woman's lips and breasts, unusually full for primates, are some of the examples furnished, the one mimicking her labia, according to Morris, the other her buttocks. This entry in Ms. Rothman's Diary provides an additional dimension to the above: *Alright, Morris, I'll buy it. But how come you never go into men & their dingdong neckties?*]

You know, enough is enough already, time you took matters in hand, Felice reminded herself. "Listen, all of you, would you just — ?"

"Archivist, honestly!" the shkhurza next to her protested. "If you cannot make her be quiet, either muzzle her or eject her!"

✋Okay, truce, she palmed, at another menacing look from the Third in the doorway. . . .

The glakh took up where he'd left off. Even more curious, indeed defying description, was the situation regarding her chest.

✋Off with that too, the Third gestured, meaning the T-shirt.

Felice sucked on her bottom lip with blinking eyes — grasped the hem, raised the shirt over her head, and turned toward the table again.

"But — but they're so big!" someone there gasped. [Ed. By comparison with the protuberances on the sides of these individuals, certainly, yes.]

✋Up with arms, the Third directed.

This is it, no more after this, Felice soothed herself, feeling the blood drain from them.

"She's got hair there too!" someone else gasped. "Just like a shmazee," remarked one more. [ʧmá·zi — Ed. the lizard-like creature that the author encountered in the woods when on her way to the first village, and Laleekh subsequently immortalized in that clay-like khalala.]

A different voice from the end addressed the brown: "So what does all this add up to, Archivist?"

Felice bent over for her things. So, now, maybe —

One of the dyspeptic types under the portholes opened his mouth. "Add up to? What does it all add up to? It doesn't require an eekhal to figure that out," he mocked. "Any fool can see whose doing this is," his neighbor chimed in. "Those da-a-amned Glakhlanders!" raged the first — he was quivering just about all over.

Felice perked up — What, Glakhlanders? There's a land where glakhs are in charge? But what've I to do with them?

"We warned you about them, co-operating with them, making binding agreements," the second accused. "We told you something like this would happen sooner or later," Number One echoed. "We opposed it each and every time," Number Two took it up, "as the record will show!" He grabbed his "xylophone-hammer," boppety-bopped on the keys of his "shoe-box" — everyone's display lighted up.

"Deeear-ar friends," said the end-one who started it all, in a conciliating tone, "never for a moment was it my intention to suggest otherwise. Of course Glakhland is responsible."

Felice's heart sank — And he struck me as being more sensible than the rest. Well, so much for him. But what do they mean exactly? Responsible how? For my existence somehow?

"I was merely leading up to this," the same end-one went on. "That in view of such a — a sad turn of events, what we ought to do is — "

"Send her down the beach and be done with it," snapped the more irritable of the pair under the portholes.

You know, Felice mused, considering how things're going down here, I wouldn't mind forgetting about telling them who I am and so on and doing just that, going for a trot along the seaside, for real. But judging from their overall technical expertise, that's probably not what he meant. It must refer to some ultra-sophisticated way they have of getting rid of folks down here.

There was a lot of discussion, most of it in vehement opposition to "giving her the gas-pipe," she was happy to hear. . . .

"Archivist" — it was the first one on the end — "have any mental evaluations been done of the subject?"

"Objection! Objection!" bellowed the badgering pair under the portholes in unison. "This party is in no way qualified to meddle in such affairs," Number One pointed out. "Nor is anyone else here," added his neighbor. "We had such an individual here once if you'll recall," Number One went on, "but now that he's defected — "

"He did not, he did not defect!" the one next to her shouted out. "He was de-PORTED!"

"DE-FECTED!" Number Two thundered. "We know what we know." He snatched his hammer again and brought it down with the full force of his being this time. All the displays blazed.

It became very still.

"May he rot there in Glakhland wherever he is," someone

muttered. . . .

The first one on the end spoke up again — "Well, why don't we see what there is anyway."

The brown gave the Third the eye. He came and stood where the green had, and began reeling off an account of his dealings with our heroine — on the whole a highly favorable one, it seemed to Felice.

"What about gleego?" Number One under the portholes pestered. "Did you ask her if she believes in gleego?"

Felice drew in her breath. Her old teacher filled them all in.

"Well, I don't see that it makes any difference one way or another," a new one on her side commented when he was done. "Anyone would have answered yes under the circumstances," seconded his neighbor.

Felice exhaled — so I was right, in a way. [Ed. And more on this matter later obviously.]. . .

The Third was back at his post, having been excused. The first on the end spoke up anew — "Is there anything else that we should know about, Archivist?"

The eekhal gave the go-ahead to the glakh again, who stepped back up. He offered apology for the crudity of what was coming next, explaining (with extra emphasis for the brown's benefit, Felice's ear detected) that it was owing to the extremely brief notice that he'd received to get the necessary equipment ready. Then he re-activated the right tv (Lancelot continuing to pulsate on the left), and a new film began to roll, in "true" color this time, showing Felice from the back shaking her canteen at the five small glakhs in the corridor prior to taking off down the stairs into the "street.". . .

"What's that?" the second on the end wanted to know, of the circle with the arrow that Felice the Bear had just finished making on the ground with pebbles.

"Memory-marker, if I'm not mistaken," the green one answered smartly. "See?" — and fastforwarded to her later peering down at it before going back inside.

"To have such a pesky memory, is it possible?" the same

one questioned. . . .

"Who's that smart-ass?" Number One projected, a long yellow cape and tongue having appeared.

"It's on the agenda for the next meeting, sir," the brown informed. . . .

"Strange, that frantic search for water," reflected the one on the end given to fine phrases, at the height of the chase at the pool. "'Specially since it's all over," a young one beside him added.

Felice perked up — it is? "WHERE?" she blurted out — then quickly put her hand over her mouth. . . .

"So, Your Honors, what's your pleasure?" the eekhal queried when the movie was over.

"Must we come to a decision now?" someone said. "I'm hungry."

"Me too," piped up another.

The supposedly sensible one on the end was not so minded, however. "Conserver," he called over, "would you venture an opinion as to the chances of success for a — a little surgery? Nothing wildly ambitious, mind you. Let's just say, simply — corrective."

The glakh considered, ogled Felice — considered some more. She hugged her chest, completely ignoring her nose [Ed. of which more, much more, in time too] and behind in her panic.

"For the present, it's out of the question," the technical one answered finally. "You see, there are certain things — " He gave Felice another ogle. "No, I'm afraid that I would have to consult with my learned colleagues in — mm — Glakhland first."

The pair under the portholes burst out of their seats. "Treason! Treason!" they shrieked. "He just wants to go and live the good life there!" Number One threw out. "He'd never return to us, you can be sure of that!" Number Two reinforced. . . .

The glakh was as bland as ever. The eekhal queried them all afresh — what did Their Honors care to do?

What is it now, Felice wondered. The Third had fingered

something at her that she didn't catch. ✋Sorry, she fingered back, would you be so kind as to render it again, please.

"OUT!" he hissed.

•

What a kinky lot, and things sure don't look very healthy for me, let alone promising, I gloomed, back in the room . . . settled on the bed with arms behind my head, legs crossed. But the important thing is not to despair. So what'll it be, what's the next step? Nothing, everything was out of my hands, I saw at once.

But supposing you had free rein, what then? It was an academic question, but for the sake of passing the time, with nothing else to do, I indulged myself.

Clearly the solution lies with that mature green, the fiddler with machinery or whoever he is, it came to me after some mulling. If only there were some way of getting hold of him alone. I could take him inside the ship and show him a thing or two, tell him, and then —

But his field appears to be animal biology, at least he seems to lean that way. It's possible that my spiel would go right over his head. Yes, but he must have some associates who are really into things mechanical, and all he'd have to do is relay what he's seen and heard to them. Then, after they've come inside with me and I've explained it all to them, to clinch things we could have a test-run upstairs.

And then once everyone becomes aware of who and what I am. . . .

That's as far as I got . . . after that I fell asleep. . . .

I forgot to wind the watch. Now I'm lost, really lost in time. Let's say I was out for an "hour," it's 10 a.m.

The Third Assistant was just here, opened the "door" and stuck his head in. Said I was in luck, Council had reached a decision. Was in a positive ecstasy over it, a cheeky devil, not an ounce of fellow feeling in him.

What was the decision? Something stark-raving whacko, you better believe it — I'm to go down to the Third Stage (whatever that is) and

appear before the Council there. This Council'll go along with what-
ever they decide.

I threw him a curve: "How come they're not sending me to the
Second Stage?"

He batted it back, easily: "They're on the outs with them for the
moment." Then he was gone, ducking his head right out again and
making the door-parts clang together.

I jumped up & ran over there, realizing that he's the only thing I
have right now till I get the "ear" of the right individual. But when I
pushed the switch, nothing happened — the "door"'s locked.

I'm a prisoner here now for sure.

Boy, this is some fix you're in — I was prone once more.
But really when you begin to think about it, things are not
that bad, I tried to buck up with. You seem to have completely recovered from your affliction, as the Head Archivist
or whoever he is called it. You've still got plenty of food —
I'd hefted the pack not long before — and the water's holding nicely too. Let's face it, the only thing lacking is more for
when the canteen begins to run low again. And of course,
you could stand a bath, the duds a good scrubbing.

Just then I had a sinking feeling — for real! The room'd
begun to move . . . downward. Not very fast, mind you, by
inches . . . still, down.

I began to sweat — I'm going down further . . . further
yet from the surface — clenched and unclenched my fists.
Better get busy with something . . . something, anything.

A thought came, I brightened. That junior shkhurza at
the end of the table said that there was water all over, which
must mean here too.

Okay — I was up, digging for the flash. Let's have a look,
a really good look and see if we can find it. . . .

10:30. Taking a break. I've just finished covering the wall beside
the bed & the section of the other behind my head. Climbed up and
went up-down, up-down in tight vertical rows from tip-toe to a squat.
Didn't come across anything, not even a hint, but I'm not discouraged,
not yet(!), there's plenty more to go. . . .

11:05. Break-time again. The whole of the left wall's done. Still

nothing, only — and note this, it's a good lesson for you: there's a
rectangle (8"x 10") of thinner-than-hair cracks where that glakh was
fiddling—a plate, in other words. (I found the cracks by staring very
hard at the place, then looking away, then staring again.) I tried
digging my fingers in & prying with the driver, but couldn't get the
thing to budge nohow. Now am going to move on. There's probably no
water there anyway, so close to gadgetry very likely to be electrical . . .
and water's what we're after, still. . . .

You know, it's perfectly possible we're going about this all
the wrong way — I was in the middle of the wall opposite the
bed, just past the pail and the peepee place.

I dropped my hands and about-faced, and just stayed
there like that, swaying sort of. Gradually everything in the
room faded from my sight, and then this came, from Col-
eridge's "Rime of the Ancient Mariner" or "Water, Water
Everywhere," as we used to call it when kids:

> The very deep did rot: O Christ!
> That ever this should be!
> Yea, slimy things did crawl with legs
> Upon the slimy sea.

Then everything faded back into view, and there it was.

"Has to be, there's no other place," I murmured, right
there on the spot the next moment . . . the end of the bed. I
hooked some toes under the dustruffle, flipped it up.

Sure enough — there was something resembling a soda
fountain spigot and a drain. [Ed. During one of our later
meetings, when in a better frame of mind, Ms.Rothman speculated that this facility may have served very sensibly for rinsing one's feet before retiring.]

"Now to work" — I hopped to it with soap and tooth-
brush. . . .

"More like it," I mumbled, lounging at last with hair limp
(feat of the year under that little faucet). Clapped my feet,
in only the sneaks — socks and everything else drying on a
spanking new sheet on the floor.

The room was still going down . . . slowly down.

●

Felice was right at the "door" all dressed early the next "morning" when the parts separated.

An eekhal was there, a shorter, leaner (and thus probably younger) version of the Third Assistant. "We'll have to move right along, running late," he said very fidgety-like, and spun on his heel rightward.

Felice clip-clopped after him, down yet one more corridor just like hers, with a Council room at the other end.

A smallish glakh, of the same generation, was stationed at the entrance. Felice sized him up as being of a rather benign disposition.

"The Chief Conserver had to oversee the works today," he offered pleasantly as she drew up.

"The Head Archivist's otherwise occupied too?" she as pleasantly asked in her turn.

✋Check, he signed.

The brown in the meanwhile had plowed inside, faced leftward, and begun holding forth. "Psst, now!" he whispered, with the preliminaries disposed of. . . .

Inside, it was much of a muchness with the Council room above, Felice saw at once, moving along leftward at his direction — except that the purple jowls at the table down here were puffier andeyes more protruding . . . also, the table-surface looked dull and "shoe-box" contraptions with their displays seemed worn. When she faced round, at the same spot as upstairs, it was to find the young eekhal and glakh before her likewise "froggier"; the tv's, which were set close together, had seen better days as well. . . .

Quite a number of vigorous conversations had erupted at the table on sight of her.

"Would you come to order, please!" the eekhal called out shrilly.

No one paid any attention — the talking went on as loud as ever.

A brown head knew when it was licked. ✋Alleyoop! he

semaphored to his associate, the glakh.

That one turned toward the tv's and stretched both arms across them—worked both sets of controls on the sides at the same time with hands right-angled at the "wrists."

Both screens blinked on, the left with a rust-colored Lancelot, the right with the "x-rays." Ribbons of script danced along both, above and below, those on the top moving rightward. [Ed. Leading one to believe that they were summaries of the proceedings above.]

All eyes at the table began to follow. Things there calmed down. . . .

It seemed utterly black outside, to Felice sneaking a peek at the portholes. Is anything out there or what, she wondered. The shkhurzas remaining engrossed, she eased round and hiked herself up on her toes a bit . . . a bit more.

Nothing was there. It was truly like real night. Oh well.

But just then two shadowy figures sort of floated into view. One was outlined in red-hot red and brandishing a flickering light-blue rod with a wire or cord of the same attached to it; the other glowed bright yellow — but only to the "waist." The rest of his body was obscured by a silver "puddle" glittery with pink and lemon patches.

A purple under one of the center portholes happened to notice Felice looking. "What does she find so interesting out there?" he asked.

Let's try not to ruffle anybody's feathers — Felice turned to seek instruction from the eekhal.

❦ Tell, he ordered.

She described the scene, haltingly.

"Is there anything else, is that all?" the same shkhurza cross-examined.

Well, Felice considered — the red-rimmed one had just dangled the end of the light-blue line to his companion, delineated in yellow and half-immersed in silver —it sure would be nice to know what the story is, are they fishing or mining outside there? But you just better play it straight, no fooling around. "Yes, the colors are most unusually vivid," she responded.

"Vivid?" the purple sneered."Vivid, is it?" he echoed contemptuously. "Imagine, those Glakhland slimes gave her all that" — he pumped his fist at the tv screens — "and brains in addition!"

Everyone else there at the table broke into derisive howls — "Gee! Gee! Gee! Gee! Gee!". . .

At least I'm not gonna have to strip again, Felice was consoling herself not long after.

A split-image of herself naked, shot from overhead, had just come on to succeed the feature film.

One-two-three . . . the girlee show was over.

"So, Your Honors, what's the good word?" the eekhal queried.

A neighbor of the purple on the other side of the table spoke up: "Believe you me, this mischief is not Glakhland's alone. Those Eekhallanders had a hand in it too."

Felice took careful note of this — Well, well, it seems some browns also have a country of their own.

"A bunch of creeps, they are," a new one on his left reinforced.

"Yes, but the Glakhlanders are the real culprits," put in the original one.

"Their gleegos don't hatch together," his neighbor raved on concerning the Eekhallanders. [Ed. The word here obviously being used in its literal sense of "egg."]

Felice fell to speculating — Hm, what form might their perversion take?

"May they all croak," a voice beside her added by way of summing up.

The eekhal seized the moment — "Well, Your Honors? I'm waiting, Your Honors."

"Would you kindly shut up and stop interfering!" someone on the end spat out, then addressed those around him in a milder but as firm a tone — "My friends, I for one refuse to be a party to this."

"I'm with him," another there joined in.

"After all, they're the ones up there on One who're always insisting that we play ball with those Glakhland scumbags" — it was a third.

"Now they want us to do their dirty work for them," a fourth rounded it out.

Stools scraped all over. Everyone was on his feet filing out.

"But, Your Honors, don't leave like this, give a hint first!" cried the brown in a panic. "What shall we do with her?"

"Ship her to Five," said he who was at the "door" just then. He hurried away. "Yeah, that's a good idea," agreed the next in line. He vamoosed too.

"Not Four?" the brown persisted, to be absolutely certain.

"Wouldn't give'em the satisfaction," muttered the last, before he was gone.

"Any idea what Five's like?" Felice asked some little while later, after the eekhal and glakh had tidied up. She was bustling back to her room with the two of them in tow.

"A li'l on the noisy side," answered the latter, a real sweet one.

Noisy, schmoisy, she scorned. And when I'm there, what then? Will I be shuttled around some more, sent down further yet, or what? Reaching the threshold, she darted in . . . whirled on them. "Must be quite a number of stages, huh?"

The brown's hand went up. "Too many," he snapped, and flicked the switch out there.

•

BOOM!

I'll say noisy, Felice thought, jolted into awareness. It was like a blast from a couple of tons of TNT at the very least. In fact, so ear-shattering had it been, with everything jittering so, that a couple of minutes passed before she realized that the room was no longer moving.

Now that's funny — she was at the "door." It remained closed. God helps those etc. She pushed to do the honors herself.

Now that's even funnier — no one was there to greet her.

What can be? She stepped out, made a sharp right — and went right smack into a wall!

"Gee! Gee! Gee!" someone cackled behind her.

She turned about, patting her nose. So far so good.

There was a corridor with a Council room at the end. An eekhal and a glakh were standing midway down, neither one of them exactly a spring chicken, she guessed.

"Everyone's always confused the first time," the brown cheerily explained as she made for them. "You'll get used to it before long," the green added. [Ed. They were, of course, referring to the fact that the corridor ran leftward down there.]

BADA-BOOM! A cloud of dust descended from the ceiling — to cover layers of it already under foot, Felice now noticed.

Get used to it? Let's hope not, was her thought. "What's going on anyway?" she inquired, coming up to them.

"Don't ask," said the glakh bubbly-like.

Besides getting on in years, he was not in the best of shape, she noted, his breath issuing in wheezes. The eekhal also had problems, to judge from his face, the skin lackluster.

✋Let's not dawdle about, shall we, the latter diddled with a wee flourish. They brushed off heads and shoulders with a swip-swipe, wheeled around, and fell to marching sort of, back toward the Council room.

She was supposed to follow, naturally. . . .

Inside — as she proceeded rightward — purple eyes were sunken and "cheeks" sucked in. Also, the table top was a collection of rude logs lashed together and no "shoe-box" data-boxes were in evidence on it, while above on the wall a row of painted black circles served in lieu of portholes.

"'Bout time those shits [Ed. lit *pakhapa*] upstairs realized they needed us," someone at the table muttered, when she'd faced forward. . . .

The old green was puttering with the controls of the right tv.

"Well?" a purple one behind her demanded.

"Here we are, here we are," the green warbled.

Ke-rack! the tv coughed. The screen became filled with bouncing balls, beige ones.

"Can't you get that damn thing to work properly?" the same purple growled.

"I'm trying, Your Honor," the old green squeaked, and touched here and there on the tv's side some more.

Ke-rack! The balls ballooned into mushroom puffs, like sand-colored stars bursting.

"If you don't get it going soon, I'm leaving, dya hear?" the severe one threatened.

"Doing the best I can, sir." *Tick-tick-tick,* green nails worried the "glass." *Mmf,* the old one blew, almost out of patience himself — sidestepped over to the other tv, the left.

WHOOM! — that was more "TNT" going off.

"Look!" someone at the table yelled.

The right viewer was on — the plane was there in all its glory.

"Her bagaba?" the shkhurza beside her queried.

"Believe so," answered the old eekhal.

Felice smiled — Sure will be interesting to know what that word means some day. . . .

"Gotta hand it to them, those Glakhlanders," the same shkhurza remarked, after he'd had his fill. "They sure are ingenious."

WHA-OOM! — was another explosion.

"Oo-ookh!" everyone cried.

The image was gone, screen dark again . . . the room was hazed all over.

Tick-tick-tick, went the glakh again with his nails.

"Is that it?" demanded the growler.

"'Fraid so, sir." The old one was very down.

"Well, send it all back then," the growler's neighbor on the end said with a kind of sigh. "And tell them," another there picked it up. A "youth" under the "portholes" finished it for him — "Tell them we'll be glad to go along with whatever they decide."

The old eekhal wanted to be sure — "Send it to Three?"

"No, no, of course not! Whatever gave you that idea!"

snarled the growler irritably. "He's a moron," a new voice piped up. "They're nitwits, both of them," added the growler.

WHADA-OOM! The lights in the walls winked, the raining dust grew brighter by a notch.

A fourth on the end introduced a new topic for discussion . . . the feasibility of creating "hold-fast sites."

Well, guess it's over, Felice said to herself, much relieved. ✋What say you? she sent the eekhal.

✋Meet you outside, he signaled back.

The two of them, brown and green, slowly rotated toward the "door," went a step, froze, went another. . . .

Felice did the same. . . .

"Whadya suppose'll happen upstairs?" she asked in a low voice, once the three of them were safely back in the corridor.

"Oh, they'll p-p-pack you off to G-G-Glakhland, I should think," answered the old eekhal, his "nerves" still frazzled, like hers, from that last dynamite wallop.

"It's the only logical thing to do," the green twittered.

●

Hallelujah, I rejoiced, as the room snuggled up to where I'd started, Stage One. I felt so light of heart, could have kissed anyone, even the Third Assistant, skunk though he was. My chest was less constricted too, I seemed to be able to breathe more easily.

The "door" split at once. A brown face inserted itself.

"Well, hello," I said, taking it to be him, and hot-footed it over there. But was it he? I wasn't sure. Closed my left eye, opened it, closed the right. "You are different, aren't you?" I still wasn't willing to swear to it.

✋Correct, he tapped out, he was the new Third.

"What happened to the old one," I asked. "What did he do, go and get himself canned?"

No, he resigned, came the answer. He was in Produce

now.

[Ed. Employment and training were likewise matters that I had requested the author to explore further — alas, in vain. As I understand it from our conversations, an elaborate civil service system existed for each of the types, in whose ranks one could rise or shift from job to job after a suitable period of apprenticeship.]

He seemed alright; his bearing was perhaps a trifle stiffer than my former teach's. But there we are, this one had the same old trouble with his "sniffer" — suggested that we step outside out of the range of my "privy" to discuss matters further. [Ed. One assumes that glakh-porters on the different stages had been by to clean The Place from time to time when she was gone.]. . .

"So what's up?" I asked, out in the corridor — quite sure of myself after that chat with the old eekhal and glakh on Five.

Well, they were about to celebrate their holiday, this new Third began very soberly.

"It wouldn't be called Bagaba Day by any chance?" I kidded. Who ever would have thought, such a wild guess.

"Indeed — it — would," he answered huffy-like, having a very low tolerance for interruptions it seems. I let him spiel his spiel, which he'd obviously been instructed to do by the Head Archivist, if not by the Council itself — to wit, Their Honors earnestly recommended that I spend the time until they reconvened diverting myself at the festivities, from which they felt I stood to benefit considerably.

"Well, I'll certainly be glad to oblige," I said. All I needed to know was where to go and when.

It was simple: the place, the chief place anyway, was the Bagaba Hall. As to the time, I'll tell you for the life of me I just couldn't make it out — when the something flows into something else and turns orange, I don't know. But not to worry, he assured, after repeating it all for a third time without success. All I had to do was check out the "street" from time to time, and go on down and join the crowd when it began to collect.

There was another directive from the Council. As some time remained before the official start of Bagaba Day, they felt that I might also find it worth my while to attend a meeting of the Head Archivists' Council, which was just then getting under way down the hall.

Ayayay, more meetings, I thought. Seems that's all everyone does around here. Well, there's no harm in it. ✋Sure thing, why not, I agreed.

Oh boy, if this isn't a jake-the-fake, I've never seen one, it came to me, stepping through the "door."

The table was three-quarter's full of mature-looking eekhals (including the one who'd presided over the Council meeting I presumed, though he was indistinguishable from the others). An empty stool waited for me by itself on the near end, where a camera in the ceiling could easily record my every action and reaction.

I had this urge, once I sat down on it, to give the powers-that-be a good show by making funny faces and so on. But a word to the wise, my better self advised, let trouble come to you, which so far it has a-plenty down here.

All the "shoe-boxes" with their little hammers had been pushed into the center, and a serious debate was in progress, with each Archivist in turn offering his view. The object of their concern, as I soon gathered, was a circular dais at which the three major councils would be dining later in the Bagaba Hall. At issue was whether the Archivist tier of this dais should be stationary or not.

Oh wow, I groaned after hearing out three of those senior brown individuals — two pro, one con. I'll never make it through this — my eyelids were getting heavy. Maybe you should change positions — I shifted from one ball of my behind to the other.

A new speaker had just come to the fore — he was of two minds.

Please take heed, this bodes for ill, I warned myself — lids were sagging again in earnest. Best get up — go on — and so it shouldn't look odd, mosey on over to the "windows." 'Fact, you should do it anyway, see what's what with the plane.

I stood up, carefully . . . sidled over to the closest port-hole . . . raised my chin to look out, the lower edges of those things on a level with my eyebrows as previously stated.

Ah, Lancelot. There its silvery self was, sitting pretty on the same ledge as before . . . a chasm maybe ten feet in width separated it and my building . . . everything was a dreary grey, the "sky" above, that pinkish-brown.

So, shall we have another go at it, I proposed after lingering there for a few moments.

But just then I spotted one of those small glakhs over there on the ledge — he'd popped up from somewhere to the right . . . was making straight for it, the plane, my precious. One-two-three — he scrambled onto it and planted himself upright on the nose!

I just lost my cool, that was all — forgot where I was, everything. Boy oh boy, he's got some nerve, I fumed — applied my knucks to the "glass." ✋Get off of there! I thumped at him.

See-no-evil, hear-no-evil. The fool started jumping up and down, like a baboon — a green baboon!

I rapped some more, and shook my fist, still with no results. Then all caution went to the winds. Looking desperately around, lo, in the back of the room, beyond the far end of the table, I spied a looping door I hadn't noticed before. Flying to it, I yanked it open, and found myself in a kind of pantry — that is, a small room lined by white cupboards with white plastic-faced counters. Odds and ends of recently cut lumber were lying about all over in sawdust.

Another looper was dead-ahead. I charged through that one too, onto a terrace from which a narrow wooden bridge had recently been built over the chasm to connect with the ledge.

"Off! Get off!" I shouted, bowling along.

The baboon's "knees" folded sideways like a grasshopper's. He sprang into the air extra high.

"Didje hear me?" — I'd gotten across the footbridge, was

almost upon him.

The green shoes with their pointy toes landed hard . . . an "ankle" twisted, which came as no surprise when one considered the short, tight skirt and cape flying in his kisser. He slipped to the ground, and skedaddled away limping, to a door in the wall.

I stopped short, all tuckered out — well, that's that — and turned round to go back inside. "Holy moly!" Inside, staring out of each porthole, was a head — a green head! Looked to be more juniors.

They were all at the table, including someone in my seat, when I strolled in moments later, fully recovered. Everyone sat with heads down . . . silent. You couldn't hear a single hard breath from hurrying to move the stools back from the portholes and so on.

"What happened to the Archivists?" I inquired, having paused in my old question-and-answer spot.

"Finished," the small glakh in my seat answered without looking up.

Hm, this has all the appearances of being another test of some kind — I squinted up at the "cameras." Well, you didn't do so well in the last one, that's for sure. Let's see how you make out here, with these types. "What was decided?" I further inquired.

"Who cares," one catty-corner to him shot back.

Well, if that's the way things're going to be, might as well go, I decided — took a few steps.

The green in my seat spoke up again — "You think you are so high and mighty, just because of your bagaba outside there."

His neighbor joined in — "We can make one just as good, and out of prakholga [p $\mathrm{\kappa^3 a \cdot \chi^9 \, \mathring{o} \, \mathring{l} \cdot G^3 a}$] too." [Ed. A one-time usage of this term, which was never explained. Whatever prakholga was, one should consider that it need not have been valued for the properties that we routinely prize in our materials, such as strength, durability, and eye-appeal.]

"And bigger at least by a goomee [G⁴ŭ·mi]," that one's neighbor added. [Ed. A unit of vertical as opposed to horizontal, quadrilinear rather than common linear measurement of the same general magnitude as our meter.]

"Is that so? How interesting," I said, with a frog in my throat. As with everything else, one didn't know whether to laugh or cry.

"How much longer do you think we have to stay here?" my ears picked up from the murmuring original neighbor.

"How should I know," the green in my seat murmured back. Then he pulled one of the "shoe-box"-contraptions toward him and picked up a hammer — impishly in his right hand—began tapping on the keys.

Everyone else followed suit.

I looked over the nearest one's "shoulder." They were playing a game on a grid like tictactoe.

"Gee!" the whole table went — someone'd dropped out. "Gee!" — someone else."Gee! Gee!" — more. . . .

The one on the near end in my seat was the winner, fair and square too as far as I could tell. They all got up and made tracks.

o

It's time you were going too — the last of them had just disappeared through the "door." Yes, surely it's time, all the Bagaba hoopla must have begun by now.

But first, a brief precautionary stop back in the room was in order. . . .

Well, well, another mystery unraveled, I saw not long after, amidst a huge holiday swarm down in the "street."

There was no longer any question what a bagaba was. (I had sort of guessed already, hadn't you?) Each trio was in possession of one; in some cases where the thing was cumbersome or heavy, two or all three were lugging it together. Purely and simply, they were gewgaws meant to be used for decorating building interiors, similar to the "horrors" hanging on the living room walls and from the ceilings that I got a gander at when I was stuck in the elevator that time and the "door" kept clinking.

Unforgettable:

— *some very life-like busts, in profile. Perhaps of themselves, lizards, snakes? Hard to tell — I'm serious. All of them made of garara, I imagine.*

— *glossy plastic-like orange and red plaques of the same size as the tv screens with more of those rounded corners. Pictures were traced on them in outline in some darker color, brown I should think. Of those I got a more than passing glance at, most showed the Supreme Council in action — on occasions when they were handing down landmark decisions maybe. Other popular subjects included scenes from previous Bagaba fetes and something someone in the crowd referred to as Re-return Day.*

— *fist-sized light-gray, possibly metallic, slivers, dangling from the tips of twig-like rods. Let's say schematized gleegos — I'm guessing, haha.*

And what was the object of schlepping all of those *objets d'art* to the Bagaba Hall? Well, as it soon became apparent from keeping an ear peeled as she went along, they'd grown tired of them and were hankering to get rid of them, which they could do in the Hall by swapping them for somebody else's — the object of the holiday. According to the rules, also gathered on the way, only one such thing could be offered for exchange by each family, and the transaction had to be completed in situ. But of course, things varied considerably in actual practice. [Ed. The attitudes manifested by various individuals heretofore with respect to the plane, canteen, and even wristwatch are good cases in point — to put it delicately, a declaration to trade having been assumed on the heroine's part because of her anomalous position in the community.]

Needless to say, everyone was dressed up in their very best — the more mature folks decked out entirely in white, red, or yellow, the others just in capes or sometimes simply shoes of those colors. They were all sort of giving me the eye too, sidelong-like. . . .

Quite a crush developed before the entrance, and as I got closer, it turned out that an elder-type eekhal was checking bagabas for their condition before letting the owners in.

✋Mine's on the roof, I told him, when I finally reached the head of the line.

He gave me a quick once-over — ✋Capeesh — flagged me in.

Inside was a vasty cavern-like place, bigger even than the hall where they had those purple-tinged scrolls or tongues or whatever they were hanging down.

[Ed. The following late entry from Ms. Rothman's Diary (dated just before her precipitate departure for Texas) provides another dimension.]

I've been sitting here all night trying to come up with a better way of describing the girth of that place, & now (it's 4 a.m. or thereabouts) I believe I have it.

Revise & Insert

Conjure up that barn or gross barnyard, the Metropolitan Opera House at Lincoln Center, or else the Sun Yat-Sen Concert Hall, in Mainland China or on Taiwan, makes no difference. But if you can't for some reason, perhaps never having been privileged to view any of them in the flesh in one form or another, just think of, in all its glistering untarnishedness —

THE EVER-LOVIN' TITANIC!....

It was already pretty much packed, with many holding firmly onto their bagabas, considering deals.

So what's the story here? In the thick of it all, I craned my neck this way, that. "Well, get a load of that!"

In the rear, slightly to the right of center, stood the aforementioned dais for the machers, the executives — with its three tiers, it looked like an enormous wedding cake. The shkhurzas' level, on top of course, was rigidly stationary; the glakhs', bottom, was merrily twirling clockwise — and as decided at long last apparently, the eekhals' tier, in between, kept swinging a half circle to the left and back again. . . .

More and more threesomes were arriving momentarily with their bagabas, and it was getting rather close all around me. So do yourself a favor and go on over to the side somewhere out of the thick of things. I headed for the opposite wall up front, where there seemed to be a little more lebensraum. Unpursed my lips to give forth with a little ditty as I did so:

The Shang- hai ran off and the cat - tle all died.

That morning the LAST piece of bacon was fried.

Ike was disgusted and Betsy got maid,

The dawg hung's haid and looked won - der - ous said.

A Shanghai is a rooster, 'case you weren't aware. It's important for the meaning, you understand. Makes the picture of utter desolation complete.

Hey, hey, why not join me in a chorus? C'mon, do ya good. Look, it's easy, weaves up and down nice and regular-like:

The SHANG- hai ran OFF and the CAT- tle all DIED.

"Hello, there, green-one all-by-yourself!" someone hailed.

Who? — I was sort of startled out of a reverie. Does he mean me? Whoever could it be? The light wasn't all that great — I peered.

"Over here," the same voice sounded to the right.

Of all things. "Mercy me," I let out. It was the Third, the original Third Assistant.

His brown form, clad in a brown cape with red piping, separated itself from the crowd. "You do remember me, don't you?" Right behind him were a shkhurza, all in purple with white tips to his shoes, and a glakh with piping and tips of yellow, his rigmakhans without a doubt [$\texttt{в}^2\text{I}'\text{G}^9$· ma· χ^4an — Ed."mates," but rendered "brother" henceforth, as it seemed closer to the literal truth]. The first looked like a real kvetch, a sour puss, if ever there was one; the green was a kid and a mite on the shy side, or so it seemed at the moment.

Cradled in the arms of those two, front and back, was a silvery-green "fish" with pink splotches, oh, about four feet long — with a single blood-shot eye plunk in the middle of its forehead, and a bright blue sack with a rock-like something in it hanging from its belly by a thread.

I hadn't forgotten about the Third and the wicked turns he'd done me; just decided to let bygones be bygones, so there'd be someone to pass the time o' day with for a while — tired of being by myself when everyone else had someone. "I hear you're in Produce now," I said.

"Gee, gee. Quieter there," he acknowledged, reminding of how he'd been with me in the beginning, so ingratiating. "Tell me" — his tone changed a teensy bit, facial expression with it — "could I possibly interest you in our makhpeezoo here [maχ^9· p i ′ · z u]?"

What? He had to be kidding. That piece of khazzerai [in Yiddish, "pigfood"]? In return for what, Lancelot? "Is it real?" I asked.

"Gee, gee, gee," the purple and green tittered together, "fish" shaking too, ball and all.

"Naturally," said the Third. In fact, it had been quite a fighter in its day, as one could see for instance from the left snout, where some teeth and whiskers were missing. "But of course," he went on to assure, "if one doesn't like it that way, one doesn't have to have it that way." His glakh-brother was very clever with his hands and would restore it however the new owner wished.

"No. Thanks," I made it clear. Gads, better get a move on before he sweet-talks you into it, prodded myself. I began to back away.

But just then the glakh's eyes met mine, and it occurred to me there was something familiar about him. And then the shkhurza chose to come closer with the "fish"'s head, causing him to move up with the tail — and favor one of his legs in the process, as someone might who'd turned an ankle! It was he — it had to be — the Green Baboon!

My cheeks grew red-hot, I raised a finger and admonished with it. "You! You!" I spluttered.

"Sorry about that," the Third apologized, almost with a ring of sincerity. "And so is he."

The eyes of the guilty one turned light grey.

✋Alright, no harm done, I relented. After all, reasoned to myself, he probably wasn't the main one to blame — the caper was staged, just like the others more than likely. I couldn't help being curious about him. What did he do, what field was he in, I asked.

"Plumbing, Fourth Level," answered the Third, meaning the fourth floor of this Stage. "But he's been moving up steadily."

"Indeed" — I managed a straight face — "you and your shkhurza-brother must be very proud." And that one? He looked to be not too advanced in years either. "Serves on a council of some kind, I suppose."

Right I was. Fourteenth Sub-District.

And how did such a loving threesome find one another? Did they all meet in the gleego-house or what?

The Third sensed that I was trifling with him — "Rather not discuss it if you don't mind."

The shkhurza and glakh, busting a gut with their piscine burden, sent him stern and plaintive looks.

Their eekhal-brother renewed the assault on his "prospect," me — It was not your everyday bagaba, and honestly, in A-one condition, more or less.

Oh, I was in full command, never fear — except that suddenly I got this inspiration. Unstrapped my watch (a Timex), told them that I had need of a certain receptacle for my greater comfort. If the glakh-brother made it for me, it was theirs.

The Third and His Honor looked dubious, but not so the Baboon. Let's hear more, his eyes registered.

I appealed to my old teacher: "Listen, I realize this is somewhat irregular. However, if your glakh-brother is willing and as talented as you claim — "

A green finger rose from off the dorsal "fin."

Settled. I got out pen and pad from the back pocket of my jeans (where I'd taken to carrying them of late), and sketched in the object of my desire, indicating the dimensions by raising and lowering my hand from the floor. It was to be like a large tea kettle with the spout just so — capable of fitting into the opening of one of those pneumatic tube-like devices and yet large enough to accommodate. Whatever he chose to fashion my potty of (hereafter so called) was fine with me, just so long as it was sturdy, uncorrodible, and light.

The small green one had followed my every word and gesture intently. ✋No problem, he gave me to understand.

I tore the sheet out to hand it to him.

He waved it away — ✋Unnecessary. Had it all down pat in that noggin of his, he did. . . .

"So what would you all have done with that other possession of mine?" I inquired, with the pen and pad re-stowed, watch refastened — I was referring to the plane, of course.

The Third acted as their spokesman again. Glakh-brother belonged to a choral group that met in another big hall; he and his friends had thought that it might be nice to ornament one of the walls with it. Just a matter of getting hold of some strong wire.

"He sings too?"

The purple's pruny features ironed out. "Beyootifully," he gurgled.

The Green Baboon grew all shiny (reminding of Laleekh in his "cups").

"Are you sure I couldn't persuade you?" the Third began. . . .

●

No one came to bother Felice the next "morning," so she went to push the switch for the "door" straight from sleep.

Now we'll see a thing or two, she thought — the "door" on the other end was wide, the new Third on duty there. The lights were on inside, and so it had to be another business day with the Council in session one assumed; she could just make out the Archivist and Conserver in their customary positions within.

Felice reminded herself of the necessity of seeking out that older, more technically knowledgeable glakh, and decided that the best thing to do was to get dressed and go over, wait for a recess or an adjournment — corner him then. But first she was of a mind to consult with the Third at once, life being what it was in those parts, ever unpredictable. . . .

I sure said a mouthful, was her feeling when she was there before him.

Inside, the Council was meeting alright, but presiding over it was a different Archivist and Conserver, both a shade younger.

Well, there's nothing for it, it's him or nothing, Felice brooded. The important thing is not to let our hopes get up beyond reason — this one might turn out to be a geologist or something like that with very narrow interests and friends of the same ilk. . . .

"So whadya think," she asked the new Third, "will Council finish their deliberations 'bout me today?"

"Possibly, but I rather doubt it," replied the acrid one.

Felice felt herself starting to tremble, but squelched it somehow — "Why not?"

The new Third's lips remained as they were — like two dark crayon lines.

Don't falter, keep at it, Felice urged herself — "When will they then?"

He stepped over to the switch, made the "door" slide to. "You must realize that Their Honors have other matters to attend to besides you."

Felice's chin began to sink to her chest — she jerked her head back, deliberately.

"They'll get around to it sooner or later," he added softly.
With a touch of concern? It was hard to believe.

I suppose it's so, there is a lot for those shkhurzas to do,
Felice conceded, on her way back to her room. Still — She
regulated her breathing, forced herself to swallow. . . .

Inside she sought the bed, its edge. Okay, time for a strict
accounting. She reached for the pack on the floor beside the
bed's head and dragged it to her. Turned it upside down and
stuck her hand in, scooped things out until it was empty. Laid
the food tubes in rows by themselves, like little dead bodies.

There were nineteen in all. . . .

Well, that doesn't leave you with much of a choice, does
it?

Chapter Six

[Ed. "I can't go on with it!" These were the desperate words that assailed my ears when I telephoned the author to inquire what the trouble was now — why the due-date for this chapter had also been missed.

Sanity eventually prevailed, of course — after I insisted over and over that it would be a pity to abandon a work that had progressed so far, which indeed it would have. But this particular chapter continued to prove troublesome — I received it little-by-little over the course of several months, and at times the narrative was so disconnected as to be almost incoherent (which I have since remedied with substitutions from the Diary).

Be it known that once I had all the pieces in hand, by mutual, tacit agreement Ms. Rothman and I never discussed or even so much as alluded to them in our subsequent dealings with one another.]

Awright, let's get organized, I prompted myself, with everything back in the pack the way it had been. From now on, you're on short rations, meaning three feeds per twenty hours maximum. Not only that, you're gonna lick yourself back into shape — one and a half hours of running in place etc. spread out over that same period.

I began then and there. . . .

Now for a modus op — had just finished toweling down (with a sheet) after the swabbing courtesy of the faucet.

Before lunch. Here it is:

— I'll try & get above to the surface, where with Laleekh's help, I'll make an effort to live off the land, & hide out somewhere whenever a party from this place comes inspecting — size things up if & when

reps from those other countries turn up.

     — Alternatively (& I imagine more easily), I'll see if I can find a way to that Glakhland, where one can only hope the types are a little more reasonable & will be interested in learning who I am & so on. . . .

     Tea-time (with plain water, unheated). I've turned it all over several times, & let's face it, it's a tall order. I don't even know what to look for. An elevator with a decompression chamber? A train? Some combo thereof? Something else I can have no knowledge of?

     So it'll have to be another scouting expedition. I'll go down into the "street" & head leftward again . . . or two hours tops past the furthest point I've been, the building with the indoor pool. If something turns up, I'll take it from there; if not, I'll come back here of course & see if anything's changed. . . .

     Dinner. No one's been by or anything. I just hope this is not another of their tricks, tests. That'll be a fine howdyado. But what can one do. Carry on.

     So let's see. I'll take along ONLY food & water, leave behind everything else — or just about.

     Sure would be nice if I could stop by the plane somehow & load up on more food tubes. Just a matter really of keeping an eye peeled to see when clean-up's finished after the business day's over.

     The Meeting Room'll have to be parked there for me to go thru, of course. . . .

     "pm." I dunno, on second thought, I'm not sure sneaking into the plane like that is a good idea. Supposing there are cameras still trained on it & some of those handy little glakhs happen to be watching, spot me doing it & follow suit soon as I'm gone — and begin messing around with the controls! Talk about jollies. They're liable to have more'n they Bar-Gained for, one helluva Roman candle.

     So, we'll pass on that phase of the operation, okay? Now the next question is — when? Easy: the night after I nail down when their night is. . . .

     I just looked outside. The "door" down there's closed, those little glakhs are close by it, puttering. I've re-set the watch to 6. . . .

     8. The corridor's empty, the lights're lower by a smidge. So. . . .

     10. Just checking (for the hell of it). Everything's the same. . . .

     12. Ditto. Ditto. . . .

8 a.m. Meant to keep it up all night, but dropped off. Anyway, the "door"'s open, new Third's back monitoring it. (When I stuck my head out, he didn't even look my way.) If this is more of their chicanery, so help me, I'll absolutely scream. . . .

2 p.m. The Council's just left, via the stairs. A clean-up team is coming on by the same. The Third gave'em hell 'bout something & beat it too. . . .

3:32 p.m. There we are. Everything's battened down . . . silence.

Morning. (The time's all screwed up, so have decided to forget about it.) The important thing is a new day's begun, and this is it, tonight's the night. . . .

Aft. The pack's all ready, canteen too. Now for a little shut-eye. I'll lie down with everything on, even the sneaks. That way I only have to get up & go when the time comes.

Achtung: I've taken a snippet of a certain white pill from the first aid kit [Ed. Morphine probably] . . . washed it down with the dregs of the brandy-for-emergencies.

•

I'd just come out of the deepest of dreamless sleeps. Carramba, what an inspiration that boilermaker was, I feel wonderful!

Sat, stood, heaved on the pack, slung the canteen. Okee-doke, we're off.

At the "door" I paused, as who wouldn't have. Maybe they're going to tail me with their cameras like before. Maybe that's what this is all about, that's why they've been studiously avoiding me.

Doesn't matter, my better self argued. HAS to be done.

And Lancelot? I considered, after stepping out into the corridor. You may well be leaving good ole friend-in-need, the one link to home, for keeps this time.

Same scene, self repeated.

How quiet it all is, I couldn't help marveling, once I was through the stair-door. Practically danced down the stairs. . . .

The "street" when I reached it was the same. Not a sound came from anywhere, it was dead-like . . . also, a little darker, the sky a deeper shade of pinkish-brown.

What's going on in the "scroll"-hall, I wondered, approaching the entranceway. Peeked in . . . nothing . . . completely black.

I passed the Bagaba Hall . . . then the building with the silvery lobby. Boy, that was some adventure you had out here with that ridiculous glakh and the long yellow tongue . . . then you had to go and follow him and his mates in, and there was that runaway elevator.

Here is where you were so distraught about still being without water . . . the pool-building was coming up.

Now we'll see something, I hoped, having put that entrance behind me too.

At first there were just more buildings with their marquees. But gradually they became fewer & further between, till there was just rock-face on my left; a road continued on my right below (probably belonging to the Second Stage). Wasn't long before another wall of rock began rising there too, so that finally it felt as if I were passing between two pyramids, endless with rounded surfaces, & was "out of town" or in the "outskirts."

Soon the road took to curving in the other direction, as if it were making the bottom part of an "s." And then everything began to close in, the "cliffs" on either side of me to grow closer together, till the road was hardly more than a path.

Just as I was getting ready to give up & turn around, I spied a notch in the wall on the left about a hundred feet ahead — like a way through. The only thing is, it turned out to be really narrow, so much so that I would've had to enter in there sideways. It seemed to me where there was one, there had to be more, & I kept on going.

Sure enough, in a while there was another "cut" like that, also in the left wall. Only it too turned out to be cramped. But then, after another short while, came a third, this time on the right, & I don't know, I decided even at the sight of it coming up that this was it, the way through at last.

When I got there, though, it wasn't that hunky-dory either — wide enough for me to negotiate forward alright, but going up rather abruptly, which could make for some very tricky legwork it seemed to me. I decided to take ten on the ground there at the opening, & had me a good feed, certain to need all the strength I could muster.

When I got going, hadn't covered more than five or six yards before I was back — the way was full of loose gravel under foot, & having the pack on my back proved to be an added hindrance. I hid it under some stones, except for half a dozen tubes, which I stuffed in my jeans pockets to be on the safe side. Even then, when I went in there to begin the trek up once more, kept backsliding every few feet almost, & had to dig in constantly with my heels.

Every now & then, to give myself a breather, I grabbed hold of a wall, clawing, & somehow managed to hang on for a few moments. Damp and clammy the wall-surfaces were, & when I listened closely, thought I heard trickling nearby, like from an underground stream. The "cuts" through would seem to be the result of erosion then, I figured. Only they were deep and straight up & down — so maybe that's how they got started, then some individuals came along & finished the job.

Eventually the steepness began to level off, as if I were approaching a summit. Huffing & puffing, took a break there, & shined the flash back down to where I'd left the pack.

Everything was A-ok as far as I could see: there was no motion anywhere . . . and it was that same before twilight dark — 'cept for a single tiny glint, which I assumed to be one of the buckles peeping out.

Striving to get the best of that gravel again, soon I was going down, which was just as difficult as up & dangerous — constantly had to brake myself, which nine times out of ten sent me slamming into one or the other of those hard-rocky surfaces on either side of me. Once I had to stop and shear away one of the jeans legs, which had shredded at the knee and was dangling, a nuisance — did it with the knife, which, don't ask me how, I sorted out from among the tubes in my pocket. Then a jagged rock punched through a sneaker sole, & lest another pierce my foot, I had to stand there & hold on & fashion a new inner sole, doing so out of a piece of the cut-away denim.

At long last I made it — was down on level ground and out of that pass.

However, what was my reward for all the suffering I'd endured?

Zilch. Before me was only a boulder-strewn beach and a sea beyond it — the sand pinkish-grey, the water crimson (like on the American and British flags but duller).

I felt completely drained, and sat down, then lay back. And then, really bushed & disheartened, of all things, I fell asleep.

"Here we are," I sighed, not long after — awakened by a pebble sticking in the back. Checked the time, no harm done, only ten or so minutes had passed. The important thing is that you've got the energy now to make it back over that rugged trail. Felt almost as good as when I set out.

My hands, though, were another story, with both palms scraped at the heels and the nails torn and bloody. I'll tell you what, I proposed in my best Flora-voice, why don't you go on down to the water and take a look — if it seems okay, wash them off in it. Maybe the deep dull red color is only a reflection from the sky, not a chemical dye or something like that.

Good idea — I sat up, scuffed off the sneaks, and undid the watch and stashed it in one of them, slipped the flash into the other, and unslung the canteen beside them.

But what's this? On my feet, I made out that the water had receded some, the shoreline was about a block further out than when I looked before.

Now that's odd, let's face it, I acknowledged — decided to pick my way through the boulders to the old water's edge. But not that odd really, considering all . . . that this is another world with natural laws of its own, and living beings that have evolved in response to it. . . .

Still, where can all that stern redness be heading, I wondered. The waterline had retreated a mite more yet, and was still doing so.

Well, why not tag along with it for a while, maybe something'll be there in the end. I tapped the mud with my foot — seems firm enough. . . .

Boy, this is fun, I couldn't help admitting in a matter of moments — reminded of ice skating, squushy ice skating. Only, try as I might, I simply couldn't catch up with that red band ever-shrinking toward the horizon. 'Fact, I had a feeling that it had recently speeded up some and was really beginning to outdistance me. . . .

Better take a reading now, I decreed not long after — and turned around. The mountain (or actually range) that I had come through was ever so far away . . . it stood like a tall, dark, pinkish shadow.

This'll have to be it, you've got to go back now. No contest, I would. But first, before that, had to do something about the one jeans leg, which had gotten all soggy on the bottom and was annoying.

Only the funniest thing, when I bent over, it was to find the mud surrounding my foot full of ripples — and they were all in motion, like little squirming worms.

Now this I definitely don't like the looks of. Made quick work of the jeans leg, folding it up to below the knee. . . .

It sure is spooky, I thought somewhat later, while stepping along. The ripples had grown some, they were mini-waves now, on a par with my insteps . . . all moving toward the horizon like the water before.

It'll really be tough going if they get any higher, I predicted. . . .

Within seconds it seemed, that's what happened — they were up to my ankles. I decided to take off leftward for a spell to see if maybe there was a way around them so I could proceed faster. . . .

No luck. But whatever you do, don't panic, I warned, with them slapping against my shins. Everything'll be alright, you'll see.

The dark pink mountain, my goal, was closer now, but there was still quite a bit to go, ten blocks at least, and I was beginning to sag from all that slogging. Well, why not turn around and skip along with the waves for a while, until another solution for making progress against them presents itself (a crazy idea in retrospect, but at the time seeming to make perfect sense).

No sooner done than a blow caught me in the hollows behind the knees and sent me sprawling!

Wow, I'll be swamped by these mud-waves in no time flat

if they continue on the rise like this. I hauled myself up and tried to run — another one hit me in the same place and knocked me down again!

The jeans, it came to me, I must get rid of them . . . they and the stuff in them're weighing me down, like wet cement. I rolled over onto my back, quickly pulled them off, kicked them away, and got to my feet again, thinking just to keep up with the wave-onslaught in a trough.

No success there either — I was bowled over, struggled back up, was bowled over yet once more. They were now up to my hip, those awful things, and coming ever onward relentlessly!

Relief, however, was not far off, I saw the next time I rose up after going down. There was a small neutral area, like a tiny island, maybe fifty feet away to the right. It was my only chance, I had to give it my best shot — tore off the T-shirt, bra, even the underpants — staggered on, ever-falling. . . .

I can't, I can't do it anymore, I agonized, at one point. Still, forged ahead . . . on my knees, crawling.

"It's all over — you're safe — you're alive," I gasped, flat on my back with dry sandy fineness under me. Those things, those horrible mud things, were oozing all around — *ya-pup, ya-pup.*

I leaned on an elbow to see — they were cresting, shoulder-high, a dozen or so feet in front of me and on either side (behind me too, of course), slimy grey with a pink tinge, disgusting.

Rest, sleep, I ordained, the tears welling. I settled back.

But now there was something new, a new sound, coming from somewhere close by to the left, a boulder there. It was like a voice . . . a human voice . . . a female one. I could've sworn that it had called me by my name.

Be careful, I alerted, still stretched out with eyes closed. This is some kind of hocus-pocus to be sure. In fact, now that one thinks about it — The call came again, this time distinct — "Felice?"

Answer, answer it, I told myself. "Yes — yes, here I am,"

said from where I was, still not looking . . . to gather reserves.

The thing was now before me, directly before me — "Felice, it's Mother, Mommy."

My reaction was immediate — "My mother's gone, and the dead do not come back." But I went on lying there, blindly.

"All the same, it's me-ee," she said, using Flora's tone.

Don't fight it, I advised myself, ride it out — "What do you want?"

"Oh, noth-iiing," she answered with the same lilt.

I don't know what got into me. Suddenly I couldn't help myself — couldn't! "You know," I began, now with eyes deliberately squeezed tight and at the same time smiling, in a way, "I wrote this poem once. Well, it wasn't quite. Anyway, it sang and sang, but — "

Enough! I told myself. It's absurd, utterly absurd! I unglued lids — at last.

There was nothing — only the same yupping pinkish-grey mud-waves, now way over my head for sure, and the island with its fine white sand.

I scrambled up, brushed a grain from a cheek . . . irritating, like a hair, a fly.

"Listen, whoever you are — whoever you are doing this." I made a fist, raised it to the sky . . . that pinkish-brown canopy, of stone probably. "I've had enough, okay? Enough!"

●   ●   ●

Clang!

Felice sprang up out of bed as if she were shot, looked wildly around — "What? How?"

She was fully dressed down to the sneakers; the pack and canteen were right by the bed's head, where she'd put them before taking the snooze. I never left here, that's what. It was all a dream.

Brought on by that itty bitty piece of pill and drop of booze? Possibly. She took a step forward — and dropped to the floor, spun there by the suddenness of her movement. No, they were not entirely the cause, was her conclusion now. No, something else much stronger was added; I've been drugged.

Angry's not the word, Felice was fit to be tied. "What the hell!" She hoisted herself to her knees, wedged one leg under her, intending to rise — but the leg buckled. She sort of slithered over to the "door," stuck a brow out.

"Yooow!" — she'd been sucked over the threshold, the mat had whisked her away. She was hurtling toward the other end of the corridor.

"What's going on? Are you all crazy?" Felice was screaming at the New Third the next moment.

❧Shush, enough, he waved. The "door" was open, room "bright" behind him; Council was in session.

She looked around him to see who was who, what what. "Oh man," she softly let out — the original eekhal and glakh were there again.

It took a few moments to recover from the surprise. Now were they relieved temporarily and then brought back, or what, Felice wondered. Who knows, the possibilities were endless. It's even conceivable that their absence was a part of this last caper. . . .

The Archivist was talking, and gesturing behind him at the right tv set, which was probably on. Felice caught a word or two — something about The Subject's inability to interact in a group.

On and on he went, and then dribbled off.

"So where does all this leave us?" someone to the left asked, perhaps one of the shkhurzas on the end of the table.

"But that's not all, sir, there's more," the brown one reminded, and looked Felice's way.

❧Get going, the Third motioned.

Okay. Okay, I'll do it, Felice said to herself. But for my part, they can all go to hell — all of them!

Both tv's were on, she noted en route to her spot. The

right one was spieling footage of herself at the Head Archivists' meeting just before the start of the Bagaba festivities. The plane was pulsating in sepia and tan on the left again.

The last frame of the Subject standing by while those small glakhs tictactoed on the "shoe-boxes" slid off as she was facing round.

"Well, what are you waiting for?" demanded one of the irritables under the portholes. "Everything drags on here so," his neighbor complained by way of support.

"Maybe we oughta do a review of our procedures one of these fine days," suggested the young one at the end, he of the ubiquitous water.

"That's beside the point!" snapped Number One Irritable.

"It is NOT!" his nemesis beside her countered.

The eekhal interfered — "Your Hon-oors, plee-eeze!" — the strain telling. . . .

The Conserver took the floor, and began by wishing to make it very clear at the outset that he and his colleagues had not entered into this matter lightly. "You see," he tried to explain, "it was essential, as I'm sure you can well understand, that the compound we finally decided to go with yield reliable and conclusive data and at the same time — "

"Is all this really necessary?" someone yelled out. "C'mon, get on with it!" another seconded. "Absolutely disgusting," muttered a third, "they do exactly what they want with us, this crew."

The brown interfered again, at the top of his "lungs" — "Plee-eeze, Your Honors, plee-eeze!" — at the end of his tether. . . .

The Conserver in the meanwhile had gone to reactivate the right tv, as calm as can be. Another film began to roll, featuring someone resembling Felice mightily but not quite her — with a flatter chest and rear, and suppler waist. Her "double" on the screen had just bounded out of the bed and swooped upright with the gear, was now making for the "door," with an unfamiliar lightness of step.

Felice gazed — gazed harder. So, as I thought, they induced it, that dream . . . and then somehow managed to tape it. Was difficult not to be fascinated. . . .

"She has a pretty fair conception of herself, wouldn't you say?" one of those on the end gave it as his opinion, as "she" pranced down the stairs.

"You think so? I don't think so," Number Two Irritable challenged. . . .

"Where's she off to anyway?" someone else on the end asked, as "she" loped past the despairing place.

"You'll see in a moment, sir," the Archivist put in, snivelly-like. "There" — the second "pyramid" had appeared.

"But — but!" someone else sputtered. "There's no such place!" a new voice finished it for him.

The Conserver slipped his oar in — "In all fairness, sir, subject has never been beyond that pool."

"Yes, but she should have an inkling at least of what's there," another end-one argued. . . .

The odyssey went on, with more of the same at each juncture.

"What in the world!" exclaimed Number One Irritable — "she" had just come out of the pass, and the sea, that dull crimson expanse, was before her.

"Look at that!" Number Two Irritable shouted out. The "mud-waves" had commenced. "Sheer madness!" he added. "She" was writhing and flopping and floundering.

The Conserver stepped over to the set and turned up the sound.

YA-PUP . . . FELICE, IT'S MOTHER, MOMMY.

Felice's eyes scanned hither and yon . . . looking . . . looking, in vain, for the owner of that voice . . . as her "double"'s eyes soon would. . . .

YOU KNOW, I WROTE THIS POEM ONCE —

"What's that she's yammering?" yapped Number One Irritable.

"Sorry, sir, it was impossible to make out," said the Archivist. "Subject has a nasty speech impediment, as you yourselves have borne witness to," the Conserver picked it up. . . .

LISTEN, WHOEVER YOU ARE — DOING THIS —

"She certainly seems wrought up about something," commented Number One's arch-enemy beside her, he who had formerly been so disturbed by her speaking out of turn and jitteriness. . . .

"There it is, Your Honors," said the Archivist — the show was over.

Brown fingers signaled from the doorway — ✋Let's go.

Trembling visibly, Felice closed the distance between her and the Third with determined strides. "You-ou-ou — !" she began to curse him, with quavery voice. And indeed now that she knew what passed for profanity in those parts, what could she not say.

Only for the life of her, nothing came — but nothing!

"You, makhpeezoo, you!" she choked out, belly-laughing inside in spite of herself.

●   ●   ●

[Ed. Let this charming reminiscence from Ms. Rothman's early childhood, which I found on a loose folded sheet in one of the composition books belonging to the Diary, serve as a transition here.]

It's Only a Movie

I couldn't have been more than four at the time — TV wasn't around yet, not seriously anyway. At our neighborhood "arts" house there in Brooklyn they were playing for just one day, a Wednesday, a revival of Lost Horizon, *which someone told Flora to be sure not to miss. Who knew from baby sitters in those days; Flora took me everywhere. But there was no reason to worry, as there might have been if we were going shopping downtown, which I found "baw-ring"; I'd already demonstrated that I could sit through a whole afternoon of Bugs Bunny and the like, which to her way of thinking (long before others began to notice, incidentally) contained some rather "raunchy" stuff.*

So off we went to Lost Horizon, *and at first everything went swimmingly, with the handsome stranger arriving in Shangri-la and meeting with the beautiful lady who looked something like Mommy, & of her deciding to go along with him when the time came for him to say goodbye. But then as soon as they left Shangri-la's precincts, just like that the beautiful lady began to shrivel up into an old crone — boy, did I let out a howl.*

Felice, it's only a movie, Flora softly said.

That worked, and it didn't work — I left off with the howl and fell to wailing with my mouth open, Ooooooh.

People all around — in the dark, where they were just voices, remember — started shushing. An old grandfather down front yelled, Kvyet — with an accent. And a woman quite close by us commented to the person she was with, Who brings a child to see such a thing.

Flora didn't want to miss the final moments of the debacle either, and all the complaining hadn't made the least impression on me — I was still Oohing, now with hot burning tears running down my cheeks.

Felice, please, she pleaded. It's a picture — she put a hand up in front of my eyes and fluttered it — just a picture.

Get rid of me Their Honors will now most certainly want to do, I reasoned back in my room, with head on arms, left leg crossed over. But it seems to me there are only two real possibilities — either they'll send me to Glakhland or that other country where eekhals run things.

A passing thought came, like a leaf falling — Sure would be a riot if they opted for the surface. But don't go getting your hopes up 'bout that. Things haven't come your way easily in this particular world so far, and there's no good reason to believe they're going to at this juncture.

A new thought succeeded that one, 'nother leaf — Sure wish I had more food 'case Lancelot and I get separated again. I was now down to eighteen of those precious tubes, having just polished off yet one more. Maybe as soon as Council's through, I could — It's even possible I can yet collar that Conserver and see what can be done with him.

Up, up — I swung myself up and made a beeline for the

door, touched the switch. Well, well — it didn't budge, I was locked in again — something's in the works.

+10 minutes. The suspense is killing, I'm ready to flip. Think I'll climb up on the bed with the flash & see if I can find where they let the drug in — had to be thru the ceiling, no? . . .

I've done six rows. Stuff it, I can't anymore — I just can't concentrate. Besides, what difference does it make. They did it, that's all, and if you choose to make yourself miserable worrying whether they're going to do it again with something more lethal, be my guest. . . .

+10 minutes. Yeah, a hum like from a motor just started underneath somewhere.

+1 minute. Hell's bells, it stopped, and there are voices, loud ones, two or more, coming from out there in the corridor.

"I assure you it will take only a moment," someone was pleading. Unless my ear pressed flat against the "door" was hearing things, it was the old Third. "You don't even have to — "

"But you realize I have my orders," someone else said, in a very clipped way — the new Third, dollars to donuts.

"Of course, of course," the old Third smoothed over, in that ingratiating way of his. His voice dropped, so I could just barely make out the rest — something about the glakh-brother finding himself with far more patching to do than'd originally been reckoned on and before they'd fairly looked around —

The top "door"-part whipped up, like a window shade.

Ye gads! I let out to myself. The two of them, the two Thirds, were there before me side-by-side — as alike as two puppies from the same litter.

"Here we a-a-are," the old Third singsonged, on the right. He had a dull black metal vessel like a large tea kettle with a wide spout — extended it by the handle above the lower "door"-part edge, but kept it slightly on his side.

So. I took off the watch, dangled it his way by the buckle — held my other hand out, palm spread, to receive, you better believe it.

He set my potty there, light like balsa . . . snatched his prize, greedily.

"Look here, there are some things you oughta be aware of concerning that new bagaba of yours," I offered, when he was satisfied as to its condition(?) — and explained about keeping it wound. "That is, if you want the little sticks to keep going round."

The old Third became his old indignant self — "That's the main point of it, isn't it?"

I went on — it was strongly recommended that the case remain untampered with. However, should a certain green party and/or his intimates be so inclined, under no circumstances were they to interfere with the round, toothy gidget moving back and forth (like the Head Archivists' tier in the Bagaba Hall), or else the whole proposition'd go "down the beach" for sure. . . .

Next case, I declared to myself, with him gone. The new Third was still there, with trigger-finger itchy for the switch.

"Say," I ventured, "will that big thing of mine out there on the roof be coming with me — to Glakhland?"

✋Neg, he poked. His finger started forward — to push.

Now there's something. "Any chance of allowing me a last — ?"

●

" — guess not." Felice grimaced chimp-like at the descended upper door-half. "Tried at least." . . .

So, let's have a really good look — a long moment had passed. She held the "kettle" out at arm's length, balanced it on her index finger. The Green Baboon had outdone himself, it was an excellent piece of workmanship, beautifully rounded, without a dent or scratch.

But that's really neither here nor there, will it work? She flipped up the cover of the pneumatic-tube-like device, took the potty by the handle, and thrust the spout in the "toilet" opening, drew it out — "Yes, indeed."

She tugged at a finger-sized knob to remove the potty's lid, clapped the lid back on. The thing was fine in that respect too — a good, snug fit for if and when the pot would have to be carried over a distance.

[Ed. Possibly a swords-into-ploughshares motif was being hinted at above. A colleague of mine in Chemistry seems to think that the author had in mind as the material for this item carbon fibres embedded in epoxy resin, the current basic ingredient of American fighter planes.]

Felice sought the bed with the pot against her bosom — sat down with it. "So," she said to the wall opposite . . . her old peepee place, "now what?"

Now we wait again, it seemed to reply in its fashion. She reached over, dragged up the pack and canteen beside her — set it, the nice new possession, on her lap. "'Kay."

●

Here we go now for sure. The motor'd started up again soon after.

There — the room was moving, downward like before but faster. Ah — it had changed course, was now going to the left.

But what's this? We'd stopped again . . . ground sharply to a halt. Oh boy! The room was rocking back and forth now, like swaying . . . over what, I didn't even want to try and imagine, yuck!

"I'd sure like to get my hands on whoever's doing it," I muttered. Has to be some of those little glakhs, the imps, of course. . . .

At last, it'd stopped — someone, maybe the new Third, came along and caught'em I hope.

Everybody's gotta have their kicks . . . innards, forget. We're off!

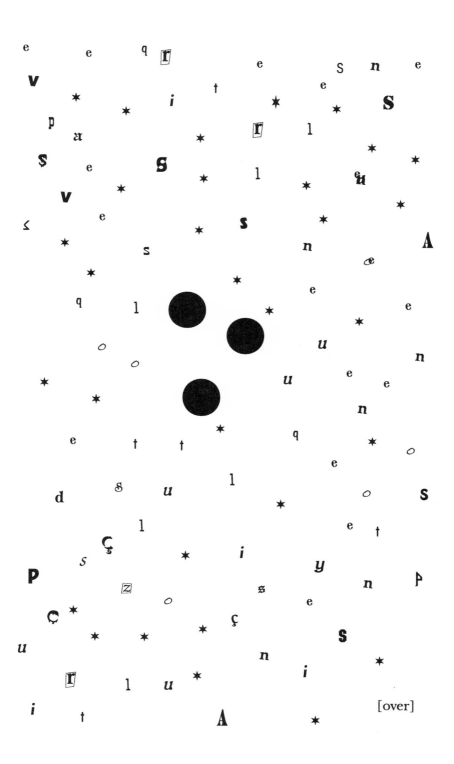

[over]

[Ed. This works out to:

"On est deçu si souventre par les apparençes qu'on s'estonne les quelquez voy qu'içelles sont veritelles."

Anon., Fourteenth Century.

"We have been deceived so often by appearances that we are indeed astonished when they turn out on occasion to be reality."

I was unable to locate it in any of the standard anthologies of the period.]

Chapter Seven

[Ed. Needless to say, I was relieved beyond measure when this chapter arrived on time. Still, I could not help noting something different again, only it was not a matter of the strategy this time — that remained the same — but of the tone, and I ventured to mention as much to the author in not-too-pointed a way when next we met.

Ms. Rothman's reaction was as to be expected I suppose. "Oh, do you think so?" she said with a penetrating gaze and wry grin. "Well, if you think it will make for difficulties, why not suggest to readers in a headnote that they partake of some bubbly alcoholic refreshment before proceeding further."]

The "room" eased to a standstill, as if into a berth. Felice was right by the door, having recently awakened from a long unnatural sleep (to conserve food).

"Hello, in there, can you hear me?" someone on the other side called very softly.

Now that's odd, Felice thought — the individual had employed the shkhurza form for her. And purple I'm not, not by any stretch of the imagination, so what's up? Let's play ball with him, and try and find out. "Yes," she answered full-throatedly, "yes, I can" — using shkhurza-endings for herself as well.

"Listen," the same one said with the same hush in his voice, "we're going to have to perform a rather ticklish operation to get you out of there, and we'd prefer not attracting any attention to you in this area. So if you don't mind, we'd appreciate your being as quiet as possible."

Ticklish, huh? Well, I'm sure I've been through worse. "Whatever you say," Felice answered back in a whisper, using the glakh form for him, as he had for "we." "You on the outs with'em here?" she asked as an afterthought.

"Something like that," he said, as if already preoccupied with the ticklishness.

Well, kiddo, lessons galore you've learned here — now don't shilly-shally, out with it, badaboom, Felice urged herself. "I'd like to get a message through to your Council or whoever officiates here," she projected considerably louder.

"There's only the Chief," he returned with a warning edge. "I'm Second Vice, Exec Com, A-Tube, if that's of any use to you."

Now that augurs well, was Felice's thought. She modulated her tone: "Look, I've pretty nearly run out of food." Which was the truth; in spite of all her stringent measures, she was down to four tubes.

"No problem," he shot right back. "I'll attend to it personally, as soon as we arrive."

Another good sign, as Felice saw it. But we've heard that song before, haven't we? So let's reserve opinion.

From outside, there came muffled sounds, possibly of a chest or something being opened. Felice quickly turned away to go and put on clothes and get the gear together. . . .

Riggle-riggle-riggle went a new thing out there, like a chain being gently wound round a drum.

Felice scooted back over with the T-shirt round her neck.

KONK! something rang out.

"Watch that!" hissed the Second Vice.

"Sorry, sir," another apologized lugubriously. "The prier slipped."

"I DON'T CARE!" the Second spat out. "So help me, if you foul this up, you'll live to regret it — even if you are my shkhurza-buddy." [Ed. The word for spouse here is a shade different from what it was in Shkhurzaland — rigmak-hal [$ᴮ^{3\prime}$G^9·ma·χ^4a$\underset{\circ}{}$l]] instead of rigmakhan — hence my rendering of "buddy" instead of "brother."]

Mniff, sniffed the clumsy one. "I'll endeavor to be more careful in the future." The attaching or whatever continued.

Felice added a sniff of her own — least it didn't turn into a brawl right away. Put one arm through a sleeve, the other, and pulled the hem down. . . .

The final link of chain *riggled* around a while later. "I believe we're ready," the Second Vice said to her through the "door." "What's the good word?"

"Whenever you say," Felice responded, waiting with pot and pack beside her. Boy, it sure will be nice to get out of this place, take some of whatever they have that passes for fresh air into my lungs, she thought. How long have I been cooped up here anyway? Who knows.

The bottom half of the door descended — *Clank-ull.* In the space was a thing that looked like a corrugated sewer pipe. "Go ahead," said the Second.

Felice dragged up the pack, put it on, got down on her knees, and began crawling forward into the darkness there, nudging the pot ahead of her. "Gads, what's that?" she let out under her breath, a foul odor like three-day-old garbage having assailed her nostrils. It's you, that's what, was her conclusion. A real bath is most definitely in order.

After ten or so feet, she left the "sewer pipe" and blindly entered something as narrow with a smooth feel — tapped ever so lightly in the blackness with a knuckle. The wall was of wood. Now for the dimensions — she raised up on her haunches, tried to spread arms, had to crook elbows at vertical surfaces. Touched a ceiling easily. Scrambled to an end, another flat surface. The thing she was in was four by four by eight feet.

"How're we doing?" inquired the Second Vice from outside.

"'Kay." A fourth "wall" came down vertically behind her. "I think," she added.

"Don't worry, you'll be there before you know it," he cheerfully reassured her. "In the meanwhile, may I suggest that you relax and make yourself comfortable."

"Right." Felice shrugged off the pack, shifted from knees onto rump, lay back — crossed arms over chest — uncrossed.

Meer-eer a machine whirred. She felt herself — that is, the box she was in — rising. *Plip*, the crane lifting it stopped. The box was slid back onto a smooth surface, like a coffin into a hearse.

"Now you do remember where to go," the Second said to the shkhurza, his mate. "You won't forget, will you?"

The other snapped to: "Yes, sir. No, sir."

Fancy that, Felice marveled to herself, they have memory lapses here too. Let's hope the purple's telling the truth. A fine howdyado if. . . .

Weer-eer purred the vehicle that her container was in, rolling slowly as if on wheels. It continued at that snail's pace to a curve, which it took at a slower crawl yet, and then went upward even more hesitantly, after which there was a fresh curve.

Still flat on her back, Felice counted four such bends. The atmosphere inside there had become really foul.

Finally, after several more climbs and windings round, the vehicle came to a halt.

"Easy does it," cautioned the shkhurza-buddy to three or more other purple ones standing by.

The box, with Felice in it, was slid out, hiked up, and hauled along for ten or fifteen feet, then neatly set down on a floor it would seem.

"What are we supposed to do now?" one of the bearers asked, almost accusingly.

"Wish I knew," the buddy answered. "He didn't say."

"I'm for leaving it then," another voice proposed.

"No, I think we should open it," countered someone else.

A regular coffee klatch it was out there in Felice's judgment. She was really beginning to sweat and gasp. "Hey, c'mon, what is this, let's have some air!" she yelled.

"I dunno, I dunno," whined the buddy. "I wouldn't want anything to go wrong. I'll catch it but good if anything goes wrong."

What the hell, Felice grouched to herself. "Hey!" — *dum, dum*, she rapped weakly. "Will you open up already?" Bells were beginning to ring in her head. . . .

Heavy footsteps came that way.

"Hiya, Chief!" all the purples shouted more or less together — there were maybe six of them.

"Where is she?" demanded the individual who was obviously the Chief from a short distance away. "What!" — he was closer. "You mean to say you haven't let her out yet?"

The first purple from before took it upon himself to try and explain.

"Told? Told?" echoed the Chief. "No one should have to tell you that, where's your sense? There's a living being in there."

"Just 'bout," Felice mumbled, in English.

"Do it now, get it open now, dya hear!" the Chief ordered.

"Okay, Chief! Okay! Don't get excited!" some tried to pacify. "No harm done, you'll see!" a lone sad one added.

"Bad enough to have to be transported in that — that absurd contraption," the Chief muttered, amidst a lot of feet lighter than his running away somewhere. "Now this" — the pitter-patter returned.

Bop-bop-bop hammers clopped over Felice's groggy head. *Creeek!* — the top of the box squeaked, being wedged up. Felice fought for a breath . . . found it. The top came completely off, and — *Whack!* — was tossed aside. Her lungs drew in another breath, a good one.

Smack! — the end by her feet was down. *Bobble-bobble-bobble* — the other three sides.

"Dear, dear, dear," crooned this tall, robust glakh standing over her. He bent down, got hold of her ear-flaps — and tugged her up toward him!

"Ow, that hurts," she complained weakly.

"Dear, dear, dear" — the Chief gently laid her head to rest again — *bunkle* — leaned way over and gave her — her NOSE! — a swipe with his tongue, an ooky yellow rag.

Felice's schnoz wrinkled. Her fist went up to smear.

The Chief regarded her indulgently.

He was wearing a knee-length apron topped by a cape, both green, she noted . . . a little group of shkhurzas, pint-sized rolypolies like Laleekh's neighbors the purple "twins," stood huddled in a corner to the far right . . . also in short aprons and capes, of their color.

"So-o-o?" — the Chief was glaring in their direction — "Where's the bed? Why's there no bed here?"

The small, fat ones were galvanized into action — "Awright, awright! Comin' right up!" There was a general stampede out a door directly before her . . . two of them came rushing right back with a sort of cot sans a dustruffle . . . dropped it at right angles to a wall on her left . . . the four others, who had followed hard behind, came and got her, each by a hand and a foot . . . dragged her over there . . . dumped. . . .

The Chief was beside her again, much concerned. "Is there anything — would you like something?"

Bonk, bonk, the two bed-schleppers konked at the bed's foot, seeing to the faucet very likely. Their pals were back in the corner, buzzing.

"Well" — Felice's bosom was still heaving — "as I said to the Second Vice — "

"Yes, yes." The Chief, with many things to do no doubt, wheeled around and began hi-stepping toward the door.

"Hey!" Felice hollered. "Hey, wait a minute!"

The Chief kept on going, right out. The fatties trooped after him, the last one pressing something outside — to close her in with a horizontal slider.

Felice sighed — looks like it's going to be more of the same in this land, with variations.

●

So-ho, whatdawe have here exactly? It was a while later.

From what I was able to make out — the lights had been turned down or off — I was in a room of about the same size and shape as my elevator room in Shkhurzaland, except that the corners where the walls met were at true right angles, not curved. The surfaces, including the floor, seemed to be a kind of yellowish white, such as one might find in some old hospital, say, left over from the days of British colonial rule in Rangoon or somewhere.

Dead ahead on the floor were the remains of my container, in the midst of which still lay the pack, canteen, and pot. Along the wall beyond (opposite my bed) were other broken-up boxes it looked like.

Maybe these quarters are just temporary then, I speculated. On the other hand, maybe not. Except that if not, perhaps after I've had a little "heart"-to-"heart" with the Second Vice when he comes to see about my food or sends someone —

But first things first. I sat completely up and reversed myself so my head was at the bed's foot, feet the head — the same soda fountain spigot and drain were there as in my old room. I reached down and depressed the lever. Ah, that's progress for you, really advanced types here — the water ran clear.

So is this another elevator I'm in or what? I don't think so, but let's verify. I got up on my hinds, jumped up and down on both feet. It was as solid and substantial as bedrock.

I went over to the wall behind the bed's head — prickled it smartly with my nails — *tonk-tonk* . . . re-prickled higher — *tonk-tonk* . . . again to the right — *tonk-tonk* . . . danced them on the floor — *tonkety-tonk* . . . again elsewhere — *tonkety-tonk.* That's that, all metal.

Now for the main event — I skipped over to the door. "Hm" — there wasn't a pneumatic-tube-like thing there. And what was there was quite different:

— an "aluminum" wheel two inches in diameter, reminding of the much larger ones in our bank vaults, with a white button like an aspirin in the center

— to the left of it, two dozen tiny silvery toggle switches, arranged in a tiny circle.

The wheel must govern the lights, I theorized, remembering the knobs in Shkhurzaland. I grasped it, and twisted a wee smidge, leftward of course. No siree, controlled the door — it had slid to the left a couple of hairs. I twisted the wheel some more — the opening widened.

What purpose does the button serve then? I touched it. So — the door had sprung completely open with a *ssst.* I touched it again. There — it had closed with another *ssst.* Chiaro (as they like to say in Italian opera from time to time) — it's for a fast entrance or exit.

The toggles are for the lights then, it stands to reason. I flicked one outward, the only way it would go. You bet — a section of the wall opposite the bed had gone grey. I flicked it back — it went back to its original antique white. I tried another of those togs — yes. I flick-flicked the whole batch of them "in." Not great but not bad, as the story goes in these below-surface parts — the room was lighted up to 75 watts, give or take a few.

Toggle switches, as you perhaps know, are made up of balls attached to the sticks. To see if anything further would happen if the former were swiveled in their sockets, I took hold of the tog-stick controlling the lights in the wall opposite the bed again and twirled it. As I somehow suspected, it was for really fine tuning — the light there had grown more intense, then darkened. Just for the fun of it, I tried driving the stick in plunger-like. Isn't that interesting — the light there had begun to flicker.

Enough for now . . . rest.

So where is everybody, how come nobody's come, I pondered, after waiting for ever so long in my usual position. Let's have a look-see outside. Maybe there's a national emergency or something, and everyone's run and hidden somewhere, and forgotten all about dear you.

I hopped to it over to the door, stabbed the button.

Was nothing much there — only a road like a tunnel, equivalent to about one and a half of our lanes in width, all of it including the roadbed of the same straw-colored white as the surfaces inside. To the left, it curved abruptly leftward; on the right, there was a shallow descent of several hundred feet to another leftward curve.

I'll wait here for five minutes. If no one appears at the end of that time. . . .

A little leery on account of the quiet, I opted to go right for the sake of greater visibility.

Now here's a blessing, I declared, in front of a pair of doors forty or so paces down, conventional ones with "aluminum" hoops for handles. The first was covered over by small green-and-yellow and smaller brown-and-red in-and-out circles of dots resembling gear wheels. The second had the same design in purple-and-white, except that the dots were really minuscule. I pulled Number One open, quickly closed it ('case of cameras). [Ed. Not to be the case ever again during our heroine's sojourn in this world, to anticipate.] Sure enough — there were two rows of "pneumatic-tubes" inside. . . .

I'll continue on to the bend, that's all, I schemed, not wanting to lose sight of my room lest someone at last turn up, and worried about the expenditure of energy with so little food to fuel it.

That's what I did . . . and nothing of any great moment was there. Just more tunnel, again going down . . . maybe three blocks, to another curve.

Back we go. . . .

"How now," I alerted, by the toilet rooms.

The funniest thing: a vehicle had come round the bend up ahead, beyond my room. Come is not the word for it, careened is more like it — careened around on two and a half of four fenderless wheels, as fast as it could go — a good ten miles an hour, I figured. Now it was catapulting toward me, at maybe twelve — a spidery stainless-steelish affair calling to mind things we Earthlings've sent into space now and then.

High up in the rear, like in an old-time touring car, a glakh of the same big build as the Chief sat shoulder-to-shoulder with a skinny eekhal, both dressed in their colors. Another of those fatty shkhurzas was down front center by himself, somehow maneuvering the thing — no steering wheel in sight!

Which side of the road should one step to, I considered, and moved over leftward.

Onward the car bore, straight for me. But then suddenly, just before reaching my door, it veered sharply to the left, and hit the wall there head on — *bum!* — causing the green and brown to pop up in the back there.

"Are you crazy!" the glakh screamed at the chubby.

That one turned his head. "Sorry, I was thinking of something else!" he shouted — then backed up, and they were on their way again.

So it seems they do suffer from absent-mindedness here as well, I was happy to see . . . flattened with my belly against the right wall.

They "raced" by without appearing to take any notice of me.

[Ed. Corresponding to the change in power structure, the glakhs and shkhurzas in this land were then more or less opposite as to physical type from their counterparts in Shkhurzaland. Here is a comparative table by way of summary.]

	Glakhland	**Shkhurzaland**
glakh	Tall and robust	Short and slender, the older ones (Chief Conservers) her size, the younger ("sweepers") smaller
eekhal	As tall but very thin	Tall and thin
shkhurza	Short and plump	Tall and burly

•

So what's going on, why hasn't anybody been to see me, I mooned, in my old position on the bed. A longish spell, maybe as much as a whole night, had passed, and yet one more tube had been consumed, bringing my total down to two.

Don't tell me I'm going to have to take matters into my own hands again. My guts were really squawking — I got up to do just that, thinking to try going to the left outside and see what was there. If anyone comes along in the meanwhile, screw'em, let'em go look for me, I thought.

But just as I'd stepped out after fastforwarding the door, this small crowd of shkhurzas, more porky's, rounded the corner below there to the right. A pair in the lead were lugging something humungously heavy between them; the rest were along for the company to judge from the yaketty-yack. Let's wait up and see what it is, I decided. . . .

Hey, get a load of that, I couldn't help crowing when they'd gotten closer. It was an all-purple crocodile of sorts, with heavy eyelids and its white tongue dangling . . . dripping strings of gooky saliva.

"We're going to Surgery," the bearer on the head side said, very pleased with himself. He cutchicooed the "croc" under the lower jaw — one of its hind legs lashed out viciously.

"Isn't that nice," I answered back congratulatorily. Well, surgery we've had more than enough of down here, so best give that area a wide berth, advised myself, confine our foraging to back yonder . . . just penetrate further this time. . . .

I turned to head rightward again, but now something new came round the bend and began up the "hill" — another spider-vehicle, bulkier than that car with the trio in it before . . . and lumbering . . . with another of those round-faced purples at the helm.

Somehow I have a feeling this is for me, I further advised. . . .

Sure enough, the shkhurza drew up by me. "I'm s'ppose to 'scort you to the meeting," he said, leaning out of the cab-part.

"Meeting?" I squeaked. There are meetings here too, is it possible?

"Staff meeting, 'specially convened, only the bigshots," he explained. "I'll make room for you."

He got out and went round to the back of his vehicle, where there was a cargo bay. I followed to see what was there. The whole floor was full of glass jars of various widths, from a foot on down; each contained a cigar-shaped something resting on the bottom.

"It'll take a sec" — he began shoving the jars aside. A larger one toppled over, and a small brown "alligator" floated to the edge. It was asleep, with a pinkish ribbon hanging out of its mug.

Oh brother, I groaned inside. Looks like these are more candidates for the scalpel. What if the meeting's a dodge and I too — ? "Listen," I said to him, busy poking the "gator" back in before righting the jar again — "if you don't mind, I'll go on foot, okay?" So at least, should it turn out to be as I was fearing, I'd have the satisfaction, short-lived though it would be, of knowing that I did it under my own steam, with plenty of last looks around and so on.

"Suit yerself," he agreed.

This guy's obviously waiting for me, I surmised of another brawny glakh standing in a doorway on the right, up a piece beyond the corner.

"I see that you found your way alright," he said, when I reached within earshot.

The purple continued slowly on with his load . . . disappeared round another bend up ahead.

⚘ Check, I answered, when I was up to the green one.

He looked hard at me out of dark eyes — "You do remember me, don't you?"

Remember? I sifted. Remember? Ah yes, the voice — it was the Second Vice. "Say, listen here," I said straight off, "what about my food?"

"Now, now, not to worry" — he tried to placate with his hands — hadn't forgotten. On the contrary, was seriously at work trying to get it approved.

I tried to nod their style, not too successfully — it hurt. Shades of my old friend, the Third Assistant.

"In any event," the Second continued, "you're not exactly

starving yet, are you?" — his gaze shifting meaningfully to my chest, the big boobs. . . .

Shall we go? Yes, of course. What choice was there?

Inside there was lots of loud, animated talking. As he followed me in, he told me just to "get right up," then vanished leftward into a crowd of fifty or sixty other glakhs in green aprons and capes, all standing.

Directly ahead was what he meant for me to step onto — a path-like platform about a foot above the floor. Overhead in a row were a dozen tv's with perfectly square screens, and to their right up there stood the Chief in a rounded enclosure like a stairless pulpit.

'Kay, alleyoop. Up there, I turned round to face them all, assuming that was what was wanted, noting before I did so that my platform described an oval in the back part of the room, and that the wall there was made of glass or something else see-though. Behind it was a garden with trees and a true-to-life sky — which added light to the place, the brightest yet, at least 100 watts.

Something tells me I'm in for another ordeal, I brooded, looking out over all those green beings. Many were shorter and slighter than the Chief and Second Vice, meaning younger. Well, patience. . . .

"Chaps," an amplified voice began from above my left shoulder. Was the Chief, of course. "Chaps, I have some very distressing news. Our worst fears may soon be realized" — his voice had a kind of catch in it.

Four or five glakhs in the rear called out — "What's up, Chief? What's the problem?"

Some others from somewhere else in the back there added their voices.

As I said, in for it, I repeated. But let's hear the pitch.

The Chief boomed out afresh — "As some of you are already aware, this — this individual whom you see before you arrived here yesterday from District 721."

What? I couldn't believe my ears! 721? That crazy place is a district? One of seven hundred odd others?

The Chief in the meanwhile had been filling them all in

on the details of my discovery. "Their Council demands a complete accounting," he said now. "And unless it's forth-coming within a reasonable period of time, along with assur-ances that we have those responsible in custody — they're going to withdraw from their commitments to us!"

"Oh, no-o-o!" everyone cried.

Here we go again with the responsibility bit, I remem-bered.

The Chief became grim in his chief's way — "I see I don't have to say anymore, I don't have to remind you of the many trials we've been through together, the sacrifices we've had to endure, just to locate that one — one community in a million — willing even to — "

"Whadya want us to do, Chief?" someone in the back sang out.

Did ya hear, a million, I was still chewing. But maybe he was exaggerating. Even so, imagine, just imagine if I'd fallen into the hands of one of the others, say, 720 or 722, if there is one. Why it could've been all over for me right then and there, and no one would ever have been the wiser.

The Chief was answering — "For the present just this — think. You're the heads of the units where most of the work is likely to have been done."

Lucky, I was just lucky, I meditated.

The Chief was recommending that they try and recol-lect anything unusual, like somebody of late always being on the lookout for rejects [Ed. meaning unsuitable gleegos] or scrounging for stimulators [Ed. their equivalents of hor-mones, enzymes, etc.] . . . also, staying after hours in the lab day after day. . . .

Well, it's now or never, I prodded myself, at a pause from him. I turned toward him — "'Scuse me."

♥ Later, he waved.

"But it's important. You see, I'm from somewhere else."

Hakh! he went in his throat, mildly.

And that's that, at least for now — I turned back.

"In summation," the Chief resumed, "I want each and every one of you to give me your closest cooperation. I want you to assist me in bringing to light — the authors of this ABOMINATION!" He took a gulp — nursing a cup of something up there perhaps? "Here's their data bank."

There was a *plick-plick-plick* etc. — the tv's all being activated. The platform that I was on started sliding rightward, with a *tush-tush-tush*. . . .

"What's that large metal thing on L screen?" someone in the center wanted to know.

"Not certain," the Chief answered. "A companion maybe."

You know — I'd rolled round to the back and that window with its garden beyond — if I'm not mistaken, it's all genuine, that greenery out there.

"In which case, it would have — to be — mm — mechanized," the Chief added meditatively.

Well, now, it struck me, maybe things are not as bad as —

"Why dya suppose there's only one?" another wondered out loud.

"And how's old Arthur, my mission module, faring up yonder by the by?" I wondered under my breath.

"The disposition of the metal companion's — mm — appendages is also problematic," someone else commented. "What was the point in extending them like that, dya think?"

I was gliding by them all again.

A tiny one up front began spinning round — "Br-r-r" — gyrating his arms.

"Stop that!" barked the Chief.

Tiny snapped to attention. "Sorry, Chief," he called out reedily.

"Too bad," I murmured. For all one knows, the kid might have gotten the hang of it before long. All he had to do really was straighten out his little rudder —

"Remember where you are," the Chief lectured.

Now look at that, I marveled . . . about to drift by the woods behind glass once more. Some of the branches were bobbing, leaves quivering, as if in a breeze. . . .

"How is it they didn't send the metal companion along, Chief?" someone in the rear left asked.

I was about to come round to them once more.

"Insist on our statement first," he answered.

"But that's not fair!" another from the right in the back there protested. A neighbor took up the cry — "How can they expect us to — ?"

"Plee-eeze," agonized the Chief. "DON'T belabor the obvious!"

The show was over, platform stopped.

"Chief, there isn't much to go on here, when you come down to it," the same one in the rear left pointed out.

"I'm cognizant of that," the Chief returned, "but rest assured, I intend to remedy the situation just as soon as I can."

Everyone began gabbing and scramming.

His voice rose above it all — "Which reminds me, would the heads of B-Tube and C-Tube be so kind as to remain behind?"

B-Tube and C-Tube? I asked myself, standing there sort of stunned. Ah yes, this is A-Tube, that's what the Second Vice said he was on the Exec Com of.

The Chief had whisked down to floor-level in his speaker's cabinet (thanks to no wires as far as I could tell [Ed. meaning that a motor of sorts had kept it perpetually hovering, they could fly in a way]). "Let's go to my office, shall we," he said to two other hefty greens, who'd emerged as the crowd thinned.

And me? What about me, I wondered, still on the platform . . . feeling cheated, as of old.

The Chief and his associates had begun heading for the extreme left corner of the room, where there was a door beside the glassed-in area.

Well, since no one has said me nay, I'll just tag along, I decided. Who knows, maybe I'll be able to get a word in edgewise. If not, at least I'll stay abreast of things . . . get some clearer idea of what they're going to do with me. . . .

They were already in place when I got there, the Chief facing me from a rigidly rectangular table he was leaning against, B- and C-Tube heads in vaguely S-shaped armchairs on either side between us.

Boy, they sure do have a monopoly on know-how here in Glakhland, I couldn't help admitting. Everything in the room (say, a long and narrow ten by forty feet) was either silvery like the Chief's desk, or else white — except that the upholstery of the chairs and some opposing couches further down to the left kept changing to soft marine shades like aqua and smoky-blue, then changing back again, as if they were treated "fish"-skins or something.

Oh yes, there was another glassed-in view of the garden and its make-believe sky to the right.

I took the bull by the horns, since the Chief, noticing me there in the doorway, did nothing — went and sat on the desk beside him with dangling legs . . . like a ghost.

There'd been some preliminary chitchat apparently. The Chief was now for getting down to brass tacks. "So tell me, what do you make of it?" he'd just said to the other two.

The green on the left crossed one thigh over the other — "Well, it would certainly appear to be beyond the capabilities of a single individual."

"Do you suppose . . . below somewhere?" the other ventured. He drummed nervously on his armrest, like a concert pianist playing Liszt — "Among . . . them?"

"The engineers?" the Chief considered. "Pos-sibly. But they'd surely have needed one or two from above here."

The one on the left spoke up again — "You're visualizing it as having been some sort of — concerted effort then?"

"To be perfectly blunt, yes," said the Chief. "I do hope for the perpetrators' sakes, whoever they are" — his tone darkened — "that it turns out to be — a botched experiment — not as I fear — " ✤ Someone's idea of . . . a practical joke.

Now's a good time, I thought. "May I just have your attention for a moment," began.

His hand reached up and gently descended on my scalp. "Dear, dear, dear," he murmured — the fingers with their nails scratched. . . .

"I'm simply amazed at the materials they used," the one

on the left offered after a longish silence.

Betcha he's some sort of chemist, I told myself. [Ed. To anticipate once more, that he was, his B-Tube given over to the different branches of Chemistry.] He was referring specifically to my pen and pad — the one furiously at work on the other, sketching an expanded version of that scene I'd drawn for Laleekh at first, of Arthur in the sky and Lancelot landing.

"A pity they wouldn't let us have the metal companion," the glakh on the right added. [Ed. A specialist in Physics, C-Tube the realm of same.]

The Chief grew fidgety. "Listen, what do you say to a work-up of her — I mean a really thorough one?" ☛Aside from that, I have to confess I'm completely at a loss.

"Sounds fine to me," said the Chemist.

"Me too," the Physicist agreed. ☛Only I do hope it'll be confined to our tubes, since as you're both aware, things have a way of getting out of hand below sometimes.

"Okeedoke," I said under my breath — done. I tore the two sheets out, held them up, Part I in my right, II left.

"I was afraid you'd take that attitude," the Chief said. ☛I'd kind of been counting on a little in-put from Engineering's mechanical specialists — with all due respect to the acumen of your own mechanical staff.

"It wouldn't be amiss for some of their electrical personnel to have a look at her too," the Chemist chimed in.

Electrical, huh? I faced toward the latter, jounced my hands with my handiwork in them.

The Chief's claws found my head beneath the hair afresh. "Dear-dear" — they dug in.

The Physicist was not about to yield. ☛Nothing doing, I absolutely won't have it.

"Very well," said the Chief, not all too unhappy . . . knowing when the jig was up with one of his ilk.

So there we are, no use hanging around here anymore, the rest'll be garbagey blah-blah. I slipped down from the desk — thought to leave the sheets there.

☛Away, the Chief waved.

I gathered them back up. . . .

Now what? I asked myself out on the roadway moments later . . . all alone there once more.

Why now — I spread my arms at the shoulders. Now I'll

— like Blake's Fly.

I took off for "home" . . . had me a dandy sprint with my arms out like that to the beat of that fly-tune.

●

Now that's enough of that, no more fooling round. We gotta get down to serious business ourselves. . . .

Clearly there is no use trying to tell'em a thing or two about me with a direct approach anymore — as matters presently stand anyway. Needed is a plan of some kind, with contingencies, for surviving this up-coming examination of my person . . . maybe even doing a little better than that, should opportunity knock. . . .

I have it, with an element of if you can't fight'em, join'em. It'll only be till I can figure out who the best one is to talk to among these types . . . yes, who would've guessed, we're back to that again. . . .

+ half hour. Here we go, wish me luck. A van's just pulled up — a regular tarantula! There's a brown in it beside the purple driving. He's just gotten out, loaded down with equipment . . . is coming my way. 'Bye for now.

I was lying in bed with the "covers" to my waist, hands under.

"I'm from Body Fluids," the eekhal announced, shaky-like. Was a young one, very thin, a true bag o' bones.

✋Hi, I acknowledged, with my left. Put it right under the sheet again.

He stabbed out a seat from a brown umbrella, settled on it uneasily — "Here to draw some basic from you." A brown leatherish sack, like an oversized cloth sling bag, got away from him *crack!* — hit the floor — *tinkle!*

I stared, for real — "Are you okay?"

✋Oh yes! he fluttered. "Gee, gee." He bent over, slid a hand into the bag, rummaged.

"I mean you seem to be a bit — " I worked to imitate his nervous expression.

Well, to be perfectly frank, he was — a bit. The hand continued feeling around. This was his first big job. His supervisor had chosen him for it over the other techs in his unit because of the initiative he'd shown of late — "I don't wanna ruin that impression."

"Ah!" — he'd lighted on it, the object of his search. Drew it out — a glossy brown metal something resembling an old-fashioned boot hook (the kind they once used to lace up all those boot laces) — attached the handle, fumblingly, to the end of a hose, which had been snaked in by his driver. His brown toothpick self leaned toward me — "Your arm, please."

Pash, went something out there, the purple having returned to his station — *ping-ping-ping.* Sounded like an auto tire pump.

"What's that?" I sort of shrieked.

"Separator." He leaned closer — ✋Arm.

I stayed put. "Boy, I bet you never did anything like this to the likes of me before."

"Gee, gee. I'll say." ✋Arm, arm.

He was about to pounce on me, that was for sure. "You know," I said very seriously, "I wouldn't do that, what you are about to do, if I were you."

He looked — ✋No? "Why not?"

I puffed air in my cheek and turned my head sideways to give him a hostile profile (the way I remembered the first villagers on the surface had to show annoyance) "Because it wouldn't work on me, that's why. I require another kind. If you do that, you'd only injure me, maybe even kill me" — which wasn't far from the truth, let me tell you, with that ping-schming or whatever that machine was doing out there.

The hook shook in his hand. ✋How so?

"I can't explain, you'll simply have to take my word for it."

His look had grown all troubled — he put the hook in his lap for steadying.

I had the knock-out blow all ready, sat up for it. "Another thing, once my basic's flowing, only I can stop it. Watch!" I pulled out both hands, my right with an open safety pin in it — stabbed the left pinky.

Red drops began falling heavily, each one fanning out on the sheet like a melting red snowflake (thanks to that extra .65).

The young eekhal's face became all mottled, like a relief map. [Ed. His distress was due as much to the color of her blood as the deluge it seems; their "basic" had the "look of tobacco juice to it," if one can believe the Diary elsewhere.]

I put my nose up close to him. "And you know what, I'm gonna leave it this way till someone round here does a thing or two!"

He was in a state, staggered up. "I'll — I'll go tell!" — threw down the hook with its hose, tore out.

"You do that!" I bawled after him, shoving the hand right under and clamping on a dressing.

Out in the main drag the van zoomed away — at fifteen miles per hour. . . .

Lickety-split my young brown friend was back. Almost tripped in the doorway coming through . . . knocked over his chair in an effort to catch himself. "We're suppos' to make a list of your demands!" he said breathlessly. "HOW'S THE WOUND?"

"It's okay" — I showed him.

He righted the chair and sat down, much relieved. We were to get to work right away. Hanging from his wrist was something new, to take notes on I saw the next moment — a mirror-thin oval screen in a brown frame, about eight by six inches. He recorded things on it by touching along the rims, was pretty good at it too as far as I could see.

We filled several "pages,"and he's gone off with "them." If this doesn't work, I'll have to put my thinking bonnet on again. But I believe it will. Shshsh, here he is again.

"You got the WHOLE package!" he called out, galloping in. Was so distraught, I was afraid he might faint or throw up or something.

"The Chief only ahem'd at one thing," he said after cooling it for a few secs. Who wouldn't have been amused — this brown imitated to a tee when the Chief came to that item on the list: "She wants a garden with day and night light, one blue light will do? I should HOPE so!"

He'd nearly returned to normal — a fist went up to his left brow, "Oh yes, there's one thing everyone was puzzled by. Why do you object to having your — your olfactory distention licked? Are you allergic or something?"

"Not at all," I answered — swiveled my head menacingly to a quarter profile. "Just — DON'T — like it."

•

He's assigned to me till further notice. We're to go & take care of my most immediate needs, first stop a unit of Analytical in Organic down on B-Tube (Chemistry). I asked him to step outside for a moment so I could attend to another pressing need in private. . . .

"So, shall we proceed?" he proposed when I was out there on the road with him.

"I'm with you," I said.

"Ride or walk?"

"Oh, let's stretch our legs" — that is, provided that it was not too far. We began to move rightward, side-by-side. "Say, what's your name anyway?" I inquired.

"Grig [$G^3 \text{в}^2 IG^2$]," he answered.

And mine? He never bothered even to try and find out.

They've all got one for me already, betcha, I meditated — the Monster from Shkhurzaland, something like that. . . .

As we went along, I showed him a copy of the lay-out with sketches of particulars for my new accommodations, worked up while I was waiting for him before. He asked questions & made notes on his "oval," then put the pages in his apron pocket. When we were down on B, he stepped into the first door for a moment, Communications. Then we proceeded to our destination, a block or so further.

P.S. B's around the bend at the bottom of the hill & is just like A, 'case there are any questions. Also, Analytical's reception room is something like the Chief's office but not so fancy — only the seats're covered with "fishy" cloth etc.

"We're here about the food," Grig said very respectfully but firmly to a senior glakh in the usual apron and cape, who came to meet us through a door in the back. A lab was beyond it would seem.

I handed over a food-tube that I held in readiness — my last, the very last one.

"Do you have any idea what it's composed of?" the chemist asked very seriously. "It would make everything a lot simpler."

"No, all I know is that it's a special diet," I answered as angelically as I could.

He snipped off the tip with some pincers and brought the tube's opening to his nosehole. The hole's membranes flexed, unflexed. ✤May not be as difficult as all that, he flashed, and withdrew into his inner sanctum. . . .

"How's this?" he asked, back again in a couple of minutes. Handed mine to me plus a new one.

Now who would've thought. The tubes were identical in every respect down to "Made in U.S.A." and "Patent Pending." Now for the true test — I squeezed a dab of his concoction on my index finger. It looked okay, the right shade of baby food green. I brought the finger to my lips. The taste was not bad either, not bad at all — perhaps it had a dash too much celery. I handed it back — "Could you just — ?"

He seemed to understand. . . .

"You should find this more satisfactory," he assured, before us again in another trice with another new tube.

I pressed the ersatz puree straight into my mouth this time. Was a trifle too carroty now, but why belabor the matter, as the Chief's fond of saying. ✋Fine, just fine, I made it clear.

He was all "smiles" — an order would be furthered to Processing at once. "Would you care to see how we do it?"

✋If you don't mind, some other time, I quickly scotched it. Didn't want to risk putting a damper on my appetite — in the event they used roaches or something like that for the protein part.

Our next stop was A-Exec's pool, with Grig joining me for the swim if I so wished. I did nat'rally, nice guy really, sincerely well-meaning & caring.

But first at his request we made a slight detour — was something he wanted to show me that he thought I would find interesting. We went back up to A, to an elevator (just past the Staff Meeting Room on the other side of the road). It seemed to work in the same way as the one that ran away with me in District 721 (by touching the wall), but I was too pre-occupied with filling my face with the real & fake tubes to ask how exactly — FAMISHED! . . .

Up where we ended (3rd floor?) was, of all things, a Natural History museum — a bunch of darkened rooms loaded with lighted display cases. What with all the similar small creatures I saw before in those jars in the back of the truck, it promised to be very boring — but not so. At the first case he took me to, a "salamander" world, I was just about to make some excuse for us to skip it & head for the pool when he snickered, Gee, gee. On my looking more closely, the three soft lizardy things in there — turquoise, khaki, and cerulean — turned out to be in motion . . . were slowly moving along a mossy log they'd been standing on.

Are they alive? I asked.

He snickered again — Gee, gee — meaning that they were not; they were models, mechanized ones. It seems they'd become activated by our stepping before the case; when we stepped away, they were motionless again.

After that, he led me to an aquarium full of little makhpeezoos, with dots for their single eyes and a pebble each in a sack hanging from their bellies, who became very lively at the sight of us — fakes too & great favorites of his. Then, at the next case, containing some "grasshoppers," he asked me if I'd like to have some fun & timed our stepping away to coincide with their leap across a mud puddle, so they stopped in mid-air.

I'll say it was fun — who could resist. We went back & forth several times, so they froze — hopped — froze, then tried it out on a pack of "sharklets" squaring off against a party of "squidlets," and finally on a swarm of other springing insects that I couldn't rightly see — took his word for it that they were multi-colored & quite lovely.

The pièce de résistance was a trio of puppy-sized "brontosauruses" (with pin heads, giraffe gullets, & ten-ton bodies, tails yellow, red, or white feathered), who began nibbling on some shrubs when we came up.

What's so special 'bout them, I asked, the novelty having begun to wear off, as I'm sure you can well understand.

Lookit, he said, & jumped away like before, plucking me with him.

The "brontos" kept on eating.

I: Whatsa matter, are they in need of adjustment or something?/ Grig: Gee, gee, gee! (Was quite taken with himself.) They're for real.

I: (still confused) So how is it they started chomping when they did?/ Grig: Simple, they learned it from the dummies — after an operation on the whatsis & and a suppository (up the "tail").

I: Well then, how come they didn't stop chomping when we moved away?/ Grig: Haven't mastered that part yet.

I: And how come you're such a smarty-pants about all this stuff?/ Grig: Gee, gee, my glakh-buddy's the curator. . . .

On our way back, I remarked that he seemed to have an affinity for inferior forms & asked if he had any pets. No, he answered very sadly. Get this — eekhals here aren't allowed to keep'em. Only in Eekhalland. . . .

You'll never guess what happened next — we were just about to board the elevator again when I got a glimpse of a chunky shadow flitting between some of the cases to our left. I called Grig's attention to it, my heart knocking — afraid lest something alive with snappy

*jaws'd gotten loose, or that his glakh-buddy was spying on us. But
it was neither, he let me know at once — rather his shkhurza-buddy,
who'd been tailing us for some time it appears.*

*I: What's his story?/ Grig: (with a mniff) Search me, nothing very
likely. He's just a pest, that's all. Is he bothering you?*

"Not at all," I answered, now that I know.

"Never mind "— Grig. Meef! he whistled through his sniffer-hole.
"Would you go away!" he yelled at the lurking purple.

*As Grig seemed rather glum after that, I asked him where they lived
— to get his mind off of it & also because I was curious. It isn't much,
he said, but if I liked he'd take me there, was just a matter of another
slight detour, using the elevator again. . . .*

*He sure wasn't being modest, the place wasn't much — looked
like a cross between an airplane hangar & a hospital ward, with three
long rows of triple beds. It seems the whole of A-Exec lives there.*

What do you all do for privacy, I asked him.

*It's not as bad as it looks — he. Demonstrated with his own bed
(center row center), causing a rounded canopy to swing over it like a
convertible roof with the pressing of a button.*

And the gleegos, what happens to them? — I.

*No answer to that — he was still fretting or didn't care to discuss
it.*

*Wouldn't you know it, as we were retracing our steps, the shkhur-
za-buddy appeared again, this time in the flesh, via some back stairs
. . . another purple tub o' lard.*

Would you kindly absent yourself, Grig said acidly.

*The shkhurza turned morosely away & went back where he came
from . . . but first gave me a real once-over, the way we would if we
were trying to figure out whether we knew a certain person.*

Grig and I were at the pool at last. Well, as I've said
before (and heard tell), you gotta hand it to the glakhs in
this land, they really know how to do things.

Before us was an exact replica — but I mean exact —
of the first village's pearly-green, satiny pond and its slatey
ledges, surrounded by a lush wind-whispering jungle of foliage like in the garden.

"Gee, gee," Grig tittered.

What now? I stepped forward for a closer look. "Oh my!" escaped from my lips.

Except for the water, it was all a mirage — film projections on air currents or something of that nature.

Grig was tickled at my astonishment. . . .

"Uh oh, I hate to tell ya," I said to him the next moment, ready for the plunge with all my clothes off.

Guess-who was back . . . approaching us from the other end, an entrance there as well.

Grig was on the point of pulling his cape off — yanked it back on tearingly. "What did I tell you! Leave us ALONE!" he shouted.

The purple stopped in his tracks — was maybe twenty feet away. "Look," he pleaded, "I just wanna ask her a question, then I'll go, okay?"

"Why don't you let him and be done with it," I murmured to Grig.

"'Kay, be quick about it," Grig said moodily.

The shkhurza duckwalked to right before me — his face was like a super-winey grape. "My friends and I get together every day after work and we have very lively discussions," he said. "Would you care to — ?"

Grig finished it for him — in an eekhal-buddy's furious fashion.

•

"It's time!" Grig called from the "ledge," where he'd left his "oval," to which he'd swept through the water with a few sleek strokes.

He didn't have to repeat it, I'd finished swimming ages ago.

One-two-three we were dressed and off down the elevator to the road, and trotting along as fast as our legs could carry us to where my old room had been. . . .

"Beat ya!" Grig squealed, reaching the door a hair before me — pressed to open it, felt inside and switched on all the lights at the same time [Ed. probably by inserting all his fingers within the circle of togs and simultaneously pushing the whole cluster of sticks outward].

"I'm speechless," I said, rooted there on the spot.

He was too — besides being slick in the face and gaspy. . . .

✋C'mon, I waved. It was my turn now to conduct a tour of inspection.

[Ed. Briefly, it was a one-bedroom apartment including a charming garden with a little dining patio. On the facing page is the "original" floor-plan with a key by me.]

We romped all over from pillar to post. Now he's gone. To return in the early a.m. to take me to the examination. . . .

Honestly, the place exceeds my wildest expectations. Even the food's here, in a wooden box in the kitchen. . . .

"So there we are," I sighed in bed some time later, chock full to bursting. Looked leftward to the outside through the window, which ran almost the whole length of the wall above the Parson's table.

The light had been fading, was now gone . . . only the topmost leaves and a few spots of ground were showing, powdery violet.

A pang struck me. I'll have to pay tomorrow. Yes, tomorrow it'll be payment on demand, the tariff.

Oh well, there's no use fretting about it now, is there? I rolled over on my tum, flung an arm out — like a fly.

FLOOR PLAN

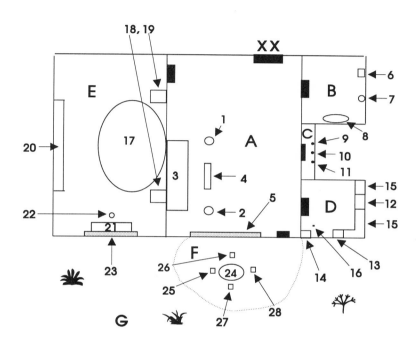

Key

A LIVING ROOM*
  1,2 Easy chairs
   3 Couch
   4 Coffee table
   5 Picture window

D KITCHEN
  12 Sink
  13 Stove
  14 Fridge
  15 Counters
  16 Crate

B BATHROOM
   6 Sink
   7 Toilet
   8 Tub-shower

E BEDROOM**
  17 Bed
  18, 19 Nightstands
  20 Dresser
  21 Parson's table
  22 Straight chair
  23 Picture window

G. GROUNDS***

C CLOSET
   9 Pack on shelf
  10 Canteen
  11 Pot

F PATIO
  24 Wrought iron
      table
  25 Matching chair
  26 Matching chair
  27 Matching chair
  28 Matching chair

*Everything faithfully modeled after the Chief's.
**Entirely in white.
***Including the lilac smell.

Chapter Eight

THIS IS THE CHIEF.

"It is?" said Felice, half asleep in bed. "Where?" Her eyes widened — she was on her side. Outside in the garden were blackish branches with leaves showing through curling white steam here and there . . . the trees shrouded in fog.

MAY I HAVE YOUR ATTENTION, PLEASE.

Felice's eyes shifted to the dresser directly before her, white like everything else. "Ah" — on the wall above it was a colored life-sized image of the Chief in profile.

That half of his mouth moved: **ALL HANDS.**

This should be rare, Felice thought, considering the deal that she and the bigwigs here in Glakhland had struck. Pulled the pillow up behind her, settled back against the headboard, quilted white velvet.

The Chief's one eye stared: **OVER THE NEXT SEVER-AL SESSIONS, AS EVERYONE DOUBTLESS KNOWS BY NOW, SOME OF US HERE IN THE UPPER TUBES WILL BE ENGAGED IN A MAJOR RESEARCH EFFORT — OF VITAL CONCERN — TO THE ENTIRE COMMUNITY. I AM THEREFORE REQUESTING — YOUR CLOSE COO-PERATION — AS FOLLOWS.**

A smile of anticipation spread across Felice's face.

FIRST, FOR THOSE WHOSE SERVICES ARE NOT REQUIRED — The Chief's cheek inflated some: **IT IS TO BE BUSINESS AS USUAL, THERE SHALL BE NO IN-TERFERENCE OF ANY KIND FOR WHATEVER REA-SON. NOW AS TO THE PARTICIPANTS —** The cheek went back to normal.

Felice drew in her breath, held it.

**THEY ARE TO DEVOTE THEIR UTMOST INGENU-
ITY AND ENERGY TOWARD SOLVING OUR COMMON
PROBLEM, AND IN SO DOING —** The cheek again in-
flated, but not quite so much this time. **THEY ARE TO
GIVE MAXIMUM CONSIDERATION TO THE SUBJECT
AT ALL TIMES. MEANING —**

Felice let go of that breath, took in another.

**AND I ASSUME THAT I'M REPEATING WHAT YOU
HAVE ALREADY HEARD FROM YOUR SECTION HEADS
— BUT LISTEN TO IT ONCE MORE, PLEASE —**

Felice's right forefinger went up to her mouth.

**NO SURGERY, TESTING PROCEDURES, OR MED-
ICAMENTS ARE TO BE ADMINISTERED TO THAT IN-
DIVIDUAL WITHOUT HER EXPRESS PERMISSION —
REGARDLESS OF — HOW — HARMLESS — THEY MAY
SEEM. IN OTHER WORDS —**

Felice's front teeth delicately clutched the knuckle.

The Chief's voice rose to new heights: **AT THE CESSA-
TION OF THIS, OUR AR-ARDUOUS TRAVAIL, I WANT
TO SEE A SHKHIBEE KHAMOR** [$\int\chi^{11}I' \cdot$ bhi χ^{10}a$\cdot$ mo^3
— "live specimen in the first degree"]! **A BLEY KHAMOR**
[bh${}_{\circ}$le — "dead even if in mint condition"] **WILL BE TO-
TALLY UNACCEPTABLE!**

"Yup, that's the ticket," Felice summed it all up for herself. Okay, time indeed, let's get a move on.

Ssst, went the front door not long after. "Anybody home?"
a voice called.

Must be Grig. Felice gulped down the half tube of puree
she had in her mouth, stuck her head out the kitchen door
— yes. "Be right with you."

Grig parked himself in the easy chair facing the window
— "No hurry, it'll keep."

"By the by" — she'd made quick work of the rest of the
tube — "should I have eaten?"

He waved the idea away, became engrossed in the doings

outside . . . the mist gradually dissipating . . . lonely trees. . . .

"Let's go," Felice said, emerging from the bathroom moments later.

They sauntered out.

"We're getting you first," he confided, meaning Fluids, his division. It was the Chief's way of rewarding him for his truly excellent handling of the sticky situation with her.

"Great," she told him. "Why the next thing one knows, they'll be moving you up in the ranks." He was at the C-level in his unit, she'd learned while they were gadding about yesterday.

He grew all wistful — "That'd be nice." His supervisor was so finicky; it had been ever so long since his last promotion. . . .

Fluids was just around the corner past the Staff Meeting Room. As they strolled along, she described the human circulatory system and explained how to tap it, and in the end offered to draw a hypo for him.

"That's very thoughtful of you, but really it's unnecessary," he let her know when she was done. Three or four drops from another petty lancing would do, he believed — that and some of her golden waste fluid and saliva, plus a soupçon from an eye socket, which he'd extract himself with a tiny dropper that his glakh-buddy, the curator of the Natural History museum, used to feed young orphaned specimens.

Felice was truly touched — how very nice of him; as I said, he's one helluva nice guy. She told him that if he really wanted to get technical, she had a number of other flowing substances in addition to the ones he'd ticked off.

Well, of that there was no doubt, he responded, didn't they all, gee gee. However, in his opinion, or actually his supervisor's she was to understand, who'd had it from his superior, it would be better if she didn't bring that up just now. She should call it to everyone's attention later, if still of a mind to — after things had calmed down and the various heads could attend to it properly without being under undue pressure, as they were now.

•

*All along the road on the right, the units involved, both Fluids &
Solids, had small flags flying, green with a yellow cube in the center.
Inside, it was much of a muchness with our medical labs, except that
everything crucial was made of that silvery stuff like the togs.*

*We spent the whole a.m. in Fluids, with Grig, the darling, hover-
ing without stint. Everybody was most cordial but preoccupied — the
heads rattling off orders to techs at instrument boards or rushing a-
bout, shkhurzas standing by to schlep or whatever. . . .*

*We're home for lunch now. Grig brought something with him to
munch on in a little pouch. He's to remain with me in Solids this
afternoon. . . .*

*When we went back, a dozen or so purple sillies were milling a-
round in the way. Broke up & ambled to their respective doorways at
the sight of us. Inside, the heads & techs too were all a little on the
snotty side, jealous of Grig's coup I suspect.*

*They took from me: a stool sample, skin scrapings from an arm
and a leg, nail parings, & hair (from my head only, on my insis-
tence). They administered: vision test, hearing etc. Achtung: measured
my temp with a pin under the left thumbnail — told me it changed
color(?).*

*I put my foot down about doing anything else, & those units af-
fected (like Excretory) were resultantly very gloomy — as if all their
equipment had blown a fuse or something. Reproductive Organs adjourned en masse to a reception room & set me in the center on a low,
round table. One of the green muckamucks then said, "The least you
can do is explain how anybody in their right minds could have expected those two bulbs on your chest to work without the orifices." Another one, younger, followed it up with: "Why did they stick one in the
middle of nowhere like that?" — meaning my navel. And a third one,
a regular Moral Majority type, wanted to know very acidly: "What
purpose is supposed to be served by the pink knobs on the bulbs' tips?"*

*I decided to try & answer from their point of view. But had no
luck even there: as soon as I opened my mouth, they started pooling
impressions.*

New day. Spent below in B-Tube.

Grig came by here first thing, all alone in a vehicle rigged specially for the occasion — looks like an aluminum baby carriage with a ball turret. The idea was for him to teach me how to drive it, so I could go down there by myself (and to C-Tube tomorrow as well), which would allow them all to monitor my reflexes etc. & him to return to work.

I had a devil of a time getting the hang of it: the controls were configured clusters of teeny holes like very shallow pinpricks, & the only clue as to their function was their occurrence on the panel in order of importance — their idea of importance, that is. (And there, dear folks, lies the secret to the operation of the elevators, Grig's "oval" too very likely.) Once I tilted over so far after sideswiping a wall, I was sure I'd topple over all the way — all this & more to the amusement of a buncha purple bellies who came to watch. . . .

When I rounded the curve below, a big crowd of greens, browns, & purples was out on the road in front of the units — all yelling, "Shkhibee Khamor! Here comes the Shkhibee Khamor" [Ed. meaning "live specimen in the first degree," it will be recalled]. *And after I braked & pushed back the hood, the crush was terrific. An older green stooped & whisked a speck of dust or something from my left cheek with a tiny brush. Then as I was getting out, someone grabbed hold of one of my boobs & gave it a loving wobble. (I mentioned it to a friendly tech later & he said he wouldn't put it past one of the "drones" — meaning purples. But I don't know, I could've sworn the hand was brown.)*

Happily the big boss appeared just then, or there's no telling what might've happened next: "Okay, chaps, let's get cracking." Ushered me in. There's good stuff in that one . . . who knows, maybe in time. . . .

Inside, there were the same kind of tests but on a chemical level, & no snags developed till Metallurgy, when I absatootly refused to part with so much as a minute flake from one of my fillings. After the last test, I went back to that unit to listen to the heads debate the possible reasons for "all that compound" in me. Dentistry & optometry too are 'pparently unknown here in the civilized part of X —from what I understand, everyone's teeth & "corneas" are replaced with each molting, which occurs annually. As for the debate, the best theories I heard advanced were: a) "An inept puerile (or febrile) attempt at ornamentation," and b) "Sheer obfuscation!"

Another new day, and oh what a day.

It began alright with Grig here again briefly for reassurance's sake, & to forewarn me about a fork in the road just beyond B-Tube, where I was to be sure to bear left to get to C.

There was a sizeable turn-out down on C too ("Here she comes" etc.), but not as enthusiastic as on B yesterday, and everyone piped down & went in as soon as I brought the "pram" to a halt.

Inside, there were physical variations on the same theme, & everything was A-okay till the last test, for buoyancy, when the big cheeses became so absorbed in the data, they utterly forgot about me, still in the tank. Boy oh boy, what with the techs busy with other things, it sure was hairy there for a while — I began to get very tired treading, & when I tried to hold on to the tank's edge, the metal cut into my hand. By chance an unaffiliated tech wandered by in search of a pal & heard me calling feebly.

While chatting with him after in his unit — where he let me dry my hair with a blower — I got this idea. Did they have any specialists in natural illumination down there, I asked him, & if so, might I see one? Bingo, there were four of them — two in Optics (one for white, the other blue light), & two more in Thermal (ditto). We went looking, & lo, found 'em all together in somebody's office playing a game (a sort of cross between chess & bridge with differently shaped spots of light of different intensities for pieces, which were maneuvered by pressing the surface of the table).

I waited patiently on a stool that friendly tech sent in, till what seemed like the right moment, a new hand or something, and launched into my spiel — "'Scuse me" etc. Never again! They can all go fry! Nobody even bothered to look up, & the one to my left stuck his claws on my head & began to scratch. . . .

Going home was something else.

La-dee-da, all in a day's work, free at last, and climbing into my chariot, extended my right arm fully for a song —

Piping down the valleys wild. . . .

giving forth fully with an original tune as Blake himself, the author, is supposed to have sung it.

Then with my left finger plunked on "forward" — I was off, back up the winding way. . . .

Now that's odd — I was about to pass the fork where Grig had been so insistent that I bear left on the way to B- and C-Tubes. The buggy had slowed down some it seemed.

Maybe my finger slipped off the spot. I lifted it, peered — no — quickly put it back. The buggy was going even more slowly.

Possibly a short's developed in the wiring or something, I theorized. Tapped with the finger there. "Now you've done it," I murmured. The vehicle had come to a dead standstill.

I pressed down with all my might now.

Yook — the wheels rolled back a notch. *Yook-yook* — they rolled some more, into the other branch of the fork.

This shouldn't be, gotta get some help pronto, I saw. Felt around on the right with my other index, a two-way radio there somewhere — "Hello, hello, does anyone read me?" I felt around some more — "Come in, please, someone!"

"Communications, B-Tube," a voice piped up, belonging to a brown probably.

"This is the Shkhibee Khamor," I said, told him what the problem was.

The voice got all excited too — "Hang on!" . . .

"This is B here," B-Tube's head identified himself a moment later, that nice chemist with some semblance of sense.

The contraption was still sliding back with my finger still heavily on forward.

"Sounds like they're using a force field on you," he diagnosed.

They? He must mean the Engineers —I trembled slightly.

"I'll get back to you," B said. . . .

In another trice the Chief was on — "Calling D-Tube, calling D-Tube" — his voice full of urgency.

There was no response.

"What did I tell you," complained someone new, C-Tube's head, the physicist. "They're always trying to horn in where they don't belong."

"Never mind that, there's no time for that now!" the Chief barked. His tone turned twittery — "D-Tube, come in please. I'd like to speak to your Number One."

"Glug-glug Glug-glug-glug!" came a different voice, raucously. (I couldn't make it out, cross my heart — too fast.)

"What do you think?" Chemical B asked Physical C.

C answered back curtly, in a snit now.

Took-took-took — the wheels took off in the same backward direction.

"Could you hurry it along?" I mumbled through jittery teeth, really in a fright.

B gave up on C, and very sensibly came back to me. "Listen, there's a grey button in the center of the panel, do you see it?"

I scrutinized that area. "Yeah, I — guess so." I'd noticed it during the lesson, taken it for a fleck of paint since Grig didn't touch on it.

The Chief snorted — something about my being blind as a whatever, and wrong-handed to boot. Also, a jerk or something like that.

"Alright," B continued. When he gave the word, I was to take either my left or right index and —

All fine and good, I hastened to point out, but did he realize that both fingers were already committed on the panel's ends.

"SORT IT OUT SOMEHOW!" the Chief shattered the air waves with.

I leaned back so I could assess the situation more comprehensively.

"Now!" the Chemist ordered.

Badaboom, I substituted my right pinky for the forefinger, and stabbed the fleck with my right thumb.

The wheels stopped . . . eased forward.

"Shit, give it some more juice!" one of the dastardly ones below cried.

"Too late," I said in English. The buggy was moving along just fine now. "Giddeyap!"

•

"All safe'n sound," Felice crowed, home at last . . . at the table in the patio with a couple of tubes. The twilight hour was coming on.

Now what, what am I gonna do with myself now — provided that the Chief and his cohorts live up to their part of the agreement, giving me this place in perpetuity, which for sanity's sake, let's say is so. There's the business of the Chemist, of course, but I don't know, I'm kinda gun-shy after so many rebuffs, need a breather to recoup my spirits.

I know — an idea had come. I'll paint some murals, liven up the walls a bit, and at the same time, by sending down for the paints and stuff, keep my hand in with him till an opportunity presents itself for a face-to-face.

Yes — Felice cottoned to it — when Grig comes, as he surely will tomorrow, we're friends now, I'll get him to show me how to put through a request.

An afterthought succeeded that one — he can help with the paint-schmearing in his off-time if he's of a mind to, his shkhurza-buddy too . . . under certain conditions.

It had been very quiet; now all at once it got stunningly so.

A pity they don't have any sweetly singing creatures here on X, Felice sighed inwardly. I wonder if — Maybe there's something, some cast-off, in Grig's lab I can have. It doesn't have to be a virtuoso, anything within reason'll do . . . just so long as the soundlessness is relieved a little.

Hey, I got it — she remembered Grig's glakh-buddy, the Natural History curator. Maybe if the situation is explained, 'bout my delicate hearing, maybe he can come up with something . . . something unreal . . . like a canary.

Dusk was now complete, and it had grown a trifle chilly. Felice transferred herself to within, to the chair facing out . . . to watch the one blue moonlet rise.

Ssst, went the door, behind her.

What? Felice looked round — it was Grig with his "oval," seeming very much in earnest. "There are some loose ends," he said very soberly.

"Like what?" She yielded the chair to him and planted herself in the other one opposite him, with the coffee table between them. "Would you care for some water, by the by?"

☙ Not right now, maybe later, he answered. . . .

"Awright, shoot," Felice said, back from the kitchen with a cup for herself on a doilied saucer. She gave him a snide look — "It wouldn't happen to pertain to those other fluids of mine perchance?"

There wasn't a glimmer of reaction from him — it was a changed Grig indeed. "No — you see — it concerns — " His gaze fell to her chest.

"But Grig," she protested, "I tried to tell'em there in Solids, you heard me yourself."

True, he agreed, but that's how things are sometimes. The Chief and Execs had reviewed her file late last night, and found it deficient in that respect. The upshot was they wanted her to feed the information to him, the tech who'd been so successful with her in the past, and he would digest what he could to report to them, record the rest for their perusal.

Why bother, she scorned internally, they'll just take whatever I say and add two and two with it, and come up with one and a half. On the other hand, there is this brown one to consider, who's been mighty kind to me in more ways than one. "Whadya say, do you think if I were to — they might — your long overdue promotion?"

☙ Check, tentative, he returned.

"Okay, let's go." She began, gave it to him from soup to nuts . . . all about the human reproductive system. . . .

"Clearly then," Grig said when he had a hefty stack of ragged-edge pages with her scrawls at his elbow, "as far as mates for you are concerned, an extrapolation like this — " He diddled the edges of his "oval," reversed it for her to see.

"Is all wrong," she pronounced, keeping a tight rein on her dimples for his sake.

On the screen were outlines of two torsos, each with a baseball-sized cavern below the collarbone, and a matching pair of their organs on a side.

Grig seemed to relax — "Now let's see if I have it all straight" — reeled off everything as she'd delivered it to him.

He certainly is conscientious, was her feeling as she listened. May he only really be a pal. "Whadya say to that water now?" she offered, after complimenting him.

🖐Thanks, no, I better go, came the answer.

"Whose brainstorm were those holes in the chest, Solids?" she tried to pry, while walking with him to the door.

Sure enough.

And how did the Chief feel about it?

He was not "in high gloss." Fluids was less so, needless to say. "Many thanks, I'll let you know how I make out," Grig said in parting.

●

What'll I do if he doesn't come, I schemed. The entire day had been spent in waiting, with no sign of him or anyone else. I was in that same chair facing the door, to which I'd gone soon after rising . . . not even interested in looking out on my greenery anymore . . . my finery.

Could it be that he too is a phony, another I'll-get-back-to-you-later who doesn't, I posed, not for the first time that day. No — I pushed it away again — when an intelligent feeling being likes someone, it comes through, human or not. Look at Laleekh and his nutty neighbors, for instance. . . .

You know, it occurred along about sundown, it's altogether possible the Chief and his associates accepted what he conveyed to them, and that was that, case closed — he hasn't stopped by because he's been too busy wrapping things up.

Tellya what we're gonna do, we're gonna go take a peek in A-Exec's dining hall. As I recall, he said there was generally a gala bash after the completion of a project, so if a ruckus of some kind is going on there, I'll know that's it. . . .

Let's see, I think he said next door to the elevator — I was out on the road, had just passed the Staff Meeting Room.

Yes, there it is — an open door in sight.

I stepped up to it. Well, well, I was right again. A-Exec was there in force, with mates, and they were all living it up, no doubt about it.

There were three circular banquet tables, one within the other — all in motion revolving leftward at a fairly rapid rate (think of the circles of a roulette wheel). The heads were seated at the outer table, techs within at the center one, and fatties crowded around the innermost. Only the greens had bowls.

On the ceiling, as if slow-echoing the whirl of the tables, giant blue-grey amoeboid globs floated around — very likely a magnified drop of unfiltered water, projected. [Ed. And here then is the secret of the infamous specks, which are nullified as soon as ingested, the author went on to say in the Diary.] Now and then, one of them swelled and divided into three . . . trivided.

❧ Hi! waved a hand belonging to a very thin brown face — Grig.

❧ Bon appetit! I waved back, managing it just before he was whipped round so his back was to me.

❧ Yoohoo! went a pudgy purple mitt in his turn, you-know-who, Grig's shkhurza-buddy, of course. . . .

❧ Be seeing you soon, Grig followed up with on the next pass. . . .

Well, that's a relief, I sighed inwardly, my faith in him fully restored.

Something changed, some signal had been given, probably by the Chief. The glakhs began flicking bits from their bowls to the two inner circles — more, more, to the point where it seemed as if a swarm of angry flies had gotten loose. Red and white tongues flashed as both browns and purples made efforts to snatch the tidbits. But clearly the lion's share went quite deliberately to the latter.

So, another mystery solved, I confided to myself — that's why the eekhals are so scrawny and the shkhurzas so porculent here in Glakhland.

Well, the units've probably all got started on another project and are keeping my pal hopping as usual, was all I could figure, after staying in the whole of the next day in the hope of setting eyes on him. . . .

You know, you have grown to depend on him a bit too much, my better self pointed out in bed later. You should strive to use your own initiative a little more as of old. . . .

He's not going to show today either, I was forced to conclude by noon of the next. He likes you, but he's just too involved. So what should I do?

Well, you could go down to B-Tube and seek out the head. But I don't know, somehow it doesn't strike me as a good idea; it needs an occasion. What then?

What else — an expedition. Everything casual-like, nothing fancyschmancy. I'll take a few tubes & the canteen, go for an hour tops, see what's beyond A-Tube if anything. Who knows, maybe there'll be — I'll just stumble on — a way up.

Better pinch myself from time to time to verify consciousness. Cameras? Well, there's nothing much one can do about'em, so we'll just have to grin & bear it. Anyway, my gut instinct is — I'm 99% sure — they don't do sneaky things like that here, & this is not a test. . . .

It's worth it just for the exercise, was my feeling on my way after breakfast the next a.m. Boy, you sure were getting out of shape sitting around like that. . . .

I'd just rounded the bend past the Staff Meeting Room. The doors of Fluids and Solids were shut tight; no one was about in the road, not even a single laboring one loitering. Must be some new project they're all on now, calling for a real all-out effort. Oh well. . . .

Curves and more curves, this is the curviest place ever, I sort of complained a half hour or so later. That is what I had been doing, winding round and round on just plain road with no doors whatsoever on either side. . . .

"Finally," I breathed, after an umpteenth bend.

There was a dead end ahead and a few feet before it on the right a conventional door with one of those aluminum

loops. A shkhurza was seated on the ground before it, leaning there with legs straight out — but such a big fat one, a
regular loin of beef, so help me.

"You're not allowed to pass without permission," he sang
out nasally (like with clogged sinuses) when I was closer.

Now there's something, I made a mental note. He'd used
the neuter form for me, meaning he didn't rightly know who
or what I was. Let's see if we can try and learn what's on the
other side of the door at least. I asked him right out.

He gave me the eye as if to say, Ya mean ya don't know?
"Next sector."

So, that figures somehow. "What is it called?" I asked.
Must be referred to by a letter or something like that, no?

His look changed to a mixture of disdain and pity —
what an idiot, he had to be thinking in other words. "B&G-
B," he answered [Ed. The B&G standing for R&D or Research and Development, it should be understood].

Aha, this sector I'm in then could be B&G-A. I sounded
him out anew.

That it was — but clearly he was beginning to lose patience with such an obvious nincompoop.

Now for a larger picture. I slid my foot forward — the left
— to just before his "heel," his eyes were compelled to fix on
my thighs. I was after the number of sectors now.

"Oh, there are eight hundred at least," he answered more
respectfully. The exact figure was hard to pinpoint right
now because of the realignments(?). There were more than
twenty B&G's alone that he was aware of.

Well, well, this extra-lumpy purple is a veritable mine of
information, I cued myself — slid my right foot up to join the
left, tensed that one as if I would next raise it and tread on
him. "What are the chances of having a look-see?" — meaning out the door.

"Rather good," he said with alacrity, properly intimida-
ted. Rolled over onto his side, pushed down with extra-chub-
by paws, up he went, up. Grasped the loop teeteringly —
tugged the door open.

"Wowee!" I cried — was brighter than the brightest earthly day in there. I'd turned right away, arms shielding my eyes — but not before I'd caught sight, as far as the eye could see, of row on row of green shoots with yellow buds standing in shallow water, some kind of crop under cultivation there in A-Tube of B&G-B it would seem.

Meanwhile he'd applied his bulk to the door to shut it again. "Zih-zih-zih," he was panting.

To keep the flow of polite patter going, I wondered aloud to which of the sectors he belonged.

Neither, was the answer. He was what one called an in-between.

"Your family too?"

He paused in his pushing — "I — didn't — say — that." Gave a final shove, spun round, plopped. "My glakh-buddy's a central figure here."

Now that's curious, I thought, could he be lying or exaggerating? I didn't recall seeing the likes of this plum pudding at the A-Exec bash. No matter, on to the business at hand, I urged. "Tell me — uh — if one wanted to, how does one" — ☞ Go up?

"Oh, I wouldn't have any idea. That's a question for" — ☞ Them below.

So, the engineers. It's elementary when one thinks about it.

●

Whatever could they all be doing in there, I wondered, passing Fluids and Solids again on the way back. It seemed quieter than before if that were possible, like deathly still. Sure would be funny — and sad too — if —

I was coming up to the Staff Meeting Room. The sounds of an animated conversation were issuing from the little foyer in there — two older glakhs stepped out onto the road ahead of me. They were congratulating one another on how swimmingly things had proceeded, singling out for particular praise the new Acceleration Process. I thought I heard my

name mentioned — Shkhibee Khamor . . . some process had
been developed in my behalf.

   How now, what's this? My place was in sight; the two
glakhs, whom I'd allowed to outdistance me, had promptly
entered, and there was a lot of loud talking inside.
   Another shindig was in full swing I saw at once on the
door-step. The living room was filled to capacity — mostly by
green faces, with here and there a brown. They were all
standing around glugging with cups in their hands.
   Someone noticed me and gave a whoop — "Here she is!"
Others around, all with oily complexions, took it up — "She's
back! She's back!"
   Grig was squeezing through the crush to get to me from
the corner by the kitchen.
   Oh boy, they're drinking booze for sure. ✋What's the
story? I hi-signed to him.
   "It's a surprise!" someone nearby cried. "In there!" Another weavingly thumbed toward the bedroom — the door
was closed, not as I had left it.
   "What is it?" I asked uneasily, a notion beginning to take
hold — I thought to make tracks for there.
   "No, no, not yet!" someone else cried. "Has to be a song
first," his neighbor chimed in. "Yes, yes," others agreed, "a
song! A pond song!"
   "It's customary," Grig explained, now before me, and not
too steady on his pins either . . . he seemed a little embar-
rassed somehow.
   A particularly tall, well-built glakh by the couch — possibly the Second Vice — started it off. Everyone else joined
in — to make a terrible caterwauling, worse even than in
the first village that time when everyone was marching in
procession to deposit their gleegos (or khreekhos as they
would have said) in the stream house. This song was all about
peace, harmony, and long life. Finally it came to a resounding raucous finish. "Lotsa lu-u-uck!" the one who'd led it off
squeak-squawked.
   They all began to file out, lurchingly. . . .

"Guess what," Grig said as the last of them was leaving, "I made B-Probationary."

My heart warmed; I certainly was happy, glad some good had resulted from all our efforts — told him so.

He looked at me with dewy eyes — "I hope I'll be able to say the same for you." No, he wouldn't stay on, would only be in the way. . . .

Whatever it is, it's gonna be a pipperoo, I'll stake my life on it, I warned myself when the front door shut behind him. Strode over to the bedroom door, gave the white button there a bip.

I'll say pipperoo — except that it wasn't an "It," there were two of them, my mates it would seem. One was my age, the other thirteen or fourteen — both were under the covers fast asleep, each with a head on a pillow.

Amazing — the faces were mine to a T, with the same almond eyes, pointy cheekbones, mouth not quite a bow, and downward curving nose. There was just one flaw as far as I could see — their chins were severely foreshortened. So viewed from the side where I was standing, it looked like two sheep snouts in bed there — one belonging to someone in his thirties, the other a teenager.

I gently pulled the covers down. They were perfectly fashioned males in every respect, again with a single flaw if you can call it that — both members were stiff, all ready for action. . . .

The boy had wakened on my re-covering them.

"Can you speak?" I whispered, in English.

"I — I think so," he answered in the same, huskily.

The man's lashes fluttered, he looked my way. "'Morning," he said in a pleasant baritone — grinned with crow's feet(!), ungrinned, closed his eyes, and fell off again.

"Whyn't you get a little more shut-eye yourself," I suggested to the other.

"'Kay," he agreed in a boy-soprano.

"Now what in blazes," I scolded a "magnolia" bush out in the garden moments later. You couldn't blame me for being upset — this was no laughing matter. One thing's for certain, I laid it down to the same shrub after pacing around some, what the Chief and his associates have in mind — for me to breed with those snaky-chinned clowns — must never come to pass.

It took a while for me to calm down, then I saw the light — that even if I wanted such a calamity to happen, it never would, for the simple reason that, clone-schmone, the green wizards could not have put together a true human male solely on the basis of the information I'd conveyed to them through Grig plus that deduced from their cockamamie examination of me. They would've had to have access to some actual sperm, and possibly a human ovum for matching purposes as well. I might also add that I'd yet to feel a period coming on, let alone have one, since the last in outer space many moons ago (which I hadn't bothered to mention to Grig during our briefing session, there having been no reason to). . . .

Well, that's a relief. Next case — what to do with them, the clowns. I went back inside, quietly, to see what was what. Maybe they'd wakened again, and finding no one around, run off like the Gingerbread Boy. No such luck. On they slept . . . like two unequal peas in a pod. . . .

Chow time, I reminded myself after tiptoeing back into the living room. It had grown dusky by then.

So this is what you'll do, I decreed, paused at the window on my way to the kitchen. You'll bunk here every night, get up early in the morning before anybody comes, tell Grig, or whoever inquires when the happy event is to be, that Rome wasn't built in a day, then after a reasonable period of time has elapsed complain that something's not right with those two in there, insist on their going back to the shop for adjustment . . . and keep on doing that till the Chief and his brood lose interest in the project, then work on collaring the Chemist alone, if nothing else to persuade him to help me get back above.

As for the clowns, they seem docile enough, but if they don't go along with what I say, there will be ways to deal with'em, heh-heh. . . .

Okeedoke, that's how it'll be — I'd polished off two tubes and settled down on the couch in the darkness, yet again to enjoy the play of violet light on the trees and ground outside. Ho-hum.

A new idea came . . . floating. You know, the two of them are there already, why not avail yourself of the opportunity. If you're so sure about not conceiving, where would be the harm?

I sat up — yeah, why not really. It's been so long since the last time, since Dave. C'mon, it'll work miracles for you, betcha.

But wouldn't it be like taking advantage, my better self argued. After all, they're innocents and probably wouldn't know the meaning of what they'd be doing. So? I argued back. For once in your life, so what? . . .

Awright, here goes — I was on my feet. Concentrate your efforts on the man — with the boy it would be going too far somehow.

I stepped to the door, heart pounding with the daring-ness of it, not from the hots, let me tell you — opened it, stepped in, and turned on the lights.

"Hi," said the kid, gave a wee hop to a sit.

The man blindly tore away the sheet. "I was having this dream," he sort of gasped. A crystal dot was on his belly . . . having dropped from his member, still ready for me.

Junior spotted it and hunched over for a better look — "Ugh."

Get rid of him, my letchy self warned. "Beat it," I said, having warmed a little to the work.

"Huh?" he shrilled. "What's the pitch?"

"No pitch, out!" I ordered, pointing.

"Fuck," he went under his breath — scrunch-scrunched to the end of the bed. . . .

Now — the brat was gone — I'll have to teach him, this one. I sat down beside him — he was snoozing again — put my hand on his chest — "Hello."

He smacked his lips pastily — "What's up?" — still with

his eyes closed.

I massaged his copious hairiness with the solid flesh beneath.

"Mm-mm," he moaned.

Now I'll just stretch out beside him and get him to lie on top of me, and then — I was actually feeling something too, the smallest flame, but the next moment it flickered out. I couldn't, just couldn't go through with it. Why? Because it wasn't me, that's all. . . .

Outside the kid was planted on the couch, leaned over with his elbow on a knee, chin, such as it was, in hand.

I came and stood over him — "Sorry I was so mean to you before." Had this yearning to smooth a lock of his hair that had strayed onto his forehead, wavy dark brown of course.

He sprang up, choked with rage — "You oughta be!" — took off at a run back in there — but promptly was in the doorway again. "HE's hogging the covers."

"Well" — I sighed, after all he's a child, they were both children —"hog'em back." . . .

Can't sleep, been thinking things over some more. You know, that's what they are & the least you can do. . . .

"I'm still up," the boy grouched, when I was before them once more. The man was three-sheets-to-the wind again, zizzing now.

"That's quite understandable," I responded right pleasantly. "Whether you know it or not, you've been sequestered here for a good long time."

The boy-eyes narrowed — "What's on yer mind?"

"Plenty," I said, "but right now I have a question for you — the TWO OF YOU!"

Hronk! the man honked — blinked.

I put it to them.

"Pee?" he pondered. His lids split apart — "Why yes, I believe I do!" "Me too!" squealed the lambkin.

They both were up, and off!

"Straight ahead!" I yelled after their string bean asses. A fresh thought struck — "Use the round bowl with the seat, NOT the one with the faucet!"

•

Morning of the first day — and the last, alas. Grig was here first thing, barging in without advance warning (as they all usually do in these nether regions). Lucky for me, I'd just gotten up from the couch & smoothed myself down.

He wanted to know what I'd named them, my new buddies. Oh man, did I have to think fast. Told him, no, guiltily, I hadn't done it yet — an understandable oversight in my eagerness to lay the groundwork, as I hoped he & his bosses would see. I vowed to make amends speedily.

New topic (an inspiration just arisen): I had it in mind to make a little spread for my mates, to keep (I twirled a finger there) cementing things — what were his sentiments? (Before you judge me to be utterly beastly for thinking of subjecting those two to X's home-grown vittles like that, be it known that I planned to partake of the risk myself just as soon as I knew that they, who were pseudo-human, could hack it.)

Oh, Grig was just ecstatic — except what about my special diet? I told him that was just till I got acclimated, I can eat anything now.

He took down a grocery list from me off the top of my head, beginning with a nice zoftig makhpeezoo (inevitably, yes?). The fixings were another matter — I had a worse time with them than with the carrots & celery down in Analytical. Anyway, he seemed to understand, at least he kept assuring me that he did with each description . . . till I got to tomatoes — after which, visibly perplexed, he said, Do my best. Oh, those "tomatoes."

"Awright, everyone, rise'n shine!" I bugled, breezing into the bedroom some little while later, after attending to a few necessities.

The man made a big stretch — "I have to pee again." "Ditto," chimed in the pipsqueak, with his wings out too.

"Fine, fine," I said, "but not just yet, I have some announcements first. I'm giving you both names, hope you like 'em." I indicated the man — "You're Meredith. And you" — jutted my chin at the boy—"you're Rooney."

The kid's nostrils flared — "You sure you don't wan' it the other way aroun'?"

I stared him down — "Positive. I'm Felice, by the by."

"Howdeedoo," warbled Meredith agreeably.

"Now hear this," I went on, "here's the program for the day — bath, chow, back to bed. And later I'm gonna cook you a beautiful meal."

Meredith became cutely starry-eyed — "You are?" "Man, I can hardly wait," said Rooney, equally ecstatic.

There, I cheered myself, it's just a matter of getting off on the right foot. And if things continue in this amicable fashion, tomorrow we'll have calisthenics, arts and crafts, and other activities as they suggest themselves.

[Ed. A "mad waterworks" scene followed here, which I thought that I would leave to the reader's capable imagination.] . . .

Neither is very adept when it comes to sucking from the food-tubes, Meredith especially. They're a little better at drinking from cups. . . .

At noon or thereabouts, while I was recovering from cleaning up etc., some purple-schleppers arrived, bearing this navy "fish" the size of a carp — so help me, with an emerald-green eye & silver whiskers — and a purple-and-white striped Santa-sack. . . .

"Heigh ho!" I sang out in the kitchen, after getting rid of those bearing types . . . practically pushing them out the door. Dragged the makhpeezoo from the counter into the sink, took up the knife.

"Maestro, some music to disembowel by if you please" — I opened my mouth, let it flow —

Ein Mäd-chen o-der Wei- ei- ei- eib-chen
Tum, tum tum, tha-da-da--da, tum!

That's from *The Magic Flute*, 'case you don't recognize it, Papageno the bird-catcher singing of his heart's desire, a sweet pretty little thing. . . .

So what's what in the fixing department, I wondered, when the corpse was sans the head, the single ball hanging down, and the guts, knife was rinsed. I widened the mouth of the Santa-sack, removed things from it by two's and three's:

— some semblance of onions, even the tomatoes, both very flat like Laleekh's jabbas, the latter much darker (bloodier) than ours.

— a collection of wooden condiment boxes the size of dice. When you scratch a side, a smelly powder trickles out of the other side — the one I settled for was a combination of "thyme" and "curry" with a dash of "peppermint." . . .

One-two-three, the head was in the stew pot covered with water and tiny-bubbling on the stove. And what, pray, are my guinea pigs up to? I trotted out and over for an inspection.

Meredith was snoring away as usual. But oh that Rooney — he'd made this remarkable discovery about himself. "I love you, Felice," he moaned, while rubbing the thing up and down.

Well, I guess the bedding'll have to be sorted out now, I sighed, after turning away. Eh, let's have a couchy lie-down till the stock is done. . . .

I've just taken the debris of the head (& eye) out, put the flesh in (with the "gizzard"), onion, tomatoes etc. Boil away, pot. Now for them again. . . .

I'll tell you that Rooney's really something . . . he's gone & transferred his affection to the other one . . . doing it to him from the back in spoon-fashion, while he slumbers on.

I thought of telling him that it's a good idea to obtain a person's permission first before doing that to him. But there's no harm in it, I suppose . . . as long as the other isn't hurting.

"Okay-ay!" I yodeled from inside the kitchen at long last. "Soup's on!"

"OH BOY!" my loved ones cried. There was a scrambling and a bumping, the two of them trying to squeeze through the bedroom door at the same time. They both came galloping toward me, Meredith loping with his longer legs, Rooney's pedaling a mile a minute — their members, soft now, jiggling.

"Take it easy, one at a time," I said with the ladle, as they reached the door to the patio.

Somehow it got open — they both plowed through at the
same time, dashed for the table, sat down at either end,
where I'd laid places.

"Here we are," I said, emerging in their wake with a
steaming platter of light purple fish-meat and a tureen of
rich maroonish sauce on a wooden tray. I set it down on the
long side between them, facing the window.

Meredith — whose skin in that superior light was pale
lime — scooped up his spoon. Rooney — with a peachy complexion—already had his clutched.

I reached over for the man's bowl, doled out to him —
he began shoveling. I served the kid — he too. "Watch out,
there are bones," I warned.

"Ooooh, you're right," Meredith affirmed, in falsetto —
drew out a truly fierce-looking one, an inch or more long.

A petite bird's nest of white needles like that began building beside each.

"Do you like it? Is it good?" I asked.

"Excellent," Meredith gave it as his judgment. "Sure is,"
Rooney cheeped.

"Do you know what this dish is called?"

Meredith's pretty brow furrowed — "It's on the tip of my
tongue." A single crease appeared in Rooney's forehead —
"Mine too."

"It's bouillabaisse. Say it after me, please."

"Bouill-a-baisse," they both dutifully repeated. . . .

"Howdya feel, wouldya like some more?" I asked after a
little — spoons and bowls licked clean.

"Thank you, I've had sufficient," said Meredith — swirled
his tongue over his lips. Rooney burped, wiped his smaller
mouth on the back of his hand.

There's something I missed, napkins. Mention it to Grig
the next time you see him, I made a mental note.

I reached over toward the man to begin tidying up — the
table rocked. "Oh dear — Merry, if I explain how to fix this,
would you, some time?"

"I certainly will," Meredith agreed resonantly.

"And you, Rooney" — I looked toward him — "would you

pitch in and lend assistance if he needs it?"

"On'y say the word," he seconded.

My fingers wove together over my chest — "Why what a sweet little family!" To myself I added: I do so hope everything agrees with them. And assuming that it will, I must remember to put some duds on the list for them, toothbrushes too. They'll have to get started on those gums right away or there'll be hell to pay. Likewise razors, for the older one anyway . . . some stubble on his handsome man's cheeks and chinlet. . . .

The bowls and stuff were piled on the tray — I was ready to go in. But just then Meredith squirmed uncomfortably. "Is anything the matter?" I asked.

He paid no attention — fixed his sights on the kid. "Did you — do something — to me — before — when I was sleeping?"

"Who me?" the Angel inquired lamely.

"Now, now," I interposed with my hands.

Meredith glowered — "Well, did you or didn't you?"

"Aw, bugger off," Rooney threw out — lighted to his feet and danced away.

"WHAT!" barked Merry — reared up, bounded after the kid, whirled him around, and let fly with his fist, catching Cheeky — pugh! — on his breastbone and causing him to recoil several yards.

"Please!" I pleaded, my hands at my breast again. "You'll hurt yourselves!"

"You bastard!" Merry shouted, a big neck vein standing out — charged toward Cheeky and bowled head-on into that one's mid-section. They both went down struggling to gain the mastery.

"Plea-ease!" I wailed, as they wrestled and rolled on the ground.

Rooney suddenly sat up and grabbed his small gut — "Oh wow!" "Me too!" Merry agreed, put his hand to his mouth. The one jumped up, then the other — they both made a frantic beeline for the inside.

"Hey," I hollered after them," don't forget, use the bowl

with the seat! PULL IT UP!"

Now what? I'd rushed after them. The bathroom door
was shut — sounds of wretching were resounding from in
there, *yuh-uhk, yuh-uhk.*

"Darn it all, the experiment's ruined," I muttered. "Meredith, Rooney, is everything okay?"

Blub-blub-blub, one or both of them answered.

A fine howdyado.

Ssst, went the front door. "Hope I'm not disturbing anything," Grig crooned.

Oh, great. "Well, actually — "

He trotted over, all eyes and ears.

There was nothing for it, the puking was plainly audible.
"Listen," I began — tried to give it to him calmly.

"Accident?" Grig echoed, dumbfounded. A patch of skin
by his left ear-button clouded over.

What else could one do? "See for yourself, it's nothing,
really." I tapped the bathroom door-button.

Meredith was lying face down on the floor with Rooney
sprawled on top of him — "Argh!" — "Uh-uh-uh!"

Froth, rich red froth, was everywhere — there was even a
dollop on the ceiling.

"Grig?" I turned to my friend. His face was blotched, just
like before with my self-inflicted wound in the pinky.

"Hey, Grig, it's not what you're thinking, honestly! It was
those — you know — those red veggies you sent me?"

Chapter Nine

Grig ran for the Second Vice. He's come & gone with some shkhurzas
& litters to bear my poor mates with their bellyaches away.

I really don't think I did anything that anyone else wouldn't have
in my position — but got a strong hunch from the way they all acted
(Grig excepted) that I'm gonna pay for this caper. The Second didn't so
much as look my way, & the fatsies weren't their usual chipper selves
either. . . .

a.m. A real up-and-down night last night. The feeling of doom
persists. Well, we'll see . . . sooner or later. . . .

mid-morning. It's continued foggy out; everything is still blan-
keted. What's going on? Is it programmed like that, to add spice to my
life, or did the individual responsible for the "sun" take off from work
today, or what? . . .

The door went *ssst* behind me. "Hi, lone one of one,"
Grig said teasingly.

Boy, was I ever glad to see him — I jumped up. And was
he alright, did he finally realize, or did someone explain to
him, that all that red stuff wasn't blood, but from the "tomatoes" he brought me? So it would seem — he was only slightly
jittery, that's all.

"C'mon and sit down," I urged — gave him my seat with
the view as of old. "I hope all that" — tilted my head toward
the bathroom — "didn't cause you any embarrassment."

He was afraid it had, a bit — suddenly put on that wistful look of his. He'd been demoted to a C again in his unit,
and his glakh-buddy the curator was, understandably, a little
miffed. As if that weren't bad enough, Yoo-hoo, his shkhurza-
buddy, had taken to spreading naughty stories about him
behind his back.

What could one do but offer profuse apologies.

That's alright, he assured. One thing was accomplished at least — he was not just a name and a stripe(?) anymore, in A-Tube or for that matter in the whole of B&G-A, including the lower reaches.

And my poor dear buds, what had happened to them?

Oh, I was not to worry on that score either — they were resting comfortably in the infirmary . . . their fate yet to be decided.

Good, they're not scheduled to return apparently. . . .

There was a longish pause. I began to realize that there was another reason for Grig's being there besides his concern for me — an official reason — and he didn't quite know how to begin.

"Do you have some instructions for me?" I inquired at length.

He seemed relieved — I was making it very easy for him. ✋Check, I was to report at once with all my gear to something called the Center for Translation.

"Translation?" I questioned aloud. "What kind of translating do they do there, Grig?" One form that I could think of was no laughing matter.

"You'll see," my friend said lightly, then noting me a little pale perhaps, added there was no need to be uneasy, not right away anyway, and if I played my "cards" right, maybe never.

More bad news: I would have to find my way to the Center by myself, as he was under strict orders to proceed directly to his lab. Worse yet, I would have to take an elevator to get there.

"But Grig — " I told him of my mad ride in 721, and there was also my ineptness in the buggy, which he himself had been a witness to.

He considered, then supposed it'd be alright if I used the stairs. "Just so long as you bear in mind that you'll come out a little differently.". . .

I walked with him to the door, as I had so many times before. "What do you say, ya think we'll meet again?" I asked when we were there.

💥Haven't the foggiest, but I'll certainly try to stay in touch, he answered.

I looked once more at his brown self — those dark eyes with their sadness and laughter . . . the belly button of a nose . . . half-moon mouth. "Guess we should say goodbye then, in case."

💥Good idea.

2 p.m. Am resting now before pulling out. The pack's crammed to capacity with tubes & canteen's filled to the brim. Seems like old times, haha. I also had me one extra hearty feed from the tubes left over in the crate, & took the liberty of stuffing two rolls of toilet paper in the pot.

For the record: I am not altogether unhappy 'bout leaving this place. Something was missing in it . . . something besides murals on the walls to relieve the monotony of the whiteness . . . something like dust, for instance . . . and maybe Flora wiping with a rag & shaking out the window while giving forth with one of her favorite arias & lieder the way she used to . . . or Dave sounding off even with that obnoxious song, "Got along withoutcha before I metcha," & doing a soft-shoe to it. . . .

Okay, ready. The stairs are the second door after the Natural History museum/pool elevator. I am to talk to no one on the way, but chances are there won't be anyone around anyway — B&G-A's really got its teeth into something new now. The Center is on the third floor. 'Case I lose count, I'm to keep a sharp lookout for a teeny-weeny dark-grey mark like a much-curlicued "y," which Grig drew for me, enlarged, on his "oval." I'll find it on the side of the banister [Ed. which turned out to be the same black pipe as on the stairways of District 721 in Shkhurzaland]. . . .

"As I live and breathe," I sort of gasped with surprise, on reaching the door and going in.

It was another museum, an anthropological-sociological one. Featured were quarter-sized glakhs, eekhals, and shkhurzas engaged in various activities, and the displays were organized according to country apparently, those in the area that I was in being given over to typical doings in Glakhland.

They're animated too, I established, in front of one. On

the point of cutting open an eel-like creature on a table, a glakh had begun pointing an admonishing finger at a tech, who had promptly fallen to shivering in his boots, while a bunch of schleppers standing by started buzzing. . . .

"Hot dog!" I let out a few rows over, in the Shkhurzaland section it would seem.

Before me in a case was a Supreme Council meeting, replete with big burly shkhurzas sitting round three sides of a table, a reedy brown archivist presiding, and a shorter green conserver touching the side of a tv set.

Boy, here's a chance for Felice to get revenge for all the insults and indignities inflicted upon her by those miserable ones. It was just a matter of waiting for the right moment to jump away, when all twenty purple mouths were open and yapping at the same time. . . .

"Is — is anyone — there?" a quavering voice called, from somewhere to the right in the dark of that room.

Jeezy-beezy, thought I'd jump out of my skin I was so startled — then realized. "Yes," I called back, "yes, it is I, the Shkhibee Khamor. Am I supposed to see you?"

"Seems so" — the voice in the dark was more confident — "I'm the head of this place. Where are you?"

I told him — and that's the end of the fun, confided to myself.

"Why whatever are you doing there?" He said to go forward three cases, to the left two etc. "Is that it?" he asked himself under his breath, meaning the right way.

Fancy that, I marveled, a green one with wandering wits too here in Glakhland. . . .

On my way, I passed through a portion of what could only be Eekhalland — the browns the dominant physical type. Interesting: they must be the ones Laleekh took me for at first — everyone's wearing "fluffy leg-coverings," i.e., long pants! . . .

"Here I am," I said, trudging up a few minutes later to the green standing in a doorway.

There was something peculiar about him, I felt at once. That is, while well-built enough, he was nowhere near as tall and fleshed out as the Chief and the other heads, yet he seemed to be of the same generation.

"This way," he directed, after getting his fill of me as well — turned on his heel.

A long narrow room was there, lined on either side by dark-wooden see-through cabinets, which were chock-full of dwarfed green legs, brown pelvises, purple feet, and so on.

He proceeded to a desk at the far end, on which stood, of all things — I recognized it from halfway down — a midget me! . . .

"Like it?" he asked, with obvious pride, from behind the desk, where he'd gone to sit down.

I was studying it closely on a stool before him, the pack and pot gratefully unloaded on the floor. Striking it certainly was — he (assuming that it was his handiwork) had managed to capture every detail down to the to the cream-colored T-shirt, blotchy jeans, and mouldy-grey sneakers. But the look on the face was something else — the eyes overly eager and mouth vacantly smiling, like one of those dopily happy Ancient Greek statues of the Archaic Period. ✺It has its points, I hedged.

He pulled open a drawer back there — "Now where is it?" — began rummaging.

"Are you going to include my buddies in the case?" I asked — meaning the poverinos Meredith and Rooney.

"Well, yes, I thought I might" — he was turning things over in another drawer — "Where? It's got to be here — or somewhere."

I studied the features more carefully — hm, is my nose really that curvy — applied my index finger to my schnozz's bridge, slid it down to the tip and back again. "Oh brother, now you've done it," I muttered.

The little Me's right hand was in action in the same way . . . vacantly grinning as before, but with the addition of a wrinkled brooding brow on the order of a Middle Kingdom pharaoh.

The ransacking eyes shifted my way — strain appeared on the face. *Mmf*— the green one reached over and snatched up the mini-Felice by the waist, yanked open the cabinet door beside him and shoved it in onto an empty shelf with its face to the wall.

❦ Sorry, I signaled him. The small Felice-arm was still pumping. "I trust it isn't anything — permanent.". . .

"There!" the doll-maker suddenly cried — a rectangular gadget in a green frame similar to Grig's "oval" emerged. "Let's begin."

"Sure thing," I said right off, hoping to win my way back into his good graces.

He began reading sort of — "I suppose — you're wondering — why you're here" — scuffed his feet as if following some stage direction . . . looked.

❦ More or less, I answered, still aiming to please.

He went on — "The Chief's exceedingly displeased with you . . . mm, mm, mm . . . wanted to render you a kindness, and what did you do but repay it with the grossest ingratitude." He simply looked this time.

Certainly nothing lost in translation there — I strove for blankness (in imitation of the expression of the Third Assistant's glakh-brother when I recognized him as the Green Baboon, if you can remember back that far).

"'Fact," this glakh continued, so distressed was the Chief that he desired to have as little to do with me henceforth as possible. "That's why you're here," he added, interpolating. "The Chief asked me to render him a favor, and I said I would gladly" — though it was to be clearly understood that he didn't have to, a center being considered on a par with a sector in many circles.

❦ Check, I smartly made him.

"As for you" — he resumed reading — opinion favored eliminating me, but a final decision respecting this had to await one of two things happening. First, the emergence of those responsible — His left cheek filled — "And they will, they always do, sooner or later!"

And the other thing?

The next assembly of the sector Chiefs, before which I'd be paraded, so that they could witness for themselves —

"All the sector Chiefs?" I managed to wedge in (to get as

complete a picture as possible).

"No, just those participating in Gleego."

Haha — my ears tingled. But first things first — when was the assembly to be?

As soon as this phase of the operation was over, in as many ?'s as it required. . . .

Now to the other matter — God helps those etc. as we say. I tried putting on a dumb shkhurza-puss—"Uh, I'm a trifle fuzzy 'bout that Gleego?" — the truth, though by now, like you, I had my suspicions. "What is it exackly?"

"What?" — he seemed genuinely taken aback. "I thought everybody knew" — beckoned for me to come round to his side of the desk, diddled on the edges of his "rectangle" — "There, Gleego."

So-ho, I pronounced internally. Yet one more mystery unraveled.

On the screen were some of the well-rounded, pristinely white domes of the first village above.

"Do you know why it's named Gleego?" he quizzed.

I kept on playing the shkhurza. ✋No-o, tell me.

He diddled again.

That image vanished — a new one faded in, offering a panoramic vista of almost all the domes in the village, as if via another scanner higher up in a treetop or something. The whole place is arranged in a shallow (egg-like) oval with the stream house a little off center, where a yolk might be.

Yolk, haha.

"Of course, it's not much now," this diddling source of priceless information confided. But one day, one fine day, it would be different. The entire surface up there would be covered with such villages, to form a single all-encompassing one stretching from coast to coast. "That is, as long as those who have agreed to participate continue to cooperate" — meaning contribute gleegos of their dominant type presumably.

His green fingers twitched yet once more — he seemed positively in ecstasy over his adroitness.

A film clip began rolling on the screen — featuring a trio

dining together in that way of theirs, flicking bits from their bowls at one another . . . shlupping it up with yellow, red, and white tongues.

"What superb physical specimens they are," my informant admired.

And that they were, as how could they not be. But now with my more experienced eye I saw that if this threesome was the norm, Gleego's residents were not quite as identical as I'd taken them to be at first — the green slightly more robust, purple tending to the portly side, and brown a trifle thinner.

Yurgh, this glakh sighed. "And how well they get on together, just as it was in the beginning."

I perked up — "Oh, have you done some excavating?"

He waved the idea away. Why bother, it was self-evident. . . .

The show was over (yet another show) — I was back in my seat. Let's see if we can really round things out, I proposed to myself. "Some Eekhallanders are involved in the project too, I assume."

Naturally, as how could they not be, gee gee. He became serious once more — "Funny you should mention it." That's what the Chief and A-Exec had decided to do with me in the meanwhile before determining my fate, I was to go and stay there . . . among my own kind.

Who? What?

"Which reminds me," he continued, oblivious — thub-thubbed on the "rectangle," peered closely as if at a schedule, rose. "You'll have to be off at once, they're holding the Shuttle for you.". . .

We started together, me with my stuff, for the door. Halfway down, he stopped, prompting me to — a brown eekhal head stared at us eyelessly from a cabinet.

"I don't mind telling you I had considerable input into that decision," this glakh-curator took it up. Indeed, if the truth be known, he saw the flaw in everyone's reasoning with respect to my identity instantly, as soon as he set eyes on me. "Yes" — his finger rose, thumped his temple — "I knew at once they all had their tails in the wrong pond." [Ed. An expression not as innocuous as it might seem, having "disgusting sexual implications," the author informed me during our review of this chapter.]

He pointed to my left arm — "Have you ever noticed those brown spots?" — meaning my beauty marks. Well, as far as he was concerned, they were a dead giveaway, arguing persuasively for something's having gone amiss in the final stages of my creation. "A kind of" — he sifted the air for the right words — "bleaching out took place." In other words, I was not really shkhurzaoid but rather eekhaloid, even in spite of the two shkhurza-like protuberances on my chest, which were all wrong anyway.

Man, thorny stuff. . . .

We went on to the door — he was about to turn away and leave me there.

"Hey, you haven't told me where the Shuttle is or anything," I reminded him.

Ah yes, all one had to do was go straight down, bearing right at the fork, to G-Tube.

I balked.

Oh, not to worry, the engineers would leave me alone now, they were just after a piece of the action before. . . .

"Goodness, I almost forgot!" he yelled, after I'd taken a few steps. A-Exec had strongly recommended that I not burden anybody there in Eekhalland with the story of my origin, as all of them, especially the eekhals, were very easily upset, and relations with them were as delicate as those with the shkhurzas of Shkhurzaland difficult.

I trotted back to him — "So who or what should I say I am?"

"Don't say anything," he lectured. An explanation had already been given — to wit, that I was a tech here whose glakh- and shkhurza-buddies had recently suffered a fatal accident, from which I myself had barely escaped. The clinic had prescribed a little change of scene for the nonce. . . .

I got going once more, but now suddenly an explanation surfaced regarding the peculiarity I'd noticed before — this green's relatively small size and obvious maturity. Of course, it has to be, I convinced myself — he's a foreigner here in Glakhland, a glakh-refugee from Shkhurzaland. Then a dim memory came of a fierce argument that had raged at the Supreme Council table over such an individual — and then it really dawned. "Say, aren't you the specialist in behavior who was deported from District 721?"

Bull's eye — but oh what I'd said. Both his cheeks puffed out, and around us it got putrid too. "I was not — WAS NOT deported!" he shouted. "I DEFECTED!" — an absolute tirade poured out of him, all about Shkhurzaland-Glakhland politics.

Cripes, if this therapist or whatever he is keeps this up, I'm liable to miss my train. But just as I was about to try and head him off, another memory flashed — of that extra-large purple at the sector door, the In-between. Hadn't he said that his glakh-buddy was some kind of bigshot in B&G-A? The exact wording he used was "central figure." "Hey," I interrupted — asked him if it were so, if he and the shkhur-za (that good-for-nothing who couldn't even do guard duty properly) made a pair.

This one's body went slack. "You saw him then," he sort of murmured.

✋ Right, right.

He became like dreamy: "Isn't he — just — something!"

Leave it to me — now the devil got into me. "You *are* married to an eekhal too, no?"

Dunder-and-blitzen, he was beside himself again. What did I take him for, some kind of pervert — like in — in Eek-halland!

Get that, will you — but we've heard that song before, haven't we? Their gleegos don't hatch together. I offered him tit for tat: "It must have made for a very sticky situation back home in 721 when you skedaddled like that." Hadn't he left behind another family?

"That was for them to work out," he retorted smolderingly.

And how had he hooked up with this family here, in the

same way I'd lost mine — that is, supposedly lost them?

His green shrinkeroo's finger playfully wagged at me — "You know, you're very nosey [*sic*], but for your information — "He grew ooky again: "After all, things have a way of happening . . . now and then." A plump one unthinkingly touches a piece of equipment in some critical place . . . a technical type after causing a stir with some picayune breakthrough on his own, becomes all filled up with his self-importance and launches into something grandiose he can scarcely understand. . . .

I had one shot left — "And do they send you messages, your old family?"

Did that set him off. "No, no, no! There are NO messages! NONE, do you hear!". . .

The meany — when I passed by the Eekhalland section of his museum again, he switched off all the lights with a glick-glick-glick.

●

Back down on the road, everything was as deserted as before, & quiet — 'cept for dismantling sounds coming from inside my former digs. I passed by without looking . . . making a single stop at the toilets somewhat further along, & opting for the green-brown room as befitted my "reassigned" status. . . .

The situation below on B- and C- was much of a muchness with A-Tube. Then after I don't know how many windings, there was a platform reminiscent of a subway station, spanking clean like in Moscow or somewhere, and sitting there, the thing that I was supposed to go on, a silvery cylinder six or so blocks long. Achtung: the tracks are on It, toward the bottom on either side, rather than on the ground — they fit into grooves in the walls down there. How it actually runs, don't ask. It ran.

Not a soul was around except for two shkhurzas on the platform's far end, having themselves a talk-fest.

"I'm bound for Eekhalland, is this the Shuttle?" Felice called.

They continued with their conversation as if they hadn't heard.

"Hey?" Felice called again, repeated.

✋Check, check, they poked, still chattering away.

She hurried up to them, noting that they weren't quite as pulletish as the schleppers above on A-, B-, and C-Tubes — "Have you any idea how I get on?" There wasn't even a hint of a door the whole length of the cylinder.

The purple on the left had just finished what he was saying — something about G-Tube's head being compelled to resign or capitulate by a "delayed count" because of a "climbing drop." He turned to her — "'Pends on which institute yer signed up fer."

Institute? Signed up? Sounds like they're into education there in Eekhalland, Felice concluded. "Well, how — ?"

Meef! someone peeped through his nosehole somewhere behind her. "Over here!" the peeper sang out. Felice turned about — an almost well-fed tech was at an opening maybe forty feet back. . . .

"C'mon, everyone's fuming," he urged, as she came up. There was a small pile of brown fabric balanced on his palm — "You're to wear these from now on." He slapped the goods onto the pot lid, which Felice was holding at her chest.

She swept past him into a small but tidy compartment, made straight for a sort of berth, and dumped everything on it — plucked up a cape from the stuff. Brown was her color, it had always looked good on her with her sallow complexion and pink cheeks. Setting that piece aside, she shook out a pair of harem pants — "Is it okay to leave my white garments on underneath?" asked over her shoulder.

"Suit yourself," the official one answered from without.

She tested the baggy pants up at the waist, some semblance of an elastic band there. It'll be a perfect fit, she judged — whisked them round to the rear. "Uh oh" — there was a slit on that side — large enough to make for an insidious draft in the small of the back. "Say, dya suppose anyone'd mind if I pinned it together?" — sewing not being one of her fortes.

Pssst went something. She spun to look — the doorway was gone, she was shut in.

"Hang on!" the tech hollered from the other side. *Roosh!* whooshed the train with her in it. "BYE-BYE!" yelled the yackers as she flew by.

Don't do anything but eat, sleep, and limber up . . . roll with the punches. Above all, don't allow yourself to get into a bad mood. Everything'll turn out alright, you'll see. (Famous last words of Flora for tight spots . . . Dave too, come to think of it.) . . .

I just find it awful being cooped up like this, unable to look out and enjoy the view, if there is one.

They keep it well-ventilated in here, though; there's plenty of fresh air circulating. . . .

•

Lolling on the cot after so many "days," Felice was suddenly alert. That's it, we're here — the train was not rushing anymore.

Now we'll see what's to be seen — she quickly donned her new outfit and gathered up the rest of the stuff, went to the "door." Just don't lose sight of what Grig said — be what they all at B&G-A want you to be, remembering that the eekhals are in charge here, difficult though that is to imagine. And above all, follow the script — a tragic accident, death of loved ones, injury. . . .

The Shuttle whispered to a halt . . . ten seconds passed . . . the door slid open.

A tall, willowy glakh in green harem pants and a cape was there on a brown platform. "Welcome to INST-360, I'm the Senior Communications Officer," he said — had a long, thin yellow-framed screen hanging down his side like a broad sword.

"Thank you," Felice responded, conscious of his having taken her in minutely, including the pack, which she'd struggled to put on over the cape, and pants, underlined by the sneakers with white socks. His gaze had finally come to rest on her hair, wild as can be in spite of strenuous efforts now and then during the trip. "It's to cover — " she explained, "you know, the flames."

"I understand," he responded, in the same soft tone.

There was a lot of commotion on the platform — groups of young greens who'd apparently arrived on the same train moving leftward behind him, young browns coming from the right as if to board.

The SCO proposed that they wait there a few moments to let everyone get where they were going. Later, after word had been passed along, she could feel free to circulate wherever she wanted without the burden of undue attention being paid to her.

Felice cradled the pot in the crook of her right arm — ✋Grateful. "Very considerate of you."

"So," the SCO began when it was all clear, "on behalf of the administration and staff, I'd like to offer you our heartiest greetings." The deans and other officials would have been there to welcome her themselves, had it not been for a new semester about to get under way.

✋Greet'em back for me, Felice answered with aplomb, "and tell them that it's quite alright, I understand."

The SCO nodded . . . slowly . . . deliberately. There'd be a little ceremony in her suite later, he added.

Hah, suite. Felice felt like balancing the pot on a finger and twirling it. ✋Splendid, she flourished, and stepped out to join him.

They began walking toward a ramp some hundred feet ahead, which led up to an enclosed bridge with windows spanning the roadbed.

Now there's a laugh — strung beneath the bridge was a huge coffee-colored banner with three fire-engine red individuals silhouetted on it, a well-filled out type holding a pint-sized one by the hand on either side. Real rah-rah goings on here, was Felice's conclusion.

"Did you have a pleasant journey?" the SCO inquired.

✋Most, she managed, shifting the pot again.

"By the by, I don't mean to be critical of your Personnel Division. They're usually more efficient than one could possibly wish them to be" — but in this instance there appeared to have been a slight foul-up, they'd neglected to forward her name with the other materials. What was it?

"Rothman," she answered unthinkingly — then bit her lip. *But what else could I have done? Certainly couldn't have given him Shkhibee Khamor.*

"Roz-mam," he repeated. His fingers traveled down to his stick-screen, keyed it in.

They were going up the ramp now . . . plod . . . plod . . . plod. Near the top he wondered if he might broach a personal matter.

✋ By all means, she waved.

He lost no time — it seems that exchange programs with Glakhland notwithstanding, the glakhs there in Eekhalland were frightfully deficient in the sciences, and when they in INST 360 heard of her impending visit, they began entertaining hopes that she could be prevailed upon to shed a little light among them. The subject didn't matter, just so long as —

"I'm sorry to have to disappoint you," Felice interrupted. "Unhappily, we're not all so privileged in Glakhland."

No? Not? He consulted his stick, raising it up by the tip — "Mm." What was her area of expertise then?

"Well — dance." *Now whatever did you do that for,* her sensible self whined. *Why you've never so much as walked a graceful step in your life, let alone anything else* — this despite her mother Flora's having scrimped and saved to provide her with ballet, tap, and ballroom lessons as a child.

"Dance?"

"Yes, I — u-uh" — Felice's ole devil pinched her—"combine it with a little brushwork." *Oh man,* Sensible groaned, *that's guaranteed to return and haunt you.*

"Dance-painting," the SCO repeated dully, his fingers as lusterlessly recording. *Everybody'd be overjoyed.*

Now, now, no reason to be upset, she tried to calm herself. *All you have to do is come up with a mode of demonstra-*

tion and have it in readiness 'case someone gets curious and wants to know more. . . .

They'd just crossed over the covered bridge and entered a tan-walled hall with oaken doors intermittently on either side — no one was about. Some two hundred yards down, they got on an elevator, rode up a floor, and walked out into a nearly identical hall, down which they headed. . . .

Okay, here it is, Sensible announced. You'll need a pink body stocking, some kegs of bright-colored paint, and a stage with a pure white backdrop. You'll come drifting on in the stocking — tra-la . . . dip hands and elbows each in orange, blue, yellow, and green . . . someone else, some kindly soul, will schmear your back with red, using a giant Q-tip — hee-haha . . . and then you'll begin writhing and churning — da-dee-da . . . glancing off the canvas with this and that — hoop -de-la . . . until eventually — voilà! . . .

Felice and her escort in the meanwhile had reached the end of that hall. "It's just a little further," he informed, leading her through a red-looper.

Before them was a brown staircase up — with more of that black pipe for banisters [Ed. which, since it was ubiquitous, quite possibly could have doubled as a water main, my colleague in Anthropology gave it as his opinion].

They went around to the side, a gilt metal door there — the SCO tapped a minuscule beige beetle-like button on the left.

Toom! the door boomed, flying up — on utter darkness.

"Make yourself at home," the tall, thin green said, not bothering with the lights. He'd be back before long with the committee — went out the way he and she had come in.

I don't know why you didn't try and make friends with him, Felice scolded herself, what's wrong with you. Oh well, it'll sort itself out . . . always does.

Now — she got on her knees, set down the pot, heaved off the pack beside it — let's not do anything sudden-like. Dug out the flash, hopped up, flicked it on.

There was indeed a room inside, roughly comparable in

size to her elevator and hospital rooms in Shkhurzaland and Glakhland.

She bowed in, and felt along the wall on the right . . . found only smoothness. Shifted the flash to the other hand, and tried to the left. Aha — there were three more of those beetle buttons, one below the other.

Let's start with the bottom one — she pushed. Eureka — three of the four walls brightened, maybe to twenty watts total, the one wall that remained dark being full of cupboards from ceiling to floor. Her eye took everything in at a glance. There was:

— a light-wooden table with something resembling a piano stool before it, parallel with the wall opposite the door and running its full length. On the table stood what looked to be two wooden crates.

— a medium-sized bed with a dustruffle, jutting out at three o'clock.

— an open door leading to a second room, at seven.

— a round viewer with a panel on a hip-high wooden stand, at five.

First things first as always, Felice gurgled. Slid her foot forward slightly, pit-patted — the floor seemed solid. Tried in another place — was the same. Stepped in with both feet, jump-jumped — fine.

Now for the walls. She went here and there to the right with her nails — tickled out all *dicks*, hence it was or seemed to consist exclusively of that garara.

And next door? There was indeed another room, similarly appointed but smaller, with a twin bed and no viewer.

"I just love moving into a new place, don't you?" Felice warbled to no one in particular — went and gathered up the gear outside, came and set it all down on the desk. "Ah" — those two objects on it were crates, and there was no question about what they contained. A large hairy "*y*" composed of jots of the same was starkly visible on each.

"My friend, dear Grig," she murmured, paused there with an arm on one of them. . . .

Water's next. Felice tripped over to the foot of the bed,

tipped up the dustruffle with her foot, bent and applied her hand to the spigot's lever. Water came out in a trickle, but it was clear — which is quite a technical accomplishment considering that glakh's are not the machers in this land.

Now for the two other beetle bumps by the door there. Felice sort of floated over to them, touched the middle one. Nothing happened. She touched it again. There was still nothing. "What's the use of having mechanical things like this if they don't work," she grouched — pressed hard, took her finger away, pressed again and again, four times in all. Suddenly the door dropped — *doom!* — shot up — *toom!*

It would seem to operate according to a code then. She pushed three times — bum-bum-bum. Sure enough — *doom!* the door fell.

Yes, one is for up, three for down. Now what does the top button have to offer? Felice tapped once, twice, five-, six-, seven-, nine-, and four-times — with no result whatsoever. So either this one's really shorted out or it's a placebo for the sake of symmetry, she reasoned.

Well, let's try it one more time with three shots, simply because it doesn't figure, being the signal to the middle button for the lights. She hit it — bum-bum-bum again. Something made her look round — "Glory be!"

The whole wall above the desk was ablaze — with a televised picture in true-color of the first village's pond, Gleego's watering hole. . . .

Three's it then, a logic beyond logic. One must definitely not sell these Eekhallanders short when it comes to such matters. . . .

All the village residents were basking there on the ledges or skimming the water . . . it was getting on toward evening . . . they'd all be fixing to go home soon. . . .

Her throat unstuck itself —

Verde, que te quiero, verde

Yes, green, how much I love you, green, Lorca-green. Felice

sighed — boy, I sure wish I was up there again.

●

TOOM!

This ox-like eekhal with a big belly was standing in the doorway — "Colleague, Colleague!" he greeted.

Me? Does he mean me, I wondered, facing him across the room from the desk, where I'd been examining the "view" from closer range after lugging all the gear in. I guess so, who else is there?

"Welcome, welcome!" he heartied — began kneeing my way.

A dozen or so other husky browns crowded in behind him, followed by the SCO, his thin greenness.

"How truly splendid of you to choose our humble INST-360 to make your convalescence in," crooned the mucka-muck, still advancing.

"What can I say, it's splendid of you to receive me," I rejoined.

At the foot of the bed his sniffer quivered — he pulled up short. The whole company stopped dead in their tracks too.

"Think" — his gullet contracted — "nothing of it. I am one of your deans, by the by."

"Pleased to meet you," I rejoined. Man, talk about ancient history — "How many deans do I have, exactly?"

"Gee, gee, gee!" he burst out. "Very funny."

"Gee," everyone else echoed.

What next, I tried to anticipate — tried but failed.

A solemn young one holding what appeared to be a small wooden cage by a leatherish thong squeezed through the crush.

"Ah yes," the Dean reminded himself, "I'm letting you have my pet lekhee to stay with you while you're here." [lɛ̆·χ'i — "a snake-like creature." We have already encountered it in Laleekh's tongue as *regee*.] "They're goo-ood company, he'll make a fi-ine companion for you."

What, a snake in my room? I was getting fidgety already.

The bearer came up to within an arm's length of me and thrust the cage toward me. I reached out to grasp the loop. He quickly let go, so his hand wouldn't touch mine.

"Well — I can't thank you enough," I said — bent over to look between the little bars. On a mossy clod, betwixt a stone grotto and a sand pile, was a foot-long brown creature about an inch in diameter. "But is't alright?" — it was lying rather stiffly on its back, with its mouth gaping.

The Dean bustled over, and stooped to look too. "Oh yes, he's just tir-red, that's all." They'd all been up very late last night, he explained, someone going on leave — "You know, that sort of thing."

Deany retreated to the foot of the bed — I deposited the cage on the desk with everything else.

"So," he said, "once more let me wish you our very best." Everyone present joined him, he was certain, in earnestly hoping that my stay with them would be both restful and restorative.

A dozen or so brown fingers stabbed the air.

I made a real effort to lower chin to shoulder — "How can I ever — " A vertebra cracked in my neck.

Mine host pretended not to hear — "One final word." If there was any way in which they could be of assistance to further my labors in — in — ? The SCO's green lips whispered something close by. The Dean's schnozz-hole contracted again. "FASC-inating," he gushed — finished 'bout my not hesitating to call on them.

There, didn't I tell you that Dance-Painting specialty of yours was going to make trouble for you, my better self crowed, as he took off, followed by the rest of the crowd. And that's just the beginning, betcha. . . .

Only the cage-bearing kid remained. "Here's the story," he said — dangled a small weighty pouch toward me by the strings, again careful to avoid any contact with me. "The fella in there gets one of these per day, no more" — double-pedaled to catch up with everyone.

I undid the pouch — was full of "snails."

Well, enough excitement for one day, I told myself, really sagging. Outa shape, outa shape, my mind beat a rhythm — unless of course it's a period coming on . . . at last. I got out the flash, headed over to the door, doused the lights, leaving on the tv.

It was velvety night up there at Gleego Pond . . . two bluish moon-ripples wavered.

I staggered back, pulling off the cape as I did so. Sat wearily down on the edge of the bed, unhooked the bra from underneath the T-shirt, and peeled the pants off — sank back and kicked everything away.

No sound from the cage over there — the creature must really be knocked out. Good. Hope it doesn't give me any trouble.

I laid the flash on the floor beside me. My eyes closed themselves. Guess they'll be showing me around tomorrow, things like that. . . .

Something's changed, I sensed quite some time later . . . the moon-reflections up above were a brilliant jewel-like blue in the engulfing darkness.

Maybe it's him on the desk, I speculated. My heart gave a knock — I hope the cage is fastened securely, it didn't manage to creep out somehow. I raised my head, peered — "Is that you, Lekhee?"

Now don't be lazy, go see what's doing there. I grabbed the flash, pushed myself up and away, and bumbled over — shined. "So it is."

He was right-side up now, with his chinlet perched atop a neat pile of coils. Twin pinhead-eyes sparkled at me . . . there was a splash of red-hot freckles on his forehead.

"Well, now," I chirped. Yuk, went to myself.

His jaws fluttered — *click-click.*

Gads, teeth, it's got teeth! "Do you want your chow, is that it?" I cooed — picked up the pouch, shook it.

Click-click.

So — "Just a sec." I took out a snail — "Here goes." Lifted the little door's latch, opened it the slightest smidge, tossed, banged the door shut, and re-latched.

Hoom-m-m-m, the lekhee hummed — began slithering to-ward it, his prize.

I gave a wave — "Have a ball." Headed back to bed-a-bye.

Ke-rack! came from behind me, his clickers cracking the snail shell open.

I hope and trust he knows what he's doing, I worried, resting back once more. A fine howdyadoo if I'm supposed to do that for him and he's gone and chipped something.

Leck-leck, my ears picked up, like a tongue licking.

Well, I guess it's alright, I tried to assure myself. As soon as he's done with his slurping, it'll be back to sweet dreams for you.

Krunch! his clickers went, obviously on the shell. *Chit-chit-chit,* they pulverized.

What! Is he foolin' around or what? I got to my hinds with the flash again and hurried back.

A piece of shell was showing between its lips, one of many strewn on the moss and sand.

"Are you supposed to be doing that, Lekhee?" I asked tenderly. All I need is for him to get sick on me or choke or something, worried now.

The chops came together — *Krunch!* Vibrated — *Chit-chit-chit.* The gullet gulped — Glup.

Well, he certainly seems to be handling it okay. To bed, to bed.

Krunch! sounded from over there, another sliver of shell about to be demolished.

I waited patiently.

Krunch! he went again.

"Darn," I grumbled, if he does all of them, it'll take all night.

Chit-chit-chit . . . glup.

Look, enough is enough, I made it clear to myself. Stick him in the other room and shut the door, that's what you should do. I sprang up and lunged for the cage.

"Yoh-oh-oh-oh!" the little mouth cried.

I winced — someone might hear and think who knows

what, come running! "Okay, okay," I soothed — put the cage down again, left him there.

"Dratted thing," I muttered, back in bed.

Krunch! Chit-chit-chit . . . glup.

I stared up at the ceiling, marking time. . . .

"Finally," I sighed, with the morning coming on . . . everything up there at the pond faded to dappled grey, with two faint blue footprints in it.

Now, quickly, to sleep. The pet to be re-negotiated first thing.

●

COLLEAGUE ROZMAM! COLLEAGUE ROZMAM! It was the SCO's voice, coming from somewhere to the left, the round viewer with the panel probably.

"Mm?" murmured Felice, still very much out of it. Her eyelids parted — upstairs the "sun" was high, with Gleego's residents out in full force again. . . .

The SCO's voice came once again, with urgency — **COL-LEAGUE, WOULD YOU PLEASE RESPOND?**

Felice rolled round. Sure enough, that one was staring back from the viewer's screen, trimly green. She dove for the panel, pressed here and there — "Hello, hello, here I am."

His face became muddy yellow in places (as Grig's had turned mottled brown before at the sight of blood or what he'd taken for it). **WOULD YOU KINDLY NOT DO THAT.**

Felice's hand skipped away — ☙ Sorry. She regarded him quizzically — "But — can you hear me without my touching anything?"

☙ No problem. **WE DO HAVE SOME AMENITIES, YOU KNOW.**

Oh swell, Felice thought, now you've gone and gotten him riled again. She changed the subject — what was up for today?

He evinced astonishment. **BUT HAVEN'T YOU CON-SULTED YOUR SCHEDULE YET? IT'S LATE!**

"Well — no. I didn't know I had one. Where is it?" she asked — spun round, and round, in the vain hope of spotting it somewhere.

The SCO became all impatience. **ON — THE — DESK.**

Okay, no need to shout, she fussed — scooted over, her boobs bobbing . . . bypassing the cape, bra, and pants on the floor. Began shoving things aside, noting that the pet was on its back once more with mouth open, still breathing presumably. "They could warn a person, a guest, a stranger," she grumbled, still frantic to find it.

"Ah" — it was under the front right corner of one of the crates, a display the size of a postage stamp, with a gossamer grid and dots like grains of fine sand in some of the boxes.

Felice scooted back — "Listen, I'm going to have to ask you to help me out." What with the explosion and smoke, her eyes, you know —

His features relaxed into a kind of pity. He read to her from a prompter — first hour (which was now), swim; second, meeting of the senior faculty of Performing Arts.

How did she get to them?

They were both in the next hall — he gave her the directions, assured he'd guide her.

Never fear — she was there already.

HURRY, PLEASE, the SCO urged from somewhere overhead, as Felice stepped through to the hall moments later.

A few paces down, she stopped at two doors next to one another, each with small red silhouettes on it, the first of a single figure, the second a pair of shorter, thinner Siamese twins. Toilet rooms for sure.

DON'T DAWDLE, the SCO's voice cautioned. . . .

Well, if I counted right, this is it, Felice asserted to herself further along.

The door that she was before, an unmarked one, glided up.

This surely has it over everything. Who would ever have thought. A huge room was there, faced throughout by large, shiny brown tiles with a band of those little-big-little silhouettes the size of colossi running clear around at eye-level . . . holding hands like paper dolls.

The pool was oval in shape, broken on the other end, right, by a tropical peninsula, whose foliage — some of it at least — looked bonafide. The water was as clear as from the tap.

Believe you me, I sure can use this. Lickety-split the cape, pants, and sneakers were off, and Felice had her behind down on the edge, toes in. Just right I'd say — it was tepid.

Her being froze — something greyly brown and as thick as a firehose was beginning to unwind into the water from among the bushes on the peninsula.

"Gads!" she let out shrilly.

It was stretching out lengthwise, the front end of it making for her.

"Wowie!" — she jerked her toes out.

A head was on that front end — and it was full of long, pointy teeth!

Felice scrambled up and looked wildly around — "Hey, SCO, are you there somewhere?"

A thin gold metal plate zipped down, oval with an indentation in the upper right (in other words, a carbon copy of the pool). The SCO's head was framed in it. **WHAT'S YOUR PLEASURE?**

She gestured at the water — the thing was before her now, showing off by snapping the air with its hatpins. "Is this lekhee vicious?"

BEG PARDON?

Hm, Felice considered, either he doesn't understand the meaning of the word, or I didn't get through because of my accent. "I mean, does he" — *click-click*, she made with her own clickers.

NOT THAT I'M AWARE. However, if she preferred to skip the swim for today, it was quite alright. The period was almost over anyway. His image faded, the plate zipped up.

Felice bent over for her stuff. . . .

"Gee, gee, gee," someone cackled over on the other end, opposite the peninsula.

Felice rose up, just finished with the second set of sneaker laces.

A small group of young browns was there — both butterballs and beanpoles — with nothing on. They'd come in via a door in the side.

"It's your turn to go first this time," a fat told a lean.

The toothy monster had turned tail . . . was steaming toward them.

"Nothing doing," Skinny protested, "I've had mine already. Lookit" — he held up his left foot for inspection — "you can still see the stitch marks."

Felice's eyes popped — strapped to his wrist was a club like a sawed-off police billy; the others were armed with them too. She tilted her head back — "Hey, SCO, I thought you said this pet here didn't bite."

The answer came from up there, sans gold metal plate — it didn't amount to much, as one could plainly see.

Attençion: No more pool, that's for sure, I'll make do with the faucet again . . . unless I can get to talk to someone. Ah, screw it. . . .

On the way to the meetin'.

Classes let out, & the hall became overflowing — with kids mostly, carrying sacks, like shopping bags, of their color.

One occasionally looked my way, sneaky-like, but everyone for the most part was too excited — it's the second day of the new term.

Note: greens & purples are also either heavy or light, but one way or another, the latter're always a hair leaner.

[Ed. For those interested, here is a table summarizing the physical dimensions of the individuals in this land.]

eekhal	Tall, and either a) thin like those of Shkhurza land and Glakhland, or b) bulky and thus on the same order as the dominant types in those lands.
glakh	Also tall, and either thin or bulky, thus in the one case unique to this land, and in the other resembling the robust glakhs of Glakhland.
shkhurza	The same but slightly smaller, and thus unique when they are thin, similar to the shkhurzas of Shkhurzaland when filled out.

Q: Do the three sexes mate here according to physical type, the fat with the fat, lean with lean, or what?

In no time flat, they all disappeared into the different rooms & it was quiet again. . . .

As I was passing one door, I heard someone within yell out: "Only inside the lines! I repeat, paint belongs ONLY inside the lines!" I decided to have a teensy look-see.

There was an enormous dome-like room in there, full of balconies going all the way up, maybe six stories — & every inch of space was taken by jr glakhs in aprons (& capes), meaning from Glakhland. Before them was a species of canvas on an easel, & they were all busily painting away with brushes attached to their knuckles by means of metal rings . . . dipping them into deep glass wells in a compartmented wooden box that stood beside them — think of a wine rack turned on end so the holes face ceiling-ward.

Presiding over this humongous brood was a young brown of the bullish type, who was somewhere in the back when I came in, & spotted me before I did him. "Come in, Colleague, come in!" he called, then hurried forward to meet me — "Highly honored." His charges were here in Eekhalland for some advanced instruction in the Arts, he explained — couldn't spend any more time with me because he was checking yesterday's assignment, & as I could see, he'd only just begun. But if I wanted to, I could make a tour of inspection on my own — which I did, or at least began to.

Boy, those kid-glakhs certainly put me & my Dance-Painting demo to shame. The teach had given 'em all an outline to follow, & they'd just gone and ignored it — with abandon. The colors, of those I saw anyway, leapt splashingly; on one canvas, the last I looked at, they actually pulsated.

Wouldn't you know it, just then the SCO began paging me, his voice echoing all over that dome-room like a bell — COLLEA-EA-EAGUE! THE MEET-IN-IN-ING!

P.S. I wonder if he saw — I'd just finished giving the creator of those pulsations a congratulatory tickle on his little green noggin. . . .

On my way again, there was another room where someone inside was yelling: "Only the notes! Remember, sing ONLY the notes!"

Now there I agree, music's a different matter entirely.

Well, well, seems like old times, I mused, on the threshold of the meeting room — in more ways than one.

It was a dimmish, low-ceilinged affair with curved rows of seats gently sloping down. I'd say there were two hundred in all — most of them filled.

Below, beyond the first row, was a very bright lit area with a half-round table centered in it. Nine eekhals, both heavy and thin, were ranged along its straight (more distant) edge.

One of them was talking — like to himself. . . .

Okay, go, I prodded, having waited until he was through, or seemed to be. Headed for an empty in the last row, five or six in — my usual parking place at department meetings and the like back home.

Boy, I sure could do with forty winks, was my feeling, squeezing by knees. The rear wall, as of old, would make a perfect headrest.

"Ah, here she is now!" pierced my ears from below there at the table. It was Lekhee's master, my dean.

I stood still.

"Colleague," his voice rang out again, "I've been filling everyone in about your most unusual specialty, and now their appetites are whetted." Would I care to enlarge upon it further?

There you are, my better self razzed. Now what are you going to do? I was really dripping with fatigue — I dunno, I'll worm out of it somehow. "Well," I began, "I — I'm truly flattered. However, you must understand — mm — that I'm not exactly — mm — accustomed to speaking extemporaneously." I looked straight at Deany — "You know, growing up in Glakhland, gee, gee."

A sparer, somewhat younger one down there spoke up — "How about tomorrow then? Would that give you sufficient time to work something up?"

Oh man, deeper and deeper, I groaned to myself. "Yes, quite," I answered. And now if they would excuse me, it was a highly complex subject and I would have to make haste if I were going to etc. etc.

You sure can put your foot in it, better self jeered, as I began pushing my way out.

Chapter Ten

[Ed. As stated in the Introduction, the author experienced another of her crises around this time — happily, not as full of angst as on that other occasion. Even so, I once again had to make do with submissions in piecemeal.

One word more: this chapter too was never reviewed by Ms. Rothman and me, nor did it ever come up in casual conversation.]

The first thing to do when one is under pressure to give forth like that, I know from long experience, is to clear everything away — on deck & in one's head. So as soon as I got back to my digs, one-two-three I stuck Lekhee, still "snoring" away, in the other room with his ration plus a few bonuses as a consolation, then had me a snooze in peace for a while.

Now I'm up, and have been thinking. It seems to me that a demo is definitely out — not for the lack of paints & stuff, which I'm sure the SCO in his communicational way could scare up if I requested it — but because I'm afraid all those senior faculty types, the recipients of my spiel, will be as sticklerish 'bout coloring inside the lines as that art teacher was with those glakh exchange students, & raise the roof. So by a process of elimination, the only thing left is to straight-talk-it. . . .

+ one hour(?). I've really had enough of Dance-Painting, & you can't blame me. So what else can I talk about? . . .

+ more time. One thing's plainly in my favor. Even if I were to do my darndest, it's unlikely that anybody'd catch more than a few o' my words now & then, and if I pitched my voice way down, hardly any at all. So as far as I can see, I've got carte blanche, can speak on any topic. It just has to SEEM sensible & in earnest, that's all. . . .

There, eureka, I proclaimed, along about supper time.

Eh, let's lube up the cords a mite. I opened my mouth, declined my lower jaw —

$$\text{𝄢}^{\#\#} \text{In } ^{\text{die}} \text{ ßen } \mathfrak{he}\text{-ei-eil' } ^{\text{gen}} \mathfrak{Hal} _{\text{len}}$$

$$\text{Kennt } \text{die } ^{\mathfrak{R}\text{-a-a-che-che}} \text{nicht. . . .}$$
$$\text{man}$$

That's from *The Magic Flute*. Sarastro the high priest is singing, the deepest of bassos — "In these holy halls,/ Revenge is unknown." The rest of the stanza goes: "Und ist ein Mensch gefallen, / Fürht Liebe ihn zur Pflicht" — "And if someone errs,/ Love leads them back to duty."

●   ●   ●

The subject of my speech, or theme if you will, wasn't exactly original; numerous others, whom I'd never for a moment hesitate to acknowledge as my betters, have expatiated on it or some variation thereof through the ages, as you'll be quick to realize — hopefully not too quick. In fact, it was not even original with me that day, I myself had used it once before — as it happens, to a single solitary soul when we were both soused to the gills.

He was that former MA thesis advisor of mine who became my boss and a friend at the Institute for a Liberal Education after I was kicked out of graduate school. Let me call him Luke, after the hero's brother in *Look Homeward, Angel*, which Luke and I had both taken to with passionate intensity when young — the two of us a pair of first class jackasses, everyone'll be thinking I suppose. Let me make the picture of asininity complete — while in college, we also both went on Spring vacation pilgrimages to Thomas Wolfe's birthplace in Asheville, I by bus from New York, Luke hitchhiking from his native New Orleans.

The occasion grew out of trouble brewing at the Institute,

which was in the last months of its existence (before the
Jersey Board of Ed forcibly merged it with the local community college). Something so unbelievable happened out
there one day that on returning to the City later and stopping off for a drink, which Luke and I did from time to time
when going home together, we stayed on at the bar until the
wee hours, and then adjourned to his apartment, near mine
in the Village, for a nightcap.

The sum and substance of the shocker was that our presi-
dent, an interim appointee, had suddenly taken it into his
head to veto a fair and square re-election of a divisional
chairman, citing some obscure clause in our Charter empow-
ering him to, and in the electee's stead appointed an old
college buddy, claiming that he was acting in the division's
best interests. As if that weren't bad enough, it seemed
to be common knowledge that the buddy was vastly inferior
in every respect — intellect, accomplishments, character, the
works — as one of the leading lights in my Humanities Division put it, he was like a satyr to the chair's Hyperion.

To me, a piccolo, and a female one at that among mostly
males, it didn't much matter one way or another — in my few
years there, I'd never exchanged more than a word with
Tweedledum or Tweedledeedee. However, I was aware that a
greater issue was at stake, going beyond the divisions' customary right to choose their own heads. The only problem
was that at that hour, slumped in one of Luke's "easy" chairs
(cracked dull-green leatherette swivels from some used furniture store) after more than one too many, it was very hard to
put one's finger on that issue. And all I could do was repeat
what I'd been saying on and off all that evening — If I were
in your shoes, Luke, I wouldn't let that man get away with it, I
just wouldn't.

Luke was descended from drinking folks with ten years
more experience than I, and so could hold his licker better.
Lighting up a Gauloise Bleue from a new pack, he sur-
veyed me with steady-brown eyes, then said roguishly — You
wouldn't, would you? And just what do you propose we do
about it?

I dunno, I answered, quite seriously. I only feel that you all ought to make a stand, that's all. (Guess I should add the whole thing became a moot point a couple of weeks later when the subject of our discussion, the ex-chair, collapsed and died of a heart attack.)

Luke wrinkled his nose, which was sloping like Robespierre's; his hair, bushed out in the back, contributed to the resemblance. You? All?

Yes . . . you . . . all. A whole bunch of (to him) enigmatic things that I'd done and said in the past, which that phrase "You, all" could well have served as a title for came welling up — and suddenly I had this driving need to explain. (Let me remind, in case you've forgotten, that this was taking place in the mid-1970's, before the Women's Movement was really well under way.) You know, I began, I've never properly understood democracy and fair play, things like that. They've always led me to conjure up things like Bruderschaft, primitive hunting societies, and so on —

So, what did we go and give you women the vote for, Luke interrupted with.

Let me finish, I insisted — reached over and parked my glass on his desk (another refugee, of dark metal, out of the same second-hand lot), somehow rose to my feet.

Luke's got a pretty fair library, he has — Greek and Roman classics in the original and translation, the Bible in a number of different versions, St. Augustine to Proust and Mann, Beowulf to etc. I went and trippingly planted myself in front of the closest wall of them, which was behind him — compelling him to rock around in his chair with a creak.

Mind you — I swayed — I go along with it, your democracy. What choice does one have, there is nothing else. But it's up to you — I drew in a breath wheezingly — YOU WITH THE POWER IN YOUR BALLS, to defend it!

To put it another way — I went on — without morality, that is, caring for one another and living by principles — I gestured at the books behind me — There is no wisdom! YOU'RE IN THE SAME LEAGUE WITH HIM, THE CANCELLER OF FREE ELECTIONS!!! I almost fell flat on my face.

Sorry to have troubled you with this unsavory tale of college chiefs and chairs (like kings and cabbages). I just wanted to make sure that what I mumbled about there at the meeting of the Performing Arts Faculty of INST-360 is reasonably clear.

●   ●   ●

[Ed. Something is obviously missing here, which I was at a loss to remedy, the Diary for once offering no clue whatsoever. A consultation with some senior member of the staff of INST-360 must have taken place at the very least.]

"Here she is now," the SCO said before Felice's door, as she stepped through from the hall returning. He'd gotten there seconds before her apparently. With him was another glakh, shorter and comparably more slender (and thus roughly her size), and a thinner purple, both with loaded "shopping bags." "These are your grenrigs [ɢ⁷ʁ³ɛ̂n · ʁ³ɪɢ⁷ — Ed. literally, "assistants," but one must not neglect to note the "rig" or "mate" component.]

Well, that was fast, Felice commented to herself. They certainly do act with alacrity round here when all's said and done.

"Two fine scholars," the SCO went on. He roughed the other glakh's shoulder endearingly — "This is Jokhrol" [já χ¹⁹· ʁ⁵oḽ].

The young green nodded, with a touch of insolence it seemed.

"And this" — the SCO patted the purple's smooth pate — "is Shkhrichig"[ʃχ¹⁸ʁ⁴Í · ʧɪɢ ⁴].

The shkhurza inclined his chin, a little on the trembly side Felice intuited.

The SCO touched the door-button — they all went in, the grenrigs immediately proceeding to the other room, where they closeted themselves with a *doom-ull*, Felice to the desk, to find Lekhee on his belly now, the last of the light at Gleego Pond fading.

"Let me briefly review their duties with you," the SCO began, from just inside. ✋So there'll be no misunderstanding, he underlined.

✋Go ahead, I'm listening, Felice diddled.

It was all very simple. Jokhrol, her glakh-grenrig, was in charge of the viewer. Shkhrichig, her shkhurza-grenrig, was to be used for clean-up, "including, mm" — the SCO gave a glance rightward at the pot on the floor — "your prosthetic device if you wish."

✋No sweat, Felice flicked.

Now he would just pop into the other room for a moment to issue some last minute instructions, then be off. He hi-stepped that way, tapped, went in, closed.

What? Secrets? The hell with that, was Felice's feeling. She hurried over and pressed her ear to the door.

. . ."Never mind that" — it was the SCO, sternly. "Now I want the two of you to promise me you'll be on your best behavior. Jokhrol?"

"Honor bright, sir," said Jokhrol huskily.

"And you?" — the SCO to the purple.

"We'll certainly try, sir," that one answered, in a higher register.

"If you will pardon my saying so, sir" — it was Jokhrol again — "this is the first time we've ever been in a jam."

Aha, concluded Felice, still listening hard, two miscreants. What did they do, I wonder?

"I'm well aware of that," the SCO acknowledged.

"It was because of him, sir, that's what did it," Shkhrichig the shkhurza piped up. "We missed him so, still do-o-o."

Him, huh, thought Felice. Was my predecessor I suppose, their former eekhal-grenrig.

"There, there, you mustn't brood," the SCO attempted to soothe. "What's done is done. One must strive to forget, carry on."

Must have met with an accident or something, Felice deduced.

"That's more easily said," Jokhrol hoarsed. "You see, sir," Shkhrichig picked it up, "we — we tend to blame ourselves."

"Well, you shouldn't," the SCO assured. "Look, you know what all that mental activity does to'em, the strain it puts'em under. If he couldn't hold his end up — "

So ho, that's how things stand, Felice commented to herself. Their brown one went bonkers.

And after this visiting Colleague went home, what then, Jokhrol wanted to know.

The SCO murmured something — wasn't able to promise anything for sure, but —

They'd be grateful for anything he could do, Shkhrichig put in. . . .

Toom-ull — the SCO emerged. *Doom-ull* — he sealed the grenrigs in again. "I'm sure you'll find them both an asset," he said to Felice, who'd scampered back to the desk and had a tube up to her mouth to hide shortness of breath.

✋ Right, right, she gave him with her pinky.

"Okeedoke, now let's get organized," Felice sang out as soon as he was gone. "Say, Jokhrol?"

Toom-ull — his green form was in the doorway. "Yes, Colleague" — his voice had a slight edge to it.

Well, we'll just nip that insolence right in the bud, we will, Felice assured herself — sauntered over to the bed, sat down, swung around with her legs, rested back. "What's the program for me tomorrow?" she asked languorously.

He went briskly over to the left side of the desk where the tiny grid was, looked down — "First period, Introduction to the Dance, INST-630," read off.

Felice became flustered — "Who? What?"

He raised his eyes — "You're on loan to'em" — consulted the display again. "Second period, Painting for Beginners, INST-25."

Another loan then. But where are 630 and 25, and how do I get there, Felice wondered. Sounds like they might be rather far apart.

Jokhrol continued — "Third through Fifth period, Seminar in Derivative Applications. That's it." He turned away, began moving away double-time.

"Applications?" Felice wondered again, aloud this time. [Ed. Their data processors were apparently subject to some of the same vagaries as ours. "Derivative Applications" can only be Dance-Painting.] "But — but where's that one being given?"

"TBA," the green projected over his shoulder.

A fresh devil, as I rather thought. But is he lying or what? I'll have it out with the SCO first thing in the morning, you better believe it.

For all his hurry Jokhrol had stopped short at the door, and was now facing her from there — "Will there be anything else, Colleague?" He seemed to have lost his cool, waited as if braced.

Well, maybe I have been too harsh, Felice considered. "Have you had anything to eat yet?" she asked, just like that.

"Yes, at the Refectory," he replied, with the same uneasiness.

Felice shrugged — what's all the fuss? What does he think I'm gonna do to him? "Well then, goodnight."

He about-faced — *toom-ull.*

Next case — the gear had to be stowed and things made shipshape, the desk was still littered with everything from yesterday. She began to haul herself up, but then all at once felt very drained, like the other day on arriving here, in spite of all that sleep on the train. I'll just take five, that should do it. . . .

"Gyo! Leggo!" reached her ears some time later. The voice seemed to belong to that purple Shkhrichig.

"What the hay, what's going on?" Felice mumbled groggily.

"Leggo! Leggo!" the same screechy voice cried.

The two of'em must be fighting. What about? She got up out of bed with a sigh.

Click-click, went the lekhee in his cage behind her.

"Awright, keep yuh shirt on," she warned — then recalled her vow to speak to the Dean or someone and get rid of him.

I'll do it tomorrow for sure.

Klop-klop, something bopped from inside the other room, like a fist on a naked skull.

Click-click, click-click, the Lekhee re-signaled.

"It sounds like an effing madhouse round here," Felice muttered — reached the "boy"s' door, punched, *Toom.* Oh brother —

Jokhrol was on the bed atop Shkhrichig with his hands around the smaller guy's throat squeezing. The poor purple's eyes were popping . . . breath was coming in gasps.

"Hey, stop that!" Felice cried, ready to jump into the fray and separate them if necessary.

Jokhrol pulled away — they both stared at her, Shkhrichig massaging his "windpipe."

Well, they listen anyway, that's something, was Felice's thought. "Now look here, you two," she admonished, "I don' wanna hear another peep outta you, dya hear?"

"Yes, Colleague," Jokhrol answered with something between sarcasm and glumness. "Whatever you say," Shkhrichig echoed.

"Okay" — Felice pressed for the door, *doom* — and began heading back, suddenly feeling very weary like before. . . .

"Yi-i-i!" she heard at the desk.

"Hey, cool it!" she yelled. "So help me, I'll report you!" A lotta good that'll do, I have a feeling. Something tells me I'm in for it, it's gonna be another gala night — I should never have let myself get talked into this. She fed Lekhee his snail.

Ke-rack! began the clickers. *Chit-chit-chit . . . glup.*

"Jokhrol, no-o-o-o!" Shkhrichig's little voice pierced the darkness.

Yes, indeedee.

●

COLLEAGUE ROZMAM, COLLEAGUE ROZMAM!
"Ah c'mon, have a heart," Felice pleaded in her sleep.
COLLEAGUE ROZMAM, WHY AREN'T YOUR GREN-

RIGS IN CLASS?

"Wow, did you hear that?" Jokhrol squawked in the other room. "Better get a move on!" Shkhrichig screeched. *Toom-ull* — their soles clattered. *TOOM-DOOM!* — they were gone.

Guess I'm up now, Felice confided to herself — opened her eyes.

The first of Gleego's residents were showing through the trees . . . arriving for another long, lazy day at the pond, which was full of gold shimmers.

Felice small-stretched, sat up. "Ooh!" — her head ached, terribly. She was sweating too, it was hot in there somehow.

The SCO began again from the viewer behind her — **COLLEAGUE** —

Felice whirled to face his thin green face on the round screen. "Now see here" — she rapped out all that had happened, very crossly.

The SCO made a stop-sign. **NOW, NOW, TOO SOON FOR COMPLAINTS**. The grenrigs needed a little time to get adjusted. His eyes lightened for a second — **AFTER ALL, IT'S NOT THE EASIEST OF ASSIGNMENTS.**

"**ASSIGNMENTS?**" Felice echoed. The true state of affairs clarified itself. Surely, she argued, they didn't expect her, an accident case, to —

WHY YES, the deans had assumed that she'd be desirous to partake of life with them fully. But of course, as she doubtless was aware or had been informed, they did things a little differently in their neck of the woods. **IT'S CUSTOMARY TO — MM — ONE AT A TIME.**

So, the perversion. Felice folded her arms — and which one of the two did he recommend that she take on first?

He waxed conspiratorial. **WELL, I HATE TO BE CARPING WHERE MY OWN KIND IS CONCERNED** — but in his opinion, for what it was worth, he believed she'd find the shkhurza more tractable.

Felice's head was really pounding now. "Okay, okay" — only if it was alright with him, could she cancel her classes for the day. I'll try and steal a march on it, whatever it is, she told herself, either a bug or my period.

TSUH-TSUH, the SCO made in his fashion. Could she stand a little music?

"No, no" — Felice put a finger up to each temple — if he didn't mind, she'd do without.

It was much later, 9 p.m. at least. Felice was feeling somewhat better, having taken some aspirins and dozed on and off.

A noise like a footfall sounded outside. That must be them now, she alerted herself in the dark — the "boys," who had been gone all day.

Toom-Doom! — the two of them scurried by to their door. *Doom-ull — closed themselves in.*

What, am I such poison as not to rate even a Good Evening? "Jokhrol? Shkhrichig?" — Felice was there in a moment. *Toom-ull* —"What's going on here?" she barked.

The green was over by their desk with one of the stools in his hands, ready to throw it — the purple stood across the room, about to duck.

"You" — Felice gestured at the slighter one — "outside!" Shkhrichig showed himself obedient. "As for you" — meaning the bully, he could have the pet to relieve the monotony, if that was to his liking.

🐦Many thanks, Jokhrol signed, but no offense intended, he'd manage alone. . . .

Shkhrichig was skulking by the desk when she joined him. "You take that side," she ordered, pointing to the half of the bed nearest him.

"Yes, Colleague," he said dejectedly — and scuffed off his shoes. "Colleague, do you have any objection if I leave my clothes on?" — felt a trifle chilly.

"No problem" — she slid in on her side, in the T-shirt, undies, and socks from last night.

He slumped down — along his edge.

"Better move in a little," she warned — squirmed slightly his way to demonstrate. Be a fine howdyado if one or both of us accidentally rolled off during the night and broke our asses.

"I'm yours to command, Colleague," Shkhrichig responded quivery-like — inched over.

Poor guy, Felice thought, he has more grounds for com-
plaint than I do really, as unlike his predecessor in every way
as a satyr is to etc. But at least there was a solution to the
basic situation, devised during her waking periods earlier.
"You know, Shkhrichig," she began, with deliberate uncer-
tainty, "sometimes — when misfortune befalls us — a curious
thing happens."

His breath seemed to come short, as if in the hope or
expectation of a reprieve.

"So if it's alright with you, how about we — don't — and
of course, not tell anybody anything?"

His share of the mattress jogged with joy — of course,
whatever she said, he'd be advised by her! . . .

Now if only there were some way of dealing with this
other bothersome thing, Felice yearned, padding back from
a clicking reminder some time later.

Lekh-lekh, the Lekhee tuned up. *Ke-rack!* — it began in
earnest.

Well — she slid in again — let's try the ole routine, think
of something else and concentrate on it.

"Yee-ee-ee!" the little mouth wailed.

"Now what?" — she hiked up her head. Her purple-part-
ner was up and had grabbed up the cage as if to dash it on
the floor. "Shkhrichig!" she screamed. "Don't!"

He gave it a rattling shake — "YEE-uh-YEE-uh-YEE!" —
and banged it down. *Plump!* bounced the little snake-body.
"Don't worry, Colleague, he'll mind his manners now."

'Runsh, came from there. *Sht-sht-sht.*

"See?"

How about that, Felice marveled, live'n loin. . . .

"What now?" she moaned, awakened out of a sound sleep
along about midnight.

Shkhrichig, who'd also fallen off as far as she knew, was
sitting up with his back to her. *Mniff,* he sniffed.

"What is it?" she asked, alarmed. Could he have caught
cold or something?

Mniff, mniff, he sniffed some more — a shiver seemed to run through him.

Let's get some light on the subject — Felice went over for them. "Oh dear!" she exclaimed on the way back — there was a dark stain on the sheet where her rump had been, menstrual blood for sure.

Shkhrichig turned toward her — his eyes were swimming.

It's the smell, she realized, remembering the sensitivity of the types here. "Listen, why don't you go on back to your room, okay?"

He bounded up — ✋How can ever I thank you enough!

"And do us both a favor," she called after him. "Tell your green pal in there that if he doesn't behave — "

On the run, Shkhrichig's finger jiggedy-jigged. . . .

Well, no great tragedy, Felice tried to console herself, over by the desk with the pack. In lieu of tampons (which had been omitted through oversight, you'll recall), there was some gauze in the first aid kit that could be wound onto a wad of toilet paper. Her draws would hold the makeshift sanitary pad in place. Perfect, all she had to do was wash (with the cape over the viewer screen like the other day), and put on a new pair.

The Lekhee was all coiled up in his grotto, with nosehole buried.

"Hello, little one," Felice saluted — applied a nail to a bar, scratched. "I'm sorry, truly I am."

"Hum-m-m," he purred — looked like a heap of choco-late licorice with red candy sprinkles.

"That's nice, my pretty."

"Hee-ee-ee-eem!"

"That's it, 'nough" — her brow achy still.

●　　　　　●　　　　　●

About 7 a.m. My grenrigs have just left with their shopping bags, & so for good, I think (& hope). But before that, I had Jokhrol come in here and use his operational skills to get hold of the SCO on the viewer

— which he did blinking for all he was worth, with his right mitt over his schnozzhole, a sight to behold, haha.

I've got permission from the Dean to absent myself from all activities till further notice — i.e., till one of my wounds, just re-opened, heals — & I've put poor Lekhee inside there for greater comfort. Now the question is, what am I gonna do with myself over the next three-four days . . . the headache's gone, oh for a book or even magazine. Maybe while I'm up & about making the bed etc. something'll occur. . . .

+ several hours. Well, it's certainly better'n just lying around, & who knows what might come of it. The other day while I was fumfing on the viewer's panel, something curious happened — when I pressed a particular spot, the pot, which was uppermost in my mind at the moment, materialized on the screen. I'm gonna see if I can find that spot again . . . for starters. . . .

+ one hour (?). I've isolated three of them(spots). Boy, they sure have a lot of channels . . . some with classes maybe for shut-ins, others with writing that scrolls down, you name it. Anyway, the thing works like this — you put your finger on the spot, and imagine something. When that thing appears on the screen, you can take your finger away — whatever it is stays there & does as you want it to. When you feel like erasing it, you just will it away. . . .

It's really a lot of fun. I did an oak tree with a squirrel underneath it on its haunches. An acorn fell & beaned him, clunk. I left him there shaking his head, & switched to Channel Two, made the Empire State Building and had someone parachuting off it singing away — "Home on the Range," what else. Then I went back to Channel One — the squirrel was still going "no," shaking. . . .

After lunch. I've got an idea for doing something serious with it now, but I don't know . . . I'm not sure I'm up to it. . . .

Aw c'mon, go ahead, it's only a caper, and if at any time it makes you unhappy, you can just up and quit.

Alright, if that's the deal — I eased up from the bed, stepped over, sat myself down on the stool. Found the first spot with my fingertip, closed my eyes. . . .

Now I was afraid to look — afraid that it hadn't turned out as it'd really been. Remember, if there's anything amiss, if you're not altogether satisfied, it can always be changed.

I peeked gingerly — opened eyes all the way. "Oh boy!" I hollered.

Flora my mother was there before me, perfect in every respect down to the dark brown hair with its natural henna tinge framing her Habanera eyes and mouth like a bow. She had on a white angora sweater set and a dark green plaid skirt, below it white tights ending in oxblood loafers, which complemented the color of her lipstick and nail polish — a particularly unforgettable outfit she'd worn when I was a child.

I couldn't stand it — withdrew to the bed and lay with face down. . . .

C'mon, more rational self pestered after a while, you know as well as I this is not over yet. Go on back there.

"Okay," I sighed — sat up, wiped my eyes . . . went. On the stool, brought my hands to my chest, twined fingers. Somehow that scene from *Twelfth Night* came to mind, when the shipwrecked Viola comes as a page to woo the beautiful Countess Olivia for the Duke of Orsino, whom she herself is in love with. "Gracious lady," I began. There was a catch in my throat — I turned away. "I can't, I can't," I whimpered.

Yes, you can, that other self maintained. Remember? It's only make-believe.

I turned back — "Gracious lady," began again. And now? Now what? I sought for the words . . . they came. "There's no point in asking you for your forgiveness, as you would not have had it any other way, I'm sure" — forgiveness, that is, for having neglected her because of Dave and my writing, when it seems that she most needed me. "My only regret is that 'Guinevere' never amounted to much as the world goes."

The dark flashing Carmen-eyes blinked, mimicking my own. . . .

"And now, my dear, I'd like to do a little something to make amends." But what, what. This'll take a little figuring. . . .

Tea time. The ground rules are as follows: the music has to be suitable for her voice; she must be, bar none, The Star of the whole shebang (which unhappily rules out The Magic Flute & Don Giovanni); and the story can't end disastrously or desperately (which, alas, eliminates other favorites). . . .

Here are three possibilities:

— Elvira from Bellini's I Puritani — the Cavalier girl whom the war separates from her true love, a Roundhead . . . she goes nuts because of it, but then pulls herself together when they're reunited.

— Poppea, the mistress who becomes wife after Nero casts out his first, in Monteverdi's L'incoronazione di Poppea.

— Puccini's Turandot, the imperial princess who plays immovable object to Calaf, son of the outcast Tartar king, but finally yields.

Well, with some reservations, I cast my vote for the last. Flora wouldn't have fancied Elvira's lunacy, even on a temporary basis, and the role of mistress, even though Poppea's finally made an honest woman of, wouldn't have appealed to her muchly either. My reservations? Turandot is overweeningly proud & unequivocally merciless in the beginning. Also, while the opera is to me Puccini's crowning achievement, I think at the same time that it's a bit of a dud, Wagner sans balls. . . .

So, done, I felt, taking my finger away not long after, and — "Tantarrah!"

Flora was completely transformed — in a flowing gown of pale peach embroidered with tiny lilacs, her make-up accordingly subdued. She stood at the top of a gently curving staircase of red and gilt wood, whose balustrades were strung round with garlands of snowy orchids.

Poised below for the long climb up was Mr. Unkindness, Barney my father, with hair restored to cover his baldness, in a blanched caftan minus the belly-bulge, his arms wide to embrace . . . the ineffable they would have sung of together thus suspended in the air forever (which is more or less what happens in the opera, Puccini having died round about this juncture in the plot).

"Well, toots, what's the verdict?" I asked Her Highness, so moved I could hardly think.

My mother's mouth, the bow, curled up at the corners.

•

Day 2. I'm rarin' to go today, & I know just what it'll be. Boy oh boy, I can't wait, but mustn't rush things . . . exercise, wash, dress, tidy up etc. first. . . .

"Okay, here goes," I said, back over there on the stool. Touched the spot for the second channel . . . looked away, with bottom lip fastened under top teeth.

"Now" — looked back. Yes, indeed, you're getting to be quite an expert at this.

Dave was there with his hair of bright carrot, in one of his many pea-green suits — to match the eyes.

"My dear," I murmured — and hung my head. Hey, come on, you're supposed to be distracting yourself, my alter ego reminded. Yes, that I am. "Dave," I murmured again, with head up. There was so much to feel . . . I had only to let myself go.

His florid face, a bit on the fleshy side, worked — **WHAT CAN I SAY? IT WAS MY PLEASURE.** The mellow tone of voice was his to a T.

"And mine too," I added feelingly.

His eyebrows arched —

𝄞 Oh, the **SHARK**, Deah, has pearly teeth--

DA-DA DAH DAH, DEE DAH

He put his index on his crown and twirled around.

•

Day 3, a little while after dawn. What's for today? There should be a new scene, but I'll be darned if I know what. Well, let's go & see what happens.

I tuned in to Channel One — "Hi, mom!"

GOOD MORNING, MY CHILD, Flora said, from way on

high.

I switched to Two — "'Lo, Dave!"

HOW YA DOIN', SWEETHEART? LOVELY DAY OUT, ISN'T IT? He wiggled his hips.

Now — I turned to the third channel. But nothing came. Eh, it'll keep. I went to put on some clothes — on a sudden whim, my old clothes, the jeans and so on. . . .

"Got it!" I shouted out, before socks and sneaks — hurried back over there. "Hi," I said to another me in jeans etc.

The "me" grinned back — so broadly that the tip of her beak almost reached her chin.

"Who are you?" I asked.

The grin faded. **MY NAME'S FELICE ROTHMAN AND — I'M NOT EXACTLY A LIVING LEGEND.**

Aw hell, I scolded myself (my own true self), you can do better'n that.

"Me"'s eyes sank into grim hollows. **I WROTE THIS POEM ONCE. WELL, IT WASN'T EXACTLY —**

Oh man, I scolded again, so help me, you're beginning to sound like a broken — "Really.". . .

Even so, it was not without possibilities, & I'm back here on the bed considering. . . .

Yup, definitely. Let's hop to it. . . .

"Good day, sir," I hailed.

AND A GOOD DAY TO YOU, MADAM, answered this middle-aged man in a get-up similar to a Pilgrim Father's, with knee breeches, hose, and buckle shoes — it was England's second greatest poet, John Milton. His hand reached up to his broad-brimmed hat and he doffed it, ruffling shoulder-length auburn waves, while his blind eyes stared vacantly.

"You were my first muse, if you'll pardon the expression."

Milton half-scowled. **I SHOULD STILL BE.**

"Well, if you don't mind, I'd rather talk about something else, your Satan, for instance" — whom I'd always regarded as a masterpiece, early on considering that leader of the Fallen Angels as the hero of *Paradise Lost*, unwittingly created by Milton (Blake's and Shelley's view), later, because of Satan's gradual degeneration into undisguised fiendishness, looking upon him as God (the character)'s unconscious instrument for good.

Milton unscowled. **PSHAW.**

"Honestly," I insisted. But when all was said and done, it was Satan's knack for saying things — the oddest things — superbly that had kept me faithful. "Listen —

What though the field be lost?
All is not lost; the unconquerable Will,
And study of revenge, immortal hate,
And courage never to submit or yield:
And what is else not to be overcome?
That Glory never shall his wrath or might
Extort from me.

"Or actually it was you, who supplied the Fallen One with the words, and the feelings behind them. Listen again —

Farewell happy Fields
Where Joy for ever dwells: Hail horrors, hail
Infernal world, and thou profoundest Hell
Receive thy new Possessor: One who brings
A mind not to be chang'd by Place or Time..
The mind is its own place, and in itself
Can make a Heav'n of Hell, a Hell of Heav'n

For surely you had your own sad situation when penning this — virtually under house arrest after the downfall of Cromwell's Commonwealth, which you'd supported to the hilt, and yet further removed from all that was familiar and meaningful to you by the loss of your sight."

I became coy — "For a brief time while in college I was turned off to you and your works, wouldje like to know why?"

Milton nodded warily.

"It was your character Sin" — whom he'd depicted as a serpent-woman ringed round by a litter of pestiferous curs, forever creeping back into her womb for comfort and yowling there. "It's no wonder that your daughters were so mean to you in the end, and their mother, your wife, left you years before. If that was how you viewed that most profound of feminine ties, what did you expect?"

His small mouth, perplexingly sensual as in his portrait, pursed.

"Anyway, as I said, my antipathy was short-lived. And all I can say now is, what a miracle *Paradise Lost* is" — not only on account of the adverse circumstances under which it was written (political exile within the exile of darkness), but also because its epic form represents a supreme compromise, his natural bent, the stage, having been wrecked by those Puritan mishugunahs, his pals!

Hey, hold on there, I reined myself in, or you won't have anything left for the others. "Sir, would you be so good as to 'scuse me for a few minutes, I see someone else coming."

My idol side-stepped leftward. . . .

"Buon giorno, signor," I greeted.

The man before me now bowed deeply, in a grey cape-like gown down to his ankles, with darker felt pumps peeping out. **COME STA, SIGNORA**? It was Florence's renowned son Dante, whose *Divina Commedia* was written largely in real exile.

"Pardonee," I said, "no parlo multo Italiano."

Dante shook his head, encased in a grey beret full of tassels, and smiled slyly — **THASS ALRIGHT, LETSA PRETEND.**

Yes, but it should be with a certain dignity, I cautioned myself. "Permit me to introduce you to a very special person who is a loyal fan of yours."

My former muse extended a sightless hand — **MI CHIAMO MILTON**. Dante hurried over and grasped it warmly in both of his — **HONORATO! HONORATO!**

"And now would you occupy yourself for a little, please. I'll be with you again shortly.". . .

This extra-rotund oriental lurched in from the right, in only a potato sack to cover his nakedness — his hair was a mass of wet black spikes. He brought the tiger-mouth of a kuang-type bronze jug up to his eye and peered — **THERE OR NOT THERE?**

"Master Li Po," I said, "as you and I are well aware, that drunkenness of yours is just a pose. So I'll thank you to spare us and be your own true self."

OH? The jug's lid clunked shut. Big-belly smiled, with dimples — **BE HAPPY TO** — bent over, stood the jug on the floor, straightened up, and began smoothing his sack-garment down. **ALL THE SAME, I'LL HAVE YOU KNOW THAT POSE, AS YOU CALL IT, WAS RESPONSIBLE FOR SAVING MY LIFE ON MORE THAN ONE OCCASION.**

"Yes, so one's inclined to suspect, reading between the lines." To wit, having had the misfortune to be born during the strife-torn T'ang Dynasty, Li Po was twice falsely branded a traitor, but probably judged relatively harmless because of his inebriation, he was punished with only imprisonment and banishment, whereas other innocent bystanders so accused, who'd remained sober, went to their deaths.

ON THE OTHER HAND, DO TRY TO UNDERSTAND, I'VE ALWAYS, AT THE SAME TIME, BEEN A FIRM BELIEVER IN TAKING A DROP TOO MUCH NOW AND THEN.

"You said a mouthful, man," I said under my breath. It's the only way really that a feeling person has of keeping a hold of him- or herself nowadays, in my opinion.

Li Po gave a wee wave to Dante, scooped up his wine, and began sort of waddling toward him. . . .

"Master of masters, Tu Fu! Venerable Wang Wei!" I cried out — at the sight of two more orientals strolling in. Also survivors from the T'ang era, both had long-wispy Fu Man-chu moustaches and pigtails dangling from skull caps, and wore charcoal-colored kimonos with curly-toed slippers.

They had both halted — Tu Fu, the younger, taller, and leaner was all attention.

"Oh, greatest of Chinese poets, I hate to be the bearer of evil tidings," I said, "but very few in the civilized parts of Earth these days, both East and West, have ever heard of you."

Tu Fu's cheeks, already quite thin, tautened — **SO BE IT.**

"As for you, sir," I said to Wang Wei, "you who excelled at everything. We still have your poetry, but of your paintings, the great ones at least, not one remains, and of your music not a single note — all fallen victim to the rapaciousness of the very souls you hoped to humanize."

Wang Wei took it calmly — still, Tu Fu put an arm round his shoulder.

"And now, gentlemen," I said, with them all lined up, "I'd like to offer you a little hospitality."

Dante swung his hands in the air — **MAGNIFICO!** Li Po held up the jug — **I'LL BE HAPPY TO CONTRIBUTE MY SHARE.** He shook it close to his ear — **I THINK.**

"But first," I went on, "maybe I should tell you something 'bout myself after all" — mindful of Milton especially, whom I'd brushed off before. "You see, I too was a poet of sorts, and I too was in exile in a way —"

Wang Wei's face expressed concern — **I DO HOPE YOU DIDN'T LAY YOUR WRITING IMPLEMENT DOWN BE-CAUSE OF YOUR — VICISSITUDES.**

"I'm afraid I did" — poet's pen anyway.

STUFF AND NONSENSE, Milton muttered.

My temper flared — "Look, sir." I wanted to point out that not everyone had his will and strength — but enough, let it be, I decided. . . .

A curtain like a stage-curtain parted behind them — to reveal a long candlelit banquet table, laden with china and silver. In the background was a huge curved picture window, looking out onto a bubbly tree-shaded brook with birds chirping in the branches.

ANDIAMO, said Dante with a flourish, then paused — **WON'T YOU JOIN US, SIGNORA?**

"Benissimo!" I agreed. "But whatever should I wear?"

Li Po dismissed this nicely — **OH, COME AS YOU ARE. LOOK AT ME** — barefooted in his sackcloth.

"Very well — that is, unless someone else has an objection.". . .

What with manipulating this whole gang on the screen and now adding myself, I was really going to have to concentrate. . . .

"Ave!" whooped Felice, in jeans and T-shirt sans sneakers

and socks.

She twitched her toes, Li Po did likewise with his . . . they both linked arms, swung round sweepingly, skipped once, and strutted, leading the way.

Felice chanted —

Hence loathed Melancholy ✳
Of Cerberus and blackest midnight born, ✳
In Stygian caves forlorn ✳
'Mongst horrid shapes and shrieks, and sights unholy.

"That's one of the *sins* of my youth," Milton eyelessly confided to Wang Wei, who was carefully steering him.

"Oh, I wrote something like that too," Wang Wei admitted, "only I tore mine up and threw it away."

"Teeheehee," tittered Tu Fu and Dante, bringing up the rear.

Felice gave forth afresh —

But come thou Goddes fair and free,
In Heave'n yclep'd Euphrosyne,
And by men, heart-easing mirth.

She and Li led them all rightward to a smaller table, where stood a softly glistening silver decanter surrounded by rare crystal goblets.

"Allow me to do the honors," said Li — set his jug down on the floor like before. The contents would be according to each one's taste, Felice explained as he poured, they merely had to envision.

Dante raised his glass jauntily — "Shall we drink to our

charming hostess?"

Felice was not so sure she liked the idea. "Whadya say to the birds instead," she offered.

"Why not, that's a good idea," Li seconded, with his glass also up.

"To the birds," they all solemnly repeated. "Long may they sing," Wang added. . . .

Skinny Tu was the first to drain his glass. "What's there to eat?" he asked, with Adam's apple bobbing prominently (he who'd practically starved to death in real life, a vrai starving poet).

Felice put her white wine down and took his arm to escort him, advising on the way, loud enough for everyone else to hear too, that the same principle was in effect for the food — they had only to wish for what they wanted. . . .

"I fancy some oysters," said Milton, when they were all there at the main table.

Wang, still by his side, uncovered a platter — "Here you are, sir" — guided his hand to it.

Milton's thumb and forefinger closed round a Colchester shell and drew it away tremulously. Felice grabbed a serviette and thrust it under. . . .

But where had Li disappeared to? Felice's eyes darted round in search of his chubby self.

"Over here!" his voice sounded from the left.

He was holding a pair of rice bowls, Fushan's finest. She went to join him with two sets of chopsticks (imitation ivory), and they exchanged.

"Some feast, huh?" he said — reached over to her bowl with his sticks and whisked off a wedge of her camphorwood smoked duck.

"And how," was her feeling too — she snagged a very slimy, garlicky morsel of his . . . originally from the sea.

Chapter Eleven

a.m. *(after the Bash). You know how sometimes you have a problem and you chew on it & chew on it, yearning for a solution — and then one morning you wake up, & there the solution is, in your head like a freshly-laid egg? Well, that's what happened to me today — I think I know how to get out of here now . . . up to the surface again.*

In brief, I'm gonna get hold of the Dean through the SCO, & tell him that the wound is not healing as fast as I'd like it to, would he contact the Chief & ask him if it'd be alright etc. etc. For a while anyway — a rest-cure like that up there proved beneficial once already, just after the Calamity. . . .

I had a bit of a difficulty locating the SCO on the panel — should have watched Jokhrol more closely the other day. Anyway I finally did, & now the matter's been set in motion. . . .

+ five minutes. Well, unless they're pulling my leg or this is another test-trick, which I'm rather inclined to doubt — I've done it. Deany came on himself, full of his usual "concern" — COLLEA-EA-EAGUE, WHAT IS THIS I HEAR? YOU WISH TO ABANDON US?

Ya damn right, I felt like saying, but played it cool, with my head hangin', "Well — I — yes."

There was no end to his solicitude — EVERYBODY IS GOING TO BE TER-RIBLY DISA-PPOINTED. And there was so much yet for me to do-o: their museums, to say nothing of their theatres & concert ha-a-alls(!).

I was all ready with the answer — could always come back after. And for good measure, I tossed in a little cough, hoik-hoik.

Boy, you should have seen what that did to his nosehole — so I could, I could certainly come back later if I wished to. . . .

Noon. Done, it's done! The SCO was just on, they got a green

*light from the Chief, and let's hope it's as legitimate & sincere as it
sounds — I'm to leave immediately.*

*All I have to do is get back to the station & onto the train there.
The SCO said not to worry, he'd direct me from his control tower —
and I expect they'll have the halls cleared "for my comfort," cha-cha-
cha.*

Bye for now.

•

*I made it, I'm here in the same compartment. They've shut the
door . . . and we're off!*

*As I was going along, the SCO told me how long the trip would
take, but as usual I couldn't make head or tail out of it . . . anyway it
can't be much longer than from Glakhland to here surely, & somehow
it wouldn't surprise if it turned out a deal shorter.*

*I'm gonna spend the time, however long or short it is, boning up
on my Geegloo (Kheekhloo), Laleekh's language. It's basically just a
matter of vocabulary now, ha. . . .*

*But first, before that, let me get out of these official brown duds &
back into the jeans — civvies! — again.*

"So here we are I guess," I couldn't help whispering
some "days" later, when the train eased to a standstill. Now
what?

A long moment passed. *Yis!* — an oval section of the ceiling slid back, oh say, big enough to accommodate someone
of my size horizontally. *Yas-s-s!* — a brass-seeming cylinder,
like the message container of a giant pneumatic tube, began
to descend through the hole . . . kept on going till it came to
rest on the floor. A part of its surface revolved open to allow
an individual to enter.

One-two-three, I had the pad and pen stowed, pack on,
canteen slung, and pot in hand. "Here goes nothing," I murmured — and walked in with studied casualness.

The cylinder's "door" revolved shut, and it began to as-
cend . . . by inches.

Oh well, you might as well make yourself comfy — I removed the pot's lid so the knob wouldn't get in the way, and with the remaining roll of toilet paper in place, turned potty upside down to make a nice little seat. . . .

"Next case," I pronounced after a good hour or more — the cylinder had stopped moving.

There was another of those long pauses, with me on my feet now poised for anything.

"Ah" — the door revolved once more. I stood before the opening peering into near-darkness. See what's out there first — seemed to be a platform with a surface of grass and rocks and other natural things.

I squatted, got the flash out of the pack, clicked it on — yes, that's what it was, a turfy platform, circular except for where it touched the cylinder, maybe four yards in diameter. I raised my eyes — there was a hole of the same size with daylit sky showing through a hundred or so feet above.

"Oka-a-ay" — I grabbed up everything and stepped out onto that platform.

Yash-sh-sh! It began to rise.

"I can't believe it, I made it, I did it," I murmured, coming ever closer to the outside. . . .

"Oh wow!" I let out, surrounded by green, Lorca-green for real. The mist had recently burned off . . . there was still a wisp of it clinging here and there.

Finished: the platform grass had fused with that on the ground, so that it seemed as if I were standing in a small clearing. So — I vaguely remembered coming upon this spot many moons ago during my solitary early morning rambles, and taking it to be a cul-de-sac.

Now where's the trail? The periphery of the clearing appeared to be made up entirely of tree trunks and bushes. C'mon, I urged — spun round. Get outta here before someone down below changes his mind or something — I spun again. Man — "Finally!" — a dead branch was lying across it.

I hopped over it. "Okay" — put the pack back on, hugged the pot to my chest — "go!" I set off at a fast trot. . . .

It was like Gilgamesh returning home from his own long

sojourn underground . . . where he went to seek answers after the death of his beloved comrade Enkidu —

❋ ❋ ❋ ❋ ❋ ❋ ❋

> Run, ferryman, run. Go run.
> See if my city, my Uruk's still there. Is
>   everything as I left it?
> Of good baked brick were the walls.
>   Clever men contrived them.
> Part of it inside was garden, another
>   part field, and then there was the
>   precinct of Ishtar. ❋ ❋ ❋ ❋ ❋ ❋ ❋

Now what about my own dear friend, is he still alive and well, or what, I worried, as I bumped along. . . .

The ashy-white domes of the village came into view—we'll soon see. . . .

Some of his fellow-residents had emerged, others were following suit — all of them on the order of the lone starveling brown, two porky purples, and spitting bear of a green and his odd lot family, plus the other souls I'd gotten a glimpse of now and again, genetic mishaps for the most part with doubtless a sprinkling of botched experiments like the Shkhibee Khamor . . . this village their dumping ground . . . the beach their final resting place, as it was that of the Gleegoites who didn't pan out, those pioneer Utopians.

And where were all these misfits heading? Where else but to their equally seedy-looking pond, full of those dark, ugly specks.

Just hope my sidekick hasn't taken off for it already himself, I yearned, cantering down a footpath.

It was only a matter of re-orienting myself according to the khreekho-house. "Hey, Laleekh!" I called out, pounding down his ramp. "Laleekh, I'm back!" — I plowed through the vines onto the landing.

His green self was there, sitting as usual on the edge of the bed, with his feet planted on the floor . . . his small round table and its single stool on one side, hamper on the other.

But what was the matter? He was lost in thought, with

both fists up to his forehead.

"Hey, Laleekh!"

He came to his senses — "Oh?" His eyes focused — "Pelice, it's you!" His skin began to slicken with happy-sweat — a tremendous improvement over when I saw him last, when he was beginning his annual molting.

Dear Laleekh, I was so happy to see him, I could have run over there and thrown my arms around him. But they don't do that here on X . . . we've got only laughter in common.

I skipped down to my old spot before him — dumped pack and canteen, plopped after them, got rid of the pot with a shove. ✋The very same.

His cheeks, the familiar green cheeks, balled and unballed — there was a dot under his left eye like a tiny golden star, I noted. "Pelice, where've you been?" he scolded. He'd searched for me everywhere, in every vacant house, after his new skin came in. Had I been hanging out at the other village or what? Surely I knew that was not the thing to do.

No, I answered, what possible interest could I have in that boring place? ✋Guess where I've been, I teased. Bent forward — "Don't you notice anything different? Like my pronun-ci-ation, for instance?"

He regarded me with astonishment, his face blotchy-yellow now — "You've been down there! 'Mong them, the Gagloos!"

✋Right you are. . . .

During the trip, I'd thought about this moment long & hard, and decided for the sake of sparing him unpleasantness (to say nothing of myself) that my accounting to him should be a very abbreviated one, consisting of those adventures of mine likely to entertain. . . .

"You know, Pelice," he said, when I was done with the last of them, about that first night with the Dean's lekhee, "there are plenty of those little regees hereabouts." If I wanted, maybe one day he could catch one for us and put together a cage out of some twigs.

"Well — "

He really got carried away — "How about a pretty green one with yellow freckles?". . .

"Now Laleekh, it's your turn," I said, after I'd somehow persuaded him to agree to a considerable rain check. What had he been concentrating on so hard before when I came in?

His hands, those deft green hands, shot up to his ear buttons — "Oh Pelice, it's awful, just awful!" — meaning his latest dealings with those miserable Gagloos, of course. "So help me, they're gonna drive me clear outta my wits one of these days."

I unscrewed the canteen, held it out to him. ✹No, he signed. I took a sip. He proceeded to unburden himself. . . .

Not long ago, a group of them showed up — of the type with the husky jegulsas (or shkhurzas, hence from District 721) giving the orders — and immediately had the eegar (or eekhal) with them set about checking the various items in the house against a list they had on the screen of their black box, a favorite activity when they weren't bawling him out for some minor offense, like the floor's being untidy, which more often than not had been caused by their own irritating little khlags (or glakhs) trekking in grass and stuff from the outside. Anyway, what should they discover but that his mattress was missing a layer of sheeting, he and the other villagers being allowed a change of linen only every three days.

Did those big purple ones fly into a fury! The shortage (probably the result of a miscounting during the period of his indisposition) was utterly unforgivable, and he was never to do it again, one of them lectured him. If he knew what was good for him, a second had drilled it in.

Then no sooner had they gone than a fresh lot appeared — this one with fat and lean browns in charge (and so from Eekhaland for sure, possibly INST-360). However, instead of giving him a puzzle to solve or something like that as they usually did, they asked him to furnish an accounting of what had taken place before with the big jegulsas and their party, and still being upset, he complied. Whereupon they all clapped their hands to their noseholes as if he were contagious and backed up to the door, and the tall, skinny green they had with them, insisted on his confessing to any other memory lapses he'd experienced, along with the symptoms.

Of course, he denied over and over that there was anything wrong with him. But it was anybody's guess now as to what they might've gone and relayed to the brawny khlags that also came to visit with a team of their own from time to time — who were generally alright, in fact the only halfway decent sorts as he, Laleekh, had endeavored to teach me on a number of occasions, but who were capable of becoming dreadful nuisances and worse at the merest hint of illness there in the village. . . .

"Well, it's possible it'll all blow over," I tried to calm him, after he'd finished. Those browns were themselves prone to absent-mindedness, and he wasn't the last one they and their green had visited that day — maybe they stumbled onto a more grievous situation somewhere else, and forgot all about him, or it just plain floated out of their minds before they got back down below.

🖐Let's only hope so, Laleekh waved moodily. And happily we'd soon see what the story was, the big green ones and their followers would be coming along to inspect any day now — after which there'd be peace for a good long while.

"Oh?" — here was an interesting piece of information. "How so?"

My friend looked his old look of "Don't you know?" — but only for a moment. "'Cause it's fixing to rain, that's how so" — that is, "everything's promising to be thoroughly doused from the sky, and it's going to carry on like that for a good long time." 🖐See for yourself.

I heaved myself to my feet and went back up to the door — poked my nose out. Yes, it did seem rather dark and foreboding out considering the time of day, barely noon. Still, what did that have to do with them, his Gagloos?

"Pish, they're scared of it" — the Eekhalanders at least. The others found it unpleasant, thankfully too much so to venture up here while it was gusting like that.

And what did he do then himself?

As he said, catch up on his peace of mind, meaning sleep for the most part, the same as everyone else.

*So, some Glakhlanders are coming, & then that's it, maybe for
months. If only there were a way . . . the plane . . . Arthur . . . home.
That would be too much to hope for, wouldn't it. . . .*

●

"I hear voices," Felice mumbled, half-asleep several mornings later.

She listened in the dark, from her old place on the floor
beside Laleekh. Yes, the noises were coming from the woods,
she could tell by the echoes . . . it sounded like a lot of loud
babbling, purple-babbling if she were not mistaken. "Laleekh, it's them I think."

He rolled over and sat up, probably having awakened
when she did. Sensing tension in him, she rose and seated
herself next to him.

They waited in silence — the party had evidently begun
its rounds on the edge of the village, as was customary. . . .

The vines parted, this tall, well-built green in Glakhland's traditional cape and apron kneed in. "Ah, there you
are, with Rareeg," he said to Felice in Khakhloo — referring
to Laleekh, of course.

Now that's what I call a real piece of luck, Felice crowed
to herself. I couldn't have done better if I'd tried — it was
B-Tube's head, the Chemist.

He moved aside — four short, fat purples schlepped in a
piece of equipment, and laboriously down the stairs made
for the table with it. A young tech followed, and beckoned
for Laleekh to come.

Felice lost no time in gaining the landing — "What's the
problem here?" If anything was wrong, she'd take her pal
and beat it into the woods with him, hide there till these
Glakhlanders all got tired of scouting around and betook
themselves home.

"Nothing, just a routine check," B answered, keeping
a sharp eye on the tech looping a wire from the machine

round Laleekh's waist. "Oh yes, I've got something for you," he remembered — motioned to the purples standing by.

Out they went, back in they came — sagging under a pair of super-duper wooden crates, marked all over with fuzzy "*y*"'s.

Dear Grig, Felice thought — and shame on you, girl. You haven't given a single thought to that brown funny face since the last time. I betcha he made a real pitch to come up here with this team. Maybe this shipment so soon after the other was his way of telling you so — or maybe he was just razzing you with it hide-and-seek fashion, "Ya ya, I know where yuh went, yuh can't fool me.". . .

The examination had entered a new phase — Laleekh, on the stool, was holding up his legs, the tech was bending over and pressing as if for swellings.

"So what's the good word in B&G-A these days?" Felice asked B, by way of making conversation.

"No harm telling you I suppose," the Chemist answered, with his attention still riveted on the tech. They'd had a number of confessions, and the Chief was expecting more.

Confessions? To what, Felice wondered. Ah yes, to concocting me. Will they all never stop chewing on that down in Glakhland, District 721 too?

B ticked off the culprits so far: they were the head of Gleegoplasmology, a malcontent who had been further disgruntled by repeated refusals to transfer his unit from Fluids to Solids, where he felt that it properly belonged; an "oval" designer from G-Tube, hell-bent on repaying D-Tube's Chief for some slight, real or imagined; and the glakh-buddies of two techs from the Center for Determination, where Meredith and Rooney were presently in residence — nabbed red-handed with a new, improved version of the Shkhibee Khamor, offering such features as perfect vision, a tongue capable of efficient food consumption, left-handedness, and flipper feet, but with the breathing apparatus still to be resolved.

"And what are you all now figuring on doing with my buddies and me?" Felice gamely inquired.

Well, as he understood it, the "boys" were to remain with them down there, a suitable play area having been erected for them at the Center. As for her, she could stay on here if it suited her. If not —

"Oh no-o-o, I'll stay-ay," Felice quickly put in.

The perpetrators were another matter. Normally the penalty for such an offense was to be saddled with extra duties, but the Chief was really angry this time, so it was anybody's guess how they'd be dealt with.

The tech, a very sober non-Grig type, stepped up to the foot of the stairs to deliver a preliminary report. Laleekh was A-ok so far, it seemed, and nothing irregular was anticipated. . . .

Hm, Felice meditated, I wonder if there isn't some way of turning that news about those phony confessions to account. An idea came — YES! — a real brainstorm. How about if the Chief handed the culprits over to District 721 for punishment and took the plane in return, in other words swapped them — the Supreme Council'd be in seventh heaven. Her inner being clouded over — yeah, sure, and then the types in B&G-A'd fall all over themselves in jubilation and pull Lancelot irretrievably to pieces. Another thought came — maybe I can somehow convince this Chemist here of its necessity to my existence. Let's see how I do. . . .

"You know, Rareeg's a good sort," she began.

Oh? He was happy to hear she felt that way, they were mighty fond of him too — still watching over things.

The only problem was, she sorely missed that metal companion of hers, did he remember it?

Of course, gee gee, how could one not.

She socked it to him, the whole deal, how as nice as Rareeg was, she had been heartsick over the loss of that other. . . .

"Well, you certainly have an idea there, if nothing else it's worth a mention," he said when she was done. Looked at her searchingly — "And you? You'd be content then?"

Oh yes-es-es. Another thing, if the Chief went along with her scheme and it wasn't too much trouble, could it be arranged for some of those dexterous little greens of 721 to leave that one main object of her affection by the big pond, where they'd found it?

Check.

He was so nice, you can't imagine how bad I felt, how close I came to dropping the pose & making a clean breast of everything. But you understand, this was my only chance of my being reunited with Lancelot & I couldn't risk it . . . I simply couldn't.

Felice had an afterthought — rare green here, Rareeg, might be a little miffed when he learned about her special gift from down below, so why didn't they send someone for him too . . . a small one like himself . . . freaky didn't matter, but had to be lots of fun.

●

Day 8. (after lights out, under the tarp by the flash). Sorry, Dear Diary, this is the first opportunity I've really had to take pen in hand. What's been happening? Nothing special — mornings before Laleekh gets up I've been pounding the trails hereabouts, afternoons are as always with him at the pond, except that I've been staying in longer . . . trying to whip myself into shape & re-acclimate myself to weightlessness for the long trip back to Earth, if it should come to that.

As for that, there's nothing so far, no word one way or another even. We've been down to the beach several times . . . maybe tomorrow.

Well, well, so there we are, I mused, once more standing at that point in the bend of the shoreline where you can look straight down to my old digs.

Lancelot's silvery self was there, maybe not so glinting because of the lowering sky . . . still, there.

"What is it, Pelice?" Laleekh asked, a little confused.

Yes, there's that to attend to as well, I reminded myself. I hadn't said a word about it or anything else yet, as why should I have while everything was up in the air. But now was a different story, and knowing me too well, my green friend here wouldn't be fobbed off with any tale of that big metal dummy's being preferred to him as a comrade, that was for sure. "It's something very special," I said for the nonce — would have to give it some careful thought. ✋Let's go a little closer, shall we? . . .

Well, it certainly seems alright, doesn't look as if it's been tampered with in any way, I had to admit, after circling round several times (with Laleekh dogging my every step). There were only a few bumps and scratches here and there, and they may have been there all along.

"Pelice, you haven't told me yet," Laleekh nagged. "What is it?"

"Well — can't you see?" I sputtered. "It's — it's something to go in, to ride in."

"Ride?" He was really bewildered now.

No, dear Felice, I warned myself, this is clearly the wrong tack to take. You really better think it through.

p.m. I'd love to tell him, I really would, & I have a feeling that he'd believe me, he's just way out enough to. But no, I can see it now, it must not be. Why? Because I don't want him looking up at the sky afterward with some kind of expectation . . . either of my returning or someone else's turning up, which he, being as he is, just might take to doing. Anything but THAT!

So? . . .

Midnight solution: Here it is, the big metal thing is something to go down into the ground in, so I can scoot off to THEM whenever I like for more assistance, instead of their coming to get me like before. In time, I'll begin dropping hints that one day I might find it more convenient just to stay below there — exasperating as quite a few of 'em are, without a doubt. . . .

I'll blast off with the first bad weather, & hopefully some good old-fashioned thunder'n lightning for cover. Leave here around dawn . . . this time without waking him up, cross my heart. . . .

As for THEM, when the various teams come back up here in the "Spring" — to find neither hide nor hair of me, to say nothing of the Companion — I can just imagine the suspicions & accusations, backbiting & vendettas . . . just imagine.

•

*a.m. (+ One week?). The sky really looked grim just now. I told
Laleekh when I came in, & he went to the door & had a look out him-
self — said for sure it's going to rain tomorrow, & he should know.
So as far as I'm concerned, this is it . . . my last day here on X. . . .*

*late. On the way back from the pond this afternoon, I asked if he
wouldn't like to stop off & load up on his favorite fruit, those luscious-
looking plummy jabbas (which for some reason he hasn't done of late).
"That would be nice, Pelice" — I used my T-shirt as a holder, going
back to the village in only the bra. By the by, besides ocher, there're
orange & plum-colored (!) ones as well. . . .*

*And a great time was had by all. Sure, I tried one. Tasted like
Liebfraumilch with a pinch of cloves, allspice, or nutmeg, and as you
can see, there was no ill-effect . . . it just left a little swirling in the
head, which has stayed with me till even now, hi* ^dee *ho.*

Plip, something dripped on the roof early the next morning, *plip*.

What else could it be but — ? I eased to a sit, grasped the
pack and canteen straps, picked up the square of green vinyl
with my left . . . and slid little by little to my feet, until I was
standing before him, my friend, my first and in the end still
best friend here.

Bye, sweet prince, I said in my mind.

Laleekh slept on, oblivious. . . .

Outside on the ramp, fine watery drops were falling. I
shook out the vinyl, flipped it over my shoulders, lifted it
onto my hair — pinched it under the chin.

A doodle of lightning flashed . . . fuchsia lightning. *Pock*,
it cracked overhead, *pock, pock* — like a popgun.

It's not exactly what was wanted, I sighed, but it'll have to
do. Took my opening stride.

Afterward
by Nancy Bogen, M.A., Ph.D.

The role of literary editor is an exceedingly trying one, indeed, often involving the last word in mediation between what an author intended and literal meaning. Alas, at times — though rare times, to be sure — taste also becomes a factor.

All in all, the situation is not unlike that of the symphonic conductor and concert virtuoso. Both are honor-bound to reproduce a given musical text as faithfully as they know how, and at the same time are driven by their own artistic compulsions, which may vary considerably from the composer's, to render those same notes feelingly.

It was in such a vein that I had hoped to put a period to Ms. Rothman's and my long labor, but as of the other day this is no longer possible. An item of gossip has reached my ears of so potentially damaging a nature as to leave me utterly dumbfounded and unable to go on. In a word, it has been bruited about that there is no Felice Rothman and never has been — that I, and I alone, am the author of this work.

The offending party, as it happens, is one of those same colleagues whom I commended in my Introduction for being so generous with his assistance. As if that were not bad enough, said individual did not have the decency to approach me directly with his piece of absurdity — no, I had to hear it from the lips of my own child, a classmate of his daughter's at the private school they both attend.

In view of this distressing turn of events, I am hereby making public the letters that I received from Ms. Rothman; if anyone cares to examine the originals, they are available in my office. These should serve as proof positive that she exists — or I don't know what will.

The first letter, as I indicated earlier, was included in the packet containing the manuscript and Diary that she mailed to me from La Guardia Airport just before her departure:

Dear Prof. B.,

By the time you get this I'll be gone — no, not dead, just vamoosed. To where you'll soon find out. I'll only tell you now — hint-hint — "vamoosed" fits.

Seriously, I needed a break from this work's pressures — or rather, I've gone as far as I can with it, now I want to move on to something else . . . something more to the point.

So please forgive. And never fear, I'll be back oon bel dee.

In the meantime would you do me a little favor? I do not deserve it, I know, so let's say for old time's sake, remembering that it was you who urged me to finish the thing many moons ago, saying what a pity it would be if I didn't etc. To be brief, it needs something more, je ne sais quoi. Could you try and figure out what that quoi is and take care of it? I've included extra in the check for your trouble, ok?

Another thing, when you're through, would you be so kind as to send copies to the folks listed on the verso — all three of whom evinced sincere admiration for my poor GUINEVERE?

Again, sorry.

Fondest regards,
Felice

This next letter was posted about a month later from Leakey, Texas:

Dear NB,

Over breakfast this a.m., I suddenly got pangs of conscience — don't laugh — somehow feeling that I owe you more of an explanation of what I'm up to.

Well, I hate harping on an old string as you know, but — it's GUINEVERE. I'm in the process of adding a whole new section, new half really, so that what was there originally will form a Part I. Surprised?

The setting will perhaps amuse you. It's in the future, on a spaceship. Sounds bizarre, but it works (I think). I'm

telling the same story of the triangle against this new background — the ship's going somewhere, but Guinevere, Arthur, and Lancelot have no idea where, or when they'll get
there. The style, which is ultra-modern, will complement
and be in contrast to the medieval flavor of Part I.

Take care.

FR

Ms. Rothman's last letter, which reached me in another
month, bore the postmark of Barksdale, Texas:

Dear N.,

The new GUINEVERE is going great guns, better than
I ever expected. I've varied Part II by giving my prima a
long solo.

You know, it's turning into a kind of opera — not li-
bretto — I mean word-opera.

Do you understand? Somehow I think that you do —
if for no other reason than familiarity, which doesn't always breed contempt, right?

Right.

'Dyos,

F.

It only remains for me to insist that the originator of that
false rumor concerning my authorship of this book spread it
no further. And my husband — who is an attorney, you will
recall — adds his voice to mine in no uncertain terms.

Honestly, it's so ridiculous — one might as well turn everything inside out and say that Rothman needed me as a
fiction. . . .

A Note on the Production

Special thanks are due Raymond Donnell for his invaluable editorial assistance.

Caroline Hagen acted as production director; the cover design and illustration were by her. The interior of the book was designed and typeset by our inimitable Karla Kraus, using Wordperfect 5.0, Ventura Publisher 4.1.1, CorelDRAW! 3.0, and Fontographer 3.5. The typefaces are Adobe's New Baskerville and Times IPA.

The music designs were based on sketches by the late Hermann Greissle, who would have done a far better job had he lived to complete them.

Camera-ready copy was prepared in-house with a Hewlett Packard Laser 4m. The printer and binder was McNaughton & Gunn of Saline, MI.

Notes